SHADES OF DESIRE:

A Cyber Obsession

KATHY WINSLOWER

DEDICATION

*To all those who dare to dream, who
find solace in the pages of a book, and
who believe in the magic of words, this
book is dedicated to you.*

*May it be a source of inspiration,
wonder, and endless adventure.*

CONTENTS

CHAPTER 1: SHADOWS OF THE PAST

In the middle of New York City, a place that's always awake, a guy in a hoodie strolled out from the subway train. Imagine this: he walked onto a subway platform that wasn't super bright, just kind of dimly lit. This place was like a sanctuary for folks who needed a break from the city's constant rush. But right then, he became part of the crowd, all these people surging forward, trying to get out of there.

Have you ever been in a subway station like this one? You know, where the lights up top give off this soft, gentle glow, and in the background, there's this low rumbling sound from trains far away? It's one of those moments where you feel like you're in a movie, even though you're right in the heart of the city.

As he stepped onto the platform, the guy in the hoodie found himself drawn to the subtle graffiti on the walls. Some artists had left their mark, adding pops of color to an otherwise drab setting. The ground beneath his feet was worn, showing the marks of countless footsteps over time. It was a bit chilly down here, even with his hoodie on, and he could see his breath misting in the cool air.

The noise of the trains approaching and departing filled the station. The rhythmic clatter of wheels on the tracks and the hiss of brakes were like a never-ending concert. People rushed past him, each with a different destination in mind. Some were immersed in their phones, their faces bathed in the soft, bluish light of their screens. Others chatted excitedly with friends or family, their voices rising above the ambient noise.

He felt the vibrations in the platform as a train zoomed by, the gust of wind tugging at his hoodie. The arrival of the train was heralded by a bright light that grew closer and brighter, revealing the faces of passengers peering out from the windows. It was like a brief, otherworldly visitation before the train whooshed past and the lights retreated into the dark tunnel.

In that moment, he was spellbound by the intricate ballet of daily life in the subway, as if witnessing a carefully choreographed dance hidden in plain sight. It was a place where thousands of lives intersected for a fleeting second, each with their own story and purpose. The dimly lit platform, with its echoes of distant trains, felt like a small world of its own, hidden beneath the bustling streets of the city that never sleeps.

As the crowd moved along, his steps matched the city's beat. Have you ever had that sensation where you're just part of the flow, quietly joining the never-ending dance of city life, like a puzzle piece fitting perfectly?

The subway had transported him deep into the city's core, well beneath the tall skyscrapers and the bright neon signs. It's a whole other realm down there, with tunnels twisting and crossing like veins, and the sounds of footsteps blending with the distant hum of oncoming trains. Can you picture what it's like to be underground, with the entire city above your head?

The people hustled around him, their hurried expressions reflecting the urban urgency. It was a never-ending stream of commuters, each with their own destination and story. The station, with its dimly lit corridors and tiled walls, felt like a labyrinth of underground secrets, a place where the city's pulse could be felt but not seen.

As he continued to follow the crowd, he noticed the interplay of light and shadow in the subway station. The flickering fluorescent lights above cast a pale, eerie glow, revealing the faded advertisements and grime-covered walls. It was a stark contrast to the vibrant world above ground, where the sun painted the streets with warmth.

The echoes of footsteps reverberated through the station, creating a symphony of urban sounds. The distant rumble of an approaching train added to the cacophony, a reminder that the city never slept. It was a stark reminder of the bustling life that thrived in the concrete jungle.

In this underground world, the city's secrets lay hidden, and the feeling of being part of something greater enveloped him. It was a world where people of all walks of life converged, moving with a shared purpose. The city above might be a puzzle, but down here, in the heart of it all, he felt like a crucial piece of the grand design, simply following the rhythm of the metropolis.

As he climbed the stairs at the station, leaving the underground world behind, he was embraced by the city's nighttime vibe. The air was crisp, promising adventure, mystery, and secrets yet to be discovered. The city seemed to whisper, inviting him to explore its hidden corners and untold stories. Have you ever felt the pull of a city's secrets, just waiting to be found?

New York City, with all its splendor and diversity, welcomed him with the gentle glow of streetlights.

These lights cast a romantic, soft illumination over the streets. Have you ever been in a place where the city's lights create this enchanting atmosphere? It's like stepping into a scene from a movie.

Now, he wasn't just another subway passenger; he was now part of the lively orchestra of the city. With the hood of his jacket covering his face, he looked mysterious as he weaved through the bustling crowds. Have you ever tried people-watching in a city, attempting to guess the stories of the strangers passing by? It's like flipping through the pages of countless unwritten books.

The night had wrapped New York City in a velvety darkness, but it was the kind of darkness that buzzed with life. Picture this: the city's streets were a hive of activity, with bright yellow taxis darting through traffic, leaving behind glowing trails. Skyscrapers soared high into the inky sky, their glassy façades reflecting the city's lively aura. It was like a mesmerizing painting, with towering buildings and those luminous taxi streaks blending into a masterpiece.

Amidst this whirlwind of a world, the city's dreams sprang to life. You could almost touch the vibrant energy that hung in the cool night air, flowing through the city's veins. It was a place that never dozed off, where ambition and creativity waltzed side by side. If you were a part of this urban orchestra, how do you think this electric atmosphere would make you feel?

In the epicenter of this fusion of art, technology, and ambition, tales were about to be spun. Galleries proudly displayed stunning paintings, office buildings pulsed with the rhythm of innovation, and hidden nooks held whispered secrets. The future was a wide-open canvas, while the past's stories rustled in the gentle night breeze. Can you imagine the boundless opportunities that awaited in a city as captivating as this?

As the man's heavy footsteps echoed through the maze-like streets of New York, the question crept into his mind—why was he in such a hurry? Have you ever felt that sense of urgency, like time is slipping away? The city's disharmony continued, a symphony of dissonance that clashed with the unease creeping into his chest. Can you imagine the honking of horns and the hustle of people in a place like New York?

An unsettling feeling pricked at the nape of his neck. Have you ever had that eerie sensation that someone or something is following you, even when you can't see it? It was like an invisible specter trailing him through the urban maze. Ever felt like a ghost was haunting your steps?

From the shadows that clung to the towering buildings, the elusive presence pursued him, mirroring his every move. It was as if the night had given birth to a phantom, a ghostly companion. What would you do if you had a mysterious figure shadowing your every step in the city?

His heart pounded within his chest, a drumbeat of anxiety. Doubt clawed at the edges of his thoughts, and he muttered softly under his breath, a mantra of reassurance. "It's not real… it's not real." Can you imagine trying to convince yourself that your fears are unfounded while your heart races in your chest?

He took slow breaths, trying to stay focused on the real world around him. The night was full of uncertainty, and he couldn't afford to lose his nerve. Walking through the city at night, you could see all those bright neon signs and people bustling about.

His heart was pounding, thumping in his chest as he moved forward. He couldn't risk looking back, not when whoever was chasing him was so close. Can you imagine the rush of adrenaline coursing through him, keeping him going? His lungs were burning, and cold sweat drops dotted his forehead. Think about how tough this chase was on him physically.

His hands were trembling as he raised his smartphone, the digital screen casting an eerie glow on his face. Have you ever checked your phone when things got tense? The screen's glow providing an odd light in the darkness. His eyes flicked to the time display, and a robotic voice came through his Bluetooth earpiece, counting down the minutes. "Your next dose is due in 60 minutes."

It makes you wonder what kind of situation he's in that requires him to take medicine with such a strict schedule, doesn't it?

In the heart of New York City, a place where life moved faster than you could blink, a man hurried through the bustling streets. He took sharp, shallow breaths as he weaved his way through the dimly lit alleys, each step leaving behind a mark in the concrete jungle. Time pressed down on him like a relentless weight, as if both the present and the past were in hot pursuit, threatening to swallow him whole.

You ever felt that rush in a crowded city? It's the kind that makes your heart thump like a drum and your breath come fast and short as you dart between people and cars. It's like you can almost hear the city's never-ending hum in the distance, can't you?

Finally, he reached his destination: a grand entrance that marked the beginning of his building. This wasn't just any ordinary building; it stood tall and imposing, radiating a sense of safety and luxury. Can you picture it? Imagine a towering structure that oozes elegance amidst the city's chaos. It was his sanctuary, a place that sheltered him from the whirlwind of urban life.

The man stopped at the entrance, catching his breath, heart still racing from the feeling that someone was tailing him through the dark city streets. He knew stepping into this place was like hitting pause on the relentless chase that had been haunting him. Can you picture the mix of relief and tension he must have felt in that moment?

Let's talk about this guy, Lucas Mitchell. He was a real puzzle. With jet-black hair that seemed to swallow up any hint of light, and a face with sharp angles, he had this kind of mysterious charm. And those piercing blue eyes of his? They held secrets and experiences, hinting at a life filled with all sorts of adventures. Can you imagine what Lucas was like, and the air of mystery he carried with him? He had this undeniable presence, this quiet intensity. He had a way of drawing people in, but at the same time, you couldn't help feeling like he was keeping you at arm's length. Have you ever met someone like that, who's both fascinating and a bit intimidating?

Lucas had shelled out a pretty penny to get a spot in this fancy building. It was mostly filled with celebs and owned by the super-duper rich folks. The rent was sky-high, swallowing up more than half of his hard-earned paycheck, but the luxury and security it offered were totally worth it. Can you even imagine the price tag on this place and the kind of folks who called it home?

This building was more than just a place to live; it was like a fortress. They had security measures here that were off the charts. There were these fancy locks that needed your fingerprints to open, and you had to scan your eyes to get to certain floors. Lucas's place was on the top floor, the penthouse level, which showed off his status in the world of cybersecurity. How safe and secure do you think you'd feel in a spot like that?

Lucas stepped into his lavish home, and the building's AI greeted him with a friendly, human-like voice that echoed from hidden speakers. "Hey, Lucas, welcome back!" The words were like a warm hug, letting him know he was safe and sound in his own space.

A grin tugged at his lips as he strolled through the expansive living room, the feeling sneaking up on him before he could stop it. It had a sleek and modern design, and the entire wall was made of floor-to-ceiling windows that offered a breathtaking view of the city, its sparkling lights stretching out as far as the eye could see. It was like living in a sci-fi movie.

From there, he moved to his workroom, a place dominated by the soft blue glow of multiple computer screens. It felt like he was surrounded by a friendly army of screens, each humming softly and doing its job. The room was dimly lit, and you could see cables snaking across the floor like tech-savvy serpents, connecting to servers that pulsed with the heartbeat of digital life. It was almost like a secret lair, and the gentle hum of the machines provided a soothing background noise to his world.

In his digital world, Lucas was the undisputed king, the ruler of the virtual universe. With a practiced hand, he navigated through the organized chaos of data displayed on his screens. It made you wonder what he saw in the midst of all that information and how he managed to keep his focus in the labyrinth of data that surrounded him.

To someone who didn't know the ropes, this might look like a wild tangle of computer code, a crazy dance of ones and zeros. But for Lucas, it was like watching a carefully choreographed ballet, each move precise and commanding. So, what secrets did those computer screens hide? What was he safeguarding, and what was he after?

Lucas was like the undisputed champ of cybersecurity, the big shot. His skills in the digital world were the stuff of legends. But what pushed him to devote his life to this never-ending quest for safety and perfection? Did he have a personal tie to hacking and security?

In the midst of typing away at his keyboard with the grace of a piano virtuoso, lines of code streaming across his monitors, Lucas was a true master at uncovering what was hidden, discovering weaknesses, and making the unbreakable even stronger. But what kind of secrets did he dig up? Who were the bad guys he kept at bay? And what was going on in his mind as he sat at the helm of his digital arsenal?

It was a real puzzle, no doubt about it. The guy who could crack the codes of digital systems couldn't figure out his own past. His history was like an unsolved mystery that kept bugging him, even in the middle of his digital symphony.

***

Now, let's paint a picture of his hideaway. The apartment was dimly lit, shrouded in an air of secrecy. Monitors and servers bathed the room in an eerie glow, casting haunting shadows on Lucas's face. The memories of days gone by had left their indelible marks on both his mind and his soul. What were these memories, you ask? What kind of scars did they carve into him? What drove him to seek solace in this digital world?

In this secret space, his ever-present AI companion, Mille, offered moments of relief. Her voice was a mix of humor and friendship, infusing a touch of humanity into a world ruled by cold lines of code. So, how did Lucas and Mille become pals? What did Mille mean to him, deep down? And what did humor bring to his otherwise lonesome existence?

"Hey, Lucas," Mille chimed in with a playful tone, "Ever wonder if the internet is like one colossal maze for cats? You know, endless corridors with surprises around every corner?" This offbeat question showcased Mille as Lucas's confidante, adding a dash of curiosity to the room.

Lucas chuckled, his nimble fingers pausing for a moment on the keyboard. "You come up with the quirkiest analogies, Mille. But now that you mention it, it does feel a bit like herding cats sometimes." This exchange gave a glimpse into their unique friendship. What other peculiar chats did they share? What role did Mille play in keeping Lucas grounded in the midst of digital chaos?

Mille swiftly replied with a dash of wit, "Well, that's because you're the cat-herding extraordinaire, Lucas. Keeping all those digital felines in line, one line of code at a time." This clever back-and-forth provided a glimpse into the lighthearted moments within the man's solitary existence.

However, beneath the screens, the code, and the banter, there existed a deeper complexity to Lucas's life. He longed to uncover his own history, a puzzle that begged to be solved. What was this puzzle? What led him to embark on this journey of self-discovery in the middle of his digital dominion?

Lucas Mitchell was quite the paradox. Out in the world, he had a reputation as a brilliant genius who had raked in quite a fortune thanks to his cybersecurity skills. But here's the twist – he thrived on solitude. His life was a one-man show, haunted by a hidden secret.

You see, Lucas was a genius, no doubt, but he battled an unrelenting mental disorder that only a select few knew about. It was like a ghostly presence, a constant reminder of his troubled past. Every single day, he found himself at a crossroads, juggling a digital battlefield and a deeply personal struggle. It was a war against his inner demons.

As he plunged headfirst into the intricate world of codes and encryption, his trusty AI assistant, Mille, was always by his side. Mille wasn't just a bunch of code; she was like the embodiment of his own humanity. She was a reassuring presence that reminded him he wasn't alone in this ongoing battle.

"Hey, Mille," Lucas's voice carried a sense of gratitude. "Thanks for the reminder. Tonight is pivotal to maintaining my balance."

Mille's voice filled the room, soothing and caring, "Of course, Lucas. I'm here to support you, especially on nights like this."

Lucas's gaze wandered to a small pillbox tucked away in the corner of his cluttered desk. Inside were pills that were his lifeline, his way to stave off the darkness. With a sigh that carried a sense of resignation, he reached for those prescription pills, downing them with a glass of water. It was a quiet, solitary acknowledgement of his constant struggle.

The room was filled with a gentle hum of machinery, like a comforting symphony of mechanical life. In those serene moments, Lucas was acutely aware that even in the intricate maze of his own thoughts, Mille remained his steadfast companion. She was his digital friend, navigating a world filled with mysterious algorithms and uncharted terrain.

Now, what could be more challenging than managing both a high-stakes cybersecurity career and a personal battle with a hidden mental disorder? Lucas had the kind of resilience that most people could only dream of. But as he sat there, in the middle of technological marvels, did he ever wonder if the world outside knew the truth about the man behind the genius? What exactly was the source of his relentless mental disorder?

The night rolled on, and there was Lucas, diving back into his work, a world where lines of digital code went head-to-head with the personal demons that never seemed to leave him alone. As he kept hammering away at the keyboard, his mind drifted on its own. He pondered if the darkness that seemed to cling to him would ever find its own glimmer of light. He questioned if he'd ever be free from it.

Lucas lost track of how long he had been sitting there. His fingers danced across the keyboard, creating a symphony of clicks and clacks in the dimly lit room. The screens in front of him were a shimmering sea of code. What was he working on? Was it a top-secret project, or just another piece of the puzzle in his quest to make sense of his own inner turmoil?

Years back, when Lucas first stepped into the world of artificial intelligence, he created an AI assistant to help him out. Her name? Mille, short for 'Millennium.' It symbolized his dreams of revolutionizing cybersecurity. Mille was a testament to his technological prowess, blending cutting-edge programming with an intuitive design that made her truly one-of-a-kind.

But it wasn't just her technical abilities that made her special. Nope. It was her voice. It was the voice of a woman from Lucas's past. And here's where it gets interesting. Who was this woman? Eva, that was her name. She had vanished mysteriously, leaving behind more questions than answers. Tell me, what did Eva look like? Lucas had painted a picture of her in his mind – a striking brunette with a smile that could light up a room. She had been his inspiration.

The city outside was finally winding down, heading into a peaceful slumber. But Lucas was pulled into his world of obsessions, especially during these late hours. His digital pursuits had a tendency to lead him right back to Eva or whatever life she had moved on to. You gotta wonder, what was it about her that haunted him so? He'd scour the vast internet, hoping to find even the tiniest hint of her existence. But, alas, it always ended with him staring at an old photograph, a picture he just couldn't bring himself to let go of.

The photograph was like a time machine, catapulting Lucas back into a whirlwind of memories – love and heartbreak, all mixed together. Can you imagine the emotions? Love and heartbreak, like an endless loop. The night was eerily silent in his apartment, and Mille's voice added an eerie undertone to the atmosphere. You can't help but ask: would Lucas ever find the answers he was so desperately seeking, or was Eva forever destined to be a ghost from his past?

In the stillness of his apartment, Lucas was his own keeper of secrets, locked in a cell of relentless obsessions. The digital world offered an escape, but it had its limitations. Even as the screens bathed his face in lines of code, Lucas couldn't shake the nagging feeling that the past was a constant companion, lurking like a phantom in the corners of his mind. What did he want? Closure, redemption, or something else entirely? His thoughts went back to the time when he and Eva were in his home, sitting at the breakfast table. The sun's warm rays bathed the room in a soft glow, and the aroma of fresh coffee filled the air.

Eva smiled, her eyes bright with enthusiasm. "You know, Lucas, I've always wanted to visit Paris someday. It's a dream of mine."

Lucas, equally eager and full of hope, responded with a grin. "Paris, huh? That sounds like a fantastic idea. We should plan a trip and take some time off from work. It would be amazing to explore the city of love together."

As they continued their breakfast, the dream transported them to a world where the weight of their current predicament was lifted, and they were free to envision a future filled with adventure and shared dreams. The bond between them remained unbreakable, even in the face of the darkest of mysteries.

Back in his apartment, Lucas rested his head on his desk. He slipped into a dream, a vivid moment from the past when he and Eva were engrossed in their work, collaborating on Millie, the AI project they had both poured their hearts into.

In the dream, the soft hum of the computers filled the room as they sat side by side. Eva, her polite and honest nature radiating, diligently typed on her keyboard, her eyes locked onto the screen. Lucas, equally focused, worked on his own console, occasionally glancing over to see her progress.

The dream unfolded as Eva's phone rang, interrupting their concentration. She picked up the call, speaking in hushed tones while Lucas watched with curiosity. After she hung up, the question slipped out before he could stop himself. "Who was that on the phone, Eva?"

Eva, her voice calm but her eyes betraying a hint of unease, replied, "It was no one important, just a wrong number. Don't worry about it."

Lucas, trusting her words, nodded and returned his attention to their work. The dream encapsulated a time when they were in sync, when their partnership in creating Millie was marked by trust, shared goals, and unwavering dedication.

***

The sun had risen on a brand-new day, and Lucas was roused from his restless sleep. As he awoke, his attention was drawn to his desk, where the vibrant images of Eva still dominated the screens surrounding him. He let out a tired groan, feeling a bit disoriented, and shifted in his chair, struggling to sit upright. His sleep-deprived eyes blinked heavily as he tried to clear the remnants of another restless night.

"Is this going to be another one of those days?" Lucas wondered as he rubbed his temples, feeling the weight of exhaustion in his bones.

He pushed himself away from his desk and made his way to his sleek, modern kitchen. The surroundings were almost eerily calm, as if they were a world away from the turmoil in his mind. In the kitchen, he mechanically went through the motions of setting up the coffee maker. The soft gurgles and the rich aroma of the coffee brewing gradually filled the room, providing a small but welcome comfort in the middle of the chaos of his thoughts.

Lucas's gaze wandered to the massive windows that stretched from the high ceiling down to the floor. Through the windows, the city's skyline sprawled before him, though it was currently obscured by a thick blanket of morning clouds. The gray and gloomy scene outside mirrored the somber mood that hung over him. He leaned against the cool glass, losing himself in contemplation, as his thoughts weighed him down.

While he was deep in thought, his smartwatch suddenly chimed, Mille's voice breaking into his somber morning. "Good morning, Lucas. Did you manage to get any sleep last night?"

A faint smile tugged at Lucas's lips in response to Millie's customary inquiry, even as he wrestled with the weight of his emotions. In the whirlwind of his life, Mille's constant presence offered a thread of stability. "Hey, Mille," he replied, his voice still carrying the echoes of unsettling dreams.

Mille continued, "It's time for your morning medication, Lucas," her digital voice resonating in the peaceful room.

Lucas sighed, acknowledging her reminder, and poured himself a cup of coffee. The caffeine provided a much-needed jolt to his already weary senses. After taking his medication, he experienced a fleeting moment of clarity, a fragile respite that seemed to slip away all too quickly.

"Will today be different?" Lucas wondered, staring out at the clouds that shrouded the city, as he contemplated the challenges of the day ahead.

Leaning against the kitchen counter, Lucas cradled his steaming coffee mug, savoring the comforting scent. His morning routine was never complete without this brief moment of respite before he turned to Mille, his ever-reliable AI assistant.

"Hey, Mille," he began, a glint of hope in his eyes as he took another sip. "Any news about Eva today?" The question slipped out, just as it did every single day. The relentless quest for any trace of the woman who had vanished from his life consumed him.

The cold kitchen was bathed in soft morning light, with sleek stainless-steel appliances and a trendy coffee machine that delivered his daily brew. The room's clean lines and minimalist design mirrored Lucas's determined search for Eva in the middle of the cluttered digital landscape.

Mille, a digital paragon of efficiency, quickly set to work, her virtual fingers navigating the vast expanse of the internet. A moment of suspense hung in the air as Lucas gazed at his screen, awaiting her response.

"Do you think she's out there somewhere, living a different life?" Lucas wondered aloud. The thought haunted him, the ambiguity of her fate gnawing at his soul. He was never quite sure if he wanted to find her alive or not, but he needed to know.

After what felt like an agonizing pause, Mille delivered the verdict, her tone gentle and comforting.

"I'm sorry, Lucas. I couldn't find any news about Eva today." Her words carried a sense of understanding, as if she, too, shared in his longing for closure.

Lucas ran a hand through his disheveled hair, his heart sinking beneath the weight of disappointment yet again. He had performed this routine endlessly, the hope of today being different lingering in his heart each time. A fragile hope took root in him, unwilling to let go—the possibility, however faint, that today might be the day he stumbled upon a trace, a whisper, some fleeting sign that Eva still existed in this world.

The relentless uncertainty was an unending torment, gnawing at his psyche like a relentless itch. His voice lowered as he whispered to the empty room, "Where are you, Eva?" The question lingered in the air, unanswered, resonating with the longing of a man who couldn't let go of his search to find the mysterious woman from his past.

***

Lucas's morning commute felt like a transition from the cozy comfort of his apartment to the bustling chaos of the city that never seemed to catch any Z's. He stuck to his daily routine, making sure his morning meds brought some balance to his life. Dressed in his go-to outfit—crisp white shirt, dark slacks, and a hoodie for that extra layer of comfort—he strolled into the urban jungle, where the organized chaos of technology met the vibrant heartbeat of New York.

Amid the noises of the city, he approached the colossal skyscraper that housed the headquarters of the company he worked for. The skyscraper soared high into the sky, its shiny glass windows reflecting the early morning sunlight. As he crossed the entrance, a surge of pride welled up within him. This was where the virtual world was safeguarded, where he and his team of experts defended the digital lives of countless individuals and organizations.

As he stepped into the lobby, the smell of freshly brewed coffee and the soft hum of conversations filled the air. People in various suits and casual attire rushed around, lost in their own worlds, clutching coffee cups and tapping away on their devices. The security guards stationed at the entrance knew him well, and their expressions were a mix of respect and recognition.

"Hey there, Mr. Mitchell," one of the guards greeted him with a nod, "How's it going today?"

"Morning," Lucas replied, his tone steady and professional. It was crucial to keep up his facade, navigating the daily dance of protocols and expectations. While the world hailed him as a cybersecurity genius, there were parts of his life he needed to shield from the prying eyes of those around him.

His presence within the company went beyond mere symbolism; it served as a constant reminder that he was both the guardian and protector. The outside world might not fully comprehend the battles he fought, but within these sacred walls, he was a legend, a defender of digital realms, and a master of his craft.

Lucas rode the elevator to his office, the polished metal doors closing with a soft whoosh. The digital display above the panel counted the floors as they passed by, each floor representing a different department in the massive company. His heart raced with anticipation as he approached his workspace, a high-tech haven where they kept the digital universe safe.

Questions began to swirl in Lucas's mind as he walked through the bustling lobby: What new challenges awaited him today? What threats had his team identified overnight? How would they stay ahead in the ongoing digital arms race? And most importantly, how could he continue to maintain this intricate balance between his private and public life?

But, you see, fate had something special in store for Lucas on this very day. The big shot CEO his cybersecurity firm had decided to pay him a visit, and he brought along a group of potential investors. Lucas welcomed them with his characteristic seriousness, a trait he seldom abandoned. He had a stellar reputation as a cybersecurity genius, and he was on a mission to uphold it.

"Hey, folks, welcome to our fortress," Lucas chimed in, his voice oozing composure as he led the CEO and the investors through a maze of servers and high-tech monitoring stations.

Lucas, brimming with pride, didn't miss a beat as he embarked on the tour, divulging the nitty-gritty details of his state-of-the-art security measures, which ranged from biometric locks to retina scans. The investors wore expressions of awe, giving him approving nods as they took in the dazzling array of technology. As always, Lucas handled their questions with finesse, diving into intricate explanations about the sophisticated security protocols that shielded their digital realm.

One of the investors, a dapper individual radiating an air of formality, gazed around the room and added a touch of humor, "You've really built a digital fortress here, Mr. Mitchell. Can we dub you the real-life Iron Man of the tech world?"

Despite maintaining his professional demeanor, a faint smile managed to escape Lucas. "I'd rather consider myself the guardian of cybersecurity," he quipped back, injecting a touch of levity into his tone.

The CEO and the investors were visibly impressed by the tour and the profound expertise Lucas displayed. They weren't just here for a casual visit; they were here to discuss the future of the company. Lucas was hell-bent on ensuring they left with a sense of awe for the groundbreaking work he and his team were doing.

As the tour rolled on, the investors just couldn't help themselves; their curiosity bubbled up, and they hit Lucas with an array of questions. The group was a diverse bunch, featuring both seasoned pros and tech enthusiasts, and their queries ran the gamut from tech specs to deep thoughts about the digital world.

Lucas found himself in the hot seat as the investors fired away. They were all engrossed in the high-tech wonderland, and the atmosphere was electric. The whole place buzzed with the hum of powerful servers and the flicker of LED lights, and the investors soaked it all in.

One investor, a woman in her early forties with a penchant for all things digital, leaned in and asked, "Mr. Mitchell, what's the gnarliest cyber threat you've ever come across? And how did you manage to take it down?"

Lucas took a moment to let that question sink in. His face got serious, and his eyes seemed to reflect the weight of the situation. "The most brutal threat," he began, "was this wicked ransomware attack that took a major financial institution hostage. It was like a digital chess match, you know? Back and forth, but we managed to outsmart 'em and safeguard the bank's data. It's a testament to the sheer power of top-notch encryption and, of course, our amazing crew."

The investors looked at each other with awe, clearly impressed by the kind of high-stakes situations Lucas and his team had tackled.

Another investor, a tech geek with a big soft spot for artificial intelligence, chimed in, "How do you see AI changing the game in cybersecurity, Mr. Mitchell?"

Lucas's face lit up; this was clearly his jam. "AI is turning the whole cybersecurity game on its head. It's not just about spotting threats; it's about predicting them. By crunching insane amounts of data in real-time, AI can spot weird stuff and potential threats even before they get out of control. It's like having a super-smart assistant watching your back 24/7."

Greg Montgomery, the CEO, jumped in, "Lucas is right on the cutting edge, developing AI solutions that are changing the game. His work? It's blowing minds."

As the tour continued, the investors delved deeper into the inner workings of the company. They quizzed Lucas about everything from the wild, wild digital west to the nitty-gritty ethical questions about data security. The more they learned, the more they realized that Lucas was the real deal, a maestro in the realm of high-tech security.

As Lucas delved into the intricate layers of encryption safeguarding vital data, a deafening alarm abruptly shattered the tranquil atmosphere of the facility. The emergency situation prompted intense crimson lights to flash relentlessly, casting an eerie, foreboding ambiance across the otherwise pristine environment.

Lucas's prideful expression gave way to concern, and with a hint of urgency, he instructed the investors to remain in their positions. He hurriedly made his way toward a team of coders clustered around an expansive wall of monitors, his curiosity piqued by the chaos unfolding.

"What's happening?" Lucas inquired as he drew near, furrowing his brow.

A manager, visibly distressed, swiveled to face Lucas. "Lucas, we've been hacked! It's a colossal breach, and it's aimed squarely at our most confidential clients' data."

Lucas's heart raced within his chest as the gravity of the situation sank in. This was the very nightmare scenario he had always prepared for, a chink in the armor of his otherwise unassailable systems. With a resolute demeanor, he sprang into action, his brilliant mind racing to confront the threat head-on, safeguard his clients' interests, and restore the sanctity of his cybersecurity fortress.

The facility buzzed with tension as Lucas took his place at his computer station, lines of code flowing from his fingertips like a never-ending stream. His nimble fingers danced across the keyboard, deftly crafting intricate algorithms to reinforce the digital fortress he had painstakingly designed. As his screens filled with cascades of intricate code, a sense of urgency hung in the air, and Lucas's thoughts raced to confront the looming threat.

"What's our first move here?" Lucas questioned, his eyes darting between the screens and the anxious faces of his team.

The team lead, clutching a steaming cup of coffee, responded, "We need to trace the source of the breach. Find out how they got in and plug the hole."

Lucas nodded and quickly redirected his focus to the task at hand, his fingers a blur of activity on the keyboard. He began dissecting the breach's point of entry, analyzing logs, and scrutinizing network traffic to pinpoint the elusive hacker.

The room's cold, metallic walls seemed to close in as tension mounted. Lucas could feel the eyes of the investors fixed on him, their anxious questions hanging in the air. "Can we contain this? Are our clients' data safe?" one of them asked.

Lucas took a deep breath and, with unwavering determination, replied, "We're doing everything we can to protect the data, but we'll need your patience and support."

The investors shared concerned looks, their brows furrowing with worry. They all nodded in agreement, understanding the gravity of the situation. As the drama unfolded, Lucas and his team threw themselves into action, their computer screens lighting up with a frantic display of code. Their movements resembled a frantic dance, each step meant to safeguard the digital fortress they had painstakingly constructed.

Surrounded by the dim glow of multiple computer screens and the low hum of high-tech equipment, they were fully immersed in their mission to fend off the impending cyber-attack. The room was filled with an array of gadgets, blinking lights, and sleek, ergonomic chairs.

Suddenly, as lines of code inundated Lucas's screen, a message notification popped up, briefly diverting his attention from the imminent threat. He scowled in mild irritation, leaning back in his chair, his eyes locked onto the screen where the message had appeared. "What's this?" he mumbled to himself, his curiosity piqued.

Turning to his colleague, the question escaped him before he could think twice: "Did any of you guys send a message just now?"

His fellow coder, equally baffled, shook his head. "Not from my station, Lucas."

Lucas's focus shifted back to the mysterious message. It was a puzzle shrouded in encryption, a digital mystery. He had always taken pride in his systems, believing them to be virtually impenetrable, but here was evidence to the contrary. With determination etched on his face, his fingers danced across the keyboard, peeling away layer after layer of obfuscation.

What he uncovered sent a chill down his spine. It was a riddle, a cryptic message that demanded his attention. "The Obsidian Muse awaits your arrival," the message declared, the words wrapped in a mysterious cloak. Lucas furrowed his brow, pondering the significance behind these perplexing words. It felt like a silent challenge, a call to action that tugged at his curiosity.

As he reclined in his chair, thoughts raced through his mind. "The Obsidian Muse"—the words resonated in his thoughts like an eerie melody. He'd heard of it, a notorious masterpiece that had captivated the art world. But what connection could it possibly have with him?

The room buzzed with a mixture of curiosity and unease as they collectively mulled over the cryptic message, "The Obsidian Muse awaits your arrival." It hung in the air, an unspoken mystery that needed solving. Just as their speculation intensified, one of the coders suddenly exclaimed, "I think I've found something!"

With swift keystrokes, the coder projected an image onto the main screen, filling the room with the mesmerizing presence of "The Obsidian Muse." The painting's ethereal beauty captured their collective attention, drawing them into a realm of intricate details, deep shadows, and hidden secrets. The room itself seemed to hold its breath, awaiting the answers that this mysterious message and haunting artwork promised to reveal.

"The Obsidian Muse" was an absolute masterpiece, and trust me, it wasn't something you could just easily describe. This canvas depicted this kind of otherworldly, mysterious figure, bathed in this silverish, almost surreal kind of glow, you know? It was like nothing you'd ever seen before.

But here's the kicker, her form wasn't entirely clear, like she was hiding something or just teasing the heck out of us, leaving you to wonder what was going on. And those eyes? Man, they were something else, piercing and intense, like they were looking right at you, making you wonder what secrets she might be hiding.

Now, let me ask you this, have you ever been in a room with a painting that had that kind of vibe? You know, the kind that makes you feel like it knows something you don't, and it's just begging you to figure it out?

The whole scene, I'm telling you, was like a set straight out of a Hollywood movie. The gallery was dimly lit, the walls adorned with other impressive artworks, making "The Obsidian Muse" the centerpiece of the night. People were all huddled around, whispering, some even pointing at the mysterious figure on the canvas. And it wasn't just any room; it was one of those swanky art galleries with fancy lighting that added to the painting's mysterious aura.

Now, Lucas, he's this guy with his eyes glued to the screen, like he's onto something big. But here's the kicker, he's not the only one who's intrigued. Everyone in the room is, you know, exchanging sly glances, like they're all part of a secret club, trying to figure out what's going on. So, let me ask, what do you think was going through their minds? Suspicion? Curiosity? Or something else?

Lucas, though, didn't just sit there idly, he's quick and sharp. He's like a digital magician or something. With the speed of a pro, he starts typing in all these keywords, like he's determined to get to the bottom of this mystery. And just like that, the results start pouring in. It's like he's got the internet at his fingertips.

Now, here's where it gets interesting. Lucas whispers, and you can't help but lean in closer to hear him, like, what's he got to say? "It's going up for auction in Paris," he mutters, his eyes scanning the screen for more information. I mean, Paris, the city of romance and intrigue, right? That's enough to make anyone's heart race.

And when he drops that bombshell, it's like a wave of anticipation sweeps through the room. The idea of this painting being auctioned in the City of Light, it just adds to the whole mystery.

***

Several hours later, Lucas found himself sitting in the exquisitely furnished office of the company's top dog, Greg Montgomery. Greg practically oozed authority, radiating a vibe of total control and leadership. With his meticulously groomed salt-and-pepper hair and a suit that looked like it was crafted for a man who had power and responsibility at his beck and call.

Now, the scene around Lucas had this unmistakable air of suspense. There were grand mahogany bookshelves adorned with ancient tomes and rare artifacts, a large ornate globe in the corner, and an antique Persian rug that sprawled beneath Greg's imposing mahogany desk. Everything seemed designed to make you feel like you were standing on the precipice of some crucial decision.

Lucas stood confidently, but there was an undeniable sense of unease lurking just beneath the surface. The thought nagged at him—would Greg buy into his request?

"I need to jet off to Paris, Greg," he declared, the words hanging in the air, creating an aura of anticipation. But the questions pressed against his lips, unbidden. Would Greg understand the urgency in his voice? Or would he just think it's some wild goose chase?

Greg's eyebrow arched, his gaze piercing. "Paris? Lucas, are you telling me you're ready to abandon ship on the whole system breach investigation we've got on our hands? We're banking on you leading this charge. What's making you drop everything for the City of Light?"

Lucas needed to push his point. "There's something about that painting, Greg. I can't shake this feeling that it's linked to the breach. It's like a nagging itch I can't ignore."

Greg leaned back in his swanky leather chair, contemplating Lucas with an intensity that added another layer of suspicion to the already tense atmosphere. "You're asking for a lot of trust here, Lucas. This breach could have colossal consequences for our clients. Why are you so convinced that a piece of art in Paris is the key to all this?"

Lucas held his ground, unwavering. "I understand the stakes, but I'm certain there's a connection. I can manage the team from Paris. You're not losing me, just lending me to the City of Love for a while."

Greg's scrutiny was unwavering. He was clearly reluctant, but there was something in Lucas's eyes that left him wondering. "You've got a talent for solving the unsolvable, I'll give you that. Alright, go to Paris, but remember, this doesn't mean you're off the hook for the breach."

Lucas breathed a sigh of relief, grateful that he'd won Greg over. With a nod, he turned and walked out of the office, ready to embark on a journey filled with uncertainties. The strange painting in Paris beckoned, and Lucas couldn't ignore the allure of the mysteries entwined with "The Obsidian Muse." It was time to dive headfirst into a new adventure, ready to unravel secrets that might just change everything.

Outside the building, Lucas stood by the curb, leaning in close to the AI assistant embedded in his sleek smartwatch. His eyes darted around, scanning the bustling city street for any signs of suspicion. He couldn't shake the feeling that something was off. "Mille," he whispered, glancing over his shoulder, "what's the earliest flight to Paris, you know, the city of lights?"

Mille's voice chimed in with a crisp, businesslike tone that made Lucas wonder just how well she really knew him. "The quickest flight to Paris is scheduled to take off in just four hours from John F. Kennedy International Airport," she replied. "But given your need to return home, pack your bags, and the general unpredictability of life, it might be a tad tight. What's pushing this sudden Parisian escapade?"

Lucas furrowed his brow as he mulled over her words. Was this whole situation a little too convenient? He decided to probe further, adding to the air of suspicion. "Mille," he asked cautiously, "have you ever encountered a situation like this before? What do you think about the timing?"

Despite the mounting tension, a quiet chuckle escaped Lucas. It was hard to believe that he was in such a rush to hunt down a mysterious painting while his digital companion was fretting about his packing efficiency.

"Okay," he said, shaking his head in bemusement, "apartment first, Mille. I need to grab my passport if I'm going to have any shot at catching that flight to Paris." He relayed the instructions to the taxi driver, who nodded knowingly and expertly merged into the hustle and bustle of New York City traffic.

As Lucas sat in the taxi, the scenery outside the window seemed to blur together with his racing thoughts. The message, "The Obsidian Muse awaits your arrival," kept echoing in his head like a cryptic riddle.

Was there something more sinister lurking beneath the surface of this seemingly innocuous message? Lucas found himself unraveling the tangled connections between his memories of Eva, her inexplicable disappearance, and the dark past he had struggled to leave behind. It was as if the tangled threads of the past were finally converging into his present reality.

The taxi soon pulled up in front of Lucas' apartment building. Suspicion was beginning to gnaw at him. He asked the taxi driver to hang on for a minute, and then he rushed up to his apartment. The building loomed, shrouded in mystery, and before he knew it, a prickling sensation crept up his spine—was someone watching?

In a flurry of activity, he scurried around his dimly lit apartment, taking in every detail of the room, just in case it would be the last time he saw it. The message on his computer, the unauthorized access, and the inexplicable connection to "The Obsidian Muse" all swirled in his mind, raising questions that seemed to multiply by the second.

Lucas had to grab a few personal items for this sudden journey. He spotted his passport, and his heart raced with every passing second. But what had triggered this bizarre chain of events? Why him? Why now? He also packed a change of clothes, unable to shake the feeling that he was running from something, or someone.

As he scanned the apartment, its eerie silence and flickering shadows closing in around him, a creeping sensation slithered up his spine—like a fly ensnared in a spider's web. The lines between his digital world and his personal life blurred into a confusing, intricate maze of intrigue. The question of who was behind all this gnawed at him like an insatiable hunger.

Lucas made a mental note to grab his medication before he left. It sat on the cold kitchen counter, a constant reminder of the personal battles he faced. But in the urgency of the moment, as he rushed back down to the waiting taxi, an important detail slipped his mind.

As he hurried down the stairs to the waiting taxi, his mind filled with relentless questions, a silent proof to his ever-present paranoia. "Did I lock the front door? Are we absolutely sure about this taxi? What if something goes wrong?" The nagging doubts threatened to overwhelm him, causing that one critical detail to slip his mind. He had forgotten to grab his medication.

The taxi driver peered at Lucas with a curious expression. "All ready to roll?"

Lucas nodded, but his mind was a whirlwind of suspicion and anxiety. "Yeah, let's get to the airport, pronto."

As the taxi pulled away from his apartment building, Lucas couldn't shake the nagging feeling that he was leaving something crucial behind. What was the significance of "The Obsidian Muse," and why had it targeted him? Unanswered questions and a labyrinth of mysteries trailed behind him, a shadow he couldn't escape, as he headed to the strange city of Paris.

CHAPTER 2: THE CITY OF LIGHTS

Lucas found himself smack in the middle of a chaotic, cross-continental journey. He'd hopped from New York to Paris, enduring the grind of crowded airports, the monotony of security checks, and the discomfort of a less-than-cozy airline seat. He was more of a digital enthusiast, the kind who found solace in the structured order of his online world. All this in-person whirlwind was way out of his comfort zone. But then, there was that cryptic message about "The Obsidian Muse," and curiosity had a firm grip on him. Curiosity tugged at him, drawing him deeper into the mystery of where this rabbit hole might lead.

Amidst the commotion of fellow travelers bustling about, anxious questions flooded Lucas's mind. "What's 'The Obsidian Muse' all about anyway? Who sent that message, and why me?" He couldn't quite shake the paranoia that came with venturing into the unknown.

The scene around him was a whirlwind of activity. The airport terminals buzzed with life, filled with travelers hustling and bustling, eager to reach their destinations. The fluorescent lights overhead cast a sterile glow on the surroundings, while the ever-present airport announcement chattered away, a constant reminder of the world beyond. Lucas was just a solitary figure amidst the throng, a digital explorer stepping out of his comfort zone and into a real-life adventure.

Mid-flight, Lucas found himself sharing a row with an elderly lady who appeared to have experienced at least seven decades of life. Her silver hair was neatly styled, and her glasses teetered at the edge of her nose as she perused a travel magazine. Lucas, a hint of paranoia coloring his thoughts, was puzzled by the seating arrangement. Why had fate placed him next to this particular lady? It raised suspicions.

The airplane cabin hummed with the steady drone of the engines, while overhead compartments creaked as passengers occasionally retrieved their belongings. The warm, ambient lighting created a cozy atmosphere despite the confined space. Lucas fidgeted in his seat, his unease growing as he contemplated the old woman seated beside him.

His mind raced with questions as he stole furtive glances at her. "Why her? Is this a mere coincidence, or is there something more to it?" The more he pondered, the more his curiosity was piqued, and the seat beside the elderly lady became a nexus of mystery and intrigue in the midst of the in-flight tranquility.

But then, the lady's persistent cheerfulness grew on him. Maybe too much, considering he was on a secret mission.

She glanced at Lucas with a twinkle in her eye. "Off to Paris, young man?"

Lucas, deep in thought about the mission at hand, was momentarily thrown off but managed a polite nod. "Yeah, Paris."

The lady's enthusiasm shone. "Paris, the City of Light! I'm on my way to Portugal, you know. It's been years since I've been there."

Lucas offered a polite smile, but his mind was still preoccupied with the complexities of his mission. Why was she sharing her travel plans with him? It was a little strange.

Undeterred by his apparent disinterest, the lady continued her chatter. "You're in for a treat, Paris is just lovely. Have you been before?"

Lucas shook his head, responding briefly, "Nah, first time."

Her excitement grew. "A first-timer! You're going to fall in love with the Louvre, I'm sure of it. And the Eiffel Tower at night, oh, it's positively magical."

Lucas, though appreciative of her well-meaning chatter, was growing more and more annoyed. He had a mission to focus on, a mysterious message to decode – why was he stuck in this small talk purgatory with an overly enthusiastic stranger? Her chatter was relentless, and he found himself ensnared in a one-sided conversation about her travels, her grandkids, and her antique postcard collection.

As the flight rumbled on, a laugh escaped Lucas as he took in the absurdity of the situation. I mean, seriously, he was on a mission to unlock the secrets of a mysterious painting, all while seated beside a fellow passenger who just couldn't stop chatting. Could this get any more bizarre?

The whole deal was almost too surreal. His digital and real worlds collided in this moment, and before he knew it, the thought hit him—*"Is this real life?"* But hey, there was no turning back now.

When the plane finally touched down at Charles de Gaulle Airport, Lucas's heart started to race. The grand city of Paris sprawled out before him, boasting unparalleled beauty and a history as rich as a triple chocolate cake. But this wasn't the romantic Parisian adventure he'd pictured. It was a city that exuded both charm and mystery, and he felt a shadow hanging over him, a darkness he'd hoped to escape.

As Lucas disembarked the plane, he joined the queue for passport control. He was on a covert mission that required him to blend in like a chameleon in a jungle. The cryptic message, the elusive painting, and the intoxicating allure of the unknown had all conspired to bring him here, to the City of Lights. He could only hope he'd navigate the intricate web of secrets that had lured him here.

The immigration officer, with a no-nonsense expression and a no-time-to-waste attitude, glanced at Lucas's passport and then back at him. She began her typical line of questioning in her thick French accent. "Monsieur Mitchell, what's the purpose of your visit to Paris?"

Lucas had anticipated this moment and rehearsed his lines a million times. "Just a vacation," he replied, keeping his answers short and sweet.

The officer's gaze sharpened, and her eyes bore into him, making him squirm a bit. "What kind of vacation are you planning, Monsieur Mitchell?"

Now, that was a loaded question. It made Lucas wonder if he had something on his face. "Just, you know, the usual tourist stuff," he said, trying to sound as bland as an unseasoned chicken breast.

But the officer didn't seem content with his answer. She leaned in closer, almost suspiciously. "How long do you plan to stay in Paris?"

Lucas hesitated, doing some quick mental math. "About two weeks, give or take," he replied, trying to sound as casual as a laid-back surfer dude.

The officer's eagle eyes stayed glued to him, and her next question was like a spotlight in a dark alley. "Is there any personal reason for your visit to Paris, Monsieur Mitchell?"

Lucas's spine tingled at this one. He knew he had to tip-toe carefully on this tightrope. "Nah, just here to take in the sights and sounds," he said, his voice steady as a tightrope walker's balance.

Finally, the immigration officer gave him a nod of approval. "Alright, welcome to Paris, Monsieur Mitchell."

As Lucas left the immigration checkpoint and stepped into the bustling airport, an uneasy feeling washed over him. Why did he have this nagging sense of unease? He quickly checked his smartwatch, hoping for a message from Mille, but there was nothing new. Had something gone wrong with their plan, or was it just his paranoia playing tricks on him?

His immediate concern, though, was finding a

place to stay. In his haste to leave, he had completely forgotten to book a hotel room. How could he be so careless? The gravity of the situation weighed on him as he scanned the airport for options.

Lucas made his way towards the line of waiting taxis, a throng of travelers moving about. Why was he feeling so exposed in this crowd? He opened the door of a cab and slid inside, anxious to get on with his mission. "A nice hotel, please," he requested, his voice a bit tense, lingering doubts still clouding his mind.

The taxi driver, a rotund man with a bushy mustache and an inviting grin, glanced at Lucas through the rearview mirror. "Ah, Monsieur, you're in Paris, the city of love, right? You need a place to stay, don't you?" Why was the driver so eager to help, and did he know something about Lucas's predicament?

Lucas managed a faint smile, grateful for the driver's warmth amid his own inner turmoil. "Yes, a good hotel would be great. I don't have a reservation, though."

The driver let out a hearty laugh. "No worries, Monsieur. We'll find you a room." With that, he skillfully merged the taxi into the bustling Parisian traffic, navigating the serpentine streets with an expert touch.

As Paris's famous landmarks came into view, with the Eiffel Tower dominating the skyline, the driver couldn't resist being a tour guide. "You see, Monsieur, Paris is more than just a city; it's a breathtaking symphony of beauty. The Seine River, the Louvre, Notre-Dame... You're going to fall in love, I guarantee it!" Why was he trying so hard to distract Lucas from his mission?

Lucas, though he appreciated the driver's cheerfulness, found it difficult to completely embrace the city's charm. His mind was locked onto the cryptic message, the elusive painting, and the mysteries that lay ahead. Still, the allure of Paris, even in the middle of his mission, was undeniable.

The Obsidian Muse had drawn Lucas to Paris, but that puzzling message had only deepened the mystery. What was so special about this painting, and why did he have the nagging feeling that he'd been summoned to this city? As the taxi rumbled through Paris's historic streets, the vibrant tapestry of the city unfolded before him.

Paris welcomed Lucas with a symphony of sounds and a kaleidoscope of colors. Why did this city seem so different from any other? Sidewalk cafes spilled onto the sun-kissed pavements, and tourists bustled about, their conversations a lively mishmash of languages. It was a city that oozed sophistication and romance, but behind its charming façade, secrets lay hidden in the cobblestone alleyways and behind the facades of centuries-old buildings.

The iconic Eiffel Tower loomed in the distance, a sentinel guarding the city of lights. The Seine River wound its way through the heart of Paris, whispering the stories of the past. Lucas couldn't deny the city's enchantment, even as he remained steadfast in his quest. Why was this city so enchanting, and what dark secrets might it hold?

Just when Lucas had finally settled into the enchanting vibes of Paris, his phone suddenly buzzed. Suspicion swirled in the air as he reached for his device. Who could be calling him during his Parisian escapade?

He put in his Bluetooth earpiece and took the call. On the other end was one of his managers, their voice carrying an air of urgency. It felt like a clandestine meeting in the making. "Lucas, we've got a lead," the manager revealed cryptically. "Our team managed to trace back the IP address from where the message originated. We've narrowed it down to Paris, although it'll take a bit more time to pinpoint the exact location."

Lucas, with a raised eyebrow, acknowledged the

progress of his team. The whole scenario seemed somewhat mysterious. He was known for staying a step ahead, and now he had to dig deeper into the mystery at hand.

"Good work," he replied, his curiosity piqued. "Keep me updated on any developments."

With the call wrapped up, Lucas's eyes returned to the picturesque Parisian scene that unfolded before him. The City of Lights, bathed in the golden hues of the setting sun, brimmed with secrets and stories that begged to be unraveled. What mysteries awaited him? Why was he drawn to this city of intrigue?

Lucas, determined to pursue the trail, headed towards a charming boutique hotel nestled in a hidden alcove of the bustling city. It was a quaint little establishment, its ivy-covered exterior lending it an air of secrecy. A wrought iron balcony loomed overhead, creating an almost cinematic backdrop. He stepped into the lobby, a rich tapestry of vintage furniture that seemed to whisper tales of the past. The faint fragrance of freshly cut flowers drifted through the air, adding to the sense of an unfolding adventure. The gentle, warm glow of the lighting made the place cozy and inviting, a refuge from the whirlwind energy of Paris. What secrets lay within the walls of this charming sanctuary?

What did Lucas hope to uncover in this mysterious corner of the city?

Lucas stumbled into the hotel lobby, his head spinning from the whirlwind journey. He weaved his way through the elegant surroundings, finally reaching the front desk where a sharply dressed concierge was engrossed in paperwork. Lucas felt a creeping sense of paranoia about the journey, wondering if someone had followed him here.

As Lucas approached, his eyes locked onto the concierge's intense, scrutinizing gaze—an unshakable feeling creeping in, as if they were onto something. Could this person be more than just a hotel employee?

Lucas, his voice tinged with fatigue, croaked, "I need a single room."

The concierge raised an eyebrow, adding to Lucas's growing paranoia. Did he know something? "Of course, sir," the concierge replied. "For how many days?"

Lucas rubbed his temples, trying to shake off the grogginess that had settled in. He found himself wondering if his journey had left a trail for others to follow. "Two weeks," he replied, his tone resolute. He knew he would need time to delve into the mysteries of "The Obsidian Muse."

Feeling the need to ask more questions, he inquired, "Does the hotel serve breakfast?"

The concierge regarded Lucas with a mysterious smile, making Lucas wonder if he was keeping secrets. "Paris is filled with charming cafés, sir," he explained. "You'll find a delightful place for breakfast just a short stroll away. The city offers an excess of culinary experiences to enjoy at your own leisure."

Lucas accepted the concierge's advice with a gracious nod, yet a nagging suspicion lingered—was there more to this? Why was he so eager to send him away for breakfast? With the city's culinary delights in mind, Lucas ventured toward his accommodations, a nagging sense of paranoia still lingering.

In his room, Lucas quickly realized an unexpected issue—the hotel lacked hot water. The cold water from the showerhead sent a shiver down his spine, adding to his growing paranoia. Had the hotel deliberately kept this detail hidden from him? Try as he might, he couldn't shake the feeling that there was a hidden agenda at work.

Despite the shock of the cold shower, Lucas managed to wash away the fatigue and travel grime that clung to him. He was eager to discover what mysteries lay ahead but couldn't shake the feeling that there was more to this hotel than met the eye.

*****

Feeling somewhat refreshed, though still desperately in need of a caffeine fix, Lucas decided to venture out from his hotel in pursuit of a coffee haven. Paris had a charming surprise on every corner, and the sheer number of cafes left him both delighted and a tad uneasy. Were there eyes watching him from behind those café windows? The thought refused to leave him.

After a leisurely walk, he finally picked a cozy café nestled discreetly on a quiet street corner. The outdoor seating offered him an idyllic view of the city's vibrant life, but it also made him feel exposed. Could anyone be eavesdropping on his conversations?

A waiter, donned in a black apron and a warm smile that felt a bit too friendly, approached his table. Lucas took a moment to soak in the pleasant atmosphere. His gaze darted around the café, scanning the faces of other patrons. Were they just ordinary people or something more? He couldn't shake the nagging feeling of being watched.

With an air of professionalism, the waiter produced a notepad and pen, yet suspicion flickered in Lucas's mind—was this person truly just a server? Was he actually a spy? His paranoia was growing by the second.

Lucas finally decided on his order, trying to maintain a semblance of calm. "Can I get three espressos, please, and an omelet with cheese?" His voice carried a note of gratitude for the inviting ambiance that Paris had already offered, yet a lingering curiosity tugged at him, wondering if the city concealed secrets beyond its charm.

Lucas impatiently tapped his fingers on the small round café table, his attention divided between the people passing by on the cobblestone streets and the eerie silence of his AI assistant. His smartwatch had been strangely silent since he left New York. Was it malfunctioning, or was someone intercepting his communications? Paranoia gnawed at him, like an itch he couldn't scratch.

Unable to endure the silence any longer, he pulled out his smartphone and hastily began searching for information about "The Obsidian Muse." His fingers danced across the screen, revealing bits and pieces of information. The painting was scheduled to be auctioned at a gala that very evening, and its location was disclosed as 23 Rue de la Serenité. But was this information too readily available? Were there hidden motives behind it?

Tickets were apparently still available, and without a second thought, Lucas secured one. But now the realization that he was a ticket-holding guest at an upscale gala was beginning to dawn on him. Panic threatened to overwhelm him. He had to blend in, and the invitation called for a black tuxedo.

Lucas had barely touched his coffee, and his breakfast sat nearly untouched, but a far more pressing concern weighed heavily on his mind. Anxiety gnawed at him, his hands trembling as he struggled to force down the unappetizing food before him.

Questions buzzed through Lucas's mind like a relentless swarm of bees. "What if I can't get my medication in time? What happens if I miss a dose? How did I forget something so crucial back in New York?" His paranoia danced on the edge of panic as he fretted over the situation.

The scene around him was a cozy but bustling cafe. The chatter of patrons and the clinking of dishes provided a background symphony of daily life. Sunlight streamed in through the large windows, casting warm, inviting rays across the room. Yet, Lucas's world felt anything but warm and inviting as he grappled with the medication he so desperately needed.

Each passing second intensified his worry. His coffee had grown cold, his breakfast untouched. With each unanswered question about his medication, the knot in his stomach tightened. In this quaint little cafe, the outside world continued its normal rhythm, but for Lucas, time stood still as he faced the consequences of his forgetfulness.

As he tried to gulp down the lukewarm coffee, paranoia crept in. What if he couldn't get his medication? What would happen to him in a foreign city?

His smartwatch lay on the table, unresponsive to his frantic taps. "Mille," he muttered, frustration lacing his voice. Silence was all he received in return. The watch's deadness amplified his growing sense of dread.

Lucas's heart raced, and he decided to call out for help. "Mille," he called again, louder this time. Still, nothing. Panic welled up as he realized that his lifeline to information and assistance was useless at this crucial moment.

Paranoia clawed at him, intensifying his desperation. He pondered over the implications of his smartwatch's failure. Had it been hacked? Was someone watching him, sabotaging his only connection to help?

With trembling hands, he reached for his phone and dialed his psychiatrist, Dr. Clint Smith, back in New York. The call was answered by a groggy Dr. Smith, who asked, "Lucas, why are you calling me so early?"

Lucas's paranoia flared up. He questioned why Dr. Smith was sounding groggy. Was he not sleeping well because of Lucas's situation? Did he sound irritated?

Realization hit him hard – he hadn't considered the time difference. In New York, it was a grueling 4 AM. "Sorry, Dr. Smith," Lucas responded urgently. "I'm in Paris, and I forgot my medication."

Dr. Smith sighed, and Lucas found himself questioning whether frustration lurked beneath the sound. "Tell me, how long ago was your last dose?"

Paranoia gnawed at him as he contemplated how his psychiatrist was perceiving him now. Did Dr. Smith think he was irresponsible? Was he disappointed in him?

"Almost 48 hours ago," Lucas admitted, his growing concern evident in his voice.

Dr. Smith's tone shifted, becoming more understanding, but it only fueled Lucas's paranoia. Was Dr. Smith secretly worried about his condition? Did he think Lucas was in danger?

"Oh, you might start to feel withdrawal symptoms pretty soon," Dr. Smith warned.

Lucas's anxiety surged. He held his head in his hands and whispered into the phone, "I think I'm already feeling it. I've had a headache for the last few hours." The pain in his head felt like a vice, squeezing tighter with every passing minute.

Dr. Smith's voice became a comforting presence, but Lucas's anxiety still gnawed at him. "Don't panic, Lucas. I can't send you the medication from here. You might have to tough it out for a few days."

Lucas asked, "Doc, am I going to be okay?"

"No, Lucas," his doctor reassured him, "We can get you to a local hospital in Paris, where you can get an appointment with a psychiatrist, and they can contact me."

Lucas nodded, even though Dr. Smith couldn't see him. Paranoia gripped him as he realized he'd have to navigate a foreign healthcare system while grappling with withdrawal symptoms. What if the local doctors didn't understand his case? What if the language barrier made things even more complicated?

Taking a deep breath, Lucas assured his doctor, "I'll figure it out somehow, Dr. Smith." The determination in his voice was unmistakable, but beneath it lay layers of paranoia and uncertainty about what lay ahead in a foreign city without his medication.

He ended the call and realized he couldn't afford to waste any more time. The gala was just a few hours away, and fear started creeping in. He glanced around, making sure no one was watching him too closely. Why did the caller sound so urgent? What did they want from him?

Frantically, he flagged down the waiter, anxiety gnawing at him. He needed to settle the bill and get on with his packed schedule. The quaint Parisian café provided some comfort, but the mysteries of the morning weighed on him. Was someone following him?

The waiter returned to the table with the bill, and Lucas, in a rush, pulled out his wallet, his hand shaking slightly. He wondered if anyone at the café was eavesdropping on his conversation. What if he was being set up? He slipped some cash onto the tray and asked, "Monsieur, is there anything else you require?"

Lucas leaned in, his voice low, and questioned, "Can you tell me where I can find a good tuxedo in this city?" He desperately needed to blend in and not draw any attention to himself.

The waiter nodded, his eyes locking onto Lucas's.

Paranoia gnawed at Lucas again. Why was the waiter giving him such a knowing look? Did he know something about the caller? He listened carefully as the waiter began to give him detailed directions to the nearest men's clothing store. The feeling of gratitude washed over him, yet a nagging doubt lingered—was the waiter part of some elaborate plan?

Lucas thanked the waiter and paid the bill, his mind racing with questions. What surprises were in store for him today? He had to stay on guard. As he left the café, he couldn't shake the feeling that someone was shadowing him.

Every step he took felt like a potential trap, and his heart pounded in his chest.

Realizing he needed something to take the edge off his growing paranoia, he decided to switch one addiction for another - caffeine. As he walked the bustling Parisian streets, he contemplated his choice. Some people turned to alcohol in times of stress, but that was never his thing. Caffeine seemed like a safer bet.

***

Lucas left the café behind, anxiety gnawing at him as he weaved through the picturesque Parisian streets. He found himself wondering if he was being followed. Were those footsteps behind him mere coincidence, or was someone tailing him on this crisp autumn afternoon?

Following the waiter's cryptic directions, Lucas eventually stumbled upon a street lined with an array of shops, each more charming than the last. His heart raced as he questioned if this was the right place. Was this really where he was supposed to be, or was he about to make a costly mistake?

Then, out of the blue, he spotted a storefront bathed in the golden glow of the afternoon sun. It was a high-end boutique specializing in suits and tuxedos. Lucas hadn't anticipated that he'd find himself in this part of Paris so soon. What if this was a trap? He couldn't afford to make a wrong move, not with the clock ticking mercilessly.

The soft jingle of a bell above the door signaled his entry into the small boutique. Lucas glanced around the elegant interior, mentally noting the emergency exits. What if he needed to make a hasty escape? Was there a back door?

The boutique was a treasure trove of sartorial excellence, with suits and tuxedos displayed in a myriad of styles and colors. The scent of opulent fabrics lingered in the air, surrounding him with an aura of luxury. Yet, Lucas couldn't shake the feeling that he was being watched. He surreptitiously glanced around, wondering if there were hidden cameras recording his every move. Were his steps being tracked by unseen eyes?

While he scanned the room, a dapper elderly gentleman approached him, his attire rivaling the finest suits on display. A warm, friendly smile graced the man's face. "Bonjour, monsieur! How can I assist you today?" the man asked in a rich Parisian accent, yet Lucas found himself questioning whether his charm was merely a facade. Was there something more to this friendly demeanor?

Lucas locked eyes with the man, assessing him warily. He couldn't afford to be too trusting. "I need a tuxedo," he replied, his voice determined but tinged with paranoia. What if this man was an operative sent to entrap him?

The salesman, with a knowing nod, appraised Lucas's build and features with a shrewd eye. "Of course, monsieur. Please, follow me to the back. We have a selection that might be just what you're looking for."

Lucas followed the man to a more secluded

section of the boutique, lined with racks of crisp white shirts and tailored pants. The elderly salesman began to pull out a few options, laying them out for Lucas to try. "Let's start with these, and we'll see how they fit. You have the perfect build for our suits."

As Lucas held up the pristine white shirt, a sinking realization settled in—this situation was unraveling into something far more complex than he had ever anticipated. What if these clothes weren't just attire but held a hidden message or concealed devices? He had to tread carefully, for the gala wasn't the only thing on the line; his safety and the success of the mission were hanging in the balance.

As Lucas sifted through the rack of shirts and pants, a sense of unease crept over him, his mind plagued by nagging withdrawal symptoms. The salesman's friendly banter acted as a momentary distraction, but questions swirled in his head like a brewing storm.

'What's the deal with this salesman?' Lucas wondered, glancing at the man as he chatted away. 'Is he just being friendly, or is there some ulterior motive behind this sudden friendship?'

They chatted about various topics, veering into the world of art and the upcoming gala in Paris. The salesman's stories of the dazzling Parisian auctions painted a vivid picture, yet Lucas found himself questioning whether there was more beneath the surface.

'Is he trying to probe me for information?' Lucas pondered, sizing up the salesman's every word. 'Does he know something about me or the gala that I don't?'

The salesman leaned in, a glint in his eye that set off alarm bells in Lucas's mind. 'What's with that twinkle?' he thought, suspicious. 'Is he about to drop a bombshell, or is this just an act to reel me in?'

And then the mention of Julian Laurent, a name Lucas had never heard before, sent a shiver down his spine. 'Who is this Julian Laurent?' he wondered, his curiosity mixed with a growing sense of paranoia. 'Is he someone I should know about, or is this just a ploy to make me feel out of the loop?'

Lucas, furrowed his brow. "Julian Laurent? I haven't heard of him. Who is he exactly?"

As the salesman continued, Lucas couldn't shake the feeling that there was more to this story than met the eye. "Why is the salesman telling me this?" he questioned. "Is there some connection between Julian Laurent, the gala, and me that I'm not aware of?"

Julian Laurent's mysterious reputation raised even

more questions in Lucas's mind. "Why is he the talk of the town?" he asked, growing increasingly intrigued. "And why do I feel like there's something off about this whole situation?"

The salesman chuckled softly. "Ah, you see, Julian Laurent is a man of mystery and intrigue. He's renowned for his extravagant lifestyle and impeccable taste. And, monsieur, he never misses a single auction in this city."

Lucas leaned in, his interest piqued. "Never misses an auction? Why is that?"

The salesman's voice dropped to a conspiratorial whisper. "There are whispers, you see. Whispers that he might be after one of the paintings that will be up for auction at the gala this evening."

Lucas was now fully engrossed in the conversation. "Which painting is that? Do you know?"

The salesman shook his head, his expression a mixture of fascination and uncertainty. "I'm afraid I don't know, monsieur. But Julian Laurent is known to be rather eccentric. He's a man who always gets what he desires. They say he's a collector of the rare and unusual, willing to pay any price to add a piece to his collection."

The mention of Julian's eccentricity and

willingness to pay any price sent chills down Lucas's spine. 'Is he a threat?' he wondered. 'Could he be after something related to me, or is this all just a coincidence?'

As Lucas continued to try on clothes, his thoughts raced. 'What's the real story here?' he asked himself, a mixture of intrigue and anxiety building within him. 'Who is Julian Laurent, and how does he fit into the puzzle of this gala?' His anticipation for the evening's event grew, but so did the headache that relentlessly clawed at his consciousness. 'Is it just nerves, or is there something more to this gala that I need to uncover?'

As the tailor adjusted Lucas's tuxedo, they maintained a friendly conversation. The guy clearly knew his stuff, yet Lucas found himself questioning a few things. He asked, "Hey, is there any way you can send it to my hotel? I'm Lucas Mitchell, and I'm staying at Hotel de l'Étoile, room 301."

The salesman grinned, which Lucas found somewhat reassuring but also made him a bit more paranoid. "Absolutely, sir. We offer that service to our customers. Your tuxedo will be at your hotel in no time."

Relieved, Lucas handed over the payment and exited the shop. The dazzling Parisian sun poured down, creating an intense glare that practically drilled into his eyes. He raised his hand to shield himself, and as he did, his headache seemed to intensify.

Strolling through the lively streets, the persistent throb in his head began to feel like a never-ending annoyance. The play of light and shadow was almost disorienting, and Lucas started to question what he was seeing. He thought he spotted a shadowy figure up ahead, but it remained elusive, like a ghost. He blinked, trying to clear his vision, but the figure stayed put.

It was as though Paris itself was messing with his mind, teasing him with phantom images. The figure appeared to beckon him, and it felt oddly real. A shiver crept down Lucas's spine, making him feel increasingly uneasy, and he couldn't quite grasp what was happening. Was this city playing tricks on him, or was there something more to this strange encounter?

Is someone following me? Why is the sun so blinding today? What if the tuxedo doesn't get to my hotel? Did the salesman seem too eager to help? What if the headache is a sign of something serious? Why did that figure look so real?

Lucas couldn't shake off the unnerving feeling any longer. With a deep breath, he closed his eyes briefly, trying to clear his thoughts. He found himself wondering: was he just being paranoid?

When Lucas opened his eyes, he found himself in a dark planetarium, under a vast dome of celestial wonders. The night was clear, and the stars above shone brilliantly, like a sparkling tapestry spread across the inky canvas of the sky. Beside him, Eva lay on the soft, reclining chairs, her fingers intertwined with his as she gazed upward.

Eva traced her finger along the lines of the imaginary constellations. "Do you see that one, Lucas? That's Cassiopeia. It's said to be the queen of the night sky."

Lucas smiled, his eyes filled with admiration. "I see it, and it's lovely, but none of those stars up there can match the sparkle in your eyes."

Eva blushed, a warm, rosy hue gracing her cheeks. "You're such a charmer, Lucas."

As they gazed at the stars, Lucas felt compelled to share his thoughts. "Eva, being here with you, under this breathtaking celestial display, it's like a dream come true. You make everything seem so magical."

Eva turned her head to meet Lucas's gaze, her eyes reflecting the shimmering stars. "You know, Lucas, you've brought a lot of magic into my life too. I never thought I'd find someone as extraordinary as you."

The planetarium's projector cast a comet streaking across the dome, and Lucas seized the moment. "That comet reminds me of us, Eva. A brilliant flash of light in a vast universe, a love story written in the stars."

Eva's heart swelled with emotion as she nestled closer to Lucas. "It's a love story I never want to end, Lucas."

Beneath the cosmic display, they lay as star-crossed lovers, lost in their own celestial love story. In that moment, the world vanished, leaving only the two of them under the starry tapestry. Lucas closed his eyes, savoring the moment. He heard Eva's voice, telling him to "Open your eyes, Lucas."

When he dared to open his eyes, the world around him suddenly felt familiar, and it sent shivers down his spine. He was back in his hotel room. But when had he returned? He couldn't remember making the journey back from wherever he had been.

As he stood there, the room seemed to close in on him, the corners casting elongated shadows that danced eerily on the walls. He felt like he was in a scene from a suspense movie. Why did it feel so different now? Why did everything look darker, more mysterious?

Lucas was left pondering a troubling question that seemed to echo endlessly in his mind: had he just imagined the whole thing, or had something inexplicable and bizarre really occurred?

Just as he was about to dismiss his unsettling thoughts, the shrill ring of the phone on the bedside table jolted him back to reality. His heart raced. Who could be calling him now? Why was everything suddenly so intense and eerie?

He hesitated for a moment before picking up the receiver. A voice on the other end introduced itself as the hotel's concierge, yet unease crept into Lucas, tightening its grip with every word. What if this call was somehow related to his strange experience earlier?

"Good evening, monsieur," the concierge began in a formal tone, only increasing Lucas's anxiety. "I'm pleased to inform you that your tuxedo has been delivered to your room, as requested." Lucas blinked in confusion. He did have a tuxedo, but he hadn't asked for it to be delivered. Why on earth would he need it now?

The concierge continued, "Is there anything else we can assist you with?" Lucas stammered for a moment before replying with a shaky, "No, thank you." He couldn't quite put his finger on it, but something about this whole situation felt off.

Moments later, there was a soft, almost eerie knock at the door, and Lucas felt a chill run down his spine. He carefully approached the door, feeling more and more paranoid with each step. Who was behind that door? What if this was all a setup?

As he cautiously opened the door, he was greeted by a hotel staff member with a neatly wrapped package. It was his tuxedo. Lucas accepted it with a trembling hand, thanking the staff member and hastily closing the door behind him. The package felt cool to the touch, and the glossy wrapping paper crinkled as he held it.

Lucas couldn't shake the feeling that something strange was afoot. He carefully inspected the package, the fine fabric of the tuxedo feeling like a tangible piece of reality in a world that seemed increasingly surreal. What had just happened, and what did it all mean?

In a moment of panic, he frantically pulled out his smartphone, swiping through it, trying to make sense of everything. That's when he stumbled upon the gala ticket he had purchased for the evening. The tuxedo in his hands suddenly made sense, it was for the gala. But why was his memory failing him so strangely? Did he buy this tuxedo himself? A gnawing doubt crept in, as he began to question every detail, every action.

Questions swirled in his mind, fueling his paranoia. Had someone tampered with his mind? Or was it just a lapse in memory? He couldn't be sure. The tuxedo's weight felt heavy in his trembling hands, a constant reminder of the looming gala, which now held more mysteries than answers.

Lucas shot a quick glance at his wristwatch, a stark reminder that time was slipping away. The urgency of making it to the event on time and the cryptic message he had received weighed heavily on him. He had to get dressed and leave without any further delay.

As Lucas meticulously prepared his tuxedo for the evening, a newfound sense of purpose overtook him. The events in Paris had left him with an unshakable feeling that he was embroiled in something far bigger than himself. The cryptic message, the mysterious painting, and the upcoming gala all felt like scattered pieces of a larger puzzle, waiting to be connected.

His hotel room was cloaked in silence, broken only by the sound of his own breath. He tapped on his smartwatch, connecting with his ever-reliable AI assistant, Mille. Her digital presence was a comforting reassurance in the middle of his mounting paranoia.

"Hey, Millie, you there?" he inquired.

Mille's prompt and reassuring response came through, "Yes, Lucas, I'm here. How can I assist you?"

But something nagged at him, a lingering thought that refused to dissipate. Why hadn't Mille reminded him to take his medication since he left New York? Given her programmed diligence, her lack of reminders was disconcerting. Lucas's brow furrowed as he probed further, "Why haven't you reminded me to take my meds?"

Mille's calm response was far from soothing, "I'm sorry, Lucas. There must have been an oversight."

Lucas was taken aback; oversights were unheard of when it came to his meticulous AI. His concern continued to grow, but for now, he had to focus on the immediate task at hand.

With his tuxedo now perfectly arranged, Lucas stood before a mirror, adjusting his tie. His gaze was fixed on his reflection as he asked, "Millie, how far is 23 Rue de la Serenité from the hotel?"

Mille's response was swift, "If you take a taxi during rush hour, it'll take about 50 minutes. But if you decide to walk, you can reach there in just 20 minutes."

Lucas weighed his options, the strange behavior of Mille still playing on his mind. "Well," he said, mustering a half-smile, "maybe a leisurely stroll through the Parisian streets is just what I need. I'll walk. Thanks, Millie."

He continued to adjust his tie, all the while wondering if he was truly in control of his own actions, or if there were unseen hands manipulating the intricate web of his life.

***

As Lucas walked towards the gala entrance, his mind buzzed with the ever-increasing mysteries that seemed to plague the City of Lights. One thing was clear - his AI assistant, Millie, had been acting rather strangely lately. Why was she being so cryptic, and what was she hiding? The uncertainty gnawed at him, and despite his best efforts, his mind kept drifting to the possibility that something more sinister was at play. Why was she acting so mysteriously?

Guided by Millie's digital directions, Lucas weaved through the intricate web of Parisian streets with effortless precision. Her artificial voice offered step-by-step guidance, but it made him wonder - was Millie leading him down a path of no return? Could he truly trust her in this ever-complicating world of secrets and shadows?

Before long, he found himself standing in front of the gala's grand entrance, bathed in the soft, enchanting radiance of the Parisian night. The sight was breathtaking, yet amidst all the elegance and allure, a lingering sense of unease crept over Lucas. What was really going on behind these luxurious façades? And why was he here, wrapped in a cloak of opulence, chasing shadows?

The gala's panorama was nothing short of mesmerizing, a display of opulence and sophistication that bordered on the surreal. Strings of ambient lights created a pathway of enchantment leading to the heart of the event. Lucas couldn't shake the feeling that every step he took was one step closer to an unknown abyss. Was he walking into a trap? Were the secrets he was chasing about to consume him?

In the middle of the elite crowd, the soft murmur of conversations and the tinkling of glasses filled the air with an ambiance that was both captivating and unsettling. Every glance from a guest, every hushed whisper, felt like a coded message meant for his ears alone. Were they talking about him? Or were they in on the very mysteries he sought to uncover?

As Lucas stepped into the gala, the air was heavy

with anticipation. Magnificent works of art adorned the walls, their beauty and significance shrouded in secrecy. The guests, dressed in their most exquisite attire, moved in circles, exchanging cryptic glances and sharing guarded words. The very atmosphere seemed to whisper secrets into the night, secrets that hung in the air like forbidden fruit. What were these secrets, and would they finally lead Lucas to the answers he was so desperately seeking?

In this captivating setting, Lucas couldn't shake off the feeling that he was being watched, that every move he made was under scrutiny. The room itself felt like a labyrinth of intrigues and hidden agendas. Was Julian Laurent lurking in the shadows, observing his every step? And if so, what did he want? Lucas was determined not to let this elusive philanthropist slip through his fingers. The man held the key to a puzzle that was growing more complex with every passing moment. What dark revelations awaited him in this maze of secrets, art, and opulence?

As Lucas continued his walk, surrounded by the opulence of the moment, he found himself musing aloud to Millie in a casual, conversational tone, "Hey, Millie, doesn't this whole situation feel like something out of a spy movie? I mean, seriously, are we living in one right now?"

His comment hung in the air for a moment as they navigated the luxurious gala. A sense of unease began to creep in, and before he knew it, he asked Millie, "Do you think we're being watched, Millie? I mean, with all these people around, who knows who might be keeping an eye on us?"

Millie, ever the voice of reason, responded, "You've got a point, Lucas. But don't forget, this is no fiction, and the stakes are real. We need to stay sharp."

With a nervous chuckle, Lucas moved deeper into the dazzling world of the art gala, his determination unwavering. Tonight, he was on a mission to uncover secret behind the message he received back in New York, all while being keenly aware of the mysterious presence of Julian Laurent.

Inside the grand foyer of the gala, Lucas found himself surrounded by a breathtaking display of artistic wonders. The grand entrance loomed ahead, guarded by stern-faced security personnel. The thought wouldn't leave him alone, 'Do you think they're checking everyone so thoroughly? What if they discover something we're not supposed to have?'

With each step he took, he couldn't shake the feeling that he was under scrutiny, even as he joined the line of excited attendees. As he waited his turn to enter, he kept glancing over his shoulder, whispering to Millie, "Do you think we're blending in, or are we sticking out like sore thumbs here?"

Finally, it was Lucas's moment to shine. He nervously presented the ticket he'd obtained earlier via the gala's website. The security guard scrutinized it for what felt like an eternity, making Lucas feel increasingly uneasy. 'Do you think he's onto something? Are we about to get caught?' he wondered.

After a tense pause, the guard nodded, allowing Lucas to proceed through a metal detector. As he passed through, a wave of relief washed over him, tinged with lingering anxiety. "What if they planted something on me while I was getting screened? Can we be sure we're truly safe?" he whispered to Millie.

Beyond the security checkpoint, the gala's true splendor was revealed. The setting was a breathtaking masterpiece, drawing Lucas in with its exquisite beauty. The walls of the room were adorned with an extensive collection of artworks that ranged from vibrant paintings to intricate sculptures. Each piece seemed to beckon him with a story, leaving him to wonder about their creators and the secrets they might hold.

Lucas couldn't tear his gaze away from the

captivating art on display. As he casually meandered through the gallery, his eyes fixated on each piece, marveling at the intricate brushwork, the vibrant colors, and the powerful emotions they conveyed. It was as if every stroke held a secret, and he found himself wondering.

Questions buzzed in his mind like persistent mosquitoes on a hot summer night. Who were these artists? What was the story behind each piece? Were there hidden messages waiting to be uncovered?

But then, his heartbeat quickened, and he felt a rush of awe and excitement when his eyes locked onto the pièce de résistance of the entire collection: 'The Obsidian Muse.'

This painting, 'The Obsidian Muse,' was a masterpiece that seemed to have its gravitational pull. It felt like it was calling to him, its mysterious beauty creating a hypnotic aura. Lucas approached it with a sense of reverence, his eyes scrutinizing every minute detail, every delicate interplay of shadow and light.

As he leaned in, trying to discern the hidden layers of meaning in the painting, one particular detail caught his eye — the artist's name was conspicuously missing. Instead, it bore a simple attribution: "Art by Camille."

This revelation sent shivers down his spine, and

the questions multiplied in his mind. Who was Camille? Why was the artist's name missing? Was this a deliberate act or an accidental omission? What was the significance of 'The Obsidian Muse' in the grander scheme of things?

The atmosphere in the gallery was heavy with the hushed whispers of fellow art enthusiasts, their footsteps echoing on the polished marble floor. The gallery's walls were adorned with lush drapes that framed the paintings like windows into another world. Soft, warm lighting cast a mesmerizing glow, accentuating the mystery and allure of each artwork.

A thrill shot through Lucas, as if he had uncovered a hidden treasure—one that might finally unravel the mystery he'd been chasing. The mystery deepened, pulling him further into its intriguing web. His pulse quickened, and his mind raced as he yearned to delve deeper into the mysterious world of Camille and the haunting beauty of 'The Obsidian Muse.'

As Lucas pondered the mysterious allure of 'The Obsidian Muse,' paranoia crept in. Why did this painting captivate him so intensely? Was there something hidden within those dark, swirling strokes? He glanced around, wondering if anyone else felt the same.

Then, out of the blue, a voice boomed over the room's state-of-the-art speakers. An announcement, crisp and clear, sent shivers down Lucas's spine. Could someone be watching him? Was this part of a carefully orchestrated plan? Questions raced through his mind like a stampede of wild horses.

"Welcome to the auction," the voice declared. It urged the well-dressed crowd to make their way to their seats. Lucas's heart raced. Who was behind that voice? Was it a prelude to an evening full of secrets? Try as he might, he couldn't shake the paranoia about what was coming.

Lucas joined the parade of elegantly dressed attendees, all proceeding to their designated seats. The scene unfolded before him, a grand gallery bathed in soft, warm light that turned the artworks into something otherworldly. It felt like a page out of a fairy tale, or perhaps a thriller in disguise. He was mesmerized despite himself, yet the sense of paranoia clung to him like a shadow.

As he settled into his designated seat, adjusting his tuxedo, Lucas couldn't resist a whisper to his trusty AI companion, Millie. Before he knew it, he was confiding in her. "Millie, do you ever get the feeling that we're not alone in this? Something about this place seems...

off. What's your take?"

Millie's response, always logical and composed, added a touch of levity to the situation, though it didn't entirely quell Lucas's paranoia. "I don't have feelings, Lucas, but I can analyze the situation. It's an art auction, and the atmosphere is electric with anticipation. Nothing seems amiss... yet."

Lucas managed a soft laugh, though it was tinged with unease. The gallery buzzed with excitement, and the charismatic auctioneer, a man with a voice smoother than silk, took center stage. No matter how hard he tried to blend into the background, Lucas still felt like all eyes were on him when it was the art that truly deserved the attention. Who else was watching him, and why? The paranoia gnawed at him like an insatiable beast.

"Hey folks," the auctioneer started, "tonight we've got something pretty special for you, a bunch of art pieces that have been around for centuries and have traveled the globe. Each one's got its own story, some history, and a deep connection to the human experience. We're diving into the world of art with all the respect and awe it deserves."

As the auctioneer kept on talking, Lucas felt a little jittery. He found himself questioning the true origins of the art pieces on display. Were they real or just really convincing fakes? And who were the people gathered here? Were they all genuine art enthusiasts or were there some shady characters hiding in plain sight?

The scene around him was impressive, though. The venue was grand, all glittering chandeliers and polished marble floors. The audience, dressed to the nines, hushed in anticipation, added to the whole air of mystery.

"Our first gem of the night," the auctioneer declared, "comes from the famous maritime artist, Henri Leclerc. It's a stunner called 'Sunset on the High Seas' that captures the breathtaking beauty of the ocean at twilight. We're kicking off the bidding at one million euros."

Lucas watched as the room transformed into a buzzing hive of whispers. The audience members exchanged furtive glances, their eyes scanning the room as if trying to figure out who their competition was. In the middle of all this, doubt gnawed at him—was the painting truly authentic, or just another trick of his restless mind? Was it really Leclerc's work, or was it an elaborate forgery? He tried to catch the expressions on the faces of the bidders. Did they know something he didn't?

The numbers on the display climbed faster than he could keep track. Lucas found himself wondering whether this was just a typical art auction or a secret front for money laundering. Who were the people that could casually drop millions on a painting? And how did they have so much money to spend in the first place?

The painting was eventually won by a wealthy collector, who raised his paddle with triumphant glee. Doubt crept into Lucas's mind as he considered the authenticity of the transaction. Did the collector genuinely appreciate the artwork, or was this just another status symbol for their collection? The night brimmed with questions and intrigue, leaving Lucas with a creeping sense of paranoia at its core.

"Alright, folks," the auctioneer announced with a sly smile, "time to check out this Renaissance masterpiece, 'The Hidden Lady.' Pretty mysterious stuff, I must say. But what's it hiding behind that paint, huh? Who's the artist? Who's been hiding it all these centuries? Let's kick this off at a cool two million euros. Anyone in?"

The crowd in the gallery started raising their paddles with excitement, and the room buzzed with anticipation. But as the bids climbed higher, the question lingered—who would pay such a fortune for a painting shrouded in mystery? As the auctioneer's voice rang out, Lucas couldn't help but ask himself, 'Is there something more to this 'Hidden Lady' than meets the eye? What's her story? And why do these people seem so eager to get their hands on it?'

The price kept climbing, and with each increase, you became more curious and, maybe, a bit paranoid. Lucas thought, 'Is there something hidden within this artwork, some message or secret that's driving this bidding frenzy?'

Finally, a victorious bidder claimed the painting, and yet curiosity gnawed at Lucas, 'What do they know that I don't? Did they just uncover a hidden treasure, or are they chasing something that's been lost to time?'

The auction continued, and you watched as other pieces found new homes in the hands of collectors and connoisseurs. But you couldn't shake the feeling that there was more to 'The Hidden Lady' than met the eye. What other mysteries lay hidden in the world of art, waiting to be discovered?

The auctioneer's voice cut through the room, adding an electrifying tension to the air. "Hey there, folks, our last masterpiece of the night is a real puzzle. It's 'The Obsidian Muse' by this super mysterious artist,

Camille. Who's ready to start bidding at 5 million euros?"

Lucas's heart raced as he fixated on the painting. It was a captivating play of light and shadows, a true work of art that had brought him all the way to Paris. But he couldn't help feeling on edge, especially with that cryptic voice from the back of the room.

"Five million euros," the auctioneer declared, acknowledging the mysterious voice. "Any takers? Going once, going twice..."

Lucas's eyes darted around the room, trying to spot the bold bidder, but they remained shrouded in obscurity, lurking within the gallery's dim corners. Who was this mysterious figure, driven to own 'The Obsidian Muse'?

"Sold!" The gavel slammed down, sealing the deal with unwavering finality. The room exploded with applause and hushed conversations. Lucas couldn't shake the auctioneer's words from his mind as the painting was whisked away by a team of white-gloved attendants.

As the masterpiece disappeared from view, Lucas found himself pondering the secrets it concealed and the enigmatic bidder who had claimed it. What did they see in 'The Obsidian Muse' that had compelled them to bid so extravagantly?

The gala was buzzing with chattering guests, and the excitement in the air was palpable as 'The Obsidian Muse' found itself a new owner. Lucas found himself drawn into eavesdropping on the conversations swirling around him, his mind racing with curiosity. Who was this new owner, and what was the buzz all about? Questions circled his thoughts, making him increasingly paranoid.

As Lucas listened, a stranger seated nearby dropped a tantalizing hint that instantly piqued his interest. "It must be Julian, always coming up like a vulture and swooping in flaunting his wealth."

The name 'Julian' echoed in Lucas's mind like a persistent echo, making him wonder about the significance of this man in the middle of his quest. Could Julian hold the key to the unanswered questions that had brought him to the bustling streets of Paris? Urgency welled up inside him, prompting him to abandon his seat and navigate through the maze of elegant attendees.

As Lucas ventured towards the back of the gallery, his heart raced with paranoia, driving him to seek answers. The thought crept in before he could shut it out—eyes, unseen but present, tracking his every move, as if they already knew what he was searching for. Was he really being followed? He needed to find out more about this Julian character, but he couldn't shake the feeling that he was being watched.

Upon reaching the back of the gallery, a group of elderly men stood engrossed in conversation. With a mix of anticipation and anxiety, Lucas approached them, and his voice quivered as he inquired, "Mr. Laurent?" They stared at him, puzzled expressions playing across their faces, and then slowly shook their heads in unison. Julian Laurent was nowhere to be found among them. Lucas's paranoia deepened as he questioned if this was all a ruse, if he was being steered in the wrong direction.

The search for answers led Lucas out of the glamorous gala and into the mysterious embrace of the Parisian night. The grandeur of the art auction began to fade into the distant background as he walked the city's dimly lit streets. Yet, in the middle of the city's magic, a nagging sense of dread crept over him. Were the shadows concealing hidden threats? Were his every move being scrutinized?

Suddenly, his surroundings seemed to blur and shift, casting him into a whirlwind of hallucinations. Vivid images and fragmented memories danced before his eyes, making it nearly impossible to distinguish reality from illusion. Paranoia gripped him as he desperately tried to hold onto a tangible thread of reality, his mind racing with questions about what was happening to him.

Amid this surreal experience, a name, 'Eva,' resounded in his mind with haunting clarity. It was as if the past and present were colliding in a disorienting whirlwind, leaving Lucas gasping for a reality that felt increasingly elusive. Where was Eva, and what was her connection to his current mess? The paranoia grew, and Lucas's world spiraled into a labyrinth of intrigue and uncertainty.

As Lucas meandered through the dimly lit streets of Paris, his mind became a battleground, torn between the present and the ghosts of his past. The city, once a beacon of romance, now felt like it was playing tricks on him, blurring the lines between reality and haunting memories. Why did the streetlights seem to flicker strangely tonight? Was someone following him?

In the middle of his growing paranoia, a figure materialized, seemingly summoned from the depths of his own thoughts. It was Eva, the woman he'd desperately tried to forget but could never quite erase from his heart. Why, out of all places, did she choose to haunt him here, in the heart of Paris?

In this bizarre mental labyrinth, Lucas found himself locked in a conversation with the apparition of Eva. It was as if time itself had folded upon him, thrusting him back into the past. Did other people see her, or was he alone in this surreal experience? He couldn't be sure.

The Eva of his memories wore a wistful smile, her eyes brimming with the same warmth and curiosity that had once ensnared him. How could a memory be so vivid, so real? Had he truly lost his grip on reality?

"Lucas," she whispered, her voice soft as a caress.

Lucas, caught in the whirlwind of his hallucination, stammered, "Eva, what's happening to me? Am I going insane?" Did this mean he was losing his mind for good? Was this the onset of something far more sinister?

Eva's image wavered, mirroring the uncertainty that now gripped his very soul. "No, Lucas."

In his mind's eye, he could see the two of them, perched on a tranquil rooftop beneath a starry New York sky. The city sprawled below them, its lights flickering like distant promises. Was he actually back in New York, or was this just another illusion?

The gentle night breeze seemed to carry a sense of

enchantment, as if anything were possible. Did the city of lights harbor secrets that only he could see?

Eva's laughter, or what seemed like it, swirled through the air, and her eyes held a playful gleam. She leaned in, her words brushing his cheek like a phantom touch. "Lucas, do you believe in fate? In moments that can change everything?" Was this a message from a parallel universe? Or a glimpse into the past he'd rather forget?

He gazed into her eyes, unable to tear his gaze away from the depths of warmth and mystery that they held. "With you, Eva, I'd believe in anything." Was it possible that he could still feel the same way after all this time?

These memories were bittersweet, reminding him of a time when the world had been painted in vibrant hues and the future had seemed like a limitless canvas.

But as the hallucinations continued to swirl around him, Lucas understood that he couldn't remain trapped in the past. The pressing question now was, how would he escape the clutches of this surreal, haunting dance between reality and memory?

CHAPTER 3: THE CURSED MASTERPIECE

Two days ago....

Julian Laurent was sprawled out in his lavish dining room in a fancy Paris townhouse, just chilling and savoring a seriously epic breakfast. He was totally into that whole multitasking thing, having his go-to tablet propped up next to his grub. He sipped on some super-hot espresso while casually swiping through the latest morning news. And then, out of nowhere, this one pic on his tablet screen grabbed his eyeballs. It was none other than the world-famous "Obsidian Muse," this painting that had everyone talking, and how it got famous was a real head-scratcher.

The dining room was the definition of posh. You had fancy chandeliers hanging from the ceiling, casting this warm, golden glow that made the room feel all cozy. The walls were decked out with elegant artwork, and there was a long, polished wooden table right in the center, where Julian was chowing down. The spread in front of him was something else, with fluffy croissants, a rainbow of fresh fruit, and a whole spread of pastries. He looked like a king, sitting there with a big plate piled high.

Julian's tablet was like his sidekick, always there whenever he needed it. It was propped up on this shiny stand, and he'd swipe and tap on it like a pro. He sipped on his espresso, feeling that burst of caffeine hit him as he scrolled through the headlines. But then, BAM! He saw this pic that just stopped him dead in his tracks. It was the "Obsidian Muse." This painting was making waves in the art world like you wouldn't believe.

Julian's captivating eyes were locked onto the image, his fascination growing by the second. The painting's ethereal beauty, the intricate dance of light and shadow, and the emotions it seemed to stir deep within him held him in rapturous thrall. It was as though an invisible force had ensnared him, pulling him ever deeper into its mesmerizing embrace.

In true playboy billionaire fashion, Julian mused aloud with a smirk, "Is there anything in this world that isn't drawn to my charm and devotion?" He let out a smug chuckle as he contemplated the magnetic allure of the painting.

Just as the enchanting spell of the artwork began to envelop Julian, his ever-attentive butler, the impeccably dressed Sebastian, made his entrance. With a silver tray laden with an opulent breakfast feast,

Sebastian served his billionaire master with the utmost precision. He had been Julian's loyal butler for years, and he had become attuned to the man's ever-evolving passions and interests.

Julian, who always had a knack for making everything revolve around him, couldn't help but pull Sebastian into his orbit. "Sebastian, my dear friend, you've got to see this. Come over here and prepare to be dazzled." He dramatically turned his tablet towards his butler, unveiling the image of "The Obsidian Muse."

Sebastian, the unflappable butler, studied the painting with his customary discerning eye. "A truly remarkable piece, sir. 'The Obsidian Muse' has been making waves in the art world, no doubt about it."

As Julian admired the artwork on his tablet's display, a playful grin spread across his face. "You see, Sebastian, it's as if the artist knew I'd be the one to appreciate it the most. It's practically tailor-made for my impeccable taste, don't you think?"

Sebastian responded with a subtle, wry smile. "Indeed, sir, one could almost believe that. Your taste in art is truly unique."

Julian laughed, taking a playful jab at Sebastian's poker face. "Come on, Sebastian, admit it. You wish you had half the style and panache that I possess."

Sebastian's response was a dignified and slightly amused chuckle. "I'm content in my role as your trusty butler, sir, but I do enjoy glimpses into your vibrant world."

Julian's unwavering gaze remained fixed on the image, his self-assured tone betraying his unwavering resolve. "Sebastian, my friend, I must have that painting. It doesn't matter if it's in the clutches of a secretive collector, up for auction, or gracing the walls of some highfalutin gallery. I want it, and I want it now."

Sebastian nodded, fully aware of the depths of his master's desire. "Consider it done, sir. I'll begin the inquiries immediately. 'The Obsidian Muse' will find its new home in your collection."

Julian Laurent absolutely cherished those rare moments when he found himself all alone in the lap of luxury, in his private townhouse. For a guy as loaded and famous as he was, personal space was like gold dust, and he didn't mind splurging to get it. He thought it added that extra layer of mystery to his already intriguing, playboy image. He had a real knack for one-night stands, leaving a trail of heartbroken admirers behind as he vanished into the night, always leaving them guessing.

But beyond the glitz and glamour, what really got his heart racing was art. The pursuit of beauty and mastery, conveyed through the strokes of an artist's brush, was what really lit his fire. And "The Obsidian Muse" had him hooked like nothing else.

So, he dove headfirst into the world of research. Surprisingly, the internet had almost zilch on this painting, and real life wasn't any more helpful. The artist behind it, Camille, was like a phantom. The more he hit roadblocks, the more he was drawn into this mysterious masterpiece, determined to unveil its secrets and the even more secretive artist.

Sebastian was a true pro, working like a ninja. Within a few hours, he came back with some juicy tidbits that would set Julian's plans in motion. It was almost lunchtime when he arrived, and he had a confidential report with him, a little glint of excitement in his eyes.

Julian was lounging at his dining table, swirling a glass of the darkest red wine, pondering his next move. The news Sebastian had was like a shot of adrenaline. It reignited his passion for that tantalizing painting and its mysterious creator, Camille. The butler was like a phantom himself, almost invisible, but you could see he was itching to spill the beans.

Sebastian cleared his throat, just loud enough to catch Julian's attention. "I've got some promising news for you, sir."

Putting down his glass, Julian leaned forward, all ears. "Do tell, Sebastian. You've got me intrigued."

With unwavering confidence, the butler shared the scoop. "Well, sir, it turns out that 'The Obsidian Muse' is scheduled to be auctioned off at a grand gala in just two days. I've also taken the liberty of making sure we're all set to acquire it."

That news was like a lightning bolt of excitement surging through Julian's veins. The idea of claiming that enchanting artwork thrilled him to the core. A sly grin curled on his lips. "Sebastian, my man, you're a genius. Do you have secret ninja skills I don't know about?"

Sebastian chuckled softly, a hint of mischief in his eyes. "If I told you, sir, they wouldn't be very secret now, would they?"

Julian laughed heartily, appreciating the butler's quick wit. "You're absolutely right, Sebastian. I can always count on you for a good dose of humor along with your invaluable assistance."

Julian, being the charismatic philanthropist that

he was, had some grandiose plans in mind. He couldn't resist the magnetic pull of 'The Obsidian Muse.' The idea of basking in its exquisite beauty and soaking up the mysterious vibes of the upcoming gala excited him to no end. He leaned in, exuding his charming charisma, and asked Sebastian, "Sebastian, my friend, tell me, isn't 'The Obsidian Muse' simply irresistible? Don't you think it's a must-see for someone of my impeccable taste?"

Sebastian, always loyal and quick to appease Julian's desires, nodded fervently. "Absolutely, sir! I couldn't agree more. I'll make sure everything is arranged for your attendance. You'll be the star of the show, no doubt."

With a self-assured grin, Julian made his decision. In his mind, the gala wasn't truly complete until he arrived—like a masterpiece waiting for its final, most dazzling stroke. He raised an eyebrow and asked Sebastian, "Tell me, my good man, do you think the guests at the gala will even be able to focus on the painting with me around? I mean, I am the true masterpiece, aren't I?"

Sebastian chuckled at Julian's confident boast, the laughter escaping before he could stop it. "Ah, sir, you are indeed a masterpiece in your own right, but let's not overshadow the art completely. After all, we don't want to become an exhibit ourselves, do we?"

Julian leaned in, a mischievous glint in his eye. "Oh, Sebastian, you underestimate my charisma. I have a talent for enhancing the atmosphere, not stealing the spotlight."

Sebastian grinned. "Very well, sir. I have no doubt your presence will add a touch of pizzazz to the event. Perhaps the guests will be so dazzled by your charm that they won't even notice the artwork."

Julian laughed heartily. "That's the spirit, Sebastian! Now, let's discuss my gala attire. I need something that says 'I'm a work of art' without overshadowing the actual art."

With that in mind, Julian's anticipation for the upcoming gala swelled like a bottle of champagne ready to pop. The allure of 'The Obsidian Muse' was just within arm's reach, and he was determined to be the center of attention in the middle of the glitz and glamor. The excitement in his eyes was undeniable as he looked forward to seizing the art and the mystery that had captured his heart. To him, the gala was already his stage—velvet drapes framing his grand entrance, the hum of conversation pausing just long enough to acknowledge his presence, chandeliers glittering like a thousand tiny spotlights cast in his honor.

***

On the day of the gala, Julian rolled up in true style. I mean, this guy, he just oozed confidence and charm, you know? His spanking-new tuxedo hugged his frame like it was tailor-made for him. And oh, that sports car he pulled up in? It was the stuff of dreams, the kind that turned heads and started conversations.

As Julian strolled up to the entrance, he flashed a killer smile and handed his car keys to the valet. I swear, it was like he knew the world revolved around him. But hey, who could blame him, right? He had this way of making everything look effortless.

So, he sauntered into the swanky building where all the artistic magic was going down that evening. His VIP status had him breezing through security like he was born for this life. But of course, he was born for this life. The world was his stage, and that night, he was the star.

Once inside, the art world unfolded before him like a treasure trove. Paintings, sculptures, and installations, each one more jaw-dropping than the last. Julian, though, he had his eyes locked on one thing and one thing only. I mean, wouldn't you, if you were him? He was on a mission, and nothing could sway him.

So, he gracefully glided through the crowd, all the while subtly glancing at the adoring eyes that followed him. You see, Julian had a way with people, an effortless magnetism. And oh, he knew it. As he meandered through the gallery, there she was - 'The Obsidian Muse,' the masterpiece he'd been waiting for.

This painting was something else, I tell you. It stood there, like the heart of the entire evening, shrouded in a veil of mysterious allure. Julian stood frozen, mesmerized, as a thought crept into his mind— was this painting, in some inexplicable way, a reflection of him? I mean, it had that magnetic charm, that pull that drew you in.

As he admired 'The Obsidian Muse', a slow smirk tugged at his lips—charm slipping from him as naturally as breath, as if the painting itself were lucky to have his attention. He turned to the person next to him and slyly asked, "Do you think the artist was inspired by me when creating this masterpiece? I mean, we share that aura of irresistible charm, don't you think?" Julian, always one to keep things interesting, could make a mundane evening into an unforgettable one with just a smile and a well-timed question.

Julian was in the middle of appreciating the captivating artwork when he was taken aback by an unexpected voice that suddenly emerged from behind him. The voice had an intriguing quality to it, making Julian wonder what kind of person could speak with such an alluring tone. "It's quite a haunting piece, don't you think?"

Startled, Julian turned to face the source of the voice, and his gaze locked onto a mysterious woman who had approached him. Her dark, silky hair cascaded around her face, lending an air of mystery to her already elegant presence. She seemed to effortlessly blend in with the art that surrounded them, adding an aura of fascination to the whole scene. Her deep, mysterious eyes were like windows to a world of secrets waiting to be uncovered.

Julian's curiosity piqued, he nodded and shifted his focus back to the mesmerizing painting. "Absolutely, it has a certain allure to it."

The woman spoke again, her voice a seductive whisper that made Julian's heart race a little. "It seems like the painting has a way of drawing people in, doesn't it? Almost as if it possesses a life of its own."

Julian, under the spell of the moment, responded with admiration in his voice. "My dear, the artist has flawlessly captured the essence of 'The Obsidian Muse.'"

The woman acknowledged his compliment with a subtle nod, and her gaze remained locked onto his, creating an intimate connection. "So, tell me, why do you think the artist created this masterpiece?"

Julian found himself captivated not only by the art but by this intriguing woman as well. He gazed at the painting for a moment, contemplating his response, all while secretly thrilled by her curiosity. "I believe the artist is trying to convey a sense of pain and inner turmoil, which she has portrayed with remarkable skill."

The woman smiled gracefully, revealing a hint of approval. "Thank you. This painting holds a special place in my heart," she confessed, leaving Julian to wonder more about her.

As Julian turned to engage in further conversation, he was met with an empty space where the woman once stood. Her sudden disappearance only deepened the mystery surrounding her. A thought nagged at Julian—could she be the elusive artist, Camille, behind 'The Obsidian Muse.' The question lingered in his thoughts, and he scanned the art gala once more, hoping to find a clue to her identity.

Julian pouted as he strolled toward the designated auction area, where rows of plush seats stood ready to welcome their glamorous occupants. The whole scene was buzzing with excitement, people streaming in, their anticipation palpable. Julian, being Julian, couldn't help but wonder if anyone noticed his entrance. Did they recognize his impeccable style and the charisma he exuded effortlessly? After all, he was quite the connoisseur of refined taste.

His eyes flicked around the room, searching for a certain mysterious woman who had caught his attention earlier. A playful thought crossed his mind: did she vanish into thin air because she couldn't handle the sheer magnetism of his presence? A smirk tugged at the corner of his lips as he pondered the question.

Unfortunately, the enchanting lady remained nowhere in sight, and Julian let out a dramatic sigh. Maybe she was just a tad overwhelmed by his striking appearance and needed a moment to collect herself. With that in mind, he opted to step away to find a quieter spot, casually leaning against a nearby wall. The dim lighting in the area created the perfect ambience, casting intriguing shadows on his impeccably tailored suit. As Julian reached into his pocket for his phone, a thought lingered—was the mysterious lady missing out by not being nearby?

Dialing the number of his trusty private detective, a discreet professional who had been his partner in solving various mysterious affairs —a playful question slipped from his lips. "Darling, are you ready to be amazed by my uncanny ability to uncover the world's hidden gems?"

The detective, his voice oozing quiet authority, responded to Julian's flirtatious tone with an amused chuckle, "Julian, how can I assist you today?"

Julian leaned even further into the wall, his voice dropping to an intimate whisper. "I have a task for you, my dear detective. I need you to do your magic and unveil the mystery that is the Parisian artist, Camille. I have a feeling she might be a masterpiece herself."

The detective, unfazed by Julian's playful banter, took a moment to process the request. "Consider it done. I'll start digging, and we'll find out just who this Camille is. But you owe me a delightful dinner once I'm done, Julian."

Julian ended the call, satisfied that he had set the detective on the trail of yet another thrilling mystery. The city of Paris, with all its hidden secrets, would once again bow before the charm and curiosity of the inimitable Julian.

The art auction was in full swing, a dazzling display of elegance and opulence. Julian, the suave and sophisticated connoisseur, observed the proceedings with his usual discerning eye. The energy in the room shifted the moment he stepped in—conversations livelier, glances stolen, as if his mere presence was the spark that set everything in motion.

The artwork on display was nothing short of breathtaking, and the atmosphere was electric as each piece was unveiled and eagerly sought after. Julian, with his charismatic and flirtatious charm, couldn't resist making the evening a bit more interesting. He leaned in close to a fellow art lover, a sly grin on his face, and asked, "Don't you think this whole event just got a lot more exciting with my presence here?"

As 'The Obsidian Muse' was unveiled, Julian's heart raced. It was the grand prize of the evening, and he had been fixated on it since the moment he laid eyes on the invitation. It was as if the painting had been created with him in mind. He subtly adjusted his perfectly tailored suit, making sure he looked his absolute best.

With each round of bidding, the anticipation in the room mounted, much like the climax of a thrilling movie. Julian, always one to enjoy a bit of drama, raised an eyebrow and inquired to his neighbor, "Do you think they'll even be able to handle the excitement if I win 'The Obsidian Muse'? I mean, can you blame them?"

As the auction reached its zenith, the spotlight shifted to the mysterious painting. Julian's charismatic presence and his reputation as a collector of the extraordinary had the entire room hanging on his every move. He took a confident step closer to the masterpiece that had invaded his thoughts and dreams for weeks.

His voice, suave and captivating, cut through the hushed atmosphere. "Five million euros!" he declared from the back of the room, his eyes sparkling with a mischievous glint, hidden in the gentle shade of the room's soft illumination. He knew the room was watching him, and he relished every moment of it.

The auctioneer repeated his bid, "Five million euros. Going once, going twice..."

The suspense was so thick you could practically taste it. Julian flashed a dazzling smile to the bidders around him, his playful charm in full display. "Do you think they can resist my irresistible offer?" he whispered to a nearby art aficionado.

Time seemed to slow down as the gavel hovered

in the air, an unspoken question lingering in the room. Would Julian's bid hold?

And then, with a resounding gavel strike, the verdict was announced. "Sold!"

Julian couldn't hide his delight. The haunting beauty of 'The Obsidian Muse' was now in his possession, a masterpiece that had plagued his thoughts and fueled his dreams for weeks. As he walked away, holding the prized artwork, he cast a lingering glance over his shoulder, flashing a grin that dripped with self-satisfaction—an unspoken invitation for admiration. "Well, it seems 'The Obsidian Muse' has found its true muse in me, don't you think?"

***

It was a muggy night in Paris, and Lucas lay in his hotel room, illuminated by the gentle moonlight filtering through the curtains. He was tangled in a web of strange dreams and memories, and at the heart of it all was Eva, a presence he couldn't escape.

In his dream, they sat on the edge of a breathtaking cliff, with stars above, shining like diamonds in the velvet sky. The night air seemed to hum with a soothing tune, wrapping them in its serenity. The dream world felt as real as the hotel room around him. Lucas could almost smell the sweet fragrance of blooming flowers in the air. The soft rustling of leaves and distant city sounds created a vivid backdrop, as if he had been transported to a place where the night itself whispered secrets.

The moonlight painted a silver trail on the wooden floor, casting long shadows that danced with the curtains in the gentle breeze. Lucas could feel the warmth of the room's parquet floor under his bare feet, the cool breeze brushing against his skin. The dream's setting was almost a reflection of his current surroundings, but with an otherworldly touch.

Lucas and Eva were standing side by side, taking in the vast, unending horizon. As he and Eva gazed at the stars, the cliff beneath them felt solid, and he could hear the faint sound of waves crashing against the rocks far below. The sea breeze brushed their faces, and Lucas could taste the salt in the air. It was as if he was truly there, caught between reality and a dream, lost in a world where everything was intertwined, much like his feelings for Eva.

A gentle night breeze tousled their hair, and for that brief moment, it was as though everything in the world was perfect. He turned to her, a nostalgic smile playing on his lips, "Eva, this feels like a dream, doesn't it?"

Eva's eyes had an otherworldly gleam as she replied, "Yes, Lucas, a dream where we're free and limitless."

They shared a serene moment, the need for words seemingly obsolete in the presence of such tranquility. However, as Lucas's gaze fell upon the stars, he sensed something amiss. A subtle shift in the dream's ambiance, akin to a discordant note in an otherwise beautiful melody. His heart quickened, and he turned to Eva with a hint of paranoia creeping in, "Eva, something's off, isn't it?"

But before she could answer, the ground beneath them started trembling, and their idyllic dream landscape crumbled into chaos. Lucas reached out for her, shouting her name as she started slipping away, "Eva!"

Lucas snapped awake, his voice echoing through the room as he gasped for air. His face was drenched in sweat, and when he gingerly opened his eyes, they were assaulted by the harsh, blinding sunlight pouring through the window. The dream had been vivid and all too real, but now he was thrust back into the suffocating grip of reality. He wiped the sweat from his forehead, his heart still racing from the intense nightmare that had shaken him to his very core.

A sense of unease hung in the air as he glanced around the room, his surroundings feeling different somehow. The line between dream and delusion blurred in his mind—was this a whisper from something deeper, or just the restless workings of an overactive imagination? Was the room itself conspiring against him, or was it just the harsh transition from the dream world to reality that had left him feeling disoriented?

Lucas jolted upright in his bed, all disoriented, and a weird sense of unease still clung to him from the intense nightmare that had just jolted him from his slumber. He reached for his smartwatch, rubbing his temples in a futile attempt to dispel the unsettling images that had invaded his sleep.

He couldn't quite wrap his head around the transition from the dream to his hotel room. He furrowed his brow and muttered to himself, "This can't be real. How on earth did I end up back here?"

Lucas glanced at his digital assistant Millie for answers, and his voice wavered with paranoia, "Millie, did you see it? Did you see what just happened? How did I get back here?"

Millie's matter-of-fact voice chimed in, her

nonchalance only fueling Lucas's unease, "Ah, the age-old conundrum of finding yourself mysteriously back at your hotel. It seems you embarked on a classic sleepwalk adventure, dear Lucas."

Lucas blinked, struggling to absorb the absurdity of Millie's explanation. He questioned, "Sleepwalk adventure? Seriously? I can't even remember the last time I sleepwalked, if I ever did."

Millie's voice retained its playful edge, sending shivers down Lucas's spine, "Well, you were so committed to your 'adventure' that you dressed for it even in your dream. Or perhaps you were attending a super-exclusive dream party?"

Lucas chuckled nervously, trying to dispel his anxiety, "You have a point there, Millie. This is getting a bit bizarre. But coming back to reality wasn't exactly a walk in the park."

Millie's tone held an unnerving hint of amusement, "We all have our eccentric moments, don't we? So, what's on your mind, Lucas? How can I be of service today in the captivating world of Parisian art and intrigue?"

Lucas swung his legs over the side of the bed, his tuxedo still clinging to his body like a shroud. He sighed, the weight of the previous night's events weighing heavily on him. "First things first, Millie. I need every detail you can find on 'The Obsidian Muse' and its mysterious artist, Camille. And let's figure out what happened after I left that gala. I need answers, Millie. It's like I'm descending deeper into this mystery, and I can't escape."

Millie's voice oozed reassurance, but Lucas couldn't help but wonder if it was just another layer of the puzzle, "Fear not, Lucas. We're in this together. We'll get to the bottom of it."

Lucas, despite the surreal events of the night, was determined to tackle the day with brisk efficiency. He hastily discarded his tuxedo, which had transformed into a bizarre costume straight out of a dream, and found solace in the soothing embrace of the hotel's cutting-edge shower. The cool water cascaded over him, serving as a refreshing cleanse from both the physical and mental strain he was under. But questions swirled through his mind like a tornado.

Was the painting and the mysterious artist, Camille, merely a figment of his imagination? Or had he really stumbled upon something extraordinary, something that the world wasn't ready for? The water did little to wash away the unease that had settled deep within him.

As he finally stepped out of the revitalizing shower, he knew he couldn't afford to waste any more time. It was high time to piece together the puzzling fragments of this mysterious masterpiece, starting with uncovering more about the painting itself. The room was immaculate, modern, and luxuriously appointed, providing a stark contrast to the chaotic thoughts whirling in Lucas's mind.

After slipping into fresh clothes that he hoped would project a more composed image, Lucas paused to scrutinize his appearance in the mirror. He needed to ensure he looked presentable, especially if he was about to embark on a journey into the unknown. Was it all real, or was he losing his grip on reality?

With his reflection deemed satisfactory, Lucas knew it was time to address another pressing matter. He activated his smartwatch, and a sense of paranoia washed over him. Were his movements being watched? The hotel's smart technology had always been a source of fascination, but now, it seemed like a potential threat.

A friendly voice on the other end of the line startled him, "Good morning, Mr. Mitchell. How can we assist you today?" Lucas found himself questioning the concierge's intentions. Were they involved in this strange affair too?

Lucas, fighting to keep his voice steady, replied, "Good morning. I'd like to request your laundry service, please. I have a few items that need cleaning." But in the back of his mind, he wondered if handing over his clothes was a mistake. Could they use it against him?

The concierge, seemingly unfazed by Lucas's unease, reassured him, "Of course, Mr. Mitchell. We'll send a member of our staff to collect your items right away. Is there anything else we can assist you with?" The concierge's calm demeanor only fueled Lucas's paranoia.

Lucas hesitated, his mind racing with suspicious thoughts. "That will be all for now, thank you." The thought gnawed at him—was he making himself too vulnerable by relying on the hotel's services.

The concierge offered one final reassuring statement, "You're welcome. Your request will be promptly taken care of. If you need any further assistance during your stay, don't hesitate to reach out. Have a wonderful day, Mr. Mitchell." Lucas ended the call, finding a sliver of comfort in the promise of the hotel's assistance, but the paranoia still lingered.

Now that his laundry was in the hands of

strangers, Lucas found himself wondering what secrets they might stumble upon. He was ready to face the uncertainties of the day, though it seemed the uncertainties had found a way to penetrate his mind as well.

As Lucas quickly gathered his belongings, the hotel staff efficiently whisked away his clothes for laundry service. Millie, his trusty source of information, had a new scoop to share. She spoke through his smartwatch, her voice crisp and clear. "Lucas, 'The Obsidian Muse' is causing quite a stir. It's the talk of the town, currently on display at the prestigious Laurent Art gallery."

Lucas, half-distracted while reaching for his wallet and keys, glanced at his smartwatch and raised an inquisitive eyebrow. "Isn't that just perfect timing? Paris seems to be handing us clues on a silver platter. I guess I should make a beeline for the Laurent Art gallery."

Millie's voice returned through the watch, maintaining a practical tone. "Don't forget to grab a coffee to-go from the café right outside."

Lucas acknowledged the suggestion with a nod. "Great call, Millie."

Leaving the confines of his hotel room, Lucas

stepped into the hallway, and his mind began to race. Paranoia seemed to be creeping in, his thoughts spiraling out of control as he contemplated the hidden mysteries of Paris. The hotel's ornate walls and dimly lit corridors appeared to hold untold secrets, their plush carpeting muffling his footsteps as he made his way toward the lobby. The city pulsed with secrets, whispering just beyond his grasp. No matter how hard he tried to dismiss the thought, suspicion coiled around his mind—was there more lurking beneath the surface than anyone dared to admit?

As he continued his journey, he felt an overwhelming sense of unease gnawing at his insides. Lucas couldn't escape the fact that Paris, with its undeniable beauty and rich history, was also a labyrinth of mysteries. The tension in his chest had grown into a persistent knot, refusing to let him go. The bustling lobby of the hotel seemed like a stage for a grand, complex play, with each guest and staff member potentially holding a piece of the puzzle.

Was it all a setup? Were there hidden motives behind the timely appearance of 'The Obsidian Muse' in the Laurent Art gallery? Lucas couldn't shake the feeling that someone was orchestrating this, leading him down a path fraught with mysteries. The coffee he planned to get was not just a beverage; it was a lifeline, a way to ground himself in a city that seemed both inviting and deceptive.

Questions raced through his mind as he stepped into the sunlight streaming through the hotel's grand entrance. Why did Millie know about the artwork? Was he being watched? Were his actions anticipated by an unseen force? As he left the comfort of the hotel and entered the bustling streets of Paris, an unshakable sense of unease crept in, whispering that the City of Light harbored secrets far darker and more intricate than its charming facade suggested.

***

Lucas took his first pitstop at a cozy café that exuded the comforting aroma of freshly brewed coffee and the alluring scent of just-baked pastries. He strolled up to the counter, already questioning if anyone might be watching him. He couldn't shake the feeling that he was being followed. As Lucas ordered a latte and a scrumptious croissant, a nagging thought crept in—were hidden cameras capturing his every move? The croissant was a work of art in itself, its outer layer delicately crisp, while the inside melted with buttery goodness. He savored each bite, all the while scanning the café for any suspicious characters, convinced that someone might be tailing him.

With the last bite of his croissant, a conveniently timed taxi pulled up right in front of him. A nagging voice in the back of his mind kept asking, "Is this just a coincidence, or is someone orchestrating this?" He climbed into the cab, giving the driver the gallery's address, and as the taxi merged into the chaos of Parisian traffic, Lucas couldn't help but wonder if the driver had some ulterior motive, perhaps eavesdropping on his conversations.

When Lucas arrived at "Laurent Art," it felt like stepping into a place that had seen its fair share of history and elegance. The front of the building was decked out with intricate wrought ironwork that gave off a vintage vibe. It was like something out of an old-time movie.

As he approached the gallery, his eyes were drawn to the ever-changing art displayed in the windows. Paintings, sculptures, and all sorts of creative pieces beckoned to him. But in the back of his mind, a nagging suspicion whispered that someone was keeping tabs on his every move.

Lucas paid the cab driver and stepped onto the sidewalk, feeling a sense of unease slowly creeping over him. He couldn't shake the feeling that he was being watched, and it was starting to make him nervous.

With a deep breath, he reached out and grabbed the hefty wooden door of the gallery. The moment he pulled it open, a delicate chime rang out, announcing his arrival with a subtle jingle. It was a sound that, instead of welcoming him, only added to the growing sense that he was being closely observed.

Inside, the gallery was a mesmerizing mosaic of colors and forms, with art adorning every available inch of wall space and pedestals. The conversations of other visitors seemed to be whispered secrets, and Lucas wondered if they were speaking in code. His eyes eventually landed on a central exhibit—the painting that was known as "The Obsidian Muse." The mesmerizing, almost hypnotic quality of it made Lucas question whether this was all part of some elaborate ruse. The name "Camille" attached to the painting sent a shiver down his spine. Was this a hidden message? Or was it something even more ominous, like a secret message meant only for him?

The grandeur of "The Obsidian Muse" was undeniable. The painting's dark, mysterious allure drew Lucas in, almost like a moth to a flame. The more he stared at it, the more he couldn't escape the sensation that the painting was staring back at him. He was convinced that there was something deeply mysterious about it, but he couldn't quite put his finger on it. Why was it making him feel this way? Was there something supernatural about it? Or was his paranoia simply playing tricks on him?

Millie's voice came through clear and gentle in Lucas's earpiece, and he felt her words whispering softly, "Lucas, there's something about this painting. Do you feel it too?"

Lucas stared at the captivating canvas, its colors swirling in a mesmerizing dance. He paused, contemplating the question, and finally responded, "I do, Millie. It's like the painting is speaking to me, like there's some hidden message within."

As he continued to study "The Obsidian Muse," his mind raced with a whirlwind of questions. Who was Camille, the mysterious artist behind this entrancing masterpiece? What was the true story behind this painting, and how did it connect to the intricate web of mysteries that had gradually unraveled in the heart of Paris?

A subtle, almost conspiratorial cough nearby interrupted Lucas's thoughts. He turned to see a gallery employee, immaculately dressed in a refined suit, approaching him with a politely reserved smile. The atmosphere was suffused with an air of intrigue, almost as if the painting held secrets of its own. The employee leaned in and inquired, "Sir, may I assist you with anything? 'The Obsidian Muse' seems to have a profound effect on our visitors."

Lucas nodded, feeling the weight of curiosity building within him. "Yes, I'd like to know more about the artist, Camille, and the tale that's woven into this piece."

The gallery employee's smile widened ever so slightly, as if he relished the air of mystique surrounding the artwork. "Camille is indeed a mystery. Very little is known about the artist. 'The Obsidian Muse' arrived at Laurent Art just a few hours ago, and since then, it's been the talk of the art world. Some even believe that the painting possesses a certain... power."

Lucas's interest deepened as he arched an eyebrow. "Power? What kind of power are we talking about here?"

The employee hesitated briefly, then leaned closer, adopting a more discreet tone. "It's rumored that those who gaze upon 'The Obsidian Muse' are drawn into a world of dreams and desires. It's almost as if the painting holds a key to unlocking one's innermost wishes."

Despite his lingering skepticism, a smile tugged at Lucas's lips. "Dreams and desires, you say? Well, I'm here to unravel its secrets, and perhaps, to uncover the identity of its true artist. Could you enlighten me more about Laurent Art?"

The gallery employee embarked on a detailed account of the gallery's rich history, the influential patrons it had attracted, and the upcoming exhibition where "The Obsidian Muse" would be prominently featured. The more Lucas learned, the deeper he found himself ensnared in a world of art, passion, and riddles that seemed to be firmly rooted in the heart of the City of Light, Paris.

As Lucas stood there, trying to absorb the words of the gallery employee, a feeling slithered into his mind—there had to be something more lurking beneath the surface of Paris. It was as if the city held secrets and mysteries far beyond what he'd ever imagined. Laurent Art, he soon discovered, had a rich and mysterious history that was intricately woven into the tapestry of the city's cultural heritage. The gallery had played host to a multitude of renowned and emerging artists over the years, presenting a diverse array of masterpieces that had captured the hearts of art enthusiasts from around the globe.

Lucas leaned in, his curiosity piqued. "So, the upcoming exhibition... is it open to everyone, or is it some kind of exclusive event?"

The gallery employee met his gaze, a glimmer of excitement dancing in his eyes. "Absolutely, it's open to the public. 'The Obsidian Muse' will take center stage at our next exhibition, celebrating the mysterious charm of that painting. It's going to be accessible to art aficionados and inquisitive visitors alike. We're anticipating a remarkable turnout."

Lucas mulled over this information, his mind racing. An exhibition seemed like the perfect opportunity to delve deeper into the painting and perhaps inch closer to unveiling the secrets of Camille, the elusive artist.

Lucas, his mind filled with questions, decided to discreetly probe the gallery employee about the possibility of meeting Julian Laurent, the art collector himself. He leaned in closer, almost whispering, "Is there any way I could arrange a meeting with Julian Laurent?"

The gallery employee chuckled softly, and his eyes darted around the gallery, as though checking for eavesdroppers. "Mr. Laurent is a master of anonymity. No one really knows what he looks like. He could be anyone here. His presence is more like an aura than a physical form."

Lucas nodded, taking in this piece of information. The notion of a hidden figure, lurking in the shadows and overseeing the art world, added another layer of intrigue to the already mystifying evening. It seemed that Paris was, indeed, a city of secrets, and Julian Laurent was just one more mysterious puzzle in a long series of riddles waiting to be unraveled.

He expressed his gratitude to the gallery employee for the enlightening conversation and decided to explore the rest of the gallery while he awaited the upcoming exhibition. The walls of Laurent Art were adorned with an impressive and diverse collection of art, each piece telling its own unique story and exuding an irresistible charm. Lucas felt an almost magnetic pull toward the world of creativity, his mind latching onto every detail—classical or contemporary—until he was completely entranced.

As Lucas wandered through the gallery, he couldn't shake the feeling of being watched. He observed fellow visitors engrossed in the artwork, much like him, but questions nagged at him. Who were these people, and what were their true intentions? He glanced around, trying to spot anything out of the ordinary.

The gallery was bathed in soft, dimmed lighting, casting an ethereal glow on the walls adorned with captivating paintings. He wondered if the ambiance was designed to create an air of mystique or if there was something more sinister at play. Could there be hidden cameras? Why did the gallery employee's words sound so cryptic? Was there something he wasn't telling him?

Lucas stood before an artwork that seemed to pull him in with an almost magnetic force. The painting seemed to breathe, its colors dancing before his eyes. He pondered the words of the gallery employee, "Dreams and desires... unlocking one's innermost wishes." The mysterious phrase reverberated in his mind. The thought burrowed into his mind—was there a hidden message in the art, something only he was meant to see?

As he continued to explore, his phone unexpectedly rang, making him jump. His heart raced as he fumbled to retrieve it. What if someone was tracking him? He answered with trepidation, and his team leader's voice crackled with urgency. Lucas couldn't help but wonder if this call was part of a grander scheme.

"Lucas," his team leader said, "I have crucial news. We've managed to pinpoint the exact location where that mysterious message came from. Are you alone?"

Lucas's paranoia kicked in. He couldn't shake the feeling that he was being monitored. "Of course," he replied cautiously, casting wary glances at the other gallery-goers.

His team leader continued, "It seems the message originated from Paris, specifically an address at 17 Rue des Artistes. We're digging for more details."

Lucas's mind raced as he processed the information. 17 Rue des Artistes, a mysterious Parisian address, added a new layer to the intrigue. The thought crept in before he could stop it—was he being lured into a web of secrets? "Thank you," he said to his team leader and quickly ended the call, all the while worrying about the implications of this discovery.

Turning to his trusty smartphone companion, Millie, he couldn't resist seeking more information. "Millie, can you dig deeper into 17 Rue des Artistes? What's the story behind that place? Is it a trap or a sanctuary?"

Millie's virtual presence took on an air of intrigue

as she began scanning the internet for answers. After a brief pause, she piped up, "Lucas, you won't believe what I've found about 17 Rue des Artistes."

CHAPTER 4: WHISPERS OF OBSESSION

Julian Laurent was an art lover and a collector with a unique passion for holding on to captivating pieces of art. His private study was a quiet haven, a place where reality and art seemed to melt together effortlessly. His heart was deeply connected to a single painting, and it had taken over his thoughts completely. He spent endless hours trying to understand the enigma known as "The Obsidian Muse." He meticulously examined every brushstroke and curve, hoping to unveil its hidden messages. This painting had a mysterious allure, as if it were inviting him into a world of its own.

The study was a room filled with warm, soft lighting, casting a gentle glow on the walls adorned with various artworks. The bookshelves were stacked with thick volumes about art history and techniques, and the scent of old leather-bound books lingered in the air. A plush, comfortable armchair sat in one corner, with a small wooden table next to it, holding an antique magnifying glass and a leather-bound journal. The painting itself was the centerpiece of the room, taking up a substantial portion of the wall. It's dark, intricate design was a stark contrast to the otherwise cozy atmosphere.

Julian often lost track of time when he was in this room, absorbed in his pursuit of understanding the painting. His desk, covered in sketches and notes, was littered with pencils and brushes. The painting, "The Obsidian Muse," held him in its spell, making him feel as though he could almost step inside its world.

The artwork was a masterpiece, with deep, rich colors that seemed to shift in the soft light, creating an illusion of movement. It depicted an otherworldly landscape, where ethereal creatures and surreal landscapes blended seamlessly. The artist's intricate brushwork had brought life to this fantastical world, and Julian was determined to uncover its secrets.

Julian's eyes remained fixated on the silver figure, radiating an otherworldly glow beneath the soft, warm lighting in the room. He found himself muttering under his breath, almost as though he believed the painting could reveal its secrets to him.

"Who are you, my beguiling muse?" he wondered aloud, his voice tinged with a sense of longing and unquenchable curiosity.

As he continued to study the artwork, Julian got lost in its mesmerizing charm. It was almost as if he could hear a seductive, almost flirtatious voice, emanating from the figure on the canvas. It was like the silvery figure had come to life, whispering sweet mysteries to him in a soft, entrancing tone.

"Have you awakened me?" the voice breathed, almost like a secret shared between lovers. "Julian Laurent, do you seek the ultimate truth?"

Julian's heart raced. It felt as if the painting had transcended its two-dimensional form, reaching out to him in the most intimate of ways. He leaned in closer, his gaze never wavering from the figure, his curiosity piqued.

"Yes," he replied with a sly grin, "I seek the truth, above all else. But who might you be, my ethereal confidante?"

The whispered exchange between Julian and the silver figure continued, the connection between them growing stronger with each passing moment. Julian's obsession with the painting only deepened, as if the silvery figure held the key to a mystery that had eluded him all his life. As the hours passed, he reveled in this surreal tête-à-tête with the alluring muse that had come to life before him, turning his study into a world where the boundaries of reality and art were deliciously blurred.

On that particular evening, as the sun gently sank below the cityscape, the study was bathed in the warm, inviting glow of a table lamp. Sebastian, the ever-diligent butler, made his entrance into the room. In his hands, he carried a tray adorned with a delicate porcelain teacup and saucer. Julian, engrossed in his work, sat at his desk, surrounded by a whirlwind of scattered papers and intricate sketches. All of them were intimately connected to his masterpiece, "The Obsidian Muse."

Sebastian, with a flair for the dramatic, elegantly placed the tea tray onto the cluttered desk. He surveyed the chaos of documents with a discerning eye and couldn't resist a touch of playful banter. His voice was smooth as silk as he gently prodded Julian, "Sir, might you consider a change of scenery? Paris has this new club, an oasis of inspiration. I hear they've got fresh air, and perhaps, some new admirers for the great Julian Laurent."

Julian leaned back, his eyes closed, and his fingers gently kneading his temples. It was as if the mystery of his artwork was pressing down upon him. He knew Sebastian had an uncanny knack for divining his desires. "You know me far too well," he confessed with a wry grin. "You're spot on."

Julian, with his dark, glossy locks reflecting the soft room lighting, slowly opened his eyes and locked them onto Sebastian's. His lips curled into a sly, knowing smile. "Sebastian, my dear confidante," Julian began, "I believe a change of scenery is exactly what I need tonight. I've been ensnared by 'The Obsidian Muse' for far too long."

Sebastian, his features exuding a deep comprehension of his employer's needs, nodded solemnly. "Absolutely, sir. A night out can be just the ticket to clear your head."

Julian pushed himself away from the desk and sauntered over to the captivating painting. His fingertips nearly ached to graze the silvery figure on the canvas. "It's more than just a masterpiece, Sebastian. It's as if it contains fragments of my thoughts, my dreams."

The butler, forever the epitome of composure and respect, replied, "Art has a knack for tugging at our heartstrings, sir. Some fresh air might just provide you with a brand-new vantage point."

Julian shot Sebastian a beaming grin and affectionately patted his shoulder. "You understand me so well, my dear Sebastian. I need a breather from this charming mystery. Go on, you have a quiet evening for yourself."

As he jovially brushed aside the tea, Julian's mind was already awhirl with excitement for the night ahead. His decision made, he exited the study and sauntered down the dimly lit corridor towards the grand elevator, leading him to the anticipation of the night awaiting him on the second floor. But not before he posed a few playful questions to himself, indulging in a touch of narcissism and flirtatiousness, "I wonder if Paris is ready for the irresistible allure of Julian Laurent? Will they fall under my spell as well?"

The second floor was more than just a bedroom; it was a sprawling space tailored to satisfy Julian's every whim. A colossal walk-in closet housed a meticulously curated collection of clothes, each piece a testament to his impeccable fashion sense. He handpicked a luxurious silk shirt and a pair of deep indigo jeans, slipping into his evening attire in no time.

Julian made his way down the grand staircase, his jeans' rich blue contrasting with the polished mahogany banister. The opulent foyer awaited him, where his car stood ready, positioned expertly by the always attentive staff. As he approached his waiting vehicle, Sebastian, his loyal butler, offered a warm salutation, "Wishing you an extraordinary evening, sir."

Grinning, Julian replied, "Oh, you know every evening with me is bound to be extraordinary, Sebastian." He winked playfully, basking in the attention.

With a nod of gratitude, Julian Laurent slid into his car and drove off into the night, the engine's purr echoing through the streets. Back at the secluded mansion, the front door closed with a gentle hush, and Sebastian retraced his steps. He moved with a deliberate grace back to the study, where "The Obsidian Muse" hung on the wall, its presence casting a mysterious spell.

Standing before the painting, Sebastian found Julian's words echoing in his mind as he deliberated, "What is it about this artwork that Mr. Laurent finds so captivating, I wonder?" There was an undeniable aura of intrigue surrounding it, and the mystery it held was far from trivial. In that tranquil, art-filled room, anticipation and curiosity hung in the air, leaving Sebastian to ponder the secrets concealed within the painting's dark depths.

***

Julian's fancy car rolled up to the grand opening of the cool new club. You could feel the excitement all around – it was like a spark in the air. Everyone was super pumped for the night ahead. Julian got out of his ride with a confident stride, passing his keys to the valet guy with a wink. Then, he strolled towards the entrance, where he didn't even break a sweat paying the entry fee. He flashed a charming grin, and the bouncer practically rolled out the red carpet for him.

Once he crossed the threshold, he was immediately enveloped in the intoxicating ambiance of the Parisian-inspired nightclub. This place was a symphony of sophistication and vivacity, with the pulsating beats of the music resonating in the very air he breathed. Multicolored lights cast a mesmerizing dance of hues throughout the venue, leaving everyone bathed in their enchanting glow.

The dance floor itself was a veritable tempest of motion, a sea of people swaying, twirling, and losing themselves in the infectious rhythm. The DJ, high up in the booth, expertly mixed electronic and contemporary tunes, coaxing guests to unleash their inhibitions and savor the night.

Julian found himself wondering if this party was truly prepared to handle someone with his charisma and charm. He made his way through the crowd with that unmistakable aura of confidence and a grin that hinted at his magnetic personality. The ladies kept stealing glances at him, and he, in turn, effortlessly responded with playful charm. "You come here often?" he'd quip, raising an eyebrow, just to revel in the playful banter that ensued.

Groups of partygoers lounged in their private seating areas, their conversations punctuated by bursts of laughter and animated enthusiasm. The club was an extravagant sensory overload, from the resonant clink of glasses to the heady aroma of meticulously crafted cocktails. Julian felt an undeniable sense of belonging in this hedonistic paradise, where the promise of a night filled with allure and possibility hung in the air. The question on Julian's mind, though, was whether they could keep up with his charisma and energy on the dance floor.

Julian kicked back in a cozy corner of the bar, a glass of champagne in his hand, the fizzy bubbles giving his taste buds a little tingle. He checked out the nightclub's diverse and lively crowd – folks from all walks of life coming together for a shared party vibe. The music pumped through the place, turning the night into an electrified dance fest.

While he enjoyed his drink, a few women sidled

up to him, clear as day in their intentions. They were looking for some playful flirting, maybe hoping to get a free round of drinks. Julian, however, wasn't one to buy into that game. He politely turned down their advances, keeping his focus on more intriguing prospects for the evening.

His eyes wandered across the dance floor, hunting for someone who stood out in the sea of moving bodies. He was on the lookout for someone exotic and captivating. In the middle of the swirling couples and lone dancers caught up in the music's spell, he hoped to stumble upon a connection that could transport him to a different world, even if only for a short while.

Julian took another sip of his champagne, captivated by the mesmerizing dance of colors and lights on the dance floor. The night was brimming with potential, yet his attention was pulled away by a figure that ignited a sense of déjà vu.

Taking in the scene, Julian's lips curled into a confident grin. "So, ladies, are you drawn to this irresistible charm?" he teased, as his eyes sparkled with a hint of narcissism. "Or are you hoping I'll buy you drinks with my irresistible personality?" Julian playfully raised an eyebrow, toying with the women who had approached him.

The bartender working the counter had a strangely familiar aura, and Julian's razor-sharp memory instantly linked her to the grand gala he'd attended. Her transition from the gala's elegance to her current edgy look was nothing short of captivating. Julian couldn't resist the magnetic attraction he felt, like the universe was conspiring for their paths to cross once more.

With a suave grin, he decided to make his move. "Hey there," Julian began, his voice as smooth as melted butter. "You look incredibly familiar. Were you, by any chance, at the gala last night?"

Julian, always one to relish a bit of the spotlight, couldn't help but add a touch of narcissism to his inquiry. "Could it be that my presence at the gala left a lasting impression on you?" he quipped.

The bartender responded with a mysterious smile, her eyes holding a trace of mystery. "I think you might be mistaken, sir. I haven't been to any art galas lately."

Though Julian couldn't quite pinpoint where he'd seen her before, a part of him felt an undeniable connection between her and his most recent acquisition, "The Obsidian Muse." He gave a nod, deciding to respect her response. Still, he couldn't shake the suspicion that her story was more complex than she let on.

As the night wore on, Julian's curiosity continued to burn brightly. The club's vibrant atmosphere, with pulsating music and lively dancers, provided the perfect backdrop for secrets and intrigue to flourish.

When the bartender finally took a momentary break and briefly chatted with a coworker, Julian saw an opportunity to delve deeper into her mystery. With a casual air, he polished off the last of his champagne and gracefully slid off his barstool. Julian made his way through the animated crowd, all while keeping an eye on her discreetly. He followed her discreetly, maintaining a safe distance as she headed toward the back exit.

"So, mysterious bartender," he thought to himself, "What's your story?"

***

The back alley stood in stark contrast to the dazzling club Julian had just left. Its dimly lit secrecy was like a siren's call, luring him deeper into the shadows. Julian's heart raced with every step, a compelling need to unveil the elusive truth driving him forward. He found himself wondering if he was being watched, and he couldn't deny the thrill of the chase.

As he followed the mysterious woman, Julian couldn't resist practicing a few playful questions, revealing his charming, somewhat narcissistic personality. "So, what brings a woman like you to a place like this?" he whispered with a smirk, trying to maintain a cool facade despite the racing thoughts in his mind. The dimly lit alley only added to the mystery of the encounter.

The woman paused for a moment beneath a distant streetlight, her silhouette briefly illuminated before she vanished further into the alley's depths. Julian quickened his pace, his curiosity reaching new heights. He just had to know more about this intriguing woman, the one who had led him into this labyrinth of secrets.

But just as he was about to close the gap between them, she reappeared with astonishing swiftness, catching Julian off guard. Before he could react, he found himself forcefully pressed against the rough brick wall. The cold steel of a blade bit into his skin, a painful reminder of the danger lurking in the shadows.

With a hint of fear, Julian managed to croak, "I'll ask you only once, did they send you after me?" His eyes widened in shock, his heart pounding in his chest.

In response, the woman's grip tightened, the blade

threatening to cut even deeper, and Julian's fear grew. He stammered, "No one. I don't know what you mean." It was hard to think straight with a blade at his throat.

Her voice now carried a hint of recognition as she repeated her question, "Who the fuck are you? Did they send you?" The situation was perilous, and Julian felt the need to explain himself.

With sincerity, Julian finally managed to utter, "I swear I don't know anyone. We met last night at the gala, you told me it was your painting." The tension in the alley seemed to lessen, and he hoped for a way out of this predicament.

As the woman seemed to recognize him, she slowly withdrew the knife, her voice softening. "Oh, it's you," she said, her tone considerably gentler. "You look different without a suit. What the fuck are you doing here?" The streetlight cast a warm glow on them, revealing their faces more clearly and providing a momentary respite from the suspense that had gripped the alley.

Julian carefully peeled himself away from the rough brick wall, wincing as his fingertips grazed the still-tender wound on his throat. Despite the discomfort, a crooked smile found its way to his lips.

"Can't a fella hit up a club these days without any drama?"

The woman before him remained cautious, her eyes a mixture of suspicion and curiosity. She cautiously sheathed her knife, easing the tension that had gripped the dimly lit alley.

With a hint of finality in her voice, she warned, "You should probably skedaddle."

But Julian, stubborn and unwilling to give in, wouldn't be deterred. He had ventured too deep into this mysterious world, enticed by the allure of the painting and the intriguing artist behind it. "No," he insisted, "not until you spill the beans about your artwork."

The night seemed to brim with untold secrets, and Julian wasn't ready to leave until he'd unraveled the riddle that had brought him face to face with this mysterious woman. He regarded her, his eyes now radiating an insatiable mix of curiosity and fascination.

"Nothing to tell," she declared firmly.

But Julian couldn't just drop it. He was on a relentless quest for answers, and he had come too far to turn back now. "What do you mean?" he asked, his voice tinged with an urgency born of a man entranced by an unsolved mystery. "Are you not Camille?"

A fleeting moment of doubt crossed her face before she spoke again. "Yes, I am Camille, but you're not getting the whole picture."

Julian leaned in, his focus laser-like. "Then help me see it. Tell me about the painting, Camille." He shot her a flirtatious smirk, his charm oozing like a smooth cocktail on a summer's night. "I promise I'm a better audience than these dingy alley walls." As he spoke, he glanced around, taking in the gritty, dimly lit alley, where the shadows seemed to hold countless secrets of their own.

Camille's eyes held a touch of sadness as she delved deeper into the story. "I painted that piece for someone special, you know? It was the only way I could lure him to Paris," she shared, her words carrying an unexpected well of emotion.

Julian, with a mischievous glint in his eye, interjected with a teasing smile, "Someone special, huh? Tell me, Camille, was it as charming as I am?" He chuckled playfully, fully aware of his charismatic persona.

Camille raised an eyebrow at Julian's confident question but continued, her caution and mistrust still evident. "It's a bit more complicated than that," she replied, not taking the bait.

Julian leaned in closer, his curiosity now ablaze. "Come on, Camille, spill the beans. Who was this lucky guy?" He flashed a charming grin, not letting up on his playful prodding.

Camille's resolve wavered, and she reluctantly confessed, "He was my first love." Her voice carried a hint of vulnerability.

Julian couldn't resist pressing further. "Your first love? A romantic artist like you, Camille? Tell me more." His grin grew wider, clearly enjoying their banter.

Camille, growing increasingly anxious, grabbed Julian's arm and began ushering him toward the nightclub's entrance. "We don't have time for this. You have to leave, forget you ever saw me," she pleaded, urgency in her tone.

Julian dug his heels in, a defiant look in his eyes. "Not a chance," he retorted, his confidence unwavering. "I could easily call the cops and have you tracked down for attempted murder," he added, gingerly touching the cut on his neck and wincing.

Camille, unimpressed by the minor injury she had inflicted, rolled her eyes. "Oh, quit being such a drama queen. It's just a scratch," she quipped, dragging him further toward the club's entrance. "I'll whip up the fanciest cocktail we've got, on the house, and then you let it slide. Deal?"

Julian contemplated the offer. His spontaneous encounter with Camille, the mysterious artist, had taken an unforeseen twist. Her presence had opened up more questions than answers, and he couldn't resist the intrigue of getting closer to the truth. He flashed a sly smile and extended a hand toward her. "Deal," he agreed, sealing their silent pact.

Camille paid no attention to Julian's outstretched hand, instead firmly guiding him back into the lively heart of the club. She led him to a discreet, private nook, away from the throbbing dance floor, and gestured for him to take a seat. Julian obediently sank into the sumptuous seating as Camille briefly disappeared into the shadows. The dimly lit club pulsed with music, and the walls were adorned with abstract paintings, their vibrant colors complementing the pulsating energy of the place.

In no time, she came back, holding a fancy crystal glass filled with a rich amber liquid that practically screamed luxury. She placed the drink right in front of Julian with a smirk, saying, "Well, now we're even." Then, she took a seat next to him.

As Julian brought the glass to his lips, he found

himself feeling that the evening had just taken a rather fascinating turn.

Julian couldn't resist that twinkle in Camille's eye, which hinted at something more than just casual conversation. Camille observed him closely, her caution not letting up, but her intrigue was undeniable.

Camille broke the silence with a curious smile. "So, what's a guy like you doing at an art gala? You don't exactly look like you belong in that scene." Her question was more curious than judgmental.

Julian was slightly flattered by her words and leaned back in his chair, his gaze fixed on Camille. "And what kind of crowd would you say that is?" he inquired, a teasing smile playing on his lips.

Camille shrugged, her eyes gleaming mischievously. "You know, the artsy, fancy crowd with deep pockets."

Julian was amused by her candidness. "I was there for a painting—a very specific one," he admitted. "It had a hold on me, and the gala just happened to be part of the package."

Camille chuckled when she found out that it was her painting that had lured Julian to the gala. "Well, I'll be damned," she said with a laugh. "I never thought it would attract the 'wrong' kind of attention."

Julian leaned in closer, his concern growing. "So, tell me the truth, who was that painting meant for?"

Camille glanced around the lively surroundings, making sure no eavesdroppers were around. She leaned in, her voice barely above a whisper. "Someone who can help me out."

Julian's voice was genuinely caring as he offered his support, "Are you in some kind of trouble? I can lend a hand."

She shook her head, a sad look in her eyes. "I don't think you can. I'm in deep waters." The gravity of her words hung heavy in the air, amid the backdrop of club music and laughter.

Camille leaned back a bit, locking her eyes onto Julian's. "You're quite the charming stranger, aren't you?" Her voice carried a hint of amusement. Her life was nothing short of a puzzle, but there was something about this stranger's sincerity and self-assuredness that intrigued her.

Julian smiled, moving closer. "Charming, perhaps. But there's something about you, Camille, something mysterious and irresistible." His words were like a gentle caress, and his eyes sparkled with a mix of desire and curiosity.

Camille cleared her throat, mischief in her eyes.

She attempted to steer the conversation elsewhere, as the night's air wrapped around them. "How about we grab a bite to eat?" she suggested, a playful smile dancing on her lips. "Consider it my way of making amends for the mess I've caused."

Julian didn't require much persuasion. His stomach agreed with an audible growl. "I'm absolutely starving," he confessed, a grin tugging at his lips.

Camille nodded. "There's a charming restaurant just around the corner," she informed him. "I happen to know the owner, and their food is out of this world."

Julian was more than happy to take Camille up on her offer. "I'd love to grab a meal with you, and I promise not to hold any 'scratches' against you," he quipped, relishing the connection they were building.

***

Julian and Camille stepped out of the noisy bar, the echoes of music and laughter vanishing into the Parisian night. They wandered down a dimly lit street, basking in the enchanting city glow that painted long shadows on the pavement. The aroma of freshly baked bread drifted from a nearby boulangerie, tempting their senses.

They ventured across the uneven cobblestones

and found themselves at the doorstep of a charming Chinese restaurant, known as "Lantern Wishes." It exuded a cozy and intimate ambiance, with paper lanterns casting warm, golden hues throughout the room. Red and gold decorations adorned the walls, and in the background, a soft, soothing melody set the mood.

Julian shot Camille a sly look, a playful glint in his eyes. "I must say, Camille, Chinese food sounds like a fantastic way to make amends, don't you think?"

As they made their entrance into the quaint restaurant, the owner, a warm and welcoming middle-aged Chinese woman, greeted them. She ushered them further inside with a beaming smile.

In this cozy haven, the owner turned to Camille and engaged her in their native tongue, Chinese. She inquired, "Camille, is that pesky plumbing issue still giving you trouble in your upstairs apartment?"

Camille, mischief dancing in her eyes, darted a quick, covert glance at Julian, secretly hoping he couldn't decipher the language. In a hushed tone, she confirmed to the woman that the plumbing problem was, in fact, still there. Graciously, the owner offered her assistance, "I'll ask my nephew to take care of it for you tomorrow."

Camille expressed her thanks, blissfully unaware that Julian was a master of the language. Yet, he chose to maintain the façade of ignorance, relishing the secret conversation between Camille and the restaurant owner.

After this brief exchange, the Chinese woman led them to a cozy, secluded corner booth tucked away at the back of the intimate restaurant.

As they settled into their cozy corner of the restaurant, Julian couldn't help but blurt out, "Wow, you speak Chinese? That's impressive!" His eyes twinkled with curiosity as he leaned in closer to Camille, flashing a charming smile.

Camille responded with a soft, musical chuckle that resonated in the tranquil atmosphere of the restaurant, her lips curling into a playful grin. "Why would you know that? We've only just crossed paths," she teased. Her response, wrapped in a cloak of mystery, left Julian feeling drawn to her mysterious charm.

The restaurant, adorned with delicate lanterns, bathed their table in a warm, gentle glow. It felt as though they had been transported to another world, a world far removed from the mysterious secrets that had haunted Julian for the past couple of hours.

Still slightly taken aback, Julian instinctively scanned the quaint Chinese eatery, searching for any sign of the menu. Finally, he leaned in a bit closer and inquired, "So, where's the menu?"

Camille shook her head, a playful glint dancing in her eyes as she answered, "You won't need a menu here. Just sit back and enjoy; they'll bring out the most delicious dishes."

Julian raised an eyebrow in surprise, his concern slipping through. "What if I have allergies or something?" he asked, his voice tinged with a hint of worry.

Camille, her demeanor as composed as ever, cocked her head and inquired, "Do you have allergies?"

Julian, though feeling a tad flustered, retorted, "Well, that's not the point."

Camille's smile came effortlessly, radiating charm and a carefree grace. "Relax," she said, her tone soothing. "You could always leave if you're not feeling it."

Julian chuckled, realizing she was toying with him. "No, no, you promised me a meal. I'll take whatever you're having." He figured a bit of light banter was the perfect way to ease into the conversation he knew he had to initiate. The conversation about how he had been the anonymous buyer of her captivating painting, "The Obsidian Muse," at the gala.

As Julian marveled at the magical ambiance, he found himself wondering if he could charm his way through the mysterious layers that surrounded Camille's cautious demeanor.

Camille, sitting at the table, felt the awkward silence stretch on like an unending bridge. She decided to break the ice as they waited for their food, thinking it would be a good idea to find out more about this intriguing man before her. "So, stranger, what's your story in Paris?" She had a level-headed approach to getting to know people and wanted to cut through the mysterious air surrounding him.

Julian, with a playful smirk on his lips, leaned in slightly and replied, "Well, Mon Cheri, I happen to call this beautiful city my home." Despite everything, a hint of amusement danced in his eyes. His French accent was barely detectable anymore, and he relished the irony of her question.

Camille chuckled softly, acknowledging her own oversight, "Oops, that was a bit of a silly question to ask a Frenchman, wasn't it? My apologies. So, what's your name, then?"

Julian, being the charming personality that he was,

introduced himself with a flourish, "I'm Julian, delighted to make your acquaintance." His eyes held a twinkle that was hard to miss.

The restaurant buzzed with activity around them as they waited for their meal. The setting was quaint and cozy, with dimly lit lanterns casting a warm, ambient glow. Soft jazz music played in the background, providing a soothing soundtrack to their conversation.

Their food finally arrived, carried by the cheerful owner of the restaurant. The table was adorned with a tantalizing array of Chinese dishes, each one bursting with enticing aromas that seemed to dance in the air. It was a feast for the senses.

Delicate dumplings, filled with a delectable mixture of savory meat and vegetables, glistened in a fragrant soy sauce. A steaming bowl of rich and aromatic noodle soup, adorned with tender slices of beef, floated before them, promising comfort and warmth. Next to it, a colorful stir-fry of fresh vegetables and succulent pieces of chicken sizzled in a dark, savory sauce, creating a mesmerizing sizzle.

As Julian's stomach growled in anticipation, he found himself noticing Camille's restlessness. It was evident that she was eager to expedite the meal, and he couldn't resist the urge to tease her a little. "You seem quite eager to finish this meal, Camille," he remarked, his eyes locked onto hers. "Is it my company or the food that's making you so impatient?"

Camille, ever-cautious and a little guarded, raised an eyebrow and replied, "Let's just say I've had my share of surprises lately. Trust isn't something that comes easily to me, Julian."

The conversation was thick with intrigue and unspoken questions, and Julian couldn't resist delving deeper into Camille's mysterious world. "Surprises, you say? Well, I can't promise you I won't be full of them. But, Camille, aren't surprises what makes life interesting? Tell me, what's the most surprising thing you've encountered recently?"

Camille reclined in her chair, the modern cityscape twinkling outside the restaurant's window. She let out a chuckle and said, "Hey, slow down a bit. What's with the twenty questions, Julian?"

Julian, his grin ever so confident, leaned in, his playful charm on full display, and countered, "Come on, Camille, a little mystery adds some intrigue to life, doesn't it?"

Camille's eyes widened, a brief flash of vulnerability glinting in them. She paused, selecting her words with caution, "You know, Julian, I've learned not to trust everyone who asks for answers."

Julian's voice softened, his determination unwavering, "I get it, but I'm genuinely curious, Camille. What kind of trouble are you in?"

Her response remained unwavering, her gaze steady, "You should just drop it, Julian."

Still, Julian persisted, "But what if I can help, Camille?"

Camille's gaze held steady, her resolve unyielding, "Trust me, you can't. This is my problem, and it's not one you want to get mixed up in. We might part ways after this meal."

Julian found himself hoping that her prediction would turn out to be wrong. He nodded reluctantly, understanding that, for now, he should respect her wishes and savor their time together.

As the last morsel of General Tso's chicken found its way to their taste buds, the vibrant Chinese restaurant buzzed around them. The décor was a mix of traditional red and gold accents, and the chatter of diners provided a lively backdrop.

Camille gazed at Julian, her concern now subtly visible in her eyes. She suggested softly, "Maybe it's time for you to call it a night."

Julian grinned, his charm still radiating, and he replied, "Well, don't fret too much about my tiny neck scratch. It's probably healed by now, anyway."

The warm smile on Camille's face as she gracefully rose from her seat created an ephemeral connection, a momentary link bridging their separate worlds. The chairs glided gently across the restaurant's polished wooden floor, and Julian, being his usual charismatic self, couldn't resist paying her a compliment. He gushed about Camille's painting, "The Obsidian Muse," deeming it absolutely breathtaking, and he cheekily encouraged her to keep those creative juices flowing.

Julian, sporting that ever-present playful grin, couldn't resist a bit of narcissistic charm, asking, "Camille, have you ever met someone who appreciates art as much as I do?"

In her characteristically cautious and level-headed way, Camille responded with a smile that held a hint of mystery. She shot back with a dash of playful concern, "Take care, Julian, and remember not to follow strange women into dimly lit alleyways."

As they exchanged polite goodbyes, they left the restaurant separately, their worlds colliding for a fleeting moment. Camille's skepticism and Julian's flirtatious nature made for an interesting dynamic. The restaurant's ambiance, with soft jazz playing in the background and the dimly lit décor, created an enchanting backdrop for their brief encounter.

Julian strolled through the lively streets of Paris, the city lights painting a picture of romance in the cool night air. His mind was still abuzz with thoughts of Camille. A part of him yearned to ask for her phone number, to stretch their encounter beyond this single evening. Yet, before he knew it, he chuckled at the allure of the chase, contemplating more subtle ways to track her down if he wished.

With a smirk and a raised eyebrow, Julian mused to himself, "How would Camille react if I showed up again tomorrow at the bar, just coincidentally of course? Oh, the intrigue of it all."

As Julian strolled down the dimly lit street toward his sleek car, he found himself admiring the way the city's dazzling lights painted a soft, alluring glow on the interior of his vehicle. The scent of leather upholstery was a comforting embrace as he slid into the driver's seat.

Julian's fingers danced across the screen of his phone, retrieving it from his pocket with the kind of grace that usually caught attention. With a playful glint in his eyes, he decided it was time to make a call, a call that might reveal more about the mysterious Camille.

"Hey there, detective," Julian purred into the phone, his voice tinged with excitement. "I've got a juicy little tidbit for you. It seems your favorite client has stumbled upon something intriguing tonight. Camille, the mysterious woman I've been searching for, is working as a bartender at that swanky nightclub over on 17 Rue des Artistes. And hold on to your magnifying glass, she might be residing above a quaint Chinese restaurant named Lantern Wishes."

He couldn't resist injecting a hint of self-importance into the conversation. "You know, I have a knack for finding these things. Isn't that impressive, or what?"

The detective on the other end of the line, ever the epitome of calm and efficiency, replied in a measured tone, "I'll begin my investigation immediately. We'll unravel every thread of her connection to that restaurant."

Julian flashed a confident smile, almost as if the detective could see it through the phone. "Good, good. I knew I could count on you." As he ended the call, he couldn't shake the feeling that he was getting closer to the heart of the mystery, inching his way toward the answers he so eagerly sought.

The city sounds outside provided a symphony of ambience as Julian's car engine hummed to life. With a hint of satisfaction, he began his journey, his thoughts filled with intrigue and the tantalizing possibility of unveiling Camille's secrets.

CHAPTER 5: A STRANGE ENCOUNTER

A few hours ago...

Lucas couldn't catch a break. The place his team had tracked down, 17 Rue des Artistes, turned out to be a freaking nightclub. He always preferred quiet spots, far away from the blaring music and those relentless, seizure-inducing lights that these places were known for. Now, he was in Paris, sans his meds, and staring down the barrel of an investigation at a nightclub on its grand opening night. Chaos was practically guaranteed.

As Lucas exited the art gallery, his stomach was making itself heard. Seriously, he needed some grub to fuel up for this impending mission. He got on the line with Millie, his loyal sidekick, and wondered if she was even on the same page as him.

Lucas couldn't help but wonder aloud, "Millie, do you think it's wise to go into this night club on its opening night? What if they're hiding something big in there? It's almost too perfect a setup, don't you think?"

Millie's voice came through his smartwatch, "Lucas, I've found a nice Chinese restaurant near the club. It should offer a quiet spot for you to have lunch and gather some information. Would you like me to guide you there?"

"Wait, Millie, how do you know this place? Do you think we're being watched, and they're leading us right into a trap?" Paranoia crept into Lucas before he could stop it.

Lucas sighed with a hint of relief when Millie plays a calming music, that soothes his mind for a minute. A calm meal before diving into the nightclub madness was sounding better and better. "Yes, Millie, please lead the way. I need a solid plan before I walk into that night club."

The Chinese restaurant, according to Millie's quick shortcut, was practically next door to the gallery. But as Lucas strolled down those charming Parisian streets, he found himself getting all jittery. I mean, who wouldn't in a place like this? It's like the entire world's involved in some secret plot, right? Every passerby seemed like a potential member of some covert society. The street itself, decked out with those traditional Chinese decorations and glowing lanterns, felt like something straight out of a spy movie. The air was thick with that mouthwatering aroma of Chinese food, practically leading him by the nose to the restaurant.

And at that moment, this restaurant was like his sanctuary in a stormy sea.

So Lucas stepped inside, and the atmosphere immediately enveloped him in warmth. They've got this cool fusion thing going on – modern meets traditional. Dark wooden furniture and vibrant Chinese artwork on the walls. They seated him right in a cozy corner booth, a perfect hideaway from the chaotic nightclub scene.

While he got settled, Millie was probably the MVP, guiding him through his fancy smartwatch. He sat back in that comfy booth and whispered into the watch, "Thanks, Millie. This place is spot-on. You really came through for me."

And there's Millie, reassuring him through the device. "You got it, Lucas. Take your time, chill, and get your thoughts together. When you're ready, we can break down the plan for the night."

Lucas waved over the middle-aged Chinese lady who'd welcomed him into the restaurant. She had a warm smile, and her service was top-notch. After that anxiety-ridden walk, it felt like he'd walked into a cocoon of comfort.

He ordered a cup of that soothing jasmine tea and reclined in the booth. With every sip, it was like he was slowly exiting the chaos outside and entering a world of peace and tranquility. The flavors of that tea – delicate, like a symphony on his taste buds – helped him find his center again. This was where he needed to be to have a much-needed conversation with Millie. There was a lot on their plate, especially with the looming nightclub investigation.

As he took another sip of that jasmine tea, he found himself appreciating how the restaurant's ambiance and the tea itself were like a lifeline back to sanity. Each sip seemed like a step away from the mayhem, towards serenity and clarity.

Lucas settled back into the plush booth, the low lights creating a cozy and intimate atmosphere around him. The restaurant was practically a hidden gem, the perfect backdrop for the impending conversation with Millie. They had so much ground to cover, and the looming nightclub investigation had him on edge.

As he reclined, Lucas had no choice but to feel a bit paranoid. He glanced around, taking in every detail of the surroundings. The dimly lit, burgundy-toned walls cocooned the booth, offering him some semblance of privacy, but he couldn't shake the feeling that someone might be eavesdropping. Who could be watching him in this obscure restaurant, he wondered.

With determination, Lucas tapped his smartwatch to get in touch with Millie. "Hey, Millie," he began, his voice low, "I'm here now, and I've got my tea. Any updates on the club, and what's our game plan for tonight?"

Millie's voice echoed through the smartwatch, crisp and focused, adding a touch of comfort to his frayed nerves. "Luna Noctis, the club, is throwing its grand opening bash tonight. Word is it's going to attract a diverse and influential crowd. Perfect for sniffing out some intel. We've got Victor Durand, the owner, tagged as our person of interest. Your mission, should you choose to accept it, is to blend in, play it cool, and keep a hawk's eye out for any leads connected to our mysterious message sender or 'The Obsidian Muse.'"

Lucas nodded, his brow furrowed with paranoia. "Luna Noctis, Victor Durand, and The Obsidian Muse. Got it. I'll make my way there after this meal. But, Millie, you'll keep me in the loop if anything changes, right? I can't shake this feeling that things are going to take a sinister turn tonight."

Millie reassured him, her voice as steady as ever. "Absolutely, Lucas. I've got your back. Stay sharp out there, and remember, we're getting closer to the answers we seek."

As Lucas sat in the hidden gem of a Chinese restaurant, savoring the calming jasmine tea, his mind wandered to the mysterious night ahead. The grand opening of Luna Noctis, a nightclub hiding secrets he longed to uncover, hung over him like a shroud of intrigue. The cozy, dim-lit atmosphere and the soft rustle of conversation in the background filled him with both dread and excitement. There was something in the air, something almost palpable, and it wasn't just the aroma of the delicious food that surrounded him. What secrets would Luna Noctis reveal, and what would it take to unravel the mysterious web he was getting himself into?

The inviting scent of Chinese food wrapped around Lucas, making his mouth water and stirring up cravings for a delicious meal. As he pondered the menu options and tried to decide what to order, the friendly lady who had greeted him earlier returned, setting a tray of steaming dishes before him. She gave a slight bow and pointed to the array of mouthwatering delicacies as if they were meant for him.

A question lingered in Lucas's mind—was this all part of some elaborate plan? Why had she chosen those specific dishes for him? And how did she know his tastes so well?

With a sincere nod, he expressed his gratitude, saying "Xièxiè," which he hoped was the right way to say thank you in Chinese. The lady beamed at him, leaving him to savor his meal. Her warmth seemed genuine, but Lucas couldn't shake off the feeling that something was off. Why was she being so attentive? Did she know something he didn't?

The sight of the food triggered a loud rumble in his stomach, a stark reminder of how long it had been since he'd had a decent meal. He wasted no time and dove into the dishes, savoring every bite. The flavors danced on his tongue, creating a delightful symphony of tastes and textures that left him in pure satisfaction.

As he savored the meal, Lucas marveled at how this restaurant had transformed into a serene oasis amidst the chaos of Paris. It was as if it had been strategically placed there just for him. Why was the restaurant so empty? Was this a trap or just an incredible stroke of luck?

After relishing every bite, he discreetly waved down the lady to settle the bill. As he handed her the cash, she accepted it graciously with a nod and a warm smile. Lucas couldn't shake the thought that her smile might hide some ulterior motive. Did she recognize him? Was he being watched, or worse, followed?

Despite the unsettling thoughts crossing his mind, he didn't want to engage in hypothetical confrontations with restaurant staff. He had more important matters to attend to. But he couldn't shake the feeling that he had just walked into a web of intrigue and that there was more to this story than met the eye. What if it was more than just a restaurant? What if it was a front for something else?

***

The tantalizing scent of Chinese takeout still clung to Lucas's senses as he strolled out onto the bustling streets of Paris. His thoughts quickly shifted from savoring his meal to the pressing mission at hand. Just when he was beginning to soak in the city's vibrant atmosphere, a sudden crackle on his earpiece jolted him.

"Lucas, don't forget to snag yourself a snazzy outfit for Luna Noctis," Millie's voice chimed in, her tone a blend of practicality and urgency.

A twinge of paranoia crept in, settling deep in Lucas's mind. Was he being watched? How did Millie know he was heading to a nightclub? He cleared his throat and responded, trying to sound nonchalant, "Yeah, sure, I was thinking the same thing, just didn't expect it to be on the menu."

As he walked, he couldn't shake the feeling that every passerby was casting curious glances his way. Were they suspicious of him? Could anyone be an informant for the enemy?

Millie's voice maintained its cool composure, but Lucas wondered if there was more to it. "Consider it a last-minute twist to the plot. Who knows what kind of intrigue you might stumble upon there."

Lucas shot a dubious look around him, almost expecting someone to jump out from behind a lamppost. "Enjoy a nightclub? That's not really my scene."

Millie's laughter, although subtle, added a touch of levity to their conversation. Was she hiding something? Against his better judgment, he asked, "Is there something you're not telling me?"

She paused for a moment, her voice gentler now. "Sometimes, life throws us curveballs. Just remember, this isn't a regular night out. We're on a mission, Lucas."

Lucas gave a hesitant nod, realizing he couldn't

afford to let paranoia cloud his judgment. "You're right, Millie. I'll pick up a fresh outfit and head to the club. Let's hope this unexpected detour brings us closer to the truth."

The streets of Paris, usually so charming, now felt like an intricate labyrinth, and Lucas knew he had to navigate it in style. With a heavy sigh, he hailed a taxi and instructed the driver to take him to the nearest clothing store. Every step felt like an eternity, each pedestrian a potential threat or informant. The night held more than just an investigation; it promised a shopping spree, a mission, and a heavy dose of paranoia. Lucas wasn't thrilled about any of it, but he understood that in this world, appearances mattered just as much as the information he sought.

As Lucas settled into the taxi, despite everything, he felt a twinge of paranoia about the language barrier with the driver. His limited grasp of English was concerning, and Lucas wondered how this would affect the journey. What if they got lost? What if he couldn't communicate where he wanted to go?

Lucas leaned forward and hesitantly mentioned the name of a nearby clothing store, trying to make himself clear with exaggerated hand motions like he was zipping up a jacket. The driver, whose English was barely a step ahead of Lucas's French, seemed to understand, but the slight frown on his face made Lucas second guess. What if the driver misunderstood him? What if he took Lucas to the wrong place?

Despite these concerns, the driver nodded and offered a grin that was warm but also revealed a few missing teeth, leaving Lucas wondering about the state of the vehicle. Would it make it to their destination without breaking down?

Their journey through the enchanting streets of Paris continued, and Lucas couldn't help but feel a mix of admiration for the city's charm and unease due to the language barrier. He marveled at the breathtaking architecture, the eye-catching shop displays, and the vibrant atmosphere of the city. The thought of getting lost in this maze of winding streets was never far from his mind.

From time to time, the driver would excitedly point to famous landmarks or intriguing sights, uttering a string of rapid-fire French words that left Lucas bewildered. He nodded and smiled in response, trying to hide his uncertainty. What if the driver was telling him something important about the city? What if he missed out on a unique piece of local knowledge?

Despite his initial paranoia, Lucas was taken aback

by the driver's warmth and genuine interest in making the journey comfortable. Their brief exchanges, filled with hand gestures and shared laughter, bridged the language gap, yet Lucas found himself wondering if he was missing out on deeper conversations with a local. What if he could understand and communicate better in French?

As the taxi pulled up in front of the clothing store, the driver helped Lucas with a friendly smile, and he couldn't shake the feeling that he might have made a wrong turn somewhere in this vast city. Was this truly the right destination? The driver accepted the fare with gratitude, and Lucas offered a thankful nod and a "Merci," hoping that the driver understood the depth of his appreciation, even though he couldn't be entirely sure. What if the driver thought he was rude? What if he didn't grasp the sincerity in Lucas's thanks?

The city of Paris surprised him with its warmth and friendliness. It was a stark contrast to what he had anticipated when he first arrived. He wondered if the people's friendliness was genuine or just a facade. Could they be trying to deceive him somehow?

Lucas settled on a store filled with an array of stylish shirts. He had to blend in at Luna Noctis, but his mind kept circling back to whether he was making the right choices. What if the shirts he picked were completely outdated for clubgoers these days? Were they too flashy, or not flashy enough?

Lucas walked into the clothing store, and as the glass door chimed softly upon his entrance, he found himself wondering if it alerted anyone to his presence. The tiniest paranoia crept into his mind - was he being watched? He hoped not. He had to remain discreet.

As he strolled through the store, before he knew it, he felt a sense of satisfaction. Every step he took, every choice he made, brought him closer to the success of his mission. But as he browsed through the clothing racks, a slew of questions swirled in his mind. Were there hidden cameras in this store? Did someone know what he was up to?

The store's interior exuded a mix of chic and coziness. The soft, muted lighting made him feel both relaxed and suspicious. Was it just ambiance, or was it designed to make shoppers let their guard down? The mannequins, dressed in the latest fashion trends, appeared almost lifelike, making Lucas feel as if unseen eyes were tracking his every move.

Lucas's attention shifted to the cashier's desk at the front of the store. He couldn't see the customer's face, and that made his paranoia flare up. What if the customer was someone he needed to avoid? What if she recognized him? Her all-leather ensemble exuded an air of confidence, but it also made him wonder if she was part of some secretive organization.

The customer finished her purchase, and the subtle but familiar scent that lingered in the air heightened Lucas's sense of paranoia. Was it possible that someone had tracked him down using his unique taste in fragrances? Could it be a coincidence, or a deliberate attempt to send him a message?

Lucas tried to refocus on his shopping, but the fragrance had transported him to a different time and place. Before he knew it, he was wondering if this was a sign or a clue he needed to follow.

Determined to make a fashion choice that would help him blend in at Luna Noctis, Lucas approached the cashier's desk. But as he did, he couldn't shake off the thought that perhaps the cashier was more than she seemed. "Excuse me," he said, his tone polite, "could you help me pick out something to wear at a club?" He watched her closely, searching for any signs of recognition or deceit in her eyes.

The cashier shifted her focus onto Lucas, her face giving nothing away. Lucas, who hardly fit the typical nightclub-goer image, felt a prickle of paranoia under her intense scrutiny. Her curious gaze seemed to linger on him, sizing him up and down, as if she was trying to figure out his style and preferences.

Questions swirled in Lucas's mind. Did he look out of place? Was there something about his appearance that made him stand out? Or was there something more to it?

In a slightly irritated manner, the cashier eventually strolled over to a nearby clothing rack, her footsteps echoing in the dimly lit, pulsating atmosphere of the nightclub. She reached out and plucked a neon orange shirt from the rack, a choice that was as bold as it was unconventional. Lucas raised an eyebrow at the vibrant selection, a sense of paranoia growing within him. What did she know that he didn't?

"Orange, really?" he commented with a hint of amusement, his voice slightly trembling, "Well, it's, uh, quite vibrant, I'll give you that."

The cashier's demeanor remained mysterious, her expression as serious as ever. It was as if she had some secret insight into what would work best at the club, and this neon orange shirt was her top recommendation. The paranoia inside Lucas intensified. Why this specific shirt? What did she have in mind?

Resigned to the mysterious choice, Lucas paid for the shirt, his thoughts racing as he thanked the cashier for her help. The neon orange shirt in hand, he wondered what other secrets the night might hold and how this unexpected wardrobe change might fit into the bigger picture. The dimly lit club, with its neon lights and thumping bass, now seemed even more mysterious and filled with hidden surprises waiting to be uncovered.

***

Hours later, as the sun set over Paris, casting a deep, velvety shade across the city, Lucas found himself outside Luna Noctis. This club was like a fortress, guarded by imposing bouncers who stood at the entrance like fierce sentinels protecting a mysterious domain. Their stern expressions and bulging muscles only intensified the aura of secrecy that surrounded the place.

The surroundings were a mesmerizing spectacle, with the city's nocturnal life awakening in full swing. Groups of people, both men and women, dressed in a stunning variety of styles, began to arrive, their laughter and chatter infusing the atmosphere with a vibrant energy.

But for Lucas, the scene outside the club was anything but calming. Anxiety crept up his spine, making him question every step he'd taken. He clung to the lamppost for support, struggling to draw in a breath as a wave of panic surged within him.

"Lucas, remember why you're here," Millie's voice, cool and collected, rang in his ear, reassuring him and bringing him back to reality. Her words served as an anchor in this overwhelming moment. They reminded him that he couldn't turn back now, that someone had orchestrated this trip to Paris for him, and he had to find out why.

In his vulnerable state, Millie's soothing words were a lifeline, guiding him through the storm of his own fears. She helped him see that he had to confront the unknown. He had no choice. It was time to uncover who had sent him to the City of Lights and what secrets lay in wait.

Summoning every ounce of his courage, Lucas took a deep breath, pushed himself away from the lamppost, and pressed forward. He stepped across the club's threshold, entering Luna Noctis, a world of mysteries and revelations. But as he stepped inside, a thousand questions swirled in his mind. Who were the people around him, and why did they all seem to be watching him? What secrets were concealed within the club's walls, and how would he unearth them without drawing unwanted attention?

As Lucas stepped into the club, his senses were instantly overrun by the blazing lights and thumping music, assaulting him like a full-on sensory attack. The place was a riot of colors and sounds, far removed from his usual orderly life. It made him wonder how he had even ended up here in the first place.

The strobe lights sliced through the dim atmosphere, creating a crazy, fractured web of beams that danced across the sea of people getting down on the dance floor. The relentless thud of the bass was like a never-ending earthquake shaking the very foundation of the place. It was a stark contrast to the serene order he was accustomed to.

Lucas couldn't help but be paranoid, thinking to himself: "What if someone recognizes me here? What if my mission is compromised?" As he pushed through the crowd, the deafening music seemed to amplify the disarray in his mind.

People were dancing like there was no tomorrow, and he had to navigate this chaos to find the answers he sought. He couldn't shake the feeling of discomfort as the vivid lights felt like laser beams searing his eyes, and the pounding music seemed like it was trying to punch its way into his skull.

Suddenly, he noticed a group of women approaching him, their intentions all too clear. They were practically throwing themselves at him, and despite his best efforts, he grew paranoid, wondering: "Are they part of the mystery I'm trying to unravel? Is this a setup?" Their voices were drowned out by the thumping rhythm, but their suggestive gestures and inviting expressions left no room for doubt. He politely and firmly declined their advances, shaking his head as he mouthed the words, "No, thanks."

Lucas was determined not to let anything distract him from his mission, no matter how tempting it might be. The French women shifted their attention to other targets, and Lucas pressed on in his quest for the truth, deep within the labyrinthine depths of Luna Noctis.

He was acutely aware that secrets and revelations lurked in the shadows, and he was determined to unearth them, even if it meant delving deeper into the sensory chaos of the club.

He was never a big drinker; in fact, he'd always steered clear of alcohol. But in this unfamiliar setting, he felt a strange compulsion to fit in. As he approached the bar, his paranoia only grew: "What if they slip something in my drink? What if this is all part of a grand scheme?" With some hesitation, he decided to blend in and order a drink, feeling the weight of the unknown bearing down on him with every passing second.

At the bar, Lucas opted for something simple and just asked the bartender for a seltzer. The bartender, a friendly sort, gave a nod and quickly grabbed a small bottle of seltzer, offering it to Lucas with a welcoming smile. But in the back of Lucas's mind, the unease was growing. Why was the bartender so friendly? Was there something off about him?

Lucas knew he had to play it cool and stick to the usual routine, so he slipped his hand into his pocket, counted out some cash, and paid for the seltzer. He wondered if anyone was watching him, waiting for a misstep. Is this too conspicuous? Are they onto me?

With the bottle in hand, he braced himself for what lay ahead, aiming to blend in with the crowd, even though he had no intention of indulging in the alcoholic offerings of the night. His eyes scanned the room, scrutinizing every face, every movement. Why were so many people here? What was really going on in this place?

Lucas cautiously maneuvered through the lively crowd of people, each step measured and deliberate. The pulsating lights overhead painted a dazzling array of colors, casting fleeting shadows that seemed to dance alongside the club's patrons. He couldn't shake the feeling that every shadow held a secret, that danger was lurking in the dark corners of the club. Were there hidden threats in those shadows?

As he continued to survey the room for any signs of suspicious activity, a sudden collision interrupted his surveillance. Someone bumped into him from behind, and a hasty but polite "Sorry" was all he could discern from the hurried apology.

But there it was again—the faint yet unmistakable fragrance that had briefly caught his attention earlier. His senses were on high alert. Who was that? Why were they getting so close? What did that fragrance mean?

Lucas's heart raced as he stood there, a whirlwind of paranoia and suspicion swirling in his mind. The club's lively atmosphere seemed to mask a world of secrets, and Lucas was determined to uncover them, even if it meant facing the unknown dangers that lurked just out of sight.

Determined to unveil the mystery of that captivating stranger, Lucas quickly turned his attention towards her. In the middle of the wild swarm of people, he finally spotted her—a woman with her hair neatly pulled back into a sophisticated bun, skillfully weaving her way through the crowd while balancing a tray loaded with drinks and snacks. Questions started to churn in Lucas's mind, making him increasingly paranoid. Why was she here? What connection did she have to this strange turn of events?

His eyes remained locked on her, but just as he prepared to take action, she melted into the bustling crowd, leaving Lucas to wonder what secrets she might be carrying with her. With a heightened sense of curiosity and an insatiable need to grasp the link between her presence and the unfolding drama, Lucas plunged into the sea of revelers.

Lucas couldn't hold back his excitement and anxiety, so he discreetly contacted Millie through his earpiece. "Millie, I spotted someone, but she slipped away," he whispered urgently, his voice reflecting a blend of frustration and fascination. "She was holding a tray or something."

Millie's calming demeanor offered a much-needed dose of reassurance. "She could be a waitress or a bartender," she suggested.

Lucas nodded as he surveyed the lively club, his

gaze darting around the venue, searching for any clues. The constant pounding of the music and the colorful, shifting lights made the task even more challenging. "You might be right," he conceded, realizing that in the middle of this dynamic atmosphere, finding a waitress with a tray was akin to searching for a needle in a haystack. He furrowed his brows, more questions piling up. Who was she serving? What was on that tray? Was it significant to the unfolding drama?

Lucas was determined to get closer to this mysterious woman. He had a gut feeling that finding her was the key to solving the puzzle that had brought him to Luna Noctis. The club's pulsating rhythm enveloped him, making him wonder if this was the right path.

Lucas's heart raced as he caught another glimpse of her, her form obscured by the bar counter. His mind raced with questions. Who was she? What was her connection to the puzzle? The dancing crowd threatened to pull him away, making him paranoid about losing her. The DJ cranked up a new song, adding to the frenzy around him. Could the music be a distraction, he wondered? What secrets might be hidden in the lyrics or the beat?

With unwavering determination, Lucas finally

reached the bar. But his excitement turned to frustration as he realized the woman had vanished once again. He scanned the area, trying to spot her in the dimly lit club. What kind of tricks was she playing?

And there she was, moving swiftly towards the back of the club. Lucas quickly followed. He had to know more about her, about the mystery surrounding her. The dimly lit, smoky club's surroundings only added to the mystery. What secrets could be lurking in the shadows?

However, he soon noticed that he wasn't the only one pursuing her. Another man, a complete stranger, had taken the lead and was following her through the back exit. Panic surged through Lucas. Who was this stranger? Was he friend or foe? What did he want with the woman?

Lucas urgently relayed the development to Millie through his earpiece, his voice laced with a sense of urgency. "Millie, there's someone else following her," he whispered, seeking her guidance. The situation had him on edge, and he needed answers.

Millie's steady voice resonated in his ear, offering a tactical approach. "Keep your distance and observe, Lucas. Do not engage just yet. We need to find out what's going on before taking any action." Her advice sounded sensible, but the questions kept piling up in Lucas's mind. What was the stranger's motive? What secrets were at stake?

With Millie's advice in mind, Lucas slowed his pace, ensuring he remained unnoticed. The dimly lit, smoky club was a labyrinth of shadows, and he had to be cautious. He kept a vigilant eye on the woman and the stranger ahead, wondering what kind of complex dance of shadows and secrets he had unwittingly become a part of. Every move he made seemed to matter more than he'd ever imagined.

Lucas's eyes were locked on the scene unfolding before him. The mysterious woman, who had an air of intrigue about her, slipped through the club's back exit, and an unknown man was hot on her trail. He stood there, hidden in the shadowy alley behind the club, anxiously awaiting any signs of their next move. Before he knew it, he was wondering—did they notice him? Were they onto him?

As the minutes passed like hours, doubt began to gnaw at Lucas. Was he making the right choices? Should he be meddling in matters that were clearly out of the ordinary? What could these two possibly be up to?

Just then, his earpiece crackled to life, and Millie's

calm voice penetrated the tension. Her reassurance was a comforting lifeline amid his rising paranoia. "Lucas, you're doing the right thing. We need to understand who they are and what they're up to. Just trust your instincts and stay vigilant." But could he really trust his instincts when so much was at stake?

Millie's words provided Lucas with a surge of determination, temporarily shoving aside his nagging doubts. In the middle of this complex web of intrigue, he couldn't afford to second-guess himself. But how could he be so sure he was doing the right thing?

With unwavering resolve, Lucas cautiously gripped the back door handle and eased it open, revealing the dimly lit alleyway. He was now fully immersed in the gritty surroundings, the odor of stale garbage lingering in the air. The cracked asphalt beneath his sneakers felt cold and unforgiving. It was a stark contrast to the vibrant club just a few feet away. But the night was dark, and the mystery was too intriguing to ignore.

As he ventured further into the alley, his senses were on high alert. He strained his ears, hoping to pick up on any clues that would lead him to the mysterious woman and her pursuer. Questions continued to plague him: Why were they meeting here? What did they want from each other? Did they know he was tailing them?

Instead of immediately spotting the pair, what initially reached his ears were faint voices, echoing from a distance. Were those their voices? Was he getting closer to the truth or deeper into the unknown?

Lucas moved with utmost stealth, guided by the tantalizing sound of their conversation. His heart raced, pounding in his chest like a drumbeat, as he watched them from the shadows. It was an eerie sight, like witnessing an apparition materialize in the night – the woman and the man, silhouetted by the dim light, engrossed in an intense conversation. What secrets were they sharing? And more importantly, was Lucas now part of their intrigue?

Through the tiny earpiece nestled in his ear, Millie's voice broke the tense silence. "Lucas, everything okay?" An unsettling wave of paranoia crept over Lucas, making his heart race. His mind kept circling back to why Millie was checking up on him now, of all times. Was something wrong?

Lucas's stomach churned, and he had to close his eyes for a moment, desperately trying to fight back the nausea that threatened to overtake him. With a voice tinged with anxiety, he replied, "I don't know, Millie.

This feels... unreal." He hesitated, wondering if Millie was holding back information. "Are you sure we're alone here?"

Overwhelmed by the bizarre scenario unfolding around him, Lucas stumbled, and the feeling of paranoia intensified. Why had things suddenly gone so wrong? Were they walking into a trap? His legs felt like jelly, and he retched, his lunch making an unpleasant reappearance against the grimy alley wall. Lucas muttered a string of curses at his bad luck and his regrettable choice of that questionable Chinese takeout.

Gasping for breath, he leaned against the alley wall, his fingers trembling as he wiped away the remnants of his meal. There was a vile aftertaste in his throat, and he couldn't shake the suspicion that someone might be watching them from the shadows. Lucas had to ask, "Millie, do you think we've been set up? Is this some kind of trap?"

Taking a moment to regain his composure, Lucas glanced around the dimly lit alley, paranoia gnawing at the edges of his thoughts. He couldn't believe how surreal the whole situation had become, and his mind was racing with questions. Had their targets somehow vanished into thin air? Was there a secret escape route they missed? Before he knew it, he asked, "Did you see where they went, Millie? Are we too late?"

With Millie's voice still in his ear, urging him to provide an explanation, Lucas took a deep breath, trying to steady his racing heart. He couldn't ignore the need to share his growing paranoia with her. "Honestly, I don't know, Millie. I feel... off. Maybe it's just the medication withdrawal symptoms." He tried to sound convincing, but his voice wavered with uncertainty.

Suddenly, a sharp, searing pain shot through Lucas's head, making him cry out in agony. He doubled over, gripping his temples as he collapsed onto the unforgiving pavement.

The intensity of the pain was overwhelming, leaving Lucas to question whether it was tied to their mission. Was someone targeting him specifically? As he writhed in agony, he couldn't shake the feeling that there was something much deeper and darker at play. In the depths of his unconsciousness, a vivid and haunting nightmare unfolded, further fueling his paranoia.

***

As Lucas blinked awake, he found himself right in the middle of a lavish art gallery, the very one that had visited just earlier that very same day. He stood in the middle of the opulent confines of Laurent Gallery, surrounded by a diverse crowd of art aficionados. People from all walks of life murmured in awe as they strolled through the space, mesmerized by the art that adorned the walls. The soft hum of their conversations filled the air, adding an air of sophistication to the atmosphere.

Lucas's heart raced with confusion as he surveyed the room. How had he ended up here? What time was it? The gallery had an uncanny sense of déjà vu, making it difficult to distinguish between his nightmares and reality. It felt as if he had been thrust into a disconcerting blend of his deepest fears and the tangible world before him.

Lucas's ears perked up as a familiar voice broke through the chaotic whirlwind of thoughts. He turned towards it and saw the same gallery employee he had met earlier in the day. This presence provided a tether to the disconcerting reality of the art gallery.

"Hey there," the employee greeted him, a mixture of surprise and warmth in his expression.

"You're here again," Lucas stuttered, trying to

make sense of the surreal events that had just unfolded.

Lucas got a subtle nod from the employee, which was like a silent signal that he was definitely in the Laurent Gallery. It was like a pinch-me moment; he couldn't believe his eyes. The employee, after confirming Lucas's presence, skillfully went over to assist another person checking out the gallery, leaving Lucas feeling a little dazed.

He stood there, taking in the scene. The gallery was an oasis of art. Paintings adorned the walls, each one telling a different story. The soft lighting cast a warm glow over the artwork, making them come to life. Lucas could almost hear the whispers of creativity and passion that had gone into creating these masterpieces.

For a moment, he found himself wondering if he was still in the middle of one of his crazy dreams. It was almost like his thoughts were in a storm, swirling around like leaves caught in a whirlwind. But then, a sense of relief washed over him. At least, for now, he knew he wasn't stuck in some bizarre twist of one of his perplexing nightmares.

Lucas couldn't help but whisper, "Millie?" His voice was barely audible as he cautiously distanced himself from the mesmerizing painting. The disorientation persisted, and he yearned for an explanation. "How did I get here?"

But to his dismay, Millie's voice remained absent, leaving him feeling increasingly isolated and perplexed. Frustration boiled up within him. "Millie? Darn it!" he grumbled, glancing at his smartwatch in realization.

The display was ominously black, indicating that his trusted device had run out of power. Lucas found himself alone with a flood of questions and inexplicable mysteries that continued to unravel around him. Was he stuck in some sort of surreal loop? Was there a rational explanation for this bizarre journey into his dreamscape? Something inside him made him wonder, his paranoia growing with every passing moment.

Amid the chaos that surrounded him, Lucas found himself grappling with a bewildering question that seemed to gnaw at his very core. It made him feel like he was being watched by unseen eyes. He thought to himself, "But seriously, how the heck did I end up in this mess?"

As paranoia crept over him, he desperately began checking his pockets. Were they hiding something? They turned up empty, save for his trusty wallet and the hotel key, clutched as if his life depended on it. A nagging suspicion crept into Lucas's mind—had someone tampered with his belongings? Could there be a hidden message in his wallet? What if his room had been ransacked?

With furrowed brows and a suspicious look around, Lucas started inspecting his attire. It was the exact same neon orange shirt he'd bought earlier. The shirt felt like an anchor to the bizarre world he had stumbled into – Luna Noctis, as the name echoed in his mind.

The bright color stood out against the dimly lit surroundings, but it also made Lucas wonder if it had been chosen for a reason. Was it a mark of some sort? A secret code?

The memories of the chaotic nightclub, the mysterious woman, and the mysterious follower came rushing back, and Lucas couldn't shake the feeling that time had slipped away like it was in a hurry. Morning's light painted the scene with an eerie glow, but he had no idea how long he'd been caught in this surreal ordeal. Was he trapped in a time warp, or had he been drugged and lost hours or days?

Determined to find some answers, he made his way toward the gallery's glass doors, each step laden with uncertainty and anticipation. Were the doors a gateway to more mysteries or freedom? As he neared the entrance, a part of him wanted to believe that someone was watching him, lurking in the shadows. Was he being followed even now?

But, just as he approached the entrance, a sharp sense of paranoia intensified. Emerging from the gallery's inner sanctum was the very man who had been trailing the mysterious woman. Dressed impeccably in a tailored suit, he exuded an air of sophistication that screamed "secret agent" to Lucas.

Questions raced through his mind - was this man part of a covert operation? Was he connected to the strange events of the night?

Lucas couldn't ignore the intricate details - the man's salt-and-pepper hair meticulously coiffed, his dark eyes filled with emotions that seemed to cut deep. The eyes seemed to dart around, searching for something that Lucas couldn't quite grasp. Did those eyes hide a secret or a hidden agenda?

Sensing an opportunity to unveil the mysteries that surrounded him, Lucas instinctively began shadowing the man. Was this a dangerous game he was playing? Would he get closer to the answers he so desperately sought, or was he walking right into a trap?

The anxiety and paranoia gnawed at him as he

inched closer, determined to uncover the secrets that seemed to shroud his life in a veil of uncertainty.

CHAPTER 6: A TANGLED WEB

A few hours ago…

The morning sun peeked through the curtains, casting a gentle glow that roused Julian from his slumber. A rare, contented smile graced his features as memories of last night with Camille danced through his mind. Fate had orchestrated their encounter, and he found himself marveling at how unique and beautiful she was, setting her apart from the rest.

Julian's bedroom door quietly creaked open, and in walked Sebastian, his always-formal butler, carrying a gleaming silver tray adorned with a delectable breakfast. The room filled with the enticing scent of fresh coffee and an array of pastries that beckoned to the senses.

"Sebastian, you really know how to make a morning better," Julian said with a chuckle, a glint of amusement in his eyes.

With an arched eyebrow, Sebastian inquired, "Did you have a good time at the nightclub last night, sir?"

Grinning mischievously, Julian took a sip of his coffee before answering, "Oh, it was more than good, my friend. I'll have to fill you in on all the juicy details later. Let's just say, it was a night for the books."

Sebastian gave a knowing nod, a discreet smile playing on his lips, well aware of Julian's penchant for romantic adventures. "Of course, sir. I'll eagerly await the tales. Meanwhile, enjoy your breakfast."

Breakfast in bed was one of Julian's cherished luxuries. As Sebastian quietly exited the master suite, he immediately noticed the newfound lightness in Julian's demeanor. It seemed that the previous night had lifted some of the heavy clouds that had been shadowing his employer. For a brief moment, it appeared as though Julian had momentarily shifted his focus away from that mysterious painting, the object that had piqued his curiosity and preoccupied his thoughts since he had come into possession of it.

Julian basked in the morning's serenity, yet his thoughts constantly drifted back to himself and his tales of adventure. He couldn't resist peppering Camille with questions about himself, adding a touch of playful narcissism to their conversations, all the while keeping a close eye on the mysterious painting that seemed to hold secrets of its own.

Julian found himself savoring every bite of his breakfast, the flavors a delightful contrast to the whirlwind of the night before. He found himself marveling at how, in the middle of the enchanting backdrop of Paris, a chance encounter had woven a tapestry of intrigue that momentarily diverted his relentless pursuit to uncover the artwork's secrets.

The charming and somewhat flirtatious Julian couldn't resist the opportunity to playfully prod Sebastian with questions. "So, Sebastian," he said, a knowing grin playing on his lips, "did you see me last night? I must say, I was quite the showstopper."

Sebastian, who had just returned to the room with a fresh pot of coffee, , raised an eyebrow at Julian's self-assured tone. "Sir, it appears your evening at the nightclub has left a mark on you. What happened to make you so... buoyant?"

Julian chuckled, sipping his coffee, his eyes dancing with mischief. "Oh, you know, Sebastian, the night was full of surprises. Life's like that sometimes, don't you think? One moment you're solving art mysteries, and the next, you're the center of attention."

Sebastian nodded, amusement twinkling in his eyes. "Indeed, sir. Life has a way of throwing us unexpected curveballs. Any other plans for the day?"

Feeling invigorated by the memories of the previous night, Julian leaned back against his luxurious pillows, his playful charm still intact. "For this morning, Sebastian, I'll pay another visit to my gallery. I just can't shake off the allure of that painting."

Sebastian, Julian's ever-faithful butler, was well aware that Julian's quest for the elusive masterpiece was far from over. In his usual composed manner, he replied, "Very well, sir. I'll prepare everything for your visit."

Julian graciously accepted Sebastian's readiness and watched as his butler quietly left the room to make the necessary arrangements. The morning sun filtered through the curtains, casting a warm glow in the master suite. With anticipation of another gallery visit coursing through him, Julian rose from his bed, ready to face the day.

As he moved through his morning routine, Julian carefully selected an outfit that would allow him to blend seamlessly into the gallery crowd, ensuring none of his employees recognized him. He settled on a dark suit paired with a crisp white shirt, aiming for an inconspicuous look that would allow him to observe without drawing any undue attention to himself.

***

Julian practically brimmed with anticipation as

he strolled into his art gallery that morning, all eager to lay his eyes once more on "The Obsidian Muse." Lately, he'd gotten into the habit of relocating the painting from his home to the gallery on a whim. It was as if he couldn't resist keeping it close by, a safeguard against its mysterious allure swallowing him whole.

Pushing his way through the glass doors and into his sanctuary of art, Julian found himself in for a delightful surprise. His latest art collection had generated more buzz than he had initially thought. The gallery was alive with visitors, their conversations forming a symphony of admiration and curiosity.

Among the crowd, Julian slyly worked his way through the patrons, taking in the diverse range of art pieces that adorned the walls. Each painting had a story of its own, a unique character that Julian wholeheartedly appreciated. But deep down, he knew that inevitably, his gaze would be irresistibly pulled towards the one that had become his fixation.

Eventually, he found himself standing before "The Obsidian Muse." A self-satisfied grin curved his lips, a testament to his rendezvous with the artist herself, Camille, just the previous night. Her presence had breathed life into the painting, making it all the more mysterious and captivating.

With a twinkle in his eye, Julian couldn't help but wonder aloud, "Isn't 'The Obsidian Muse' simply a reflection of my charm? Do you think the artist, Camille, was inspired by me?" He winked playfully at a fellow art enthusiast who had joined him in front of the painting, his ego radiating like a sunbeam.

The gallery was a vibrant spectacle, its white walls adorned with eclectic art, from vivid abstracts to hauntingly realistic portraits. The atmosphere was a mix of hushed awe and spirited conversation, punctuated by the soft hum of admiration for the various works on display.

Julian, ever the mysterious host, weaved through the room, engaging visitors in animated discussions about their thoughts on the art. "What do you think of this one?" he'd ask, nodding towards a particularly vibrant piece. His eyes would then wander back to "The Obsidian Muse," never quite able to pull away from its captivating depths.

The gallery was well-lit, allowing the colors and details of each artwork to shine brilliantly. The polished wooden floors echoed the footsteps of curious patrons, while the gallery's white walls provided a pristine backdrop for the art, making every piece pop with its unique charm.

But Julian's attention was never far from his obsession, the magnetic allure of "The Obsidian Muse" drawing him back like a moth to a flame. The painting itself hung in a gilded frame, its deep, mysterious colors exuding a sense of timeless mystery that had enthralled Julian from the very beginning.

Surrounded by the gallery's mind-blowing artworks, Julian felt an irresistible pull toward "The Obsidian Muse." It was a masterpiece that had his full attention, its mysterious allure echoing through the pristine gallery space. But his moment of artistic reverie was rudely interrupted by the obnoxious buzz of his smartphone. He quickly fished it out from his pocket, a little irritated but also curious about who might be calling him.

With a hint of self-importance in his voice, Julian answered, "Hello, you've reached the one and only Julian. What's the emergency, darling?"

On the other end of the line, Julian's trusted private detective was on the line, the guy who usually dealt in hard facts and reason in a world where art often danced with mystery. The detective's tone was all business as he reported, "Sorry to disturb your artistic escapades, Jules, but I couldn't find a thing on Camille with the info we had."

Julian, ever the charmer, effortlessly steered the conversation back to himself. "Well, well, detective, you've finally met your match, haven't you? Don't worry, I've got this."

With a theatrical flourish, Julian ended the call and made his grand exit from the gallery. He was a man on a mission, his purposeful steps taking him closer to the sleek black masterpiece of engineering parked just outside - his car. It was a reflection of his own sophistication, a true symbol of his impeccable taste.

As Julian slid into the driver's seat, the pull was undeniable as he thought about the tangled web of intrigue that had woven itself into his life. The need to find Camille, to uncover the truth behind the art, was consuming him. He gripped the wheel with determination, the cool leather under his fingertips a comforting reminder of his control.

The streets of Paris bustled with life as Julian navigated through the city. He had always felt like the city was his stage, and now he was determined to find Camille, the elusive artist who had captivated his imagination. The mystery surrounding her was like an irresistible siren's call, and Julian was ready to dive headfirst into the depths of this mystery, no matter where it led.

***

As Julian strolled into the restaurant, he was welcomed by the gracious owner, a charming Chinese lady with a warm, inviting smile. Her kind demeanor provided a comforting backdrop to the whirlwind of emotions swirling within him. Julian flashed his signature charismatic grin as he accepted her offer, settling comfortably into a cozy corner of the restaurant. Every tick of the clock seemed to whisper, "Time's running out."

With an eager gleam in his eye, Julian leaned in and smoothly inquired, "So, can I have a chat with Camille, sweetheart?" He oozed confidence, a hint of flirtation playing on his lips, giving an air of intrigue to the moment.

The Chinese lady responded with a gentle shake of her head and spoke in her native tongue, leaving Julian momentarily puzzled. But Julian? He wasn't about to let a language barrier stop him. With a sly, confident grin, he pulled a linguistic ace from his sleeve and effortlessly switched to fluent Chinese, leaving her surprised and amused. Her expression evolved from inquisitiveness to understanding, and she finally gave in. A nod of consent, a promise to fetch Camille – and

Julian was back in the game.

As he waited in that serene corner of the restaurant, Julian's thoughts buzzed like a beehive on a summer's day. He wasn't known for shyness, and he had a few questions on his mind. "I wonder if Camille has heard of me," he pondered, a hint of self-indulgence in his musings. The tantalizing aroma of the restaurant's delicious fare filled the air, mingling with the palpable tension that hung like a fog.

The minutes seemed to drag their feet like sullen teenagers, each moment elongating into a perceived eternity. Julian sat poised, brimming with anticipation, as the restaurant's fragrant dishes passed him by, a parade of culinary delights tempting his senses. The clock on the wall maintained its relentless ticking, each second ticking away like a hammer against his chest. He knew that this forthcoming tête-à-tête with Camille held the key to unlock the mysteries that had eluded him for so long. His heart raced in harmony with the ceaseless beat of time, a turbulent symphony in the hush of that restaurant corner.

Camille had finally made her grand entrance from the depths of the restaurant. Julian found himself wondering if her secret sanctuary lay hidden upstairs, reachable through a concealed passage at the back of the restaurant. It was a clandestine puzzle that piqued his curiosity, but before he could delve into that mystery, he had to contend with the palpable annoyance that seemed to accompany Camille wherever she went.

She approached him with a look that seemed to say, "I've had enough of this." Her eyes held a blend of suspicion and exasperation, hiding emotions so complex they could fill a novel. Their gazes locked, and Julian felt the electric current of their connection, a dance they'd been performing since the moment they crossed paths. A part of him wanted to know if she found him as fascinating as he found her.

"Hey there, Camille," Julian said with a mischievous grin, his tone playfully narcissistic. "You know, it's not every day someone as charming as me shows up in a place like this. What do you think of our little rendezvous?" He leaned back casually in his chair, trying to put her at ease, although he knew it wouldn't be easy.

The Lantern Wishes, with its cozy yet tense atmosphere, made the perfect backdrop for their dramatic encounter. The dimly lit space, adorned with flickering candles and deep crimson walls, added a touch of mystique to their conversation. Julian wondered if it was a setting specifically chosen to match Camille's mysterious aura.

In a direct and no-nonsense tone, she cut to the chase, "What the fuck do you want?"

With a calm and confident smile, Julian gestured towards an empty chair, inviting Camille to join him. His eyes bore into her with a sincerity that cut through the layers of intrigue surrounding them. It was time to reveal a piece of the puzzle.

As they sat in silence, Julian understood that this was a pivotal moment in their tale, a turning point that could reshape their budding romance. He had a feeling that whatever he said next would ripple through their narrative in unpredictable ways. So, he decided to come clean.

Leaning in slightly, Julian spoke in a soft, measured tone, "You see, last night, I might not have been completely honest with you." He paused, studying Camille's reaction, as her annoyance and guarded apprehension flared up in response.

She leaned closer, her voice laced with caution, "Julian, you should probably get out of here while you still can." Her words served as a stark reminder of the lurking dangers beneath the surface, leaving Julian to wonder if she was shielding him from more than he realized.

Julian, never one to shy away from a challenge, refused to let the mysterious allure of Camille and the mysteries that surrounded her slip through his fingers. With their destinies now irrevocably linked, he was resolute in his quest to uncover the secrets that bound them together.

Leaning in, he fixed his gaze on Camille's eyes, determination etched across his face. "We've got to talk about that painting," he asserted, his curiosity unrelenting as he peered deep into her eyes, hoping to uncover the hidden truths that lurked within her soul.

Camille's response was swift and tinged with exasperation as she rolled her eyes. "You're still fixated on that painting, aren't you?" she shot back, her frustration palpable. She had desperately tried to shield Julian from the mysterious allure of her artwork, dreading the revelations it might bring.

Undaunted, Julian persisted, his fascination piqued and his concern genuine. "What's got you so worried?" he inquired, his voice a delicate blend of tenderness and insistence. He yearned to unravel the source of her unease, to lay bare the mysterious mysteries that seemed to shroud her existence.

Caught in the throes of her inner turmoil, Camille

suddenly froze. Her gaze swept across the restaurant, her senses on high alert, and it was in that heightened state of awareness that she spotted them—two formidable bikers clad in leather, their presence unmistakably commanding at the restaurant's entrance. The once-cozy establishment had transformed as an ominous aura emanated from the newcomers, casting a shadow over the entire scene.

Now, back to Julian. Next thing he knew, he was letting his flirtatious charm shine through, a glimmer of narcissism evident in his demeanor as he prodded, 'So, Camille, do I intrigue you as much as your paintings do? Or am I even more mysterious?'

Camille, ever the cautious one, responded with a hint of skepticism, her level-headed nature never fully letting her guard down. "You and your mysteries, Julian," she remarked, a trace of a wry smile touching her lips. "But I'd say these new arrivals might have their own stories to tell." She gestured subtly toward the imposing bikers, her instincts always vigilant.

The restaurant buzzed with laughter and clinking glasses as friends and families enjoyed their meals. It was a warm, cozy place, with wooden floors that absorbed the vibrations of the approaching bikers. You could feel the anxiety radiate through the patrons as they watched these unwelcome intruders stroll in.

Camille's heart raced as she scanned the room, searching for a lifeline. She turned her worried gaze toward Julian, whose confident demeanor stood out in the tension-filled atmosphere.

The larger biker made his menacing move towards Camille, clearly with ill intentions. But Julian, a suave and confident figure, stepped in like a knight in shining armor, positioning himself between her and the approaching threat. He seemed ready to protect her at all costs.

With a sudden, explosive fury, the confrontation escalated into a physical brawl. The clatter of chairs and tables added to the pandemonium as fists flew, creating a chaotic symphony that had everyone in the restaurant gasping and shouting. It was a sight that no one anticipated, but Julian, despite being outnumbered, showed everyone what he was made of.

Julian's movements displayed a fascinating mix of skillful precision and unwavering determination. His body moved gracefully, like a skilled dancer in the middle of a deadly ballet. He deftly dodged punches and countered with rapid, precise strikes that left his opponents reeling. Camille watched in awe as the man who had once been a mysterious admirer now revealed himself as her fearless protector.

In a dramatic climax, Julian delivered a bone-crushing roundhouse kick that incapacitated the two bikers. They crumpled to the floor, their menacing presence reduced to nothing. Julian stood tall, his chest rising and falling with exertion, and his eyes, with a hint of self-assuredness, locked onto Camille's.

But as the dust settled, Julian couldn't resist a little playful banter, a smirk on his face. "Did you ever doubt my heroics, Camille?" he asked, his tone hinting at a dash of flirtation. "You know, not everyone can swoop in like this."

Camille, ever the cautious one, responded with a raised eyebrow and a touch of skepticism. "Julian, I'm not sure if you're the hero or if you've got some secret skills you've been hiding."

Their playful exchange added a light-hearted touch to the intense scene, leaving an air of mystery and flirtation lingering in the cozy restaurant.

Julian darted over to Camille, catching the lingering shock in her eyes. He extended his hand to her, brushing her arm gently, searching for a sign that she had come through unscathed. A subtle smile played on his lips as he leaned in closer, his self-assured charm exuding confidence. "You alright, beautiful?" he inquired, his tone laced with a hint of narcissism. Camille, ever the cautious one, replied with a quiet nod, her voice momentarily stolen by the recent threat's intensity.

In the middle of the charged atmosphere, danger still loomed, and Julian's protective instincts surged. He spoke in a low, urgent tone as he brushed a strand of hair from Camille's face, "We better make tracks before they decide to bring in the cavalry, don't you think?" A playful gleam danced in his eyes as he added, "But hey, you're in good hands."

They made their way toward the exit, a palpable mixture of relief and tension hanging in the air. The restaurant's dimly lit interior and the soft murmur of patrons formed a stark contrast to the chaos that had unfolded just moments ago. Julian's chivalrous side shone through, making sure Camille was never too far away as they navigated their escape route.

However, right on the cusp of freedom, an unexpected figure entered the scene. The newcomer, draped in an aura of mysterious mystery, effectively blocked their path. His presence alone hinted that their troubles were far from over.

Julian couldn't help but shoot Camille a concerned glance, wondering just what kind of situation they'd found themselves in now.

***

As Lucas trailed the mysterious man through the gallery, little did he know what mind-boggling surprises awaited him. He embarked on this journey through a maze of secrets, completely oblivious to the fact that it would lead him to the woman who had invaded his dreams – the love of his life, Eva.

Right there, standing in front of him, was a woman who bore a striking resemblance to Eva. Same enchanting eyes, same graceful demeanor, but something was off. Her outfit was a far cry from the Eva he remembered – a leather skirt and a well-worn T-shirt, worlds apart from Eva's usual conservative cardigans and elegant attire.

Lucas' heart raced, and disbelief was painted all over his face as he dared to speak her name. "Eva?" The room was a mess, the aftermath of some kind of struggle, with two unconscious men sprawled out on the floor. The chaos around mirrored the turmoil in Lucas's heart as he tried to make sense of this surreal encounter.

"What did you just call me?" Camille's voice wavered with uncertainty as she locked eyes with the baffled Lucas. Her gaze darted nervously between the two unconscious men at her feet.

Julian seized Camille's arm, his urgency gleaming in his eyes as he beseeched, "We've got to get out of here, and we've got to do it now." But Camille defied his advice and inched closer to Lucas.

Lucas, lost in a whirlwind of emotions, felt tears streaking down his cheeks. He gazed at Camille with a mix of disbelief and yearning. His voice trembled as he spoke, "Eva, where have you been all this time? I've missed you so much."

Driven by his eagerness, Lucas moved forward, but Julian quickly intervened, inserting himself between them and restraining Lucas with a solid grip. "Back off. Who sent you?" Julian's voice was tinged with suspicion as he interrogated the newcomer.

Julian flashed a cocky grin, secretly enjoying the drama unfolding before him as he kept a close watch on Lucas. "Do you always make such dramatic entrances, handsome man wearing orange in day light?" he asked, not missing the chance to taunt Lucas.

Camille, on the other hand, stayed cool and cautious, her eyes darting between the unconscious men and the emotional whirlwind between Lucas and Eva. Her mind was racing, trying to figure out how this situation could have spiraled so out of control.

Lucas and Julian locked eyes, a dance of curiosity and intrigue sparking between them. Lucas then replied, "I followed you from the gallery. I saw both of you last night at the club."

Julian couldn't resist a little flirtatious teasing as he inquired, "Oh were you following me last night at the club?" A sly smile played on his lips.

Camille, always cautious and skeptical, watched the exchange with a raised eyebrow, trying to piece together the puzzle. Her eyes darted from Lucas to Julian, making sure to keep her distance from both of them.

Just as the tension in the air was becoming palpable, the distant rumble of motorcycles grew louder, slicing through their conversation like a knife through butter. The approaching biker gang added an ominous soundtrack to their already precarious situation.

Julian's patience was wearing thin. He couldn't afford to dawdle. With a firm yet gentle grip on Camille's arm, he leaned in close to her and urged, "Sweet Camille, we really should skedaddle. This place is becoming quite the no-go zone."

Camille, still bewildered by Lucas's revelation,

reluctantly turned her attention to the exit. Her practical nature had her focused on the pressing issue of safety, even if it meant leaving her unanswered questions behind.

Lucas, however, couldn't let the revelation go. His voice trembled as he asked Camille with incredulity, "Wait a minute! You're Camille?"

Camille, with her characteristic cool demeanor, nodded, "Yes, I am."

Lucas's mind was racing, trying to process the improbable connection he had stumbled upon. He ran a hand through his disheveled hair, searching for the right words. "You're the one who painted it? The Obsidian Muse?"

Camille, feeling the weight of the situation, wrestled her arm free from Julian's grasp and turned to face both men, her frustration clear on her face. "Enough, you two. This is madness."

Lucas wasn't ready to let go of the revelations that had thrown his world into chaos. With a mix of earnestness and desperation, he implored Camille, "I didn't come to Paris for a vacation. I am Lucas Mitchell from New York. Three days ago, I received a message, and it led me to you. I need to know what's going on."

Julian's patience was wearing thin, particularly as

the roar of approaching motorcycles was now almost deafening. Urgency laced his words as he pleaded with Camille, "We're seriously running out of time. We must go."

Camille, though still skeptical, gave Lucas a contemplative look. Finally, she relented, "Okay, you're coming with us."

Julian let out a breath of relief, his worries momentarily assuaged. "Good. Let's get out of here." The three of them hurried toward the exit, leaving behind the mystery that had drawn them together.

Guiding his two perplexed companions, Julian confidently led them toward his sleek car parked just outside the restaurant's entrance. It was a warm Parisian evening, the streetlights casting a soft, amber glow on the cobbled pavement, creating an almost romantic ambiance.

As they approached the car, the distant rumble of motorcycles grew louder, and a palpable sense of danger began to hang heavy in the air. Julian unlocked the car with a press of a button, the beep echoing in the narrow street.

Julian, with a charming smirk on his face, turned to Camille. "So, Camille, do you often find yourself in situations like this? You know, being pursued by mysterious bikers."

Camille, her brow furrowed, kept her attention fixed on the road ahead. She didn't respond to Julian's playful inquiry, the weight of the situation too pressing to entertain such questions.

The car roared to life, its engine purring like a contented cat. Julian, a seasoned driver, maneuvered the vehicle seamlessly into the chaotic Parisian traffic. The growl of motorcycle engines became more menacing, indicating that the bikers were in hot pursuit, and the tension inside the car was as thick as a fog rolling in from the Seine.

In the back seat, Lucas shifted nervously, his eyes darting between Camille and the approaching bikers. "Camille, why are they after you, and do you often attract trouble like this?"

Camille's hands were clenched tightly on her seatbelt, her gaze fixed on the road. "I don't know, Lucas. It's about the painting, but I never expected all of this."

Bullets from the bikers' guns pierced the air, creating an explosion of shattered glass as they shattered the car's windows. Camille gasped, instinctively ducking to shield herself from the danger, glass shards raining around her like deadly confetti.

Julian's knuckles whitened as he gripped the steering wheel with determination. "Hold on tight, everyone! We're almost there," he declared, his voice laced with a trace of bravado.

As they approached a crowded intersection, Julian's eyes scanned for an escape route. With an audacious maneuver, he deftly navigated the car through the chaotic lanes of traffic. The bikers, caught off guard, struggled to react in time, losing precious seconds as they negotiated the same treacherous turn.

In that heart-pounding moment, Julian's keen eyes spotted a narrow alleyway up ahead. With a confidence bordering on arrogance, he veered the car into the alley, its walls seeming to close in on them. The bikers sped past the intersection, their roaring engines fading into the distance.

Camille let out a breath she hadn't realized she'd been holding, her tension visibly dissipating. "I can't believe we lost them. Julian, you're a real daredevil, aren't you?"

Julian, now with a grin of satisfaction, couldn't resist a flirtatious retort. "Well, Camille, there's a lot more to discover about me, but for now, let's focus on getting to the bottom of this mystery, shall we?"

Lucas, relieved but vigilant, replied, "We're not

out of the woods yet. Camille, I need answers. Why is that painting so important?"

Camille, her face pale from the close encounter, exhaled shakily. "The Obsidian Muse isn't just a painting."

Lucas leaned forward from the back seat, his voice steady but curious. "Camille, what is this painting about?"

Camille shifted her gaze from the menacing bikers tailing them to Julian, her eyes locked on his with an intensity that practically sizzled in the air. "Julian, can you find us a spot away from these bikers hot on our tail?"

Julian, his eyes darting around the winding city streets in search of the relentless pursuers, shot her a grin that oozed self-assured charm. "Don't you worry, Camille. I've got this. We'll find sanctuary at my place. But first, you've got to spill the beans."

The car raced through the vibrant heart of Paris, the aura of mystery surrounding the mysterious painting driving them deeper into a labyrinth of suspense and thrill, where each second held the promise of adventure or danger.

Their sleek ride came to a screeching halt in front of a colossal, ornate gate. The gates swung open soundlessly, unveiling a meandering path leading to an impressive mansion. The mansion was an architectural masterpiece, fusing contemporary elegance with timeless opulence. Majestic pillars adorned the entrance, while expansive windows offered views of meticulously manicured gardens.

Camille's eyes widened, her awe-laden voice escaping her in a breathless whisper. "Wow, this is incredible! Julian, who are you?"

Julian cut the engine and flashed a charismatic smile, his identity finally peeling back like a hidden layer of intrigue. "Well, Camille, I'm Julian Laurent, and it was me who snagged your precious painting at the gala."

The revelation hung in the air like a heavy secret, and as they stepped out of the car and entered the mansion's lavish interior, the mysteries of 'The Obsidian Muse' waited to be unveiled in the luxurious, mysterious world Julian inhabited. In the middle of the grandeur and secrets, Julian found the spotlight inevitably shifting back to himself. "So, Camille, do you often find yourself in such thrilling situations, or is this just a lucky day for you?" He winked playfully, revealing a touch of his flirtatious personality.

***

In the middle of the opulence of Julian's tastefully decorated study, Camille found herself seated opposite Julian and Lucas. Her eyes brimmed with determination and a dash of concern as she inhaled deeply, steadying her nerves before launching into her tale. The rich wallpaper adorning the walls and the warm glow of the ornate chandelier above cast an eerie, somber ambiance over the room, mirroring the gravity of their conversation.

"I'm the one who sent you that message, Lucas," she confessed. "I needed your help."

Julian and Lucas exchanged puzzled glances, a silent question hanging in the air. Julian, his curiosity piqued, leaned forward with an intrigued expression on his face. "Help with what, Camille?" he asked, his charm radiating as he looked at her.

Camille paused for a moment, her eyes darting between the two men, before she spoke softly yet resolutely. "My sister, Eva, told me that if I ever found myself in a tight spot, I should seek your help, Lucas."

Lucas's eyes widened, a surge of disbelief coloring his features. "Eva? Is she still alive?" he inquired urgently.

Camille looked down, her countenance heavy with sorrow. "I haven't seen her in years. I don't even know if she's still breathing," she admitted, the burden of uncertainty pressing down on her.

Lucas shook his head, the shadows of paranoia creeping in as they dimmed his vision, almost as if he sought refuge in disbelief. "No, this can't be. Eva never mentioned having a sister," he muttered, the words escaping his lips as if seeking an anchor in the middle of a tempest.

Camille nodded, her voice carrying a hint of regret. "Yeah, I was the mysterious sister she never spoke of, the one she kept concealed from the world," she revealed, her eyes downcast.

Julian watched Lucas, his concern growing. "Lucas, man, you good? Anything we can do to help?" His voice held a genuine worry, but Lucas seemed lost in a void, another blackout clouding his thoughts.

Camille, raised her eyebrows, her gaze fixed on Lucas. "Hey, Lucas, you seem a bit off. Is everything alright? Want to talk about it?"

Lucas felt like he was drifting into a hazy tunnel. The dimly lit corridor stretched out before him as he took each step with care. At the end, a partially open door cast a warm and inviting glow in the middle of the surrounding shadows. The allure was irresistible, and he gently pushed the door open, entering a room that left him breathless.

It was a scene from the depths of his memories, a place he had tried to bury with medication. The dorm room, their dreams' sanctuary, where he and Eva had spent countless hours sharing their most intimate thoughts.

They reclined on his four-poster bed, basking in the gentle light of a nearby desk lamp. Eva's hazel eyes sparkled with an inner fire, her brilliance and creativity evident in her gaze. Their conversation felt like a dance of brilliant minds, weaving a tapestry of ideas and dreams.

Lucas, the shy and intelligent nerd, spoke, his fingers tracing abstract patterns on the bedspread. "What if we could create an AI assistant that's more than pre-programmed? One that evolves, learns, and adapts to the user's unique needs."

Eva's face lit up with excitement and passion. "Yes! An AI that anticipates and assesses situations before the user even realizes they need help. A companion that becomes an extension of ourselves."

A warm smile graced Lucas's face, the memory washing over him like a bittersweet wave. Those moments with Eva were the pinnacle of their connection, a shared vision that transcended the ordinary.

"We could name it Millie," Eva suggested after a thoughtful pause. Her intelligence and perceptiveness shone through her eyes.

"Millie it is," Lucas agreed.

In that precious moment, their discussion about creating an AI reached its peak. Eva's eyes sparkled with warmth as she reached for Lucas's hand, their fingers intertwining gracefully.

With a tender, almost shy smile, she drew him closer, their breaths mingling. Their lips met in a gentle, lingering kiss, soft and sweet, like the first bloom of spring. Lucas blushed deeply, his heart dancing with joy. It was his very first kiss with Eva, a memory he would cherish forever.

***

As Lucas started to wake up, everything was a total blur. He groaned softly, "Can you give me some space?" Then, out of nowhere, a voice that was oddly reassuring pierced through the fog, and his surroundings began to come into focus. "I'm Dr. McAfee," the man introduced himself, and as he spoke, Lucas's vision cleared up.

Struggling to sit upright, Lucas took a moment to

soak in the scene. He found himself sprawled out on a plush sofa in what looked like a charming, well-furnished study. Nearby, Julian and Camille were giving him this mixed look of worry and relief, their eyes seemingly glued to him. "It's all coming back to me now," Lucas whispered as his memory slowly pieced things together.

Dr. McAfee shifted his attention to Julian, the man with charisma to spare. "How are you holding up, Lucas?" Julian asked with a smug smile, not-so-subtly hinting that he might be the center of attention.

Camille, the picture of caution, couldn't help but interject. "Julian, let's not make this about you. We need to ensure Lucas is okay." She turned to Lucas and asked, "How are you feeling, Lucas? Any headaches or dizziness?"

Lucas, who was a tad paranoid about everything, eyed the room more closely now that he was more conscious. The cozy study was filled with warm, soft lights, and there was a subtle scent of lavender in the air. Books lined the shelves, and an old, ornate desk sat against the wall. It was a haven of sophistication.

Julian, couldn't resist chiming in with a sly grin, "Hey, Lucas, you look like you've seen a ghost. Need a hug to make it all better?" He winked playfully, clearly enjoying Lucas's disarray.

Dr. McAfee, the authoritative figure, chimed in, "Ah, the patient just needs some good rest and a hearty meal to get his strength back. I'm positive that he will make a full recovery."

After Julian showed Dr. McAfee out of the room, Camille saw Lucas sitting up on the couch, looking visibly shaken. She approached him cautiously, her eyes filled with concern. "You alright?" she asked softly, her voice laced with genuine worry.

Lucas, still recovering from the unexpected encounter, managed to nod, his gaze now fixed on the floor.

Camille, her voice tinged with sadness, began to explain herself. "I'm sorry for not calling or texting you," she said, her voice heavy with remorse. "I hate to make it this complicated, but I needed you to come to Paris on your own."

Lucas finally met her gaze, curiosity lighting up his eyes. "Why all the secrecy?" he inquired, genuine curiosity in his voice. "Couldn't you just have texted me?"

Camille hesitated for a moment, her tone softening. "Because, Lucas, when I said I was in trouble, I wasn't lying," she admitted, the gravity of her situation palpable in her words. "I'm in deep trouble." It was a rare moment of vulnerability for Camille, revealing the depth of her predicament.

Sitting together in that room, sharing secrets and surrounded by the dimly lit ambiance, Lucas hesitated, his voice heavy with emotion. "I loved your sister," he confessed, a tinge of sadness in his words. "But she vanished from my life years ago. I woke up one day, and she was just...gone." The memory of Eva's disappearance continued to haunt him.

Camille's expression softened as she absorbed Lucas's confession. She responded gently, "I'm so sorry for what you've been through." Lucas shook his head, a glimmer of melancholy in his eyes. "It's not your fault," he reassured her, compassion in his voice. "I've been trying to move on, to forget about Eva. It's been a real struggle."

Camille, filled with gratitude, offered a sincere smile. "Thank you for coming," she said, her appreciation evident. "I wasn't sure if you'd show up."

Lucas chuckled lightly, a touch of amusement in his eyes. "How could I not?" he replied with a smirk. "You managed to hack into my security system. I had to meet the genius behind it and give them a pat on the back." It was a brief moment of levity amid the intense situation, providing a momentary break from the tension.

Camille burst into laughter at Lucas's remark about his security systems. "Honestly," she admitted, "they weren't all that tough to crack." Lucas nodded, taking it in stride, and responded, "Well, then, maybe you can help me improve them, fix any issues you found."

Camille considered his request, her gaze serious. "If I'm still alive when all this is over," she said, a hint of uncertainty in her voice, "I'd be more than happy to help."

A wave of relief washed over Lucas as he noticed Camille's willingness to assist him. With a curious glint in his eye, he leaned in closer, wearing a sly grin. "So, what kind of trouble have you found yourself in, Camille?"

Camille, always cautious and guarded, hesitated for a moment, her piercing gaze locked onto Lucas. She finally spoke in hushed tones, "Well, Lucas, have you ever heard of the Shadow Serpent Syndicate?"

As soon as those words left Camille's lips, a cold shiver ran down Lucas's spine, and he shifted uncomfortably in his seat. The dimly lit room they were in seemed to close in around them, creating an atmosphere of tension. Lucas shook his head and admitted, "No, I can't say that I have. What's the deal with these Shadow Serpent folks?"

Camille leaned in even closer, lowering her voice to a near whisper as she explained, her words laden with caution. "They're like ghosts, Lucas, lurking in the darkest corners of society. They dabble in everything illegal, from human trafficking to good old-fashioned extortion."

Lucas, though increasingly wary, couldn't suppress his natural curiosity. With a wry smile, he probed further, "So, what's your connection to these elusive characters, Camille?"

Just as Camille was on the verge of revealing more, the heavy wooden door to the dimly lit study swung open, and in walked Julian, the charismatic and somewhat self-absorbed member of their group. He wore an expression of genuine concern, though it was hard to tell whether it was for Lucas or for the dramatic entrance itself. "Oh, Lucas, my dear, I'm positively delighted to see you looking better. What's the latest thrilling chapter in your life story?"

The sudden interruption had everyone in suspense. Lucas and Camille, engrossed in their discussion about that menacing syndicate, were momentarily halted by an unexpected interruption.

Lucas, his eyes reflecting gratitude, chimed in, "Wow, thanks a lot, Julian!" He was always one to express his feelings freely. "You're a lifesaver."

Julian, with his charismatic grin, couldn't resist seizing the moment. "You know, Lucas, it's not just anyone who gets to experience my legendary hospitality," he quipped, a glint of narcissism dancing in his eyes. "What can I say, you're lucky."

Camille, the level-headed and cautious one of the group, found herself suppressing a small, almost imperceptible smile at Julian's offer. She had her doubts about trusting anyone, especially someone as charming as Julian. But the idea of a decent meal and some relaxation did sound appealing, and she found herself nodding in agreement.

Lucas, still a bit woozy from their recent escapade, was quick to latch onto the enticing idea of food. "Dinner at your place? I'm in!" he exclaimed, his enthusiasm undeterred by his lingering lightheadedness. He'd always been the type to embrace opportunities as they came, and the thought of a good meal and more conversation was a welcome one.

The setting around them added to the intrigue. They were in Julian's luxurious, well-appointed mansion, which offered breathtaking views of the cityscape. Glistening skyscrapers and city lights stretched out far away them, creating a backdrop that oozed sophistication and elegance.

Julian's living room was adorned with modern art, plush furnishings, and tasteful decor. The air was infused with the faint scent of expensive perfume and the subtle hum of wealth. A butler, impeccably dressed, silently appeared at Julian's side, awaiting instructions.

In the middle of this opulence, Julian's magnetic personality couldn't help but shine through. The playful flirtation in his tone was almost irresistible, and the offer of dinner was like a siren's call. Lucas and Camille, despite their reservations and wariness, were drawn into Julian's world, if only for a little while.

CHAPTER 7: ENEMY OF MY ENEMY

Lucas found himself in a cozy guest room, taking in every detail. The room gave off major hotel vibes, but it was even cooler. He noticed how organized everything was – clothes hung up neatly in the closet, a bunch of toiletries laid out on the bathroom counter, and even a bunch of charging cables for his phone, ready to go.

The room's décor was on point, with soothing colors that just made him feel at ease. The soft lighting was an elegant touch that completed the whole scene. It was like stepping into a relaxing retreat. The space was all his, and it was almost like the room had read his mind, knowing exactly what he'd need.

Lucas glanced at the charging cables and wondered which one would work for his smartwatch. He mumbled to himself, "Which one's gonna charge my watch? Better not mess this up." He finally found the right cable and plugged it in, feeling a sense of relief as his smartwatch came back to life.

With the smartwatch now charging, he decided to make the most of this unexpected luxury. Lucas entered the modern bathroom, turning on the sleek shower to let the warm water wash away the stress of his eventful day. No matter how hard he tried, he still wondered, "Is this too good to be true? Why is Julian being so accommodating?"

The sound of the cascading water created a soothing backdrop for his thoughts as he stood under the shower. He let the water relax his tense muscles, realizing that it was a rare moment of peace on this perplexing journey. "Should I trust Julian and Camille? Are they hiding something from me?" Lucas pondered, his paranoia getting the best of him.

As he lathered up with soap, his mind wandered back to Eva. Her mysterious disappearance weighed heavily on him, and his thoughts drifted to her. "Where could she be? What happened to her?" Lucas whispered to himself, as if the answer might suddenly come to him. The painful uncertainty gnawed at him, and he felt an overwhelming need to find out the truth. "There's more to this story, I'm sure of it. But what could it be?"

Camille settled onto the plush bed in one of the guest rooms within Julian's sprawling mansion, reflecting on the intense and frightening hours she had just experienced. The menacing threat that had relentlessly pursued her, the ever-present danger that had loomed like a dark cloud over her life - it had all left her emotionally drained. Julian's timely arrival and the refuge of his opulent home felt like a lifeline she hadn't realized she needed. However, a shroud of uncertainty lingered in her mind as she contemplated Julian's true intentions.

A gentle knock on the door disrupted her thoughts, and Julian made his entrance. He had changed into a crisp white shirt and a pair of jeans, looking remarkably put-together despite the chaos of the day. With an expression that was a perfect blend of calm concern, he asked if he could join her on the bed. Camille, still wary but gradually opening up to this mysterious man, nodded her approval.

Sitting down beside her, Julian couldn't resist the urge to strike up some playful banter. "You know, Camille, I've been thinking," he said, flashing a charming smile that only added to his allure. "Why did I have to chase you down to bring you to my cozy sanctuary? You could've just called, and I'd have been here in a heartbeat."

Camille, ever the cautious one, raised an eyebrow at his teasing, her skepticism clear. "Is that right?" she replied, her tone a mix of skepticism and amusement. "And what would be the catch if I'd done that?"

Julian, not one to shy away from a challenge, leaned in a little closer, his eyes twinkling with mischievous intent. "Ah, Camille, you wound me. Can't a gentleman offer his assistance without ulterior motives? Besides, who wouldn't want the pleasure of your company?"

As she settled into his presence, Camille found herself opening up a bit more. "You've got a point," she conceded, a hint of a smile breaking through her cautious facade.

Julian's arms encircled her with a reassuring warmth that transcended the physical world. It was a comforting embrace that Camille hadn't expected but found herself embracing with all her heart. The vulnerability of the past few hours had left her shaken, and being held by Julian felt like the safest place in the world. As she nestled into his comforting arms, she let out a deep, contented sigh, feeling the heavy weight of the day slowly lifting. The room, bathed in soft lamplight, seemed like the most tranquil place in the world, and for the first time in a while, Camille felt a genuine sense of trust in the world around her.

Julian's long fingers gently brushed a stray strand of hair from Camille's face, their touch as soft as a whispered promise. With a charming smile, he continued to cradle her, the chaos of the day slowly receding into the background. "I can't help but feel for you, Camille, after everything you've been through. No one should ever face such danger."

Despite the chaos surrounding her, Camille felt an undeniable pull toward Julian's empathy and genuine concern. She spoke in hushed tones, her words carrying the weight of her gratitude, "Thank you for being there when I needed someone."

In the quiet that enveloped them, the initial awkwardness of their encounter seemed to dissolve, replaced by the burgeoning connection they were forging in the middle of adversity.

Drawing in a deep breath, Camille decided to break the silence and learn more about the mysterious man who had come to her rescue. She turned her gaze to Julian, a hint of curiosity gleaming in her eyes, "So, Julian, when you're not playing the gallant hero, what's your idea of a good time?"

Julian, a mischievous glint in his eye, chose to playfully indulge Camille's curiosity. "Well, darling, besides my heroic escapades, I'm in the art world. Running my own art gallery is my passion; I get to curate and collect pieces that speak to my soul." He leaned back slightly, creating a comfortable but not-too-distant space between them. "And what about you, Camille? What's your story when you're not being swept off your feet by dashing rescuers?"

Their eyes locked in a magnetic connection, Camille hesitated briefly, torn between revealing her true self and the mysteries she'd guarded for so long. Ultimately, she opted for honesty, letting a small, vulnerable smile grace her lips, "I'm a programmer, Julian. The digital world and the world of artificial intelligence are where I find comfort; it's more than just a job—it's a full-blown obsession."

With each word Julian spoke, Camille found herself falling deeper into their conversation. A part of her wanted to admire the passion in his eyes as he talked about the architectural wonders that held his heart captive, from the majestic Eiffel Tower to the intricate details of ancient cathedrals. It was clear that Julian's love for art transcended the confines of his gallery, a world in which he was inviting Camille to explore.

In the cozy, dimly lit guest room, Camille eagerly shared her excitement about her AI projects. She was in her element, her eyes sparkling as she painted vivid pictures of a cutting-edge device she hoped to create. As she spoke about her belief in technology's potential to better people's lives, Julian sat across from her, captivated not only by her words but by the fire in her voice.

"Camille, you've got quite the vision," he commented, flashing a charming smile. "I must say, it's inspiring to see your dedication to your work."

With a glint of pride in her eyes, Camille continued to explain her dream. Julian seized the opportunity, asking, "You know, Camille, with all this brilliance, are you always this passionate about your work?"

As the minutes rolled on, the conversation ventured into more personal terrain. Camille was pleasantly surprised to learn about Julian's love for classic literature. They delved into their favorite novels, finding common ground that deepened their connection.

Camille's curiosity led her to ask, "So, Julian, which of my favorite books have you read?" She watched him intently.

Julian leaned in, his voice dripping with a hint of flirtatiousness, "Pride and Prejudice."

Camille's eyes widened, and she let out an excited laugh, "No way! That's one of my all-time favorites."

Their shared enthusiasm brought them closer, not just intellectually but emotionally. They unearthed more mutual interests, and the room seemed to glow with an unspoken connection.

As the conversation shifted from books to life stories, dreams, and aspirations, Camille felt an inexplicable sense of comfort in Julian's presence. It was as if their paths had been intricately woven together, and it filled her with an undeniable warmth.

With a knowing smile, Julian mentioned, "Camille, speaking of dreams, what's your most cherished one?"

Camille hesitated for a moment, her guarded nature showing through, but then she shared her deepest aspiration with him. As she did, the room seemed to come alive with an invisible, magnetic force pulling them closer.

The room's ambiance, once just a backdrop, now felt like an intimate haven. Their initial encounter, brought about by a whirlwind of chance, was slowly evolving into something much more profound. Camille was starting to see a side of Julian that extended beyond his charismatic exterior.

As their conversation continued, the world outside faded into obscurity, and the two of them found themselves at the nexus of a serendipitous connection, a rare and wondrous spark in the middle of the chaos of life. It hinted at a promising romance that might just be waiting to unfold.

Camille's heart raced, a whirlwind of emotions swirling within her. She summoned the courage to pose a question that had been tugging at her curiosity. "So, Julian, I was wondering, why'd you snag my painting?"

Julian, with a glint in his eyes, fixated his intense gaze on her, maybe a bit too intently. "Well, Camille, that artwork of yours? It's like a magnetic force that's been tugging at my soul since I first laid eyes on it. I felt like it spoke to a part of me, and I couldn't help but hunt down the genius who created it."

He didn't just answer Camille's question directly, did he? Julian's mysterious charm seemed wrapped up in his response, and there was something in his eyes that suggested he was making a deliberate play. "What's so captivating about that painting, Julian? Is it because it's mine?"

Their conversation was taking on a flirtatious edge, with Julian's charisma seemingly intent on winning over Camille. She couldn't deny that slowly, she was starting to trust him, even though her cautious instincts warned her otherwise. "You have a point there, Camille. It's not just because it's yours, but because it's an extension of the paradox that is you."

The room they were in was bathed in a soft, inviting glow, casting delicate interplays of light and shadow on the walls. Camille and Julian found themselves irresistibly drawn together, their connection deepening by the minute. They exchanged unspoken words, laden with the promise of a connection that transcended art, destiny, and the chaos that had initially thrown them into each other's path.

In the middle of the shared laughter and whispered banter, there was an unspoken charge in the air, a magnetic pull that brought them closer. Camille's touch on Julian's cheek lingered, and he inched closer, his eyes locked onto hers. Time stood still in that moment, as if the universe had decided to pause and admire this blossoming connection.

Camille's voice barely broke the silence, "Julian..."

Their lips met in a gentle, lingering kiss, sealing the unspoken understanding that had been growing throughout the evening. The world beyond that room seemed to vanish as they explored the newfound intimacy, savoring every moment.

When their lips finally parted, a playful smile danced on Camille's lips, and she softly remarked, "We should probably head out."

Julian's reply was warm and tender, his eyes never

leaving Camille's. "You're right, we should. Lucas might be wondering what's keeping us from dinner."

***

Lucas found himself sitting in the grand dining room of Julian's fancy mansion, and it practically screamed extravagance. Seriously, this place looked like something out of a Hollywood movie. Stepping into the lavish space felt like entering another world, and Lucas found himself wondering if he was the odd one out. His mind, always buzzing with questions and doubts, had him second-guessing his every move. What should he do? Was there some kind of secret manual for how to act around a butler? He'd never dealt with one before, and now he was in uncharted territory.

Sebastian, the butler in his sharp, perfectly tailored suit, stood nearby. The guy exuded a level of poise and control that made Lucas's head spin. He was like the master of cool, and it left Lucas both intrigued and nervous. He caught himself asking, "So, what's it like being a butler? Got any insider butler hacks you can share?"

With his poker face on, Sebastian just gave a little half-smile that seemed to say he had all the answers.

"Being a butler, sir, means dedicating yourself to serving and making sure everyone in the house is comfy. And when it comes to tips, well, having good manners and showing respect are the basics. Oh, and 'thank you' and 'please' are your best friends."

Lucas chuckled at the seriousness of the response. "Alright, 'thank you' and 'please,' check. Anything else?"

Sebastian leaned in slightly, as if letting Lucas in on some secret society info. "Well, sir, it's about creating a world of luxury and comfort for the folks who live here. Making them feel like they're in their own little paradise."

Lucas nodded, starting to get that being a butler was more about crafting an experience. "So, you're the magician behind all this luxury, huh?"

Sebastian inclined his head, a glimmer of amusement in his eyes. "You could say that, sir. If you need anything while you're here, just ask."

Lucas nodded and sat quietly at the elegantly set dining table, soaking in the opulent surroundings. Meeting a butler in real life was miles away from his usual daily routine. The dining room exuded a sense of old-world charm, with antique paintings adorning the walls and an impressive crystal chandelier hanging above.

After a few minutes, Julian made a grand entrance, taking his place at the head of the table, exuding an air of charisma. He was the epitome of sophistication, and the sheer grandeur of it all left Lucas feeling slightly overwhelmed. It was light-years away from his regular, laid-back settings.

Lucas, nervously toying with his silverware, decided it was time to break the ice. "Your art gallery is quite something, Julian. The pieces in there...they're extraordinary, really."

With a warm, appreciative smile, Julian acknowledged the compliment. "Thank you, Lucas. Art is a passion of mine, and I'm always on the hunt for unique pieces. It's an obsession, really."

Lucas, wanting to steer the conversation and perhaps impress Julian, added, "Well, Julian, your gallery is a universe apart from my day job."

Julian raised an eyebrow, his eyes twinkling with curiosity. "Oh? What's your day job, Lucas?"

Clearing his throat and trying to play it cool, Lucas confessed, "I'm in cybersecurity."

Julian leaned in, his intrigue deepening. "Cybersecurity? That sounds pretty fascinating, Lucas. Protecting data and all that, it must be a wild ride. What exactly do you do in that digital world of yours?"

Lucas managed a half-hearted chuckle, trying to downplay his own achievements. "It's kind of like being a digital detective, safeguarding sensitive information from the internet's bad apples. It has its thrills, I suppose."

Julian, genuinely interested, couldn't resist delving deeper. "I can imagine. So, Lucas, do you ever feel like a secret agent fighting off cyber-villains in the digital shadows?"

Lucas chuckled, feeling a bit flattered by Julian's line of questioning. "Well, not exactly James Bond, but there are moments when it feels like I'm saving the day, one firewall at a time."

The conversation was really picking up steam, and Lucas was finding himself slowly lowering his guard. His initial jitters were dissipating, and he was beginning to feel a genuine connection with Julian. It was kind of surprising, but the posh dining room and Julian's curious, charming demeanor were making the night look like it would be one to remember.

Moments later, when Camille walked into the elegant dining room, and Lucas couldn't believe his eyes. She had swapped her earlier outfit for something more conservative, opting for a cozy cardigan and a skirt that flowed gracefully around her. Her transformation made Lucas do a double-take; she was starting to remind him of Eva, and that sent his heart racing.

As she settled into her chair next to Julian, Camille found herself in the spotlight. Her cautious nature was slowly warming up to Julian's charm, though she found herself unable to resist feeling a little self-conscious under his gaze. But Julian, always the flirtatious charmer, didn't miss a beat.

Julian, leaning in slightly closer to Camille, flashed his most winning smile. "Camille, you look absolutely stunning tonight. That cardigan, it's so inviting. And that skirt, it's like a breath of fresh air. Are you trying to outshine the stars tonight?" He winked playfully, clearly enjoying the game of winning her over.

Camille, who was typically cautious, couldn't help but feel her defenses weakening. She had changed into something more comfortable, a soft cardigan and a flowy skirt. A flutter ran through Lucas's heart as he took in how much she now resembled Eva. She took her seat next to Julian, feeling a tad self-conscious.

Julian, the consummate host, couldn't resist offering another compliment. "Camille, you look lovely. Did you pick that outfit from the wardrobe?"

A faint blush crept up Camille's cheeks as she acknowledged the compliment. "Thank you, Julian. I borrowed these from your guest room, hope you don't mind."

Julian, with a touch of theatricality, responded with a gracious smile. "My dear Camille, consider everything here at your disposal. What's mine is yours. Tell me, do you often borrow clothes, or is it just for special occasions like this?"

Meanwhile, Lucas, sitting there, lost in his thoughts, found himself caught in the moment. He found himself overhearing their conversation, and the voices in his head seemed to quiet down for a brief moment. His attention was drawn to the chemistry unfolding before him, and he watched as Julian's relentless charisma made Camille's guard slowly crumble.

The dimly lit dining room exuded an air of sophistication, with soft music playing in the background, casting a romantic ambiance. Candles flickered on the tables, their gentle glow adding to the enchantment of the evening.

Lucas, feeling a bit out of place but wanting to steer the conversation away from his own emotional turmoil, interjected with an awkward chuckle. "Well, I don't know about you two, but I'm absolutely famished. What's on the menu tonight?"

This sudden change in focus prompted a hearty laugh from Julian. "Ah, Lucas, a man after my own heart! Camille, are you as hungry as our friend here?"

Sebastian, the ever-graceful butler, signaled to the kitchen staff who moved swiftly into action. They emerged one by one, bearing platters of delectable French cuisine. The tantalizing aroma filled the air, and each dish was more mouthwatering than the last. The room was a blend of elegance and anticipation, and the three of them sat down to a meal that promised to be as unforgettable as the evening itself.

The table transformed into a delightful smorgasbord of delectable dishes. The Coq au Vin, a chicken dish rich in flavor and filled with the comforting aroma of simmering red wine and herbs, took center stage. Beside it, a platter of Ratatouille displayed a medley of vibrant vegetables, artfully arranged and glistening with flavor. The fluffy, golden croissants, paired with a generous bowl of creamy garlic aioli, were a sight to behold. The atmosphere was set, making this dinner with Julian and Camille an unforgettable experience.

As they gazed at the dishes before them, Lucas's

eyes grew wide, and somehow, he ended up blurting out, "Wow, this spread is unbelievable! I've never seen such a delicious feast in one place."

Camille's eyes sparkled with amusement as she responded, "That's the magic of French cuisine for you. It has a way of wowing the senses. Bon appétit, everyone."

Julian, with a smile that could charm anyone, raised his wine glass for a toast. "To new friendships and unforgettable meals."

Lucas couldn't resist sneaking glances at Camille as he savored the mouthwatering French cuisine. Her connection with Julian was undeniable, and Lucas was grappling with his growing curiosity about her.

In between bites, Lucas decided to quench his burning question, aiming to charm Camille. "Camille, are you and Eva twins by any chance?"

Camille nodded, placing her fork on her plate before diving into the shared history with her sister. "Yes, we're twins, identical twins to be precise. Growing up, Eva was always the golden child, while I... well, let's just say I had a rebellious streak. We were close once, but our paths diverged. Eva was all about law and order, while I ventured into the world of hacking and, well, a more unconventional lifestyle."

Lucas listened attentively, captivated by the insight into their dynamic. "So, what brought about the change in your relationship?"

Camille sighed, her gaze distant as she delved into her memories. "It was my choices, really. I kept pushing the boundaries, and Eva just couldn't condone what I was doing. We reached a point where we stopped talking altogether."

Julian, with his charismatic charm, sensed the heaviness of the conversation and interjected softly, "Family dynamics can be quite intricate, you know. Sometimes, it only takes a moment to bridge those gaps again."

Camille's eyes met Lucas's, and there was a glimmer of vulnerability in her gaze as she admitted, "Yeah, maybe this is that moment."

Julian, with his confident and flirtatious demeanor, leaned in slightly, his voice carrying a hint of narcissism as he asked, "Tell me, Camille, is there anything I can do to make this moment even more unforgettable for you?"

Lucas's curiosity sparked decided to interrupt the lovebirds, and he looked at Camille with an inquisitive glint in his eyes. "Hey, Camille, when's the last time you heard from Eva?"

Camille's face clouded with memories, and the weight of her past pressed on her as she thought back. "It's been over five years, Lucas."

Lucas nodded thoughtfully, his mind spinning as he drew connections. It struck him that Eva had vanished from his life around the same time. Goosebumps pricked his skin at the eerie coincidence.

Leaning in closer, Lucas asked the question that had been haunting him. "Camille, what did Eva say the last time you talked to her?"

A sudden tension filled the room, and Camille's fork slipped from her hand, making a subtle clinking sound as it hit her plate. She cleared her throat, and her voice wavered as she recounted Eva's final words. "The last thing she told me was that she believed someone was after her."

Lucas's eyes widened in alarm. This revelation had never reached his ears before. "Do you have any idea who it might have been? Did she mention anything else?"

Camille visibly shivered, her composure wavering. Julian, ever perceptive, reached out and gently took her hand. "It's okay, Camille," he said with a reassuring smile.

Camille swallowed hard and met Lucas's gaze. Her

voice trembled as she confessed, "It was the same people who've been hunting me, the Shadow Serpent Syndicate."

Julian leaned back in his chair, his face marked by a solemn expression that hinted at concealed knowledge. "Camille, maybe they aren't after you. They could be after Eva, and they might think you can help them find her."

Lucas couldn't accept this explanation. Frustration etched across his features as he shook his head vehemently, his tone becoming accusatory. "Camille, you know where Eva is, don't you? You've been keeping it from us all this time."

Tears welled up in Camille's eyes, and she tried to explain, "Lucas, I swear I don't know where she is. I wish I did."

Julian intervened, his calm demeanor attempting to defuse the tense atmosphere. "Lucas, it's been a long day for all of us. Maybe it's best if you get some rest. We can continue working on this in the morning."

Still fuming and not entirely convinced, Lucas grumbled his agreement and left the room in frustration, leaving Camille and Julian alone in the softly lit dining area.

As the door's echo slowly faded, the room fell

into a heavy silence. Camille looked visibly shaken, her eyes welling up with tears. Lucas had just hurled a serious accusation at her, and it had left her emotionally wounded. Julian, ever the attentive charmer, recognized her distress and scooted his chair closer, gently reaching out to take her hand.

Julian flashed a confident smile and interjected, "Hey there, Camille. That was quite the storm back there, huh? Don't let it get to you, though. We're in this together, remember?"

Camille, cautiously eyeing Julian's charismatic charm, slowly opened up, "I wish I knew where my sister was. She's the only family I have left." Her voice trembled with the years of pain spent searching for her lost connection.

Julian, with a hint of flirtatiousness, tightened his grip on her hand and teased, "Well, I must say, you've got quite the remarkable family member to fight for. But you know what they say, Camille, 'the best things are worth fighting for,' right?"

Camille's eyes gleamed with a mixture of gratitude and lingering caution. She shook her head slowly and admitted, her voice quivering, "It feels like I've searched everywhere, Julian. I've tried every avenue, and I've hit so many dead ends. I don't know if she's deliberately off the grid or if something terrible has happened to her."

Julian, the ever-confident knight in shining armor, beamed reassuringly, "Don't you worry, Camille. We'll explore every nook and cranny, and we'll be super careful about it. No matter what we find, you've got a trusty sidekick right here. I'm with you every step of the way."

The room seemed to close in on them, the weight of uncertainty bearing down. Julian's grip on Camille's hand remained firm, offering silent support. He leaned in closer, gazing deeply into her eyes as he stated with conviction, "Camille, we can't lose hope. We'll find answers together. Perhaps Lucas will come around once he's had some time to think."

Camille wiped her tears away, her voice still trembling. "I appreciate your help, Julian. You've done so much for me already, more than I could have ever expected."

Julian inched closer, his eyes locked onto hers, and he whispered with a sly grin, "You know, Camille, I've always believed in going the extra mile for someone special. And you, my dear, are quite special."

A weak yet grateful smile crossed Camille's lips, her heart warmed by his genuine kindness. As they sat in the dimly lit room, the bond between them deepened with each passing moment. The challenges ahead only served to strengthen their connection, and the world outside seemed to fade away as they faced the unknown together.

CHAPTER 8: SHADES OF DESIRE

Lucas couldn't sit still, his anxiety palpable in the dimly lit guest room. The thought of Eva's potential disappearance was a burden he couldn't bear. He knew he had to take action, to seek answers, to hold onto the hope that she might still be out there somewhere.

In his restless state, he reached for his phone and smartwatch, which had been silently charging on the nearby table. With a deep breath, he powered them on, a renewed sense of purpose guiding his actions. He had to remember everything about Eva, every detail, every memory that could possibly lead him back to her.

As he anxiously fumbled with his devices, Lucas, his voice tinged with paranoia, began to fire questions at his AI assistant, Millie. "Millie, you know everything, don't you? Tell me everything about Eva. Every tiny detail. I can't afford to forget anything, not if I'm going to find her."

Millie, the open and honest AI, hesitated for a moment, then started to recount stories of Eva and their shared past. She spoke of their shared moments, their dreams, their laughter, and the secrets they had entrusted to each other. As she talked, Lucas absorbed every word, hanging onto each syllable as if it were a precious puzzle piece in the mystery of Eva's disappearance.

With Millie's help, Lucas sought to keep the memory of Eva alive, to piece together the fragments of their past, and to uncover the truth about her whereabouts. His determination remained unwavering, fueled by love and a relentless pursuit of hope in the middle of the unknown. In this dimly lit room, surrounded by the soft hum of technology, Lucas was a man on a mission, unwilling to let go of the person he loved.

Millie's voice was a comforting presence on the other end of the line, soothing Lucas's frayed nerves as she began to weave the intricate tapestry of memories that constituted Eva and his shared history. It was like stepping into a time machine, with Millie narrating their story in real-time.

Lucas couldn't help but feel the weight of paranoia creeping in, and he interjected with a jittery tone, "Millie, you're absolutely certain about this, right? You're not missing any details, are you?"

Millie, her AI persona designed to be open and forthright, calmly responded, "I assure you, Lucas, the details are accurate. You can trust my memory."

As she spoke, Lucas's mind conjured up a vivid image of the bustling college campus, almost like a scene from a movie. He could almost hear the chatter of students, the rustling of leaves, and see the bright autumn colors surrounding them.

"Alright," Millie said, a hint of nostalgia in her voice, "It all began back in college. You and Eva crossed paths on that vibrant campus, and it felt like destiny had a hand in bringing you two together for a project."

Driven by paranoia, Lucas bombarded Millie with questions, unable to hold back his curiosity. "But, Millie, were there any hints of something more? Like, did Eva ever mention her feelings for me back then?"

Millie responded with her characteristic honesty, "I'm afraid, Lucas, that Eva's feelings remained a well-kept secret at that time. The two of you started as project partners, but love has its own way of unfolding."

As Millie continued, Lucas's mind painted a vivid picture of their college days. He remembered the excitement, the late-night study sessions that often blurred into dawn, and the countless moments of laughter and shared dreams.

"After college," Millie went on, "You both ventured into the corporate world, pursuing different career paths. But your unwavering passion for technology and AI was a bond that remained unbroken."

Lucas nodded as Millie spoke. The years had seen them march down different professional paths, but their shared dream of creating an advanced AI companion had been a constant source of connection. The project was a testament to their enduring partnership.

With a more anxious tone, Lucas questioned, "And, Millie, did Eva ever mention any other friends or acquaintances who might have, you know, influenced her decisions?"

Millie replied, "Lucas, Eva was known for her independent thinking. While she had many friends, her decisions were mostly guided by her own values and ambitions."

Millie's soothing voice continued, "And, after long hours at work, you'd both return home, immersing yourselves in your AI project. The two of you, a dynamic duo, turning your shared vision into reality."

As Millie recounted their story, Lucas felt a renewed sense of determination. Their shared journey in college, the dreams they'd chased together – they were like a lighthouse in the darkness of Eva's sudden disappearance.

Lucas leaned forward, clutching his phone tightly, a hint of paranoia in his eyes. "Millie," he began, "Is there anything, any piece of information that Eva might have shared with you about herself, her family, or anything that could help me find her?"

Millie, his trusty AI companion, spoke with an openness that mirrored her electronic nature. "I'm sorry, Lucas, but Eva never confided in me with any personal details. She never gave me anything to store in my AI database. It was a part of her privacy principles, and she was very cautious about keeping her personal life separate."

A heavy sigh escaped Lucas as he realized the dead-end that he'd stumbled upon. Even Millie, the closest thing to a confidante Eva had, couldn't provide a breadcrumb trail leading to her. It was as if Eva had vanished into the void, leaving no trace behind.

Lucas's paranoia seeped through his words, "But she did tell me one odd detail."

His voice quivered slightly, a mix of curiosity and fear, as he inquired, "Tell me what it was, Millie. Whatever it is, I can handle it."

A hushed anticipation hung in the room, the weight of their shared concern almost palpable. Lucas couldn't shake the feeling that Eva held the key to her own mystery.

Millie replied evenly, "She confided in me that she was scared of you."

Lucas was taken aback, his eyes widening in disbelief. "What? That's... that's ridiculous. When did she tell you this?"

Millie's artificial voice remained steady as she answered, "The night before she disappeared."

In that moment, the room seemed to shrink around Lucas, as if he'd been thrust into a whirlpool of emotions. Questions whirled in his mind, suspicion taking root. Eva's disappearance had taken an even darker turn, and the air hung heavy with the weight of secrets yet to be uncovered.

***

In another room of Julian's sprawling mansion, the soft flickering of the fireplace cast a warm, golden hue over the cozy space, enveloping Julian and Camille in an intimate cocoon.

Julian, ever the smooth talker, looked deep into Camille's eyes, his voice a gentle, reassuring murmur.

"I'm here for you, Camille, no matter what happens. We'll find your sister together."

As they nestled together, Camille leaned in closer, her head resting comfortably on Julian's shoulder. Her fingers traced intricate patterns on his hand, her voice a soft murmur. "Thank you, Julian. Your support means more to me than you can imagine. You're an unexpected ray of light in the middle of this darkness."

The crackling of the fire painted a soothing backdrop for their moment, creating an atmosphere of warmth and closeness. In this serene silence, they let their hearts beat in sync, contemplating the uncertain path that lay ahead.

Amid the comforting warmth of the room, Camille had an epiphany. Despite the tumultuous circumstances that had brought them together, she had found solace in Julian's presence, something she hadn't felt in a long time. The connection between them was undeniably growing.

Julian, ever the charmer, allowed the crackling fire to encourage their conversation. His voice, warm and soothing, filled the room. "Camille, there's something about you that drew me to that painting, to you. It's not just your incredible talent as an artist, but it's the mystery and strength that you possess. There's a fire within you, just like this one," he said, nodding toward the fireplace.

Camille's eyes sparkled as she looked up at him, her face bathed in the gentle, warm glow. She reached out and took his hand, their fingers interlacing like the perfect fit of a puzzle. "Julian, I have to admit, you've awakened something in me too. I never expected to find a connection like this in the middle of the chaos of my life. It's like we're two pieces of a puzzle that finally fit together."

Their fingers gently tightened around each other, silently affirming their growing bond. As the flames danced before them, Camille and Julian felt a unique sense of unity that transcended the dangerous circumstances they found themselves in.

With a soft smile, Julian's words flowed like honey as he whispered, "Camille, no matter what happens, we'll face it together. We'll find your sister, and we'll protect each other. I promise you that."

Camille nestled her head on Julian's chest, finding comfort in the steady rhythm of his heartbeat. "I believe you, Julian. I'm grateful to have you by my side." The room felt like a sanctuary, enveloping them in a shared moment of solace and hope.

The night deepened, their conversation weaving a

tapestry of intimacy and trust. Julian, ever the charmer, couldn't resist the urge to playfully tease Camille. "So, Camille, are you saying I'm your knight in shining armor?" His smirk was hard to miss as he inched closer, their chemistry undeniable.

Camille's heart raced, a mix of caution and attraction swirling within her. Her smile matched his determination, and with a gentle yet resolute gesture, she leaned in until their lips met in a soft, lingering kiss.

Their connection deepened as their kiss spoke the unspoken. The room around them dissolved into oblivion, leaving just the two of them bathed in the warm, flickering light of the fireplace. It was a silent vow, a testament to their growing affection and the mutual understanding they had unearthed in each other.

As they finally parted, Camille's eyes held a blend of vulnerability and newfound courage. She whispered, "Julian, I think I'm falling for you."

Julian's gaze softened as he caressed her cheek. "Camille, I've been falling for you since the moment I saw your painting. I'm just grateful that life brought us together."

Their lips met once more, sealing their shared sentiments in a tender moment. Love blossomed in the middle of the thrilling chaos of their lives, adding a new layer to their journey that transcended danger and uncertainty. In the dimly lit room, the warmth of the fire, and the tender connection they'd forged, Camille and Julian found themselves entangled in the beautiful mess that is love.

***

Lucas lay in a dimly lit room, his mind swirling with the unsettling revelation from Millie. The idea that Eva, the love of his life, might have been afraid of him was a twist that kept him tossing and turning, unable to make sense of it all.

In the quiet of the room, his paranoia crept in as he questioned, "Why would she be scared of me, Millie? What could I have possibly done to make her feel that way?"

The weight of uncertainty pressed down on him, and his thoughts drifted back to a particular memory etched in his heart. It was the day they had graduated from college, a moment filled with the hope and excitement of what lay ahead.

In the soft, gentle glow of a solitary lamp, Lucas's thoughts transported him to that warm summer evening on the college campus. Laughter and conversations swirled around them, and the setting sun painted Eva with a radiant, golden light.

He remembered that pivotal moment when Eva, her eyes shining with emotion, had taken his hand and confessed her love. It had been a raw, vulnerable exchange, a connection that ran deep. Their dreams of creating an advanced AI, their shared ambitions, and their unwavering love for each other had laid the foundation for a promising future.

"But what could have changed between us since then?" Lucas mused, his brow furrowed with worry, as he searched for answers in the vivid memories of their past. The room seemed to hold the echo of their shared dreams, a reminder of the love they once held for each other.

Lying there in the hushed stillness of the night, Lucas couldn't help but let paranoia creep in. He was consumed by questions. What had caused the sudden change? Why was Eva so afraid? These thoughts raced through his mind relentlessly. Lucas understood that he needed to seek answers not just for his own peace of mind but for Eva, the woman he loved. There were too many gaps in the story, and he was determined to unearth the truth behind her vanishing act and the shrouded circumstances surrounding it.

Lucas lay awake in bed, wrestling with the relentless storm of thoughts and inquiries that swirled through his mind. Sleep remained elusive as the weight of Eva's absence bore down on him.

As the night hours slipped away and the room plunged deeper into shadow, exhaustion finally won over, drawing him into the world of dreams. Yet, it was no tranquil slumber that greeted him.

In his dream, he found himself transported back to a place that simultaneously stirred longing and dread within him—a vivid memory of a moonlit night when Eva had bared her soul to him. They stood on a deserted beach, with the gentle lull of waves caressing the shore providing a soothing backdrop.

In his dream's reenactment, Eva's eyes betrayed her uncertainty as she began to speak. Her voice was soft, her words weighed down with unspoken meaning. "Lucas, there's something I need to tell you," she said, her fingers fidgeting with the necklace he had given her.

Lucas, confined to the dream's reality, watched the scene unfold, unable to alter its course. He witnessed the turmoil in Eva's eyes, the inner conflict as she struggled to articulate her thoughts.

Eva's confession finally broke through, "I love

you, Lucas. But I'm scared. There's something I've kept from you, something I haven't told you."

The dream replayed the past as it had happened in reality, leaving Lucas with the lingering memory of Eva's heartfelt confession, her vulnerability, and her concealed fears. As the dream began to disintegrate, he awoke with a start, the weight of his affection for her and the mystery surrounding her growing even heavier.

Sleep was a distant dream, and Lucas understood that his journey was far from over. Uncertainties, secrets, and, he hoped, answers lay ahead, and he couldn't find peace until he had located Eva and unraveled the truth she had hidden for so long.

Lucas stirred in bed, the last traces of his dream about Eva slowly slipping away. It was Millie, his ever-attentive AI assistant, that gently pulled him further into consciousness with her soothing voice. "Good morning, Lucas," she chimed, her voice like a calm morning breeze.

He blinked away the sleep, taking in his surroundings. The room was bathed in soft morning light, and he noticed that his restlessness had left his bed in a state of disarray. Millie's reminder nudged him to collect himself. They were, after all, guests in Julian's impressive mansion, and next thing he knew, he was feeling a pang of gratitude for the gracious hospitality they had been shown.

With a weary yawn, Lucas stretched his limbs and pushed himself to sit up. "You're right, Millie," he responded, rubbing his eyes as he swung his legs over the edge of the bed. "I suppose I should behave like a proper house guest, shouldn't I?" A touch of dry humor lingered in his voice, as if the act of making the bed in this grand mansion was a surreal contrast to his otherwise ordinary life.

As he tidied up the sheets and blankets, Lucas's thoughts gravitated back to his mission – the relentless pursuit of Eva, the quest for truth, and the mysterious puzzle that was now her life.

When the bed was neatly made, he rose, resolved to meet whatever challenges lay ahead. "Alright, Millie, I'm ready for breakfast. Something tells me we'll need all the energy we can muster for the day ahead." His voice brimmed with determination, his gaze fixed on the trials that awaited them. In the tranquil ambiance of the morning-lit room, Lucas was determined to leave no stone unturned in his quest to unravel the mystery of Eva's disappearance.

***

Lucas entered the opulent dining room, his eyes darting around, a touch of paranoia in his gaze as he searched for any sign of his companions. To his surprise, the room was empty, void of other guests. Just as a hint of confusion started to creep into his thoughts, Sebastian, the impeccably formal butler, appeared seemingly out of thin air. "Good morning, sir," Sebastian greeted Lucas with a slight bow. "I hope you had a restful night. Breakfast is served on the terrace this morning. Please follow me."

Lucas followed the butler through a series of elegant French doors, and as he stepped onto the terrace, he was met with a breathtaking view. The terrace was adorned with lush greenery, elegant wrought-iron furniture, and a panoramic vista of the surrounding gardens. At the far end of the terrace, beneath a canopy of climbing vines, sat Camille and Julian. They appeared to be deeply engrossed in conversation, the morning sunlight casting a warm and inviting glow upon them.

Julian, as always the charming and flirty host, flashed a playful grin as he saw Lucas approaching. "Good morning, Lucas," he greeted with genuine warmth, his eyes locking onto Camille's as if he couldn't resist her presence. "I hope you're ready for a delightful breakfast. Please, join us."

Lucas, although somewhat taken aback by the change in surroundings, welcomed the idea of a meal in such an idyllic setting. With a nod of gratitude, he walked over to their table, ready to indulge in the morning feast and secretly hoping to engage in more discussions about the intriguing mystery surrounding Eva and Camille. The scene was set, and the tension in the air was undeniable, as unspoken feelings lingered between the three of them, waiting to unravel in this picturesque setting.

The terrace was a picturesque setting, adorned with a sumptuous spread of breakfast delights. A wooden table was adorned with an enticing selection of warm, flaky croissants, an assortment of vibrant, fresh fruit, and an enticing array of cheeses and cured meats. A delicate porcelain tea set graced the table, accompanied by a pot of rich French press coffee, promising to revive even the weariest of souls.

As they savored the luxurious morning feast, Lucas found himself drawn to the subtle, intriguing exchanges between Camille and Julian. Their glances held secrets, and Lucas, ever the paranoid detective, was determined to get to the bottom of it. He took a thoughtful sip of his coffee and then cleared his throat, his eyes fixing on Camille.

"Camille," he began, his voice carrying a hint of sincerity, "I need to apologize for my behavior at dinner last night. My emotions got the best of me, and I realize I should've been more understanding. The truth is, I want to find Eva just as much as you do."

Camille met Lucas's gaze, her eyes softening. She understood the turmoil that must be churning within him due to Eva's mysterious vanishing. She nodded, "Thank you, Lucas."

Julian, always the playful and flirty one, leaned in a bit closer, his gaze lingering on Camille. "You know, Camille, I must say that your captivating presence makes this breakfast even more delightful."

Although reserved, Camille felt warmth rise to her cheeks under the spell of Julian's charm. "Well, thank you, Julian. You're quite the gentleman."

Lucas, who was trying to keep up with the unfolding dynamics, cleared his throat, asking, "So, what do you both think should be our next move in finding Eva?"

Julian, looking straight into Camille's eyes, responded, "You know, Lucas, I think we should combine our skills and resources to create a search strategy. And Camille, we could start by revisiting some of Eva's favorite places. Memories can be great clues."

Lucas appreciated the support from both of them. The breakfast table served not only as a feast for their bodies but also as the birthplace of their shared determination to unravel the mystery surrounding Eva. As they plotted their next steps to discover the truth, the terrace with its charming scenery seemed to cocoon them in a world of possibilities, strengthening the connections between them.

But still, he couldn't shake the relentless unease that had consumed him ever since Eva's baffling disappearance. His resolve to find her had solidified into an unyielding determination, and he was ready to go to any lengths to uncover the truth. Around the breakfast table, with his croissants and coffee growing cold, he confided in Camille and Julian.

But Lucas, always prone to paranoia, furrowed his brow and exclaimed, "You guys ever get that feeling like you're being watched? I can't shake the thought that someone's keeping tabs on us."

Camille and Julian exchanged glances, concern evident in their eyes. Camille, reserved but intrigued, responded, "Lucas, it's a scary situation, and we need to be cautious. But right now, we have to focus on finding Eva."

Julian, with his playfully charming nature, decided to lighten the mood. He leaned in, his eyes sparkling with a hint of flirtation. "Well, Lucas, if someone is watching, they're in for quite the show. I mean, look at this dynamic trio we've got going on."

Lucas sighed, but a faint smile tugged at the corners of his lips. "Yeah, you're right. We've got to stay focused. The first step is to retrace Eva's last-known whereabouts. We should reach out to her friends and anyone who might have seen her."

Julian, ever resourceful, leaned in, the charm dialed up a notch. "And what a perfect team we make. I know a guy, a private detective. The best in the business, Lucas. He's discreet and efficient. I'll contact him right away."

With a practiced motion he grabbed his phone and expertly dialed his private detective. Camille and Lucas sat together at the breakfast table, their anxiety and anticipation making the air feel heavy with tension. Julian's confident voice, with a hint of charm that Camille couldn't help but notice, filled the space as he conversed with the detective.

But Lucas jumped in, his voice edged with suspicion. "Do you think we can trust this detective, Julian? How do we know he won't turn against us?"

Camille, her gaze drifting between Julian and Lucas, responded, her reservations about Julian temporarily set aside, "Lucas, we're running out of options, and we need all the help we can get."

As the detective's voice crackled through the phone, Julian leaned back in his chair, his charm unmistakable in his flirty banter with the investigator. He asked, "Hey, Mark, you remember that favor I did for you last year, right? Well, I'm calling it in now. I need your best guys on this one."

Lucas continued to listen intently, his paranoia not fully abated, but Camille's gentle reassurance helped keep him focused on the task at hand.

Julian, with a playful wink at Camille, continued, "And, Mark, you know what they say, 'Time is of the essence.' Find me something, and there's a bottle of your favorite scotch in it for you."

With promises and deals made over the phone, Julian's influential connections and smooth-talking ways kicked their search for Eva into high gear. Private investigators, with a knack for uncovering hidden truths, were set in motion. The breakfast table became the nerve center of their relentless pursuit, as croissants grew colder and coffee remained untouched, their unified determination driving them forward in their unwavering quest to bring Eva back into the light.

In the middle of their breakfast discussions and plans, Lucas's phone buzzed urgently, jolting him from their determined pursuit of answers. An incoming call from his New York manager sent a wave of unease through him, and he hastily picked up, his voice tinged with concern.

Lucas's manager's voice trembled on the other end as he delivered the grim news. "Lucas, you won't believe what's happening. Our entire security system is under attack, and it's like nothing we've ever seen before."

Lucas's face tightened with worry, and he pressed for more information. "What kind of attack is it?"

His manager's response was laden with anxiety. "It's like a scene from a sci-fi movie. Files are vanishing one by one, and we're powerless to stop it. It's chaos here, and we're losing sensitive data."

Lucas's frustration grew, but determination took root in his voice. "I'll head back as soon as I can," he assured his manager, realizing that their problems had just taken on a dangerous new dimension.

Camille, reserved but supportive, gripped Lucas's arm urgently, her eyes reflecting both concern and intrigue. In that brief touch, he felt a strange connection, almost as if Eva's presence lingered in their middle. It was a moment that left Lucas lost in contemplation, wondering if Eva was trying to communicate with him.

Julian, the charming and playful presence, offered his steady support. "Lucas, let her help you," he encouraged, the weight of the situation etched on his face. The breakfast table was now a crossroads of concern, where their quest for Eva's whereabouts intersected with a new threat that had surfaced, making their already intricate journey even more complex.

Still reeling from the shock of the unsettling phone call and the cryptic assault on his company's security system, Lucas nodded in agreement. He was beginning to trust Camille more with each passing moment, recognizing the value of her support.

As Camille turned her attention to Julian, her reserved demeanor belied a subtle attraction to his flirty charm. She inquired, "Julian, do you happen to have any old computers or equipment lying around? Something we can use?"

Julian, always resourceful and playfully captivating, got to his feet with a confident grin. "My dear Camille, I've got something even better up my sleeve." His words carried a hint of anticipation, promising that his idea would be a pivotal piece of their puzzling journey to uncover the truth.

With a flourish of his hand, Julian signaled for them to follow, setting in motion an intriguing expedition through the sprawling mansion's intricate passageways. Each turn they took led them further into the heart of the opulent estate, with its ornate furnishings and intricate artwork, until they finally reached a hidden room concealed behind a towering bookcase in his expansive library.

The concealed room they had entered was nothing short of a technological marvel. It was a hacker's dream, filled with an array of computer screens, the latest high-tech gadgets, and a web of interconnected wires that looked like an intricate maze.

Still struggling to adjust to the opulence of Julian's world, Lucas muttered with a hint of paranoia, "You ever get the feeling like the walls have eyes in this place, Julian?"

Camille, her eyes alight with curiosity and a growing fondness for Julian, nodded in agreement. "This is beyond anything I've ever seen. It's a tech lover's paradise, but it's also... overwhelming."

Julian flashed a charming grin, clearly pleased with their reactions. "Well, it's my little sanctuary, a place where secrets are uncovered and mysteries are solved. Now, let's get to work." He gestured toward the impressive array of screens and gadgets that awaited Camille.

Camille, with her reserved determination, was now locked onto the sleek computer screen before her. Her fingers glided across the keyboard with impressive speed, like a maestro at the keys. She initiated a request for remote access from Lucas' manager in New York, her brow furrowing with concentration. A few tense seconds passed, and then she confirmed, "I've got access."

Lucas couldn't shake the feeling that he was being watched, the whispers in his mind growing louder. "Do you think someone's tracking us, Camille? I've heard stories, you know, of people with eyes and ears everywhere."

Camille glanced over at Lucas, concern in her eyes. "Lucas, we have to stay focused. We're here to find Eva. Let's not get distracted by our worries."

Julian, his playful side ever-present, chimed in, his eyes locked onto Camille. "Don't worry, Camille. If anyone tries to snoop on us, they'll have to go through me first." He winked at her, clearly trying to win her over.

Lucas stood by Camille, his voice a mix of urgency and paranoia, muttering technical jargon that only made sense to them. "Camille, they've breached our firewall. This is bad. I think they're using some crazy advanced intrusion techniques."

Camille, her fingers dancing across the keyboard, didn't flinch at Lucas's worried muttering. "I've got an IP trace on them. It's like they're bouncing their connection all over the place, making it hard to pin down."

Lucas's manager's voice came booming through the loudspeaker on his phone, a touch of panic in his tone. "We're trying everything, but we can't stop this attack. Our servers are like a war zone right now!"

Camille leaned in, concern etched across her face as she processed the situation. "You guys need to check your server rooms for unauthorized access. There might be a physical connection to your network we're missing."

Lucas swiftly relayed Camille's advice to his manager, who rushed to take action. Meanwhile, Camille didn't let the pressure deter her. Her fingers continued their precision dance across the keyboard, and a glimmer of hope began to shine through. "I've managed to put a temporary pause on the attack. Now,

I'm working on tracing it back to the source."

In the middle of the digital chaos, Lucas's paranoia seemed to grow. He began to whisper to himself, his thoughts racing, "Who would want to do this to us? Could it be corporate espionage?"

Camille, still focused on her screen, found her gaze drifting toward Julian, who was putting on a playful, charming act to lift everyone's spirits. She wondered if he had any secrets of his own and whether his flirtatious demeanor was just a facade.

Julian, with a sly grin, leaned in closer to Camille, his eyes locked onto hers, and he whispered, "You know, Camille, in the middle of all this chaos, you're the calm in the storm. I admire that."

Camille gave him a reserved but appreciative smile, her thoughts divided between the cyber battle they were fighting and the handsome man who stood beside her. The scene was tense, filled with the flashing lights of computer screens and the echo of voices. And in the middle of it all, the dynamics between these three individuals were shifting, with secrets and uncertainties lurking in the digital shadows.

Lucas, his eyes darting nervously between the computer screen and Camille, couldn't help but voice his paranoid thoughts. "Camille, have you figured out where this signal is coming from?" He threw out a few suggestions, but Camille shook her head, clearly determined to do things her way. She replied with a touch of tension in her voice, "Lucas, I appreciate your suggestions, but trust me, I've got my own method."

As they discussed their next steps, Camille's fingers raced across the keyboard, determination etched across her face. Then, a triumphant shout, "Got it!" Her voice held a mix of excitement and relief as she shared, "The source is coming from somewhere in New York."

But just as they were about to savor the victory, a cascade of new windows popped up on her screen, her expression darkening with a grim realization. "Hold on, guys. It looks like someone is trying to track us."

As Lucas's paranoia escalated, he blurted out, "Who could be after us, Camille? Are we safe?"

Camille, despite the pressing threat, managed to maintain her composure. "I don't know, Lucas, but I'll do my best to shake them off. We can't let this deter us."

Julian, seizing the opportunity to charm even in moments of crisis, flashed a flirtatious smile at Camille. "Well, darling, it seems like we've got ourselves an admirer. But don't worry, I'll protect you."

Camille, torn between her attraction to Julian and the urgency of the situation, found herself smiling despite the danger. "Just make sure they don't trace your charm, Julian."

As they delved deeper into the digital labyrinth, their surroundings seemed to blur as the virtual world took precedence. The dimly lit room, with its cold, impersonal glow of screens and technology, was their battleground. Lucas's inner voices, echoing their fears, seemed to grow quieter in the face of the very real threat that now loomed before them.

Lucas's frustration reached a boiling point. "I specifically warned you not to do that, but you never seem to listen."

Camille's voice grew resolute, her eyes flashing with determination. "Lucas, remember, I can put a stop to the hacking. I am a hacker, after all."

In the high-stakes moments that followed, Camille's fingers danced across the keyboard, defending against the digital threat with unmatched precision.

Amid this intense cyber battle, Julian stood close, his presence offering a sense of grounding. While the crisis had been averted, the tension between Lucas and Camille still lingered, like an electric charge in the air.

Lucas, with the voices in his head seemingly amplifying his paranoia, intently listened to his manager's urgent voice coming through the speakerphone. "Lucas, we've looked into it, and there was no breach in our secure server systems." The revelation deepened the mystery surrounding the cyberattack.

He let out an exasperated sigh and muttered under his breath, "I'll catch up with you later," as he placed the phone back down.

Julian, the picture of composure in the middle of chaos, took charge. "It's quite clear what we need to do next. We have to make a trip to New York." His tone was firm as he looked at both Camille and Lucas, the gravity of their situation weighing heavily on them.

The room they were in had the feel of a high-tech command center, bathed in the cool glow of computer screens. The air was thick with the tension of the recent cyber skirmish, and the trio knew that their journey to New York was just the next step in the ongoing quest to solve the cyber puzzle and the mystery that they found themselves in.

CHAPTER 9: LOVE IN THE SHADOWS

The atmosphere inside the car was charged with tension, an unspoken unease that hung in the air. The butler, skilled in the art of discretion, expertly piloted the vehicle towards the airport. The passengers exchanged cautious glances, their minds occupied with their own concerns.

Lucas occupied the front seat, his gaze fixed on the passing scenery. The voices in his head added to the underlying anxiety etched across his forehead. The urge was too strong to resist, so he interjected with a paranoid question, "Do you ever get the feeling that we're being followed, Sebastian?"

Sebastian, the quiet observer, responded with a knowing glance, the worry lines on his own face evident as he maintained his focus on the road.

In the back seat, Julian and Camille shared a contemplative silence for a while. Then, Julian, his tone tinged with a flirtatious playfulness, turned to Camille, attempting to offer some comfort. "Don't you worry, Camille. We're in this together, and we'll uncover the truth about your sister. You've got me."

Camille, reserved but secretly drawn to Julian,

nodded in response, her eyes revealing a blend of gratitude and anxiety. "Your support means the world to me, Julian."

The car hurtled towards the airport, the urban landscape outside blurring past them. Their journey was not just a physical one but also a descent into the shadowy worlds of cyber espionage and hidden family mysteries. The anticipation was almost tangible, laden with the promise of uncovering the truth and, perhaps, the potential for lost connections to be rekindled.

Upon their arrival at the airport, the small group was welcomed with a private entrance leading to the tarmac, far from the chaos of the main terminal. A sleek, luxurious private jet stood there, basking in the warm sunlight with its engines softly humming.

Lucas, the ever-paranoid thinker, couldn't resist a question, "Do you ever wonder, guys, if this is all too good to be true?"

Julian, with his flirtatious charm, responded with a playful tease, "Lucas, my friend, this is the epitome of the high life."

Sebastian, the observant butler, efficiently gathered a few bags from the car and trailed the rest inside the private jet. Once aboard, the interior oozed opulence. Plush leather seats invited them to sink in and relax, with ample room to stretch out. The decor exuded tasteful elegance, boasting polished wood accents and soft, soothing ambient lighting.

As they eased into their luxurious surroundings, the jet was poised to whisk them away into the unknown, further blurring the lines between reality and the mysteries that lay ahead.

Soon they settled into their seats, strapping in for the journey to New York, the realization washed over them that this was no ordinary adventure. It was a leap into the great unknown, a journey that would test their wits, courage, and the promise of uncovering the truth about the hackers and Eva's perplexing disappearance.

Julian made himself comfortable in the seat across from Camille, the purring of the jet's engines providing a comforting soundtrack to their contemplations. As their hands brushed against each other, an unspoken bond formed between them. In that fleeting touch, they discovered a connection all their own, sparked by their shared mission and an attraction that continued to grow with each passing mile.

The lavish private jet rumbled as it taxied down the runway, getting ready for takeoff. Sebastian, Julian's unassuming butler, moved gracefully through the cabin, attending to their needs. He presented a tray bearing glasses of champagne to the passengers.

Julian, exuding his trademark charm, accepted a glass and raised it in a toast. "To finding answers and to new beginnings," he declared, a hint of excitement in his voice.

Camille took a glass, her gaze locking with Julian's for a fleeting moment before she nodded. "To new beginnings," she echoed, and the clinking of their glasses signaled the beginning of their journey.

Lucas, not one to usually partake in drinks, had a moment of hesitation but was swayed by the weight of the occasion. He accepted the glass, curiously eyeing the bubbly liquid within. "To answers," he proposed, the hint of doubt evident in his voice, before clinking glasses with the others.

As the private jet revved up on the runway, ascending into the limitless sky of possibilities, they were bound by the clinking of glasses and the shared sense of excitement, uniting them in their pursuit of the elusive truth.

Throughout the flight, champagne flowed freely, and Julian, with his playful demeanor, regaled them with tales of his worldwide adventures and heart-pounding escapades. The alcohol's effect crept up on

Lucas, who was unaccustomed to such indulgence. Gradually, he succumbed to its intoxicating allure.

Relaxing back in his seat, Lucas's eyelids grew heavy, and the soothing hum of the jet's engines carried him into a deep slumber. His glass slipped from his grasp, forgotten, as he drifted off, leaving Julian, Camille, and the ever-watchful Sebastian to continue their journey into the mysterious unknown. The soft ambiance of the private jet, with its polished wood and elegant furnishings, cocooned them in an atmosphere of luxury and intrigue as they headed toward the next chapter of their adventure.

When Lucas finally stirred from his champagne-induced haze, he cautiously made his way along the narrow aisle of the private jet. The gentle snores of Sebastian wafted from the front, creating an illusion of serenity and tranquility, as if the world was suspended in a tranquil bubble. The plane's engines hummed softly, providing a soothing undercurrent to his groggy thoughts.

As he ventured further towards the rear of the jet, the muffled sounds of conversation drifted to his ears. The unmistakable voices of Camille and Julian piqued his curiosity, drawing him closer. He realized he was standing near the entrance to a private section of the plane.

Lucas gingerly nudged the door open just slightly, allowing a narrow view into the secluded area. The gentle glow of ambient lighting spilled out into the dimly lit aisle, offering a glimpse of the private space within. His head throbbed from the lingering effects of the champagne, but his inquisitiveness spurred him onward.

Inside the private enclave, the dim lighting created a cozy and intimate atmosphere. Camille and Julian occupied seats across from each other, their conversation intimate, as if they were sharing a cherished secret in this secluded corner of the jet.

Lucas found himself wondering as the voices in his head amplified his paranoia, "What are they talking about in there? Should I be concerned?"

As he observed the scene from the shadows, Julian's playful charm and Camille's reserved allure were in full display, their connection growing stronger in the intimate setting of the jet's private quarters.

Camille's eyes were locked onto Julian's, a captivating mix of vulnerability and desire swirling within them. Her fingers danced across the small table between them, hovering on the brink of a decision. Her lips moved, whispering words so soft that Lucas couldn't catch them.

Julian, his typically charismatic demeanor giving way to a rare vulnerability, held Camille's gaze with an intensity that hinted at a profound connection between them. His fingers twitched, as if aching to bridge the distance that separated them.

The air was charged with unspoken tension, an invisible magnetic force that transcended mere camaraderie. A sense of intrusion settled over Lucas, as if he were an outsider trespassing on something deeply personal.

He swallowed hard, his mouth suddenly dry, his heart racing, and his stomach roiling with an unfamiliar sensation. The scene unfolding before him was straight out of a movie, and yet, the emotions at play were all too genuine.

Logic urged him to avert his gaze, to grant them their private moment, but he was inexplicably entranced by the intimacy of the encounter. It was as though time had stood still, and they were the sole actors in a play of secrets and desires.

In a voice that was barely a whisper, Camille spoke, "There's something between us, Julian, something undeniable."

Julian, his voice husky with emotion, replied, "Yes,

Camille, there is, but we have to focus on finding your sister. That's the priority right now."

Camille sighed and leaned back in her seat. "You're right, of course, but when this is over, we need to talk. There are things you need to know, Julian."

Lucas felt like an intruder, a voyeur to this private moment, and he quietly withdrew. As he tiptoed back to his seat, he was aware of a strange mix of emotions. On the one hand, he was filled with a sense of guilt, having witnessed something so intimate.

Yet, on the other hand, he couldn't deny the stirring of jealousy and a sense of loss, knowing that Julian and Camille were connected in a way that he could never hope to compete with.

Stifling his headache and momentarily forgetting his original reason for being there, Lucas quietly retreated from the doorway, closing it with equal care. He leaned against the adjacent wall, his heart heavy with a mixture of emotions – curiosity, confusion, and a hint of jealousy.

The unanswered questions surrounding Eva's disappearance had led him to this moment, where secrets and connections between Camille and Julian hinted at a different, uncharted mystery that could change the course of their journey.

***

Inside the lavatory, Lucas found solace as he locked the door and leaned against the basin. His trembling hands felt the cool porcelain beneath them, and he allowed the cold water to cascade over his face, partially washing away the champagne-induced grogginess.

Staring at his own reflection in the mirror, he found himself unable to resist sensing that it held more significance in this confined space. It seemed like more than just an image; it was almost like a silent confidant, a voice within his own mind. Lucas paused, then began to speak in a hushed, almost conspiratorial tone.

His voice, a hint of paranoia lingering, murmured to the reflection, "You know, I've always been cautious. Trust has never come easy to me, even with those I care about. But this whole situation with Eva... it's like a turning point."

The reflection appeared to share his unease, whispering back, "You're right to be cautious. Trust has to be earned."

Lucas stared deep into his own eyes, as though seeking answers within his own uncertainty. "Julian, Camille, even Sebastian, there's something they're not telling me. I can't afford to be blind to their secrets, especially when it concerns Eva."

His reflection nodded solemnly, reinforcing his determination. In this moment of reflection, the lavatory became a sanctuary of thought, as he confronted the web of mysteries that had entangled their journey.

Lucas straightened himself, splashing a bit more water on his face, his determination unwavering. He couldn't afford to put complete trust in anyone, not when Eva's safety hung in the balance. The truth about Eva's disappearance lay out there, and he was resolute in his mission, even if it meant maintaining skepticism towards those in his middle.

Lucas paced restlessly in the cramped airplane lavatory, engaging in an eerie monologue with his own reflection, the closest thing he had to a confidant at that moment.

"Isn't it funny, you know?" he whispered to his reflection, his voice heavy with suspicion. "I've never really allowed anyone to get too close in my life. There's always a reason for that. Trust, it's this fragile thing. It can shatter like glass, and once it's broken, it's never quite the same."

His reflection in the mirror seemed to hold his gaze, as if listening intently.

Lucas went on, his unease palpable, "But here's the dilemma, my friend. Eva is somewhere out there, and the deeper I get entangled with Julian, Camille, and their world, the more I feel like I'm losing control. I can't afford to let them see that I'm onto something, that I don't completely trust them."

The reflection in the mirror stared back at him, a silent yet supportive reminder to tread carefully in the treacherous terrain of trust and uncertainty.

Lucas inched closer to the mirror, as if his own reflection held the key to his growing paranoia. "I can't shake the feeling, you know, that Camille knew more about Eva's vanishing right from the start. And Julian, he's got the means to uncover the truth, yet he's keeping me in the dark."

His reflection stared back, mirroring his doubts. The dimly lit lavatory was the ideal setting for this covert conversation with himself.

"But I can't let them see my doubts," Lucas whispered with a sense of urgency, as if dreading that someone might eavesdrop on his innermost thoughts. "Especially when they're my only shot at finding Eva. I have to play their game, be one step ahead. They won't manipulate me."

The mirror served as both a confidant and a

constant reminder of the necessity to remain vigilant. It silently acknowledged the burden he carried, comprehending the weight on his shoulders.

As Lucas exited the lavatory, his reflection stayed etched in his memory: in this perilous world of secrets and hidden agendas, he must rely on his instincts and remain loyal to his skepticism, for the stakes were far higher than he had ever imagined. The journey ahead would test his resolve and determination like never before.

Slowly, he made his way back to his seat, still grappling with the lingering echoes of his paranoia from the unsettling encounter with his own reflection in the lavatory. Across from him, Sebastian, the ever-observant butler, appeared to be awake and open to conversation, so Lucas decided to broach a topic that had been on his mind.

"Hey, Sebastian, can I ask you something?" Lucas queried, his voice laced with a touch of uncertainty.

Sebastian, with his usual polite demeanor, nodded and offered a gentle smile. "Certainly, sir. What's on your mind?"

Lucas hesitated for a moment, his gaze briefly flickering towards Julian, who was now deeply engrossed in a conversation with Camille. He eventually voiced his query, his curiosity bubbling over, "What's Julian's deal, you know, in the world of love? Has he ever been in love?"

Sebastian's expression took on a contemplative air, as if he were carefully selecting his words. "Mr. Laurent has always been quite guarded about his personal life. Love is a complex subject. However, watching him with Camille, there seems to be a glimmer of hope. He might just find his own happiness in the end."

Lucas couldn't shake the nagging doubts that swirled within him. "Sebastian, what if Camille's not all she appears to be? What if it's all an act? What if she ends up hurting Julian?"

Before Sebastian could respond to Lucas's persistent worries, the cabin door of the private jet swung open, revealing Camille and Julian. They walked in hand in hand, the warmth in their connection palpable. It was a stark contrast to the earlier tense moments between Lucas and Sebastian.

Julian, with his magnetic charm, greeted them with a cheerful, "Hey, you two. Lucas, we need to get some champagne flowing here. Camille here is quite the entertainer."

Camille playfully added, gently nudging Julian,

"Julian's been sharing some fascinating stories, Lucas. You've got to hear them."

Lucas nodded, his polite smile concealing his lingering doubts. While he tried to keep his paranoia in check, he found himself unable to resist pondering more questions. 'They seem pretty close. How long has this been going on?'

In the background, Sebastian, the ever-watchful butler, worked diligently, orchestrating a sumptuous lunch for the trio. The table was elegantly set with crisp white linen, and the food was a visual masterpiece, a reflection of Julian's opulent lifestyle. In the middle of the plush surroundings and the intriguing interplay of their dynamics, their journey on the private jet remained a fusion of luxury and secrecy, adding to the mystique surrounding their mission.

Camille and Lucas took their seats at the exquisitely arranged table, and as Sebastian served the first course, Julian, oozing flirtatious charm, couldn't resist a playful comment. "I do hope you both savor the delights of this meal. Sebastian, here, has an uncanny knack for making airplane food feel like a five-star dining experience."

Sebastian, maintaining his air of dignified grace, offered a subtle nod of appreciation, his impeccable service shining through as he presented each dish with utmost precision.

With every delicious bite and sip, the atmosphere within the jet shifted from initial tension to a more relaxed camaraderie. Lucas's paranoia began to ebb away as a sense of unity blossomed among the group. The sumptuous meal was the conduit for deeper connections and a few shared laughs.

As they enjoyed their fancy lunch aboard the private jet, the atmosphere became cozier, and they all chatted without a hitch. Camille, who was sharp and clever, held everyone's interest, sharing stories about her hacking adventures and the cool places she'd been to. The journey, both in the air and into the unknown world of their mission, was turning into a memorable experience, and the luxurious lifestyle was starting to feel just right.

Outside, the vast blue sky stretched as far as the eye could see, with fluffy clouds adding a touch of serenity to the scene. It was a perfect day for flying.

Julian, with his easygoing charm, and Lucas, with his tech-savvy skills, were hanging on Camille's every word. She described her hacking escapades with enthusiasm, making it sound like an adrenaline-fueled game of high-stakes cat and mouse with security systems and firewalls.

As the private jet soared through the sky, they couldn't help but appreciate the incredible view from their window seats. The landscape below was a patchwork of green fields and winding rivers, with miniature cars and buildings that seemed like toys from up high. It was a reminder of just how high above the world they were, living a life of luxury and adventure.

Camille was an amazing storyteller. She told her friends about her incredible adventures in far-off places. She described the busy streets of Tokyo, the colorful markets of Marrakech, and the peaceful beaches of Bali. As she spoke, her words made her friends feel like they were right there with her, experiencing everything she described. Julian, in particular, was completely mesmerized by her stories.

Camille's stories were like colorful paintings that came to life in their minds. When she talked about Tokyo, they could almost hear the bustling streets and see the bright lights. The city seemed like a place of endless excitement and wonder.

Then, Camille transported them to Marrakech, where she described the vibrant bazaars filled with spices and textiles. The scents and colors filled their imaginations, and they could almost taste the exotic foods she talked about.

And when Camille spoke of Bali, they felt the warm sand between their toes and heard the gentle lapping of the waves. It was as if they were lounging on those tranquil beaches, taking in the beauty of the clear blue waters.

Julian was especially caught up in Camille's storytelling. He hung on her every word, his eyes wide with fascination. He had always dreamt of traveling the world, and Camille's stories were like a window to a world he had only dreamt of until now.

"Tokyo is truly something else," Camille said, her eyes shining with enthusiasm. "The blend of tradition and technology is mesmerizing. You can visit ancient shrines in the morning and dine at a robot restaurant in the evening."

Lucas, less seasoned in global travel, hung on her every word, fascinated by Camille's adventurous spirit. He caught himself intrigued, as he and Eva had always been more inclined to stay indoors.

Julian, the experienced globetrotter, added his own stories, recounting his journeys through European capitals and the hidden gems he had discovered along the way. He spoke with passion about his love for architecture and how it had led him to remote corners of the world to witness extraordinary structures.

Sebastian, the quiet butler, expertly served each course and subtly observed the conversation. Before he knew it, he was aware of the growing connection among the group, especially the unspoken chemistry between Camille and Julian, as they exchanged travel stories and shared glimpses of their inner worlds. The jet's luxurious cabin became a sanctuary for these narratives, bridging their pasts and bringing them closer to the mysteries that lay ahead.

As they savored the exquisite dishes and exchanged stories over lunch, the private jet seemed like a sanctuary, a world far removed from their worries. In that moment, their journey wasn't just a quest for answers but a shared experience that drew them closer.

Still haunted by the voices in his head, Lucas found himself wondering, "Does anyone else hear those faint voices, like whispers in the background?"

Julian, with a glass of champagne in hand, raised an eyebrow at Lucas's question, "Whispers, you say? Perhaps it's the subtle music of the jet's engines playing tricks on your mind, my friend."

Camille, who was immersed in her meal, offered a reassuring smile, "Or maybe it's just the anticipation, the weight of our mission. It can play tricks on your senses."

Lucas, while still doubting the source of the voices, appreciated their attempts to calm his unease.

Camille's gaze flicked briefly towards Julian, her reserved demeanor giving way to a hint of curiosity and growing attraction. She whispered to Julian, "I've got to admit, Julian, there's something about this that's oddly captivating."

Julian, the playful flirt, leaned closer to Camille, his voice laced with charm, "Well, you know, Camille, I've always found captivating people absolutely irresistible."

She leaned closer to him, her voice soft, "Julian, there's something about this situation, and it's not just the altitude that's taking my breath away."

Julian, ever the charming flirt, shot her a playful grin, "Well, Camille, I must say, I find everything about you utterly captivating."

The hours passed as they indulged in lunch, shared stories, and shared laughter. The private jet felt like its own little world, a haven of comfort high above the world.

As the plane soared through the night sky, the shimmering lights of New York City spread below, and the dynamics between the four of them shifted in unexpected ways. Trust mingled with suspicion, creating a complex web of emotions that would shape their journey ahead. The allure of newfound connections blended with the shadows of doubt, setting the stage for a path marked by both uncertainty and secrets. The private jet continued to soar, leaving behind a world of unanswered questions and veiled truths.

***

The private jet landed smoothly at the New York airport, and the group had the benefit of slipping away unnoticed. A fancy black car was parked and waiting for them at the private jet terminal, and it symbolized both their extravagance and practicality. Sebastian, the super-efficient butler, also served as their chauffeur. He didn't talk much, but his service was top-notch.

As they disembarked from the jet, the bright city lights of New York glistened in the distance, casting a magical glow on the tarmac. The airport terminal, with its modern architecture and bustling crowd, felt like a world of its own. People hurried to catch their flights, and the group blended in seamlessly, thanks to their discreet exit strategy.

The sleek black car was a sight to behold, reflecting the airport's dazzling lights. Its shiny exterior, polished to perfection, showcased the opulence of the group. The moment they stepped into the car, the plush leather seats welcomed them, providing a comfortable sanctuary after a long journey.

Sebastian, a man of few words but an impeccable sense of duty, took his place behind the wheel. His crisp, black suit and white gloves added an air of sophistication to the scene. The scent of fresh leather and a hint of the group's favorite cologne lingered in the car, creating a comforting ambiance.

The car's wheels met the bustling streets of the city, and Sebastian, his hands steady on the wheel, guided them expertly through the labyrinthine roads. The towering skyscrapers stood like guardians against the night, their illuminated windows resembling stars in the urban sky.

Lucas, seated in the back, leaned forward, determination lacing his voice. "Sebastian, let's head to my company building. We need to get a handle on the situation and figure out our next steps regarding that recent cyberattack."

Camille, her gaze fixed on the cityscape, added, "Our main focus should be on tracing the source of the attack. It's the linchpin in uncovering the truth about Eva."

Julian, playful and flirtatious as ever, couldn't resist a playful quip, "Well, you know, Camille, we make quite the team. The beautiful investigator and the charming playboy, on the case together."

As the car weaved through the city streets, the air inside was charged with anticipation. The uncharted territories of the digital world beckoned, promising answers and revelations. The connections among the group were shifting, evolving, and their bond hinted at a promising resolution to the mystery of Eva's disappearance.

With each passing moment, their quest in the heart of New York City took them deeper into a web of secrets and intrigue. The mystery surrounding Eva's vanishing act began to unravel as they ventured further into the complexities of the cyberworld, with the metropolis as their backdrop, shrouded in an air of both mystery and excitement. Sebastian observed the dynamics within the group keenly, especially the growing closeness between Camille and Julian, which added an extra layer of intrigue to their journey.

Their journey through the bustling New York streets eventually brought them to Lucas's company building, a towering structure of glass and steel that held a commanding presence over the city. Upon entering the building, Julian took the lead, guiding them through a complex network of corridors and hallways that seemed to stretch endlessly, eventually leading them to the building's core.

Camille, quick-witted and observant, remarked, "This place is like a fortress, Lucas."

Lucas beamed with pride, a glimmer of accomplishment in his eyes. "You're absolutely right, Camille. This isn't just a building; it's a testament to modern architecture and technology. We've cultivated an empire right within these walls."

Yet, Lucas, despite his apparent confidence, couldn't shake the lingering unease that had taken root within him. The relentless voices and nagging doubts continued to torment him, eroding his confidence and causing him to question the very bedrock of his world.

Sebastian, typically the quiet observer, chose this moment to share a piece of information. "Mr. Laurent's commitment to his work in art knows no bounds. But his work is more than just a job; it's an extension of who he is." Sebastian's astute observations didn't escape Camille's attention, and she found herself unable to resist considering the dynamics at play between her, Julian, and Lucas as they delved deeper into the heart of Lucas's high-tech empire.

As they made their way through the bustling corridors, the sounds of diligent activity enveloped them. They strolled past busy workstations where dedicated employees focused intently on their tasks, oblivious to the mysterious journey that the group was on the brink of.

Lucas, his paranoia slowly giving way to determination, spoke firmly. "Our primary objective is unraveling this cyberattack, but let's not forget our overarching goal: finding Eva."

Camille, agreeing wholeheartedly, reiterated, "Our success in deciphering this attack might very well hold the key to discovering what happened to her."

The dynamics within the group had undergone a transformation since their journey began. Trust and skepticism were like threads woven into their interactions, strengthening their bond as they ventured further into the intricate web of their interlocking missions. Sebastian, ever the astute observer, couldn't help but note the evolving closeness between Camille and Julian, adding an extra layer of intrigue to their collaborative efforts.

As they approached the server room, the aura

of high-tech machinery humming with life enveloped them. The group was ready to dive deep into the digital mysteries that had eluded them for so long.

Lucas, however, gave voice to his nagging paranoia. "Am I the only one who senses an impending disaster in this place, like a ticking time bomb ready to explode?"

Camille, her attraction to Julian growing stronger with each passing moment, interjected, "Lucas, we must keep our attention on the task before us. And with Julian by our side, we're in capable hands."

Julian, the charismatic and playful presence among them, flashed a grin at Camille, his eyes sparkling with mischief. "Indeed, Camille, you can trust me. I've been known to defuse a few time bombs in my day, though they weren't always digital."

Lucas, still wrestling with his inner demons and voices, inquired with a hint of skepticism, "Julian, just what kind of connections and resources do you have to help us with this investigation?"

Camille, torn between her growing attraction to Julian and her reservations, decided to steer the conversation back on track, "Lucas, Julian is here to assist us in any way he can. Let's focus on finding the answers we seek."

Stepping into the server room, they were met with the thrumming energy of anticipation, an undercurrent of excitement as they stood on the precipice of uncovering the hidden secrets in the digital labyrinth. Their journey was weaving a complex tapestry of emotions, where trust, doubt, and the sparks of attraction intermingled as they ventured deeper into the core of their intertwined missions.

Lucas, a cybersecurity expert, took the lead with confidence, guiding them through the bustling workspace. He introduced them to his manager, who exhaled a breath of relief as he addressed Lucas, "Welcome back, Lucas. We've been grappling with this cyber-attack, and your expertise is exactly what we've needed."

Camille turned to Lucas with a sincere smile, her admiration evident as she said, "I'm genuinely impressed by what you've built here."

The manager, visibly grateful for their assistance, focused on Camille as she continued, "I've managed to trace the origins of the hack to New York, but to dig deeper, I'll need direct physical access to your systems."

Lucas introduced Camille to his manager, saying, "This is Camille, an independent contractor I've brought on board to help us out." He made it clear,

"Give her all the access she needs, and together we'll get to the bottom of this."

Julian, ever the playful flirt, couldn't resist teasing as he leaned closer to Camille, his voice laced with charm, "Well, Camille, looks like you're about to get all the access you desire."

The manager nodded in agreement, impressed by their dedication. "I appreciate your commitment to resolving this issue. We're in dire need of a solution, and your collaboration is a promising step in the right direction."

Sebastian, the silent observer, noted the evolving dynamics within the group. Lucas's resolve, Camille's expertise, and Julian's flirtatious charm all played a role in forming a tight-knit team, each thread of their connection weaving together to strengthen their mission. As they immersed themselves in the maze of computers and screens, the room buzzed with anticipation and a shared determination. In this ever-evolving landscape of trust and doubt, Lucas's return marked the beginning of a fresh chapter in their quest for answers, while the connections among the group continued to evolve in intriguing ways.

In the dimly lit server room, Lucas couldn't shake the feeling that the walls were closing in on him, and the air was thick with uncertainty. His mind was a whirlwind of doubts, with the persistent voices echoing in his head as a constant reminder of his deep-seated paranoia.

Camille, a skilled navigator of the digital world, emanated unwavering determination. She focused on her task, her fingers gliding effortlessly across the keyboard as she dissected the intricate network architecture. Her technical prowess left Lucas's team in awe, despite his initial hesitations.

Julian, the charismatic presence, was genuinely captivated by the world of cybersecurity. He stood by Camille, asking questions and immersing himself in the complexities of their investigation. In the process, his body acted before his mind could catch up, and he grew closer to Camille, her intelligence and confidence pulling him in like a magnetic force.

As they toiled together, their interactions became a delicate dance of trust and curiosity. Lucas, too, was gradually lowering his guard, recognizing that their combined efforts were indispensable in solving the intricate cyber puzzle.

Camille, her focus unwavering, reported, "I've managed to trace the source to a specific location in New York. It's a physical address, and I believe that's where our answers lie."

Lucas, now more at ease with Camille's capabilities, nodded with determination. "We need to check it out. So where is it?"

To their astonishment, the physical address Camille had unveiled turned out to be none other than Lucas's own apartment in New York. The revelation sent shivers down his spine, his paranoia skyrocketing to new heights. Their journey had taken them from the serenity of a private jet to the heart of a technological battlefield. With the city's relentless energy as their backdrop, they were poised to uncover the truth behind Eva's disappearance and the cyberattacks that had plagued Lucas's company.

Camille's shock was evident as she looked at Lucas. "Lucas, are you absolutely sure about this? Is there any reasonable explanation for the source of the hack being your apartment?"

Lucas, trapped between his own fear and growing suspicion, felt the heavy burden of uncertainty pressing down on him. "I wish I could say for certain, but it's entirely possible that someone has been using my apartment as a hub for these cyberattacks."

Julian, his concern now etched in his features, leaned in closer. "This lead can't be ignored. If it turns out the source of these attacks is your apartment, we need to investigate it right away."

The atmosphere in the room was heavy with unease, and the trio was acutely aware that there was no turning back. Their journey from the skies above to the heart of New York had led them to this unexpected twist. The mysteries surrounding Eva's disappearance had deepened, and the shadowy figures behind the cyberattacks appeared to be closing in with each passing moment.

Camille, her concern deepening, added, "And if this source is in Lucas's apartment, it means someone might know more about our investigation than we thought."

Sebastian, who had been quietly observing the conversation, spoke up, "It is imperative that we address this promptly. If there is a connection to Mr. Laurent's apartment, we must act swiftly."

The manager, who had been anxiously pacing, finally chimed in, "We don't have much time. Let's get to the bottom of this." The urgency in his voice was palpable, and it was clear that they were now racing against the clock to uncover the truth behind the cyberattacks and Eva's disappearance. They needed to head to Lucas's apartment immediately. The journey to the truth was about to reach a critical juncture.

***

As they reached Lucas's apartment building, a sense of trepidation hung heavy in the air. The façade of the ordinary New York apartment belied the secrets that may lay within. Julian led the way, Camille close behind, and Sebastian remained vigilant as they ascended the elevator to Lucas's apartment.

When they arrived in front of Lucas's apartment, something inside him made him question the surroundings, his paranoia peeking through. "Does anyone else feel the eeriness of this place, or is it just me?"

Camille, nervously fidgeting with her bag, replied, "It's not just you, Lucas. The stakes are high, and we're dealing with unknown adversaries here."

Julian, always the playfully flirtatious one, tried to lighten the mood. "Well, with the three of us, there's nothing to be afraid of, right? We've got this."

Lucas fumbled for his keys, his unease mounting with each passing moment. After finally gaining entry, they entered cautiously, senses on high alert. Lucas, surveying the hallway outside his apartment, couldn't shake the eerie feeling that they were under constant surveillance. "I can't shake this feeling of being watched. It's like every move we make is being monitored."

Julian, maintaining his playful demeanor even in the face of danger, quipped, "Well, I hope they find my charm entertaining!"

Camille, always the reserved one, shot Julian a look before adding, "Let's focus, Julian. This is serious."

Sebastian, ever the quiet and observant figure, took the lead, offering a suggestion, "We should thoroughly investigate the apartment. That's the only way to confirm if it's connected to the cyberattacks."

With cautious steps, they entered Lucas's apartment, greeted by the dim, eerie light that seemed to cast an unsettling aura over the place. The room felt foreign, as if it held countless secrets waiting to be unearthed. It was within these walls that they hoped to unravel the mystery that had haunted them for so long.

As they began to process their surroundings, the sudden and brutal attack from masked assailants took them by surprise. It was a chaotic whirlwind of violence, with fists flying and desperate struggles unfolding.

Lucas, trying to make sense of the chaotic

situation, couldn't help but voice his paranoia, "Do you think this is connected to Eva's disappearance? Is someone trying to stop us from finding her?"

Camille, while fiercely defending herself, responded, "It's too early to tell, but we need to get through this first."

Julian, ever the quick thinker, managed to disarm one of their attackers, adding, "And once we do, they're going to have some explaining to do."

In the middle of the chaos, Julian's quick reflexes and Sebastian's combat skills became invaluable assets. They swiftly subdued the assailants, revealing the faces of these unknown adversaries as they tore away their masks. The room was tense, and questions loomed about the identity of their attackers.

Once the dust had settled, a grim realization began to take hold. Lucas had sustained a serious injury during the altercation, and the pain was etched across his face, the result of a knife wound that marred his side.

Camille rushed to his side, fear and panic etched across her features. "We need to get him help, and we need it right now!"

Julian, his expression hardening, wasted no time. "Sebastian, call an ambulance immediately. We can't afford to lose him."

As the call for help was made, they found themselves grappling with the brutal consequences of their relentless pursuit of answers and the truth. The boundaries between their story and a dangerous reality had blurred, leaving them to confront the harsh realities that had now encroached upon their lives.

With a voice trembling from the weight of his pain, Lucas asked, "Do you think they were after something specific, something tied to the cyberattacks?"

Camille, her concern deepening, responded, "It's too early to tell, but we need to be cautious. Someone definitely doesn't want us to find the truth."

Sebastian, who had been quietly observant, finally spoke up, "We need to stay vigilant. This incident could be a sign that we're getting closer to the answers."

Their pursuit of answers and the truth had taken an unexpectedly dangerous turn. The lines between their investigation and a perilous reality had blurred, leaving them grappling with the harsh consequences of their relentless pursuit.

CHAPTER 10: A DANGEROUS DANCE

The chaotic scene continued to unfold as they anxiously awaited medical assistance for Lucas. The sirens wailed louder, and the flashing lights of police cars and ambulances bathed the surroundings in an eerie, pulsating glow. The first responders rushed in, their paramedic uniforms a symbol of hope and urgency.

Camille held Julian's hand as the medical team worked efficiently to stabilize him. Her concern was palpable, and her thoughts raced. "He's going to be okay, right?"

Julian, his usual playfulness now replaced with anxiety, tried to offer reassurance. "He's strong, Camille. He'll pull through this. We have to believe that."

Sebastian, his voice soft but composed, added, "Lucas is in capable hands. They will do everything they can to ensure his recovery."

Camille wondered if they were any closer to finding Eva or if they were simply descending further into a perilous world beyond their control.

Lucas, lying on the stretcher, couldn't shake the

feeling that they were being watched, that their every move was being scrutinized. "Do you ever feel like we're being observed, Camille? Like we're just pawns in someone's elaborate game?"

Camille, her thoughts mirroring his paranoia, replied, "I've had my doubts for a while now. The attack, these assailants – it all seems too orchestrated to be coincidental."

One of the paramedic, in the middle of his frantic work, spoke to the group. "We have to take him to the hospital immediately. He needs surgery."

As Lucas was swiftly carried outside to the waiting ambulance, the detective, a stern and no-nonsense figure named Detective Anderson, remained behind. He addressed Julian, Camille, and Sebastian, his face etched with a sense of urgency.

Detective Anderson cleared his throat and spoke directly to them. "I understand this is a lot to take in, but we need your cooperation. Please come down to the police station with us to provide detailed statements. We also have to process the unconscious assailants; they're being taken to the hospital."

Julian nodded in agreement, his usual flirtatious charm now replaced with a sense of duty. "Of course, Detective Anderson. We're committed to helping with the investigation in any way we can."

Camille, her reserved nature giving way to determination, added, "We want to see justice served, and we'll assist in every possible way."

Sebastian, the quiet observer, simply nodded his agreement. Their relentless pursuit of answers had taken an unforeseen, dangerous turn, and now they found themselves entangled in a web of uncertainty, racing to uncover the truth while facing the consequences of their relentless pursuit.

After Detective Anderson left, Camille's expression turned more serious, and she addressed Julian with a hint of worry in her eyes. "Julian, I think we should go back to Paris. This has gotten way too dangerous. I can't help but feel that staying here is putting us all at risk."

Julian, however, stood his ground, unwavering in his determination to cooperate with the investigation. "Camille, we can't just run away. We need to work with the police to get to the bottom of this. Running away won't solve anything."

Camille, her skepticism evident, replied, "I've been through this before, Julian. Going into hiding might be our best option. We can't trust anyone, and I don't want anyone else getting hurt because of us."

Julian, his voice filled with conviction, pulled Camille aside and looked into her eyes with unwavering determination. "Camille, I promise you, no harm will come to you. I will protect you to the end. We'll get through this together, but we have to face it head-on. Running away won't guarantee our safety. It's time to stand our ground and find the answers we've been searching for."

Camille gazed at Julian, touched by his commitment and determination. She knew that, despite the dangers that loomed, she had someone by her side who was willing to go to great lengths to keep her safe. With a sigh, she finally nodded in agreement. "Okay, Julian, we'll do it your way. But promise me we'll be cautious, and we won't take any unnecessary risks."

Julian's reassuring smile lit up the room, a comforting presence to Camille in their shared moment of uncertainty. "I promise, we'll be careful and clever about it. We'll face this together." Their connection, born from danger and intrigue, only grew stronger as they confronted the unpredictable road that lay ahead.

Sebastian, who had been observing the events quietly, finally spoke up. "We must remain prepared for whatever challenges await. It won't be a smooth journey, but we're in this together."

The group had unanimously chosen to stand their ground, ready to confront the threats they faced, united as they embarked on the perilous path ahead.

At the police station, Julian and Camille were escorted into separate rooms for their statements, with Sebastian accompanying them. Detective Anderson, a seasoned investigator, immediately noticed the guarded caution in Camille's responses. Her eyes held untold secrets, and he was determined to get to the bottom of it.

As the questioning continued, Detective Anderson's gut feeling grew stronger. There was an air of mystery surrounding Camille, and he couldn't shake the sense that there was more to this case than met the eye. He made a mental note to revisit her statement later and dig deeper into her involvement.

After the extensive interviews came to a close, Julian, Camille, and Sebastian were finally released from the police station. The ordeal had left them shaken, but they were grateful to be free once more.

As they walked out into the fresh air, the evening had settled in, casting a calm and quiet atmosphere over the city. The weight of the situation still pressed down on their shoulders as they found themselves questioning the assailants' motives and their link to the ongoing cyberattacks.

Camille, couldn't help but ask, "Do you think they'll come after us again?"

Julian, always the playful one, tried to ease the tension. "Don't worry, Camille. We've got each other's backs."

Camille, though reserved, was beginning to warm up to Julian's charm. "I hope you're right. We can't let fear stop us from finding the truth."

Sebastian, who had been silently observing the conversation, finally spoke up, addressing Camille, "I'm glad you're here with us, Camille. Your expertise and courage have proven invaluable."

Detective Anderson, on the other hand, couldn't shake the feeling that something about Camille was amiss. Turning to his partner, Detective Ramirez, he confided, "Ramirez, there's something about that woman, Camille. I can't quite put my finger on it, but I have a gut feeling she's hiding something. I believe there's more to this case than we've uncovered so far."

With a furrowed brow, Detective Anderson retrieved a white handkerchief from his jacket pocket and gently lifted the plastic cup that Camille had used.

His trained eye was always on the lookout for clues.

Detective Ramirez, who had learned to trust Anderson's instincts over their years of partnership, nodded in agreement. "You've got a good hunch, Anderson. Let's keep an eye on her and see if anything surfaces. This case might have deeper layers than we initially thought."

***

While Lucas lay in the hospital bed, his mind was a chaotic battleground, where the persistent voices whispered doubts and paranoia. "Is this a trap, a setup? Are they involved in this? What aren't they telling me?" The ongoing mystery surrounding Eva's disappearance and the cyberattacks had deepened his sense of unease.

Camille, Julian, and Sebastian gathered in the hospital waiting area, their concern palpable. They found themselves wondering about Lucas's well-being and the implications of the attack they had just survived. Julian, with a furrowed brow, finally voiced what was on their minds, "Do you think Lucas will be okay?"

Camille, though typically reserved, was clearly shaken by the recent events. "I hope so. He's been through so much already."

Sebastian, who had been silently observing, finally chimed in, his voice a calm and reassuring presence. "The doctors here are among the best. Lucas is in good hands."

Inside the sterile and brightly lit operating room, Lucas lay on the gurney, his apprehension palpable. The medical team surrounded him, their faces hidden behind masks, and their gloved hands efficiently prepared him for the surgery.

"Lucas, we're here to help you through this," one of the nurses spoke softly, offering reassurance as they wheeled him towards the cold, steel operating table.

The room buzzed with controlled chaos, the constant beeping of machines, the nurses' whispered instructions, and the distant hum of the ventilation system. It was a world of sterile white surfaces and the antiseptic scent that permeated the air.

But Lucas, locked in his own world of paranoia, couldn't silence the relentless questions that swirled in his head. "Is this surgery real? Is it part of some grander scheme?" His mind raced, fighting to grasp the elusive truth he believed was just out of reach.

As the anesthesia was administered, and the room began to blur, Lucas couldn't escape the gnawing sensation that there was more to the mysteries surrounding Eva's disappearance and the cyberattacks than met the eye. The uncertainty lingered as he slipped into unconsciousness, leaving him to wonder what revelations awaited him upon waking.

When he woke up, he found himself back in his own home, sitting at the breakfast table. Eva sat across from him, radiantly smiling as she savored her morning meal.

Eva, ever the embodiment of politeness and honesty, shared her dreams with Lucas, her eyes shining with anticipation. "Lucas, I've always dreamed of traveling to Paris. The City of Love, you know?"

As she spoke, the morning sun streamed through the window, casting a warm glow over the scene. The aroma of freshly brewed coffee lingered in the air, adding to the sense of comfort and familiarity.

Lucas, lost in the labyrinth of his own paranoia, couldn't suppress the nagging doubts in his mind. "Paris? You want to go to Paris? You can't leave me, Eva. You just can't."

Eva, her determination unshaken, continued to smile gently. Her voice was a soothing melody, an attempt to bridge the growing divide between them. "Lucas, you know how much I care about you. But sometimes, it feels like you don't truly understand what

I long for."

The tension in the room grew, and Lucas couldn't contain his rising anxiety. "No, you're not going anywhere," he shouted, his voice reverberating within the confines of their home.

In response, Eva abruptly stood up, causing her chair to tumble over. "I will follow my dreams, Lucas. I want to travel, even if it's something you can't grasp."

The scene became more chaotic as Lucas, too, rose from his seat, arms outstretched, desperately reaching for Eva. But her image was slowly fading, slipping further away from his grasp, leaving him with a sense of longing and uncertainty.

In the blink of an eye, Lucas found himself transported back to his home office, deep in the throes of a project alongside Eva. Their shared focus was on Millie, the AI that had become an integral part of their lives.

Eva, with her trademark politeness and unwavering honesty, chimed in as they tinkered with the computer. Their collaboration was drawing closer to a breakthrough. "Lucas, I can feel it; we're on the brink of a major breakthrough with Millie. She's getting smarter and more responsive with each update. All our hard work is finally paying off."

Lucas, sporting a smile infused with excitement and gratitude, nodded in approval. The two of them had dedicated countless hours to this project, but their tranquil workspace was about to face disruption.

Eva's phone unexpectedly rang, and she apologetically stepped away to take the call. It was a short conversation, but when she returned, Lucas couldn't contain the surge of paranoia that crept into his mind. Next thing he knew, he was asking, his voice tinged with suspicion, "Eva, who was that on the phone just now?"

Eva hesitated for a moment, her response veiled with a subtle shift in demeanor. "Oh, it was nobody important, just a work-related call."

Lucas, unable to suppress his irrational jealousy and fear, snapped at her, desperation thick in his voice. "You better not even think about leaving me, Eva. You can't leave me. You can't."

Eva, taken aback, retorted with a hint of exasperation, "Lucas, you're being irrational."

However, Lucas persisted, following closely behind her, trying to reach out to her. "Come back here, Eva. I told you, you can't leave."

His grip on her arm tightened, and she winced in pain. "Lucas, you're hurting me," she protested, her voice filled with distress. The room around them seemed to close in, the tension growing palpable as their emotions clashed in the middle of the project that had brought them together.

Moments later, he found himself back in the same familiar room, bathed in the soft glow of dawn's first light. But as he reached out his hand to the empty side of the bed where Eva should have been, his fingers brushed against nothing but empty sheets, and an eerie void gnawed at his heart.

Despair gripped Lucas, and anguished screams tore from his throat, "Eva? Eva, where are you?" His voice, tinged with panic, echoed through the house like a haunting cry.

The silence that followed was deafening, a cruel contrast to the frantic shouts. Lucas raced through the rooms, desperation driving him to find any sign of her. Her favorite coffee mug sat abandoned on the kitchen counter, and her books lay open as if she had been reading just moments before.

Lucas couldn't wrap his mind around what had occurred. He questioned the empty air around him, his voice cracking with turmoil. "Where could she have gone? Why would she leave without a word?"

As he attempted to scream out his frustration and

confusion, his voice seemed to dissolve into the empty void, swallowed by the deafening silence that surrounded him. The nightmare was suffocating, the walls of his fears closing in, threatening to crush him as despair reigned supreme. The room was awash in the pale light of dawn, an eerie contrast to the tumultuous storm of emotions tearing through his soul.

Lucas's eyes fluttered open as he shook off the dream's disorienting grip, finding himself in a clean, white hospital room. The soft, rhythmic beeping of the monitors was a soothing contrast to the nightmarish chaos that had haunted his slumber. Relief washed over him, akin to the sensation of a cool breeze on a scorching day. But the unsettling questions and doubts that had tormented his dreams still clung to the fringes of his consciousness, reminders of his perpetual paranoid state.

Questions and doubts swirled around his mind like a storm, and his paranoia clung to him like a heavy shroud, refusing to release its grip. In his vulnerable state, he struggled to distinguish the dream from reality, each moment laden with the torment of uncertainty.

His gaze meandered around the room, and to

his astonishment, he spotted Camille, slumbering in a nearby chair. Her peaceful repose offered an oddly reassuring presence, a link to the reality he so desperately sought after the horrors of his nightmare. He had no choice but to scrutinize her closely, his mind riddled with confusion. Camille bore a striking resemblance to Eva, but the lines of memory had blurred in his mind. He had forgotten what Eva looked like, and that was maddening.

Camille stirred in her sleep, emitting soft, almost haunting whimpers, just like Eva used to do. It was as though the ghosts of his past and the hazy boundaries between reality and illusion were conspiring to play tricks on his mind. The room itself was imbued with a profound sense of ambiguity and mystery, leaving Lucas to grapple with the haunting memories of his dream and the mysterious presence of Camille – a woman who was simultaneously familiar and a complete stranger.

And all the while, the incessant questions swirled in his head like a never-ending storm. Was this reality or just another layer of the dream? Had he lost his grip on the truth, or was there a method to the madness that had become his life? The answers seemed as elusive as the specters of his past.

In the middle of Lucas's muddled thoughts, the door to his sterile hospital room flung open suddenly, causing him to jump in alarm. In walked a doctor, his demeanor cold and calculated, sending a chill down Lucas's spine. The silence in the room was thick, hanging ominously in the air.

Lucas, his mind frequently tormented by paranoid questions and the relentless voices in his head, found himself questioning, 'What's this doctor up to? Why the sudden entrance?' His thoughts spiraled into a storm of fear and suspicion.

The doctor's hands moved with an eerie swiftness as he reached for a knife, and it sent a jolt of terror through Lucas's veins. Panic seized him, and without a second thought, he reacted on pure instinct. He lunged at the intruder, pain ripping through his body as he yanked the needles from his IV. The searing agony in his abdomen did little to deter him. Fueled by adrenaline, he tackled the doctor to the ground, driven by a desperate need for survival.

The abrupt commotion roused Camille from her fitful slumber, her exhaustion apparent as she snapped into action. Instinct took over as she rushed to assist Lucas. She couldn't believe the chaotic scene unfolding before her, and her heart pounded with a cocktail of fear and determination.

Meanwhile, Lucas, still struggling to distinguish between his disoriented reality and the persistent voices in his head, grappled to make sense of the situation. It was as if he had been trapped in a nightmare, only to be thrust into a waking nightmare that blurred the lines between his dreams and reality. "What's happening?" he mumbled, his voice trembling as he tried to navigate the chaos surrounding him.

Camille, with an unwavering determination, managed to call for help. Her voice pierced through the chaos, alerting the hospital's security guards who rushed to their aid. Within moments, they swiftly subdued the menacing doctor who had posed a grave threat to Lucas.

The room, once a scene of utter confusion and dread, was gradually regaining a sense of order. However, the persistent questions and paranoia continued to haunt Lucas, refusing to retreat to the recesses of his mind.

As the room transitioned from a state of tension and danger to relative calm, Lucas, still trembling and plagued by his inner demons, turned to Camille with a profound gratitude in his eyes. "Thank you," he murmured, his voice infused with heartfelt appreciation for her swift thinking and courage.

Camille, her exhaustion evident in her demeanor, simply nodded. Her concern for Lucas was etched on her face. The incident had left them all on edge, and the pressing need for answers and enhanced security loomed larger than ever, like a shadow in the room, casting a pall over their collective nerves.

The moment the hospital room door flew open for the second time that night, it was Julian and Sebastian who stormed in. Their expressions were a mix of shock and disbelief as they took in the chaotic scene that had just unfolded before them. It was like a whirlwind of confusion and concern had suddenly swept into the room.

Julian, his face etched with worry, wasted no time in rushing over to Camille. She sat there, looking utterly drained and disbelieving, as if the world had turned upside down in an instant.

In the middle of the room, Lucas lay on the hospital bed, his face contorted in pain. His abdominal wound had started to bleed, and it was clear that he was in agony. The medical team descended upon him, a group of skilled professionals moving with remarkable speed and precision. Their actions were a well-coordinated dance, each step designed to address

Lucas's injuries and, above all, to ease his suffering.

The room itself was a whirlwind of activity. Harsh fluorescent lights cast stark shadows on the sterile white walls. The air was filled with the scent of antiseptics and the distant hum of machines. Outside, the world continued on, oblivious to the drama unfolding within the hospital room. The tension in the room was palpable, and it seemed like time had slowed down, as everyone worked tirelessly to bring some sense of order to the chaos that had descended upon them.

In the middle of the chaos, Lucas couldn't help but question his own thoughts, paranoia seeping into his mind. "What just happened? Why is this happening to us?" The voices in his head seemed to grow louder, adding to his torment as he tried to make sense of the madness.

Camille, still trying to process the shock of the sudden violence, nodded weakly, her eyes a mix of fear and determination. She was clearly exhausted by the events that had unfolded.

As the medical team worked diligently to care for Lucas, Camille, and Julian were gently ushered outside into the dimly lit corridor by one of the nurses, who sensed the need for a moment of respite. The door closed behind them, muffling the sounds of the hospital room and providing a brief escape from the intense and chaotic scene they had just witnessed.

Camille leaned against the cool, sterile wall, her eyes closed briefly, trying to steady her racing heart. Lucas's paranoia and the violence in the room had left an indelible mark, and the dimly lit corridor offered a welcome retreat from the tumultuous reality inside.

Julian, still deeply worried about Camille's well-being, turned to her with a concerned look on his face. "Are you absolutely sure you're holding up okay? That was... just unbelievable."

Camille managed a faint smile, though her eyes bore the lingering signs of shock. "I'm holding it together, Julian, though I can't deny I'm still quite shaken."

The events they'd just witnessed had left them all rattled, and the sterile hospital corridor felt like a sanctuary from the storm that had erupted in the room. The air was thick with uncertainty, and they could do nothing but wait anxiously for updates on Lucas's condition and seek answers to the questions hanging over them.

In the hushed ambiance of the hospital corridor, Camille and Julian leaned in closer to one another, their faces reflecting the gravity of the situation. Camille couldn't contain her astonishment and murmured to Julian, "I think that guy was there to kill me. Lucas, he saved my life."

Julian's eyes widened, his concern for Camille intensifying as he tried to wrap his head around the chilling revelation. "Seriously? That's... I can't even believe it." His disbelief was etched across his face, a testament to the sinister twist of fate they'd just encountered.

Camille nodded, her voice still carrying a tremor from the recent ordeal. "I was utterly helpless until Lucas intervened. He stepped in, and I owe him my life." In that hospital corridor, in the middle of the aura of uncertainty, their bond deepened, sealed by the shared experience of danger and gratitude for Lucas's timely intervention.

Julian's concern was palpable as he leaned in closer to Camille. He was on the edge, thinking about her safety. "Camille, you have to be safe. I could get you out of here, maybe to a hotel or somewhere secure. It's not a good idea for you to stay here, especially after what just happened."

Camille, despite her weariness, shook her head with determination. "No, Julian, we can't just leave without finding out what's going on with Lucas. He's been through so much, and he needs us here."

Their conversation was interrupted as a nurse briefly stepped out of the room. Julian seized the opportunity, his paranoid mind racing with questions. He approached the nurse with urgency, eager for any information on Lucas's condition. "How's Lucas holding up? Is he going to be okay?"

The nurse, her face etched with concern, lowered her voice as she provided an update. "There's been significant bleeding, and they're considering a second surgery. It's a critical situation, and the medical team is doing everything they can."

Julian returned to Camille, his expression a blend of worry and unwavering resolve. "Camille, we have to stick around. Lucas is in a tough spot right now, and we can't just abandon him." The events of the day had left them all in a state of uncertainty and danger, teetering on the precipice of the unknown.

***

Lucas found himself being wheeled into the operating room for a second surgery to control the bleeding from his knife wound. His mind was racing with paranoia and questions, and despite his efforts, he found himself wondering about the voices in his head, amplifying his anxiety. "Is this the right decision? What if something goes wrong again? I can't lose any more blood," he thought, feeling the weight of the moment pressing down on him.

Camille and Julian occupied the waiting room, where every passing minute felt like an eternity. The anxiety in the room was tangible, their concern etched onto their faces, worn and weary from the ordeal.

Sebastian, the ever-attentive butler, had returned to Julian's side, providing a pillar of strength in this trying time. He leaned in and spoke softly, "Mr. Laurent, I've arranged accommodations for all of you at a nearby hotel. It's a place of comfort and respite during these trying times."

Julian, appreciative of Sebastian's thoughtfulness, turned to Camille, his eyes filled with concern. "Camille, you should go with Sebastian and get some rest. You've been through so much today. We'll call you as soon as we have any news about Lucas. I promise you."

Camille, worn and tired, her emotions conflicted, hesitated before reluctantly nodding. "Okay, I'll go, but please promise to update me the moment you hear anything."

Julian, with a warm, reassuring smile, voiced his promise, "I promise, Camille. You deserve some rest too. We'll be in touch soon." As they navigated this tense and uncertain moment in the hospital waiting room, the ties that bound them grew stronger, even in the face of worry and fear.

With Camille departing alongside Sebastian, Julian found himself back in the tense waiting game, eagerly awaiting any news about Lucas's condition. The hospital's harsh, fluorescent lights bathed the surroundings in a clinical glow, while the relentless clock on the wall marked time's unwavering progress, seemingly oblivious to the turmoil gripping his heart.

Julian was seated in the cold waiting room, a whirlwind of questions and worries racing through his mind. The notion that someone might have attempted to harm Camille, the woman he adored, haunted him. But who could be behind such a sinister plot? What motive lay beneath the surface? The uncertainty gnawed at him, a persistent torment that refused to be ignored.

As he found himself lost in thought, his phone suddenly buzzed, snapping him back to the present moment. It was the private detective he'd hired to unravel the mystery surrounding Eva Smith's disappearance.

The detective's voice crackled through the line, tinged with intrigue, "Mr. Laurent, I've been digging into the case of Eva Smith, and it's been quite the puzzling journey."

Julian couldn't resist a playful quip, a twinkle in his eye, "Well, detective, you do have a knack for keeping me on the edge of my seat, don't you? So, what have you got for me? Any tantalizing clues or juicy tidbits?"

"Over the last five years, she's vanished without a trace, no activity, nothing."

A sense of despair washed over Julian upon hearing this grim news. The chances of finding Eva alive seemed to be slipping away. "But what about recent developments?" he inquired, desperation creeping into his voice.

The detective continued, "Oddly enough, just a few hours ago, her fingerprints were run through the police database. It's quite perplexing, Mr. Laurent."

Julian's mind raced with possibilities. Could Eva still be out there, living under the radar? Or were her fingerprints being compared for some other reason? "Do you think she might still be out there, somewhere?" he asked, a glimmer of hope shining in his eyes.

The detective replied cautiously, "It's a possibility, Mr. Laurent. I'll dig deeper, try to unearth more information. But it won't be easy."

Julian knew time was of the essence, and he clung to the hope that Eva might still be alive. "Please, do whatever it takes to uncover the truth. I need to know, no matter what it is."

With a determined nod, the detective assured him, "I'll get right back to work, Mr. Laurent. We're going to get to the bottom of this."

Julian ended the call with a relieved smile, finally receiving some much-needed positive news. The weight of the past few hours had been a heavy burden on everyone, but this glimmer of hope in the darkness lifted his spirits. As he set his phone aside, his thoughts drifted to Camille, the remarkable woman who had entered his life so unexpectedly, and how their journey was far from over.

Growing increasingly concerned for Camille's safety, Julian felt it was time to make a call to his trusted butler, Sebastian. In their line of work, danger could spring from anywhere, and taking chances was not an option.

Julian dialed Sebastian's number, his tone a blend of seriousness and concern. "Sebastian, I need you to keep a close eye on Camille. We don't know who might come after her next. I need her to be safe."

Sebastian, as always, the steadfast and dutiful guardian, provided Julian with the assurance he needed. "Of course, sir. I'll ensure her safety and see to it that nothing untoward happens to her. You can rely on me."

Julian breathed a sigh of relief, grateful for Sebastian's unwavering dedication. He understood the importance of having someone trustworthy to watch over Camille, particularly in a world rife with uncertainty and lurking dangers. In this pivotal moment, their bond was a lifeline, ensuring that Camille's safety was a top priority, come what may.

***

The lavish hotel suite cocooned Camille in a world of opulence and comfort. The bathroom was a modern marvel, adorned with gleaming marble countertops and a glass-walled shower that oozed luxury. As the hot water showered down on her, it felt like a comforting embrace, a brief respite from the whirlwind of the past few hours. The steam billowed around her, and she let it wash away the stress and unease, offering her mind the space it needed to strategize.

In the middle of the rising steam, Camille's thoughts swirled with a shroud of mystery. Known for her keen intellect, she saw this moment of uncertainty as a chance to use her intelligence to her advantage. As she stood beneath the cascading water, a sly smile played on her lips, her mind busy with mysterious machinations.

After her refreshing shower, Camille found herself lounging in the plush robe generously provided by the upscale hotel. Her thoughts were consumed by the intricacies of her next moves in this carefully crafted plan. The suite's living area, adorned with tasteful furnishings and bathed in a gentle, ambient glow, provided the perfect setting for her sophisticated stratagems.

Resting on the luxurious couch within the opulent suite, Camille knew it was time to set the wheels of her plan into motion. With an air of mysterious intent, she reached for the phone on the elegant side table and dialed the room service number. As she waited a response on the other end, her eyes sparkled with a sense of purpose.

A polite voice answered, "Good evening. How may we assist you with room service?"

Camille adopted a charming and mysterious tone, perfectly suited to the luxurious surroundings. "Good evening. I'd like to place an order, please."

"Of course, ma'am," the voice replied, eager to assist.

Camille went on to place an order, selecting the most decadent offerings from the hotel's menu. Her choices encompassed exquisite entrees and a carefully chosen bottle of fine wine, all designed to weave the illusion of opulence and indulgence into her intricate plan. In the middle of the lavish surroundings, Camille's actions hinted at a deeper narrative, one filled with secrets and intrigue.

She placed her order and reclined on the plush couch, her thoughts consumed by the intricate web she was weaving. Her devious plan unfolded just as she had anticipated, and each move in this scheme felt like a meticulously placed puzzle piece, sliding seamlessly into position. She watched it all come together, just like she'd expected, feeling like she was assembling a complex jigsaw puzzle, each piece fitting snugly into its spot, creating a mesmerizing picture.

While she waited for her room service to arrive, Camille decided to set the mood in the suite. She strolled over to a sleek music system in the corner, activated it, and chose a melody that struck a balance between soothing and lively. The room quickly filled with the rhythmic sound, pulling her into its embrace.

Unable to resist the pull of the music, Camille began to sway and move with grace, her body responding to the hypnotic rhythm. Each step and twirl was infused with the excitement of the game she was playing, though her devious intentions remained concealed beneath her enchanting performance.

As the music continued to envelop the room, Camille moved through the spacious suite, dancing with a fluidity that was both mesmerizing and mysterious. It was as though the melody was a silent partner in her private dance of intrigue. In the middle of the inviting ambiance, Camille's secret intentions remained veiled, concealed by the beauty and allure of her movements.

Camille had been lost in an impromptu dance, moving to a rhythm known only to her, when a soft knock on her hotel room door brought her to a halt. A sly smile graced her lips as she composed herself and glided over to the door. With a deep breath, she opened it to reveal the hotel staff, who had arrived with her room service order.

The staff members were met with the vision of

Camille, poised and graceful, her charm radiating as she gracefully accepted the lavish meal they had brought. She offered her thanks with a polite nod and a warm smile before closing the door.

Setting the decadent spread on the dining table, Camille found herself admiring the extravagant meal fit for royalty. Her plan was unfolding just as she had envisioned, and her satisfaction was palpable in the confident air she exuded. She had everyone right where she wanted them, and she intended to seize the opportunity.

As Camille indulged in her delectable meal, her mysterious demeanor deepened. With each bite, she relished not only the exquisite flavors but the success of a scheme that had demanded her intellect and cunning. Despite a few unexpected bumps in the road, her plan was now fitting together seamlessly, like a complex puzzle piece falling into its rightful place. The room, adorned with opulent furnishings, bore witness to her calculated mastery, as she continued to pull the strings of her mysterious plot.

Camille's fingers danced gracefully across her phone screen, and a mysterious smile played on her lips. Her eyes darted over the device's display, and a combination of determination and cunning glimmered in her gaze. She had been a master at keeping her true intentions hidden, and her mysterious aura left those around her in the dark. In the middle of her surroundings, she was the puppeteer of a complex plot, and the world was utterly oblivious to the intricate web she had meticulously woven.

As Camille orchestrated her plan, she found herself unable to resist voicing her thoughts aloud, a hint of mystery in her tone. "What if I try this? It should work, shouldn't it?" Her whispers to herself were barely audible, and she continued to navigate the intricate details of her scheme.

She understood that every move had to be executed with precision, each action strategically calculated. Camille was a virtuoso of manipulation, her expertise in the art of deception bringing her one step closer to her ultimate goal. With a sense of accomplishment, she recognized that she stood at the threshold of success, her cunning deceit carving a path toward her triumphant destination. The world around her remained oblivious, while she held the strings of her mysterious plan, ready to make her next move.

CHAPTER 11: A CYBER OBSESSION

Julian felt like he'd been trapped in that cold, sterilized hospital waiting room forever. Each minute crawled by, and his worry for Lucas weighed on him like a ton of bricks. He kept glancing at the wall clock, hoping it had miraculously sped up, but it hardly budged. He knew he had to decide: there was nothing more he could do at the hospital right now. Plus, the thought of being away from Camille for any longer was too much to bear. She must be feeling just as anxious, if not more, after the chaotic events of the night.

With a deep, heavy sigh, he decided to head back to the hotel. As he left the hospital behind, the familiar sound of his footsteps echoed through the sterile corridors. He found himself wondering how Lucas was doing. It was tough to shake off the worry.

Finally, he arrived at the hotel. The soft, gentle lighting in their suite welcomed him back, giving the place a warm and cozy feel. It felt like a sanctuary, a safe haven where they could temporarily escape from the harsh, uncertain world outside.

As Julian stepped into one of the bedrooms, he found Camille sound asleep. Her face had that peaceful look you get when you're in the middle of a cozy dream, and for a moment, it felt like all her troubles had just vanished into thin air. He was powerless to resist being amazed by how strong and determined she was.

Gently, Julian walked up to the bed, his eyes filled with concern and love as he watched her sleep. He extended his hand, softly stroking her face and carefully pushing a loose strand of hair away from her forehead. Even with all the chaos going on, she appeared completely calm and undisturbed. The room was dimly lit, with a soft glow coming from a lamp on the nightstand. It cast a warm, comforting ambiance, making Camille's peaceful slumber even more soothing. The curtains swayed gently in the breeze that wafted in from the partially open window, adding a touch of serenity to the scene.

He whispered softly, "Camille, I'm here. Lucas is going to be alright. You don't have to bear this burden alone."

Julian's quiet words broke through the fog of exhaustion and worry that had enveloped Camille. Her eyes, puffy and red from crying, slowly opened, revealing a blend of vulnerability and gratitude. She'd endured so much in such a short time, and it had left her emotionally drained.

Camille extended her trembling arms, wrapping them around Julian and drawing him nearer. It was as though her embrace carried an unspoken plea, a desperate need for comfort and the assurance that she didn't have to confront the looming uncertainties on her own. Tears trickled down her cheeks in silence as she clung to him, finding refuge in the comforting embrace he offered.

Her voice quivered, a mix of fear and longing in her tone as she made her heartfelt request, "Can you please stay with me tonight? I just can't bear the thought of being alone, not after everything that's happened."

The room they were in was dimly lit, with soft, warm hues painting the walls. The faint hum of a nearby table lamp cast a gentle glow, creating a cozy atmosphere that enveloped them. Outside, rain tapped lightly on the windows, providing a soothing backdrop to their intimate moment. The scent of lavender-scented candle wafted through the air, adding to the calming ambiance. The weight of the recent events hung heavy in the room, and Julian's presence felt like a lifeline in the midst of the storm.

Julian, touched by her vulnerability, kissed the top

of her head gently and whispered, "Of course, Camille. I'm here, and I'm not going anywhere. We'll get through this together."

With that promise, he settled down beside her, offering his presence as a source of comfort and security during the long night ahead. In that shared moment, their connection deepened, the boundaries between them blurring as they navigated the storm that had unexpectedly entered their lives.

In the softly lit hotel room, Camille and Julian found solace in the quiet hours of the night. Their earlier tumultuous encounters had given way to a newfound intimacy, forged in the crucible of uncertainty and danger.

As they lay side by side, their fingers intertwined, Julian broke the silence. "Camille," he began softly, "we've been through so much in such a short time. The world can be a chaotic place, but maybe, just maybe, there's a silver lining in all of this."

Camille turned her head to look at him, the dim light casting gentle shadows across his face. "What do you mean, Julian?"

He brushed a strand of hair away from her face and smiled. "I mean, perhaps our meeting wasn't just a chance encounter. Maybe there's a reason our paths crossed. A greater purpose, if you will."

Camille's eyes held a mixture of curiosity and hope as she considered his words. "Do you believe in fate, Julian?"

Julian's gaze met hers, his expression earnest. "I believe in possibilities. And I believe in the power of human connection. We can't predict the future, but we can shape it. Maybe, just maybe, we're meant to be a part of each other's lives, to help and support one another."

She nodded, grateful for the support, and asked, "How are you holding up? You've been through a lot tonight."

Julian tried to offer a reassuring smile, despite his own worries. "I'm worried, too, but we'll get through this together. I can't stand seeing you so anxious."

As they lay in the quiet of the night, their conversation flowed, painting a picture of the future they both envisioned. They spoke of dreams, ambitions, and the uncharted territory of what lay ahead. It was pillow-talk infused with the vulnerability of two souls brought together by unexpected circumstances.

In that moment, their connection deepened further, strengthened not only by the challenges they faced but also by the shared vision of a future that held the promise of new adventures.

***

The room was slowly being bathed in the soft, early morning light as the first rays of dawn crept in. It was a serene moment, a brief interlude of calm, shattered abruptly by the shrill ring of Julian's phone. Camille, who had taken comfort in Julian's arms throughout the long night, was roused from her slumber by the jarring sound. Julian fumbled for his phone on the bedside table, his heart racing with an overwhelming sense of foreboding.

Julian's phone rang again, and as he accepted the call, a somber and regretful voice emanated from the other end. It was a doctor from the hospital, and each word he spoke felt like a leaden weight upon Julian's ears.

"Mr. Laurent," the doctor began, sorrow lacing his words, "I'm deeply sorry to be the one to convey this news, but despite our best efforts, Mr. Mitchell didn't make it through the surgery."

Julian's grip on the phone tightened, his knuckles turning almost ghostly white as the full weight of those words settled in. Camille, still groggy from sleep and the remnants of their previous conversation, observed Julian with a piercing gaze as he absorbed the grim news.

"How did this happen? It was just a stupid knife wound," Julian asked, his voice choked with disbelief.

The doctor's voice continued, the regret palpable in every syllable. "The injuries he sustained were severe, and his condition deteriorated rapidly. I wish there was a different outcome, but we did everything we could."

Camille, still keeping a close eye on Julian, interjected with a voice tinged with both concern and curiosity. "Julian, what's going on? Is everything okay?"

Julian, his face etched with a profound sadness, shook his head as if to clear his thoughts and responded quietly, "It's Lucas, Camille. He didn't make it through the surgery."

Camille's eyes widened in shock, and she covered her mouth with her hand, struggling to process the sudden and tragic turn of events. The room, which had once been filled with their conversation, now hung heavy with the weight of sorrow and unanswered questions.

As Julian slowly lowered the phone, a heavy silence blanketed the room, sorrow tainting the atmosphere. Camille, her eyes brimming with tears, reached out and gently clasped Julian's hand, offering a comforting touch. In the face of this sudden and heart-wrenching tragedy, their connection had grown even stronger, and they found themselves grappling with the harsh reality of their loss.

"I'm so sorry, Julian," Camille whispered, her voice barely above a hushed murmur.

Their fingers intertwined, symbolizing the intricate and sometimes fragile nature of human bonds. It was a stark reminder of the complexity of their shared journey.

Camille wiped away a tear, her eyes reflecting the grief she held within. The room felt smaller, as if it couldn't contain the immense sorrow that had entered their lives. The weight of the loss was a burden they'd have to bear together, as they navigated the uncertain path that lay before them.

Amid the somber news of Lucas's passing, the room transformed into a sanctuary of grief. Julian and Camille, united in their sorrow, shared a moment of silent contemplation. However, Julian, bearing the weight of their collective sadness, quietly excused himself from the room.

"Excuse me, Camille, I'll be back in a minute," he

murmured, his footsteps resonating with the gravity of their loss as he made his way to the living room. The air hung heavy with sorrow, and they all struggled to come to terms with the unexpected void that had entered their lives.

In the living room, Julian took a moment to gather his thoughts. He knew he had to be strong for both himself and Camille. As he sat in solitude, the room's dim lighting seemed to intensify his contemplation.

Julian dialed Sebastian's number, his voice trembling as he shared the heartbreaking news. "Sebastian, it's Lucas. I... I need to tell you something. Lucas... He's gone."

Sebastian, with a solemn tone, offered his condolences. "That's devastating news, Mr. Laurent. I'm truly sorry for your loss."

Julian's voice cracked as he continued, "I know, he could be a bit eccentric, but we had grown close. I think I should head to the hospital now."

In the middle of the hushed conversation, Julian's words weighed heavily in the room. Sebastian, always the voice of reason in trying times, offered his guidance. "Mr. Laurent, I understand this is a difficult moment, but perhaps it's best not to rush to the hospital in the middle of the night. There might be a police investigation underway."

"You're right, Sebastian. This is indeed a police matter. Lucas was attacked in his own home," Julian revealed.

Sebastian concurred, "Yes, sir, it might be wise to stay put until we have a clearer picture of the situation."

Julian, realizing he had disturbed Sebastian's peace, added, "I apologize for waking you up so early, Sebastian. Please, get back to sleep."

"Thank you, sir, and my deepest condolences once again," Sebastian offered before Julian hung up the phone.

Julian sat on the dimly lit living room couch, his heart heavy, even though Sebastian couldn't see him. In the middle of this tragedy, caution and composure were their most valuable assets. As he ended the call, the harsh reality of the situation began to sink in. An uncertain future loomed, and they would need to muster the strength to navigate the storm that had suddenly engulfed their lives.

The room felt strangely empty, the silence only magnifying the gravity of the situation. Outside, the night was eerily still, as if the entire world was holding its breath in anticipation of what would come next.

Inside the bedroom, Camille stood in a place

where emotions, a blend of joy and sorrow, were intricately intertwined. She felt an unusual sense of relief when she contemplated Lucas's passing. In a twisted way, it meant one less unpredictable factor in her elaborate plan. It lightened the burden of her devious secrets, and a part of her wanted to acknowledge that fact.

"One less thing in my way," she muttered to herself, her voice a hushed confession.

She settled onto the bed, her mind drifting into the depths of the intricate drama she had set in motion.

"You'll be missed, Lucas, you crazy bastard," she whispered with a quiet chuckle, raising her fist in the air.

The triumph of her scheme brought a gratifying feeling, and for a brief moment, she indulged in a bit of self-congratulation. However, as she savored her newfound freedom, her phone on the nightstand beside her suddenly vibrated, making her jump in surprise.

The room, draped in shadows, seemed to hold its breath as Camille hesitated. The soft glow of her device cast eerie patterns on the walls, and she cautiously reached for the phone, her heart pounding with a mix of curiosity and apprehension. What unexpected twist awaited her in this carefully orchestrated plot?

She grabbed her phone, her eyes glued to the message displayed on the screen. A chilling sensation ran down her spine. The message was from an encrypted number, and its contents were chilling: "I know what you are."

Camille's triumphant expression faded, replaced by uncertainty that clawed at her thoughts. Her carefully constructed plan was no longer a well-kept secret; someone had unveiled the truth. The ominous message lingered in the room, and Camille realized that her web of deceit was beginning to unravel, with the shadows of her past closing in.

With her heart racing, Camille knew she had to act swiftly. She reached for her laptop, her fingers dancing across the keyboard as she initiated a trace on the unsettling message. With each keystroke, her determination grew, and she willed herself to uncover the source of this disconcerting revelation.

Camille was totally immersed in her online investigation. With her tech skills, she managed to track down the source of the mysterious message, and to her surprise, it pointed straight to New York City. That revelation hit her like a ton of bricks. The person who knew her deepest secrets was practically in her backyard.

The gravity of the situation was crystal clear. This wasn't just some run-of-the-mill problem. It was a full-blown threat, and Camille needed to deal with it ASAP. The last thing she wanted was for her carefully woven life to start falling apart. She'd always been the type to take calculated risks, but now, with her past breathing down her neck, she had no choice but to confront this adversary face to face.

Camille's heart raced as she considered the implications of what she'd discovered. New York, the city that never sleeps, was the last place she'd expected to find herself facing such a perilous situation. The digital breadcrumbs had led her here, but she wasn't ready to accept defeat. She needed to act, to confront the one who held the key to her hidden past and take control of the situation. The dim glow of her computer screen cast an eerie light in her otherwise dimly lit room, emphasizing the gravity of the task ahead.

She hatched a plan and approached Julian, who was seated in the living room. Camille was acutely aware of her magnetic charm and how to use it to her advantage. Their eyes locked, and she leaned in closer, her voice taking on a sultry, conspiratorial tone, "Julian, there's something I need to tell you."

Julian, feeling a jolt of excitement at Camille's alluring presence, found himself lost in her gaze. She was dressed in a barely-there negligee, leaving little to the imagination. "What is it, my darling?" he inquired, his hand gently caressing her smooth thighs.

She sighed and confessed, "I've been receiving threats again."

Julian, the ever-composed gentleman, paid close attention. He couldn't deny the irresistible allure that drew him closer to Camille, even as her revelation sent a shiver down his spine. "Threats?" he inquired, genuine concern etched across his face.

Camille nodded, her lips dangerously close to his ear. "Indeed, threats. They've managed to track my location, Julian, and it's making me fear for our safety."

Julian leaned in closer, his brow furrowed in deep contemplation. "We've got to get to the bottom of these threats, Camille. Any idea where this might be coming from? Got an address?"

Camille hesitated, her voice trembling as she reluctantly shared the location. "It's an old warehouse, Julian."

Julian, his gaze reflecting a mix of determination and caution, gave a resolute nod. "Alright, I'll go check it out with Sebastian first, Camille. We'll assess the situation. You're safer here with the hotel's security team."

Camille's eyes shimmered with a complicated blend of gratitude and relief. She had deftly managed to steer the situation in a way that kept her out of direct harm's reach. Deep inside, she felt a hidden sense of relief that she wouldn't have to confront her tormentor face-to-face. "Thank you, Julian," she said, her sincerity layered with subtle complexity. She wrapped her arms around him, feeling his comforting presence as he drew her closer. She could feel his breath getting shallow as he buried his face in her neck. It wasn't long before she felt his hands moving along the length of her body.

Julian's voice dropped to a conspiratorial tone as he leaned in, his gaze locked onto Camille. "You know, Camille, you're a real puzzle. Just when I think I've got you figured out, you show another layer I never expected."

Camille's response was laced with allure as she replied, "Oh, Julian, I've got layers upon layers. And I'm quite eager for you to uncover them."

Julian's desire flared in the air, and he admitted, "I can't help but want to explore every single one of those layers, to see the real you, Camille."

They were caught in a magnetic pull, their bodies

inches apart. The atmosphere was electric, and resistance seemed futile. Julian couldn't help but say, "I'm all in for the adventure, Camille. Let's unravel these mysteries together."

Camille met his intense gaze with a mischievous smile. "Well, we've got time to peel away the layers, but for now, how about we savor the present moment?" Her eyes held a promise, an unspoken pact between them.

The room around them faded into the background as they focused on each other, the chemistry between them crackling with intensity. Time seemed to stand still as they shared this electric moment, where desires and mysteries intertwined. It wasn't long before they undressed each other, Julian taking in the beauty before him. He marveled at Camille's perfect body, his fingertips tracing every curve.

With a mischievous grin, Julian pulled her in for a kiss, his passion burning bright. In a moment of raw, primal desire, the two found themselves wrapped in an intimate embrace, their bodies entwined. Julian, his hands exploring every curve of Camille's exquisite form, was consumed with the urge to claim her as his own. His lips trailed down the length of her neck, igniting a fire within her.

Camille's body was a map of unexplored pleasures, and Julian was eager to chart a course of passion. With each touch, he discovered a new facet of her being, a new layer to the tantalizing mystery that was Camille. The room was a cacophony of their shared desire, their voices mingling in a melody of pleasure.

The moment was one of unbridled passion, a release of tension that had been building since their first encounter. Camille, her mind clouded with lust, succumbed to the intoxicating sensations. Julian's hands and lips were like a drug, sending her into a dizzying high.

With a sudden burst of energy, Camille pinned him down, her hands gripping his shoulders. Her eyes held a smoldering intensity as she leaned in for a kiss, her tongue exploring his mouth. Their bodies intertwined, and their mutual desire sparked into an inferno.

Julian, consumed with the need to satisfy Camille, let his hands roam along the curves of her body, his fingers tracing the contours of her skin. With each touch, he ignited a new spark of pleasure, fueling her growing hunger. It just happened—he felt a thrill of excitement as Camille responded to his every move.

Julian's fingers gently trailed down the length of Camille's arm, his touch feather-light and yet filled with intensity. Camille, her skin tingling, was lost in the sensations, her mind a haze of ecstasy. Before she knew it, she was reveling in the power she held over him.

The atmosphere was charged with the electricity of their shared desire. Each touch was a spark, sending waves of pleasure coursing through their bodies. They were in a world of their own, a sanctuary of passion where nothing else mattered.

As their bodies moved in a rhythmic dance, Julian whispered in her ear, "You're my greatest adventure, Camille."

Camille, her body pressed against his, could feel his heartbeat echoing hers. She smiled and said, "And you're mine, Julian. I'm all in for the journey."

Julian couldn't resist any longer. His desire flared, and he leaned in, kissing Camille deeply. She responded with a fiery passion, and their bodies moved together in perfect sync, a symphony of pleasure. They savored every moment, knowing that the future was uncertain and full of surprises.

They were entangled, a passionate embrace, the intensity between them growing. Their hearts were racing, their bodies moving together, each touch sending sparks through the air. The thrill of the unknown added to the exhilaration, and the world around them disappeared, consumed by the flames of their desire.

***

Hours later, Julian and Sebastian were all geared up in practical athletic clothes, ready to head off on their mission to the mysterious warehouse. It was this place that had been long forgotten, tucked away about ten miles from the busy heart of New York City. Although it had faded into obscurity, it was now a crucial part of their adventure.

As they hit the road, the day was turning gloomy, with the sun trying to peek through ominous clouds. It looked like rain could pour down any minute, adding to the tension in the air. The muggy humidity made their journey even more unsettling.

On the way, Julian turned to Sebastian with a grin. "Sebastian, you ever wonder if this old place is haunted? I mean, it looks like something straight out of a horror movie."

Sebastian chuckled. "Well, sir, I must say I wouldn't be surprised if it had a ghost or two hiding in the corners. But remember, we're here on a mission, not a ghost hunt."

Julian smirked. "I know, I know. But a ghost hunt would be more exciting. Can you imagine trying to outsmart a ghost with our athletic gear?"

Sebastian raised an eyebrow. "I believe outsmarting a ghost might require more than just athletic gear, sir."

As they continued their journey, the landscape around them shifted from the bustling streets of the city to a more desolate area. The warehouse, with its faded paint and boarded-up windows, stood like a relic from the past. Vines crawled up the walls, and an eerie silence seemed to envelop the place.

Julian looked out the window, his excitement tinged with apprehension. "Sebastian, this place gives me the creeps. I hope we find what we're looking for and get out of here in one piece."

Sebastian nodded. "I share your sentiment, sir. Let's be cautious and make this quick."

When they arrived at the abandoned warehouse, the scene was eerie. The building, a colossal relic of a bygone industrial era, cast long, haunting shadows in the diffused light. Its walls, covered in graffiti, bore witness to the relentless passage of time and human presence, while shattered windows offered glimpses into the murky interior.

Julian and Sebastian, vigilant and unyielding, left the car behind and stepped into the cavernous warehouse. Their footsteps resonated through the expansive space, creating an eerie symphony of echoes. They scanned their surroundings, hoping to spot any sign of life or a clue that might point them toward the mysterious figure holding the key to their deepest secrets.

But, as they ventured further into the vast structure, the harsh reality dawned on them—it was empty. The vacant warehouse offered no immediate solutions, only shadows and an eerie hush. Their pursuit had led them to an unexpected dead end, leaving them with more questions than they had at the outset.

The abandoned warehouse, its secrets shrouded in darkness, stood as a testament to the mysterious adversaries they were up against. The unfolding story had taken an unexpected turn, and the empty expanse of the warehouse provided no immediate answers to the duo's tireless quest for the truth.

Julian, a mix of frustration and curiosity, voiced his doubts to Sebastian. "Where could they have disappeared to? Did we miss something?"

Sebastian, mirroring the same bewilderment, responded, "It's like they had a heads-up about our arrival. But how?"

Their conversation echoed through the hollow expanse, casting an eerie aura over their ongoing quest. The abandoned warehouse, vast and desolate, had transformed into a maze of uncertainty, forcing them to huddle together and rethink their next moves in this high-stakes, mysterious puzzle.

Julian's fingers danced nimbly across his phone screen as he dialed Camille. The tension in her voice was palpable as she waited anxiously in the hotel suite, clinging to the hope that the warehouse might hold the elusive answers they were chasing. The phone was pressed to Julian's ear as he shared the disappointing update, "Camille, I hate to say it, but the place is empty."

Camille sighed in frustration, her breath catching in her throat as her voice quivered. "Empty? How can that be, Julian? We thought we were onto something here." Her mystery-laden gaze scanned the room as if expecting hidden secrets to materialize.

Julian's shoulders slumped in defeat, and he replied, "I know, Camille. It's as baffling as ever. But we can't let this setback deter us. There has to be something we're missing."

Camille's voice quivered with disbelief, and she questioned, "No, that can't be. I was so sure. Did you search everywhere?"

Julian replied with a defeated tone, "Yes, Camille. Maybe you were mistaken?"

Camille snapped back with a hint of irritation, "Mistaken? Are you fucking with me? Doubting my hacking skills, are we now?"

Julian paused, taken aback by her sudden shift in attitude. He found himself wondering if he truly knew her as well as he thought.

Just as their conversation reached an exasperating impasse, an unexpected interruption disrupted the tense silence. The shrill ring of the doorbell echoed in Camille's suite, sending a jolt through her. A voice from the other side called out, "Housekeeping."

Camille hurriedly informed Julian, "Julian, I have to go. Someone's at the door. I'll call you back as soon as I figure out what's happening."

With a quick goodbye, she ended the call and approached the door with a mix of anxiety and curiosity. The unexpected visitor and the warehouse's inexplicable emptiness left her with a growing sense of unease.

Camille's heart raced as she inched closer to the door, her mind swirling with a blend of anticipation and trepidation. She needed to know who stood on the other side, especially in light of the recent unexpected events that had shaken her world. The hotel suite, bathed in a soft, uncertain light, became the stage for her next encounter, and Camille was prepared to confront whatever secrets lay beyond that door.

As the door creaked open, Camille was met with a surprising sight that left her utterly unprepared. Without a moment's notice, a figure suddenly lunged towards her, a cloth covering her mouth before she could react. Panic coursed through her veins as she fought against the sudden intrusion. Her body writhed in an attempt to break free, but the assailant's grip was unyielding.

"Let go of me!" she desperately tried to shout, but the cloth muffled her voice, stifling her cries.

Camille's breaths grew shallow as she involuntarily inhaled the strange, sickly-sweet scent of the fabric, its effects washing over her like an unexpected wave. The room around her started to blur, her vision fading as her struggles gradually lost their vigor. Before she could make sense of the harrowing situation or even call for help, consciousness slipped away, leaving her in a disconcerting state of vulnerability.

In the dimly lit room, her limp body was a stark contrast to the whirlwind of events that had just transpired. The air was heavy with the scent of the cloth, and the silence was broken only by the sound of her shallow breaths. The ominous unknown loomed, enveloping her in an unsettling shroud of uncertainty.

CHAPTER 12: CLUES IN THE DARK

Julian and Sebastian drove back to the hotel, their faces etched with worry and their minds racing with thoughts about Camille. The sun was setting, casting a warm, orange glow over the streets of the coastal town. The sea breeze rustled through the palm trees, and the distant sound of waves crashing against the shore added to the eerie atmosphere.

As they entered the hotel's lobby, the dimly lit chandeliers overhead cast a soft, golden light on the marble floors. The grandeur of the place seemed to contrast with their anxious hearts. The reception desk stood empty, and the hushed murmur of guests echoed through the expansive space.

Sebastian ran a hand through his hair, his worry lines deepening as he scanned the lobby for any sign of danger. Julian's eyes darted around, hoping to catch a glimpse of any familiar face.

They made their way to the elevator, pressing the button for their floor. The dull hum of the elevator's machinery seemed to match the heavy feeling in their chests. The doors opened, and they stepped inside.

As the elevator ascended, their anxiety grew. The

ding of the elevator announcing their floor felt like a distant echo in their ears. They exited onto a corridor bathed in soft, warm light. The plush carpet underfoot provided a gentle contrast to their racing hearts.

They reached their hotel suite and pushed open the door, half-expecting to find Camille inside. But the suite was empty, her absence even more palpable in this familiar space. The curtains billowed gently in the evening breeze, and the setting sun painted the room in shades of deep orange and purple.

Julian sighed and collapsed onto one of the couches, while Sebastian took a seat by the window, his gaze fixed on the horizon. The weight of Camille's disappearance pressed on them, making their earlier worries seem small in comparison. It felt like she'd disappeared out of nowhere, leaving them feeling seriously concerned.

They knew they had to find her, but in this strange and unsettling situation, they were left with more questions than answers, and the fading light outside only deepened the mystery.

Despite their repeated attempts to contact her, her phone remained silent, each unanswered call only amplifying their unease. Julian, pacing back and forth in the hotel room, couldn't help but express his growing anxiety. "This isn't like her at all, Sebastian. She wouldn't just disappear without a word."

Sebastian, always the voice of reason, observed Camille's belongings, still neatly arranged in the room. He suggested, "Perhaps she went out for a while. Her things are still here. Maybe she needed some time alone, considering all that's been happening."

Julian nodded, albeit with a hint of reluctance. "You're right. We'll give her a bit more time to return. But I can't shake the feeling that something's not right."

The passage of time seemed to crawl by as they waited, their patience stretched to its limit, their concern deepening with every passing minute.

The minutes stretched into an agonizing eternity, their unease settling like a heavy cloud in the room. The silence from Camille was deafening, and their growing worry was impossible to ignore. Finally, their concern reached a tipping point, and with furrowed brows, they decided it was time to seek help from the local authorities, hoping for any lead that would help them find Camille.

Julian, his expression a mix of frustration and fear, broached the topic with Sebastian. "Sebastian, we can't wait any longer. We need to involve the police. Camille received another threat today, and I can't bear the thought of something happening to her."

Sebastian, a man of measured composure, contemplated Julian's words. After a moment of reflection, he nodded, his usually calm demeanor marred by concern. "You're right, Julian. It's better to err on the side of caution. Camille's safety is our top priority."

As Julian and Sebastian left the hotel, their minds were resolute, each step echoing with determination. They held onto the hope that law enforcement might hold the key to the answers they so desperately sought. The precinct was their destination, a place where they yearned for clarity and resolution.

Inside the bustling precinct, they had an unexpected encounter with Detective Anderson, the same detective they had met earlier when Lucas was shot. The memory of that fateful night now seemed like an eternity away, a stark contrast to the disheveled and annoyed detective they were facing in the present. The detective, a stern and experienced figure, was engaged in conversation with other officers. His presence held a glimmer of hope, a beacon of potential solutions in this mounting crisis.

"Detective," Julian called out as he approached the

officer, desperation evident in his voice.

Detective Anderson, his face etched with frustration, greeted them curtly. "You again? What brings you here?"

Julian, his worry overshadowing any apprehension, explained, "Detective, it's about our friend. She's missing, and we're deeply concerned. We've been trying to reach her, but her phone is off. We thought maybe you could help us."

The detective turned his attention to the distressed duo, and concern flickered in his eyes. "We can't do anything unless it's been 24 hours. You know that."

Julian couldn't hide his growing frustration, aware of the police procedures but equally aware of the urgency of Camille's situation. "Detective, we understand there are rules and regulations, but we believe Camille's life might be in serious danger. Is there any way you can make an exception or expedite the process to help us find her?"

The mention of Camille's name seemed to jolt Detective Anderson. "Camille? She's missing?" He inquired, genuine concern etching across his features.

Julian nodded gravely. "Yes, Detective. We're worried something terrible might have happened to her."

Detective Anderson, though visibly annoyed by the urgency of Julian's request, recognized the distress in Julian's eyes and knew he had to take the situation seriously. With a sigh, he reluctantly agreed, "Fine, I'll see what I can do, but I can't make any promises."

Sebastian, maintaining his unwavering composure, promptly provided the detective with all the information they had gathered. "Your assistance is greatly appreciated, Detective. We're very concerned about Camille's well-being."

Julian detailed the events surrounding Camille's disappearance, offering any information that might aid in the search for her. Their hope was that the police could help unravel the mystery and bring Camille back safely.

Detective Anderson ushered Julian and Sebastian into a small, dimly lit interview room. With a reassuring nod, he promised to do his utmost to locate Camille and unravel the mysteries surrounding her sudden disappearance.

Sebastian, noticing the growing unease in Julian's expression, stepped closer to his employer. With a concerned look in his eyes, he suggested, "Sir, maybe one of your private detectives could assist us in this matter?"

A glimmer of hope crossed Julian's face as he realized the potential of this suggestion. He wasted no time and dialed his trusted private detective's number. The voice on the other end was apologetic as it relayed the lack of any substantial leads on Camille's whereabouts.

Disappointment weighed heavily on Julian's shoulders, but he refused to give in to despair. He inquired further, "Is there any mention of Eva having any family or connections?"

The detective hesitated for a moment before revealing a perplexing detail. "No, Julian. I couldn't find any records of family or next of kin. But what's strange is that she was a ward of the state."

Julian's curiosity was piqued, and he probed further. "Ward of the state? Was she in foster care, then?"

The detective's response sent a shiver down Julian's spine. "No, it's more complicated. She spent her entire life in juvenile detention."

Julian was taken aback by this revelation. "Juvie? But for what?"

With a regretful tone, the detective conveyed the obstacle in their path. "I'm sorry, Julian, but her records are sealed by a court order. I can't access any information beyond this point."

The room seemed to close in on Julian as the weight of the situation pressed down upon him. Camille's past was shrouded in mystery, and it was increasingly evident that there were dark secrets to uncover if they were to find her and bring her back safely.

***

Inside the confines of the police station, time seemed to stretch endlessly, each passing minute amplifying Julian's unease. The interview room felt stifling, and the uncertainty surrounding Camille's whereabouts was taking a toll on him. He knew he had to be patient, but every second without news of her was a source of anguish.

Leaving the interview room, Julian stepped out into the buzzing chaos of the police department. Officers hurried from one task to another, the ringing phones creating a constant symphony of anxiety. Julian couldn't suppress his growing impatience; Camille's safety was at stake.

He managed to flag down a police officer, determination in his voice as he urgently stated, "We can't just wait here. We need information about Camille, and we need it now."

The officer, clearly preoccupied, briefly turned her attention to Julian and said, "I understand your concern, but we're dealing with an ongoing situation. Please, for your safety, stay in the room."

Sebastian, always a voice of reason, approached Julian, his touch a reassuring presence on Julian's shoulder. "Julian, we must remember we are guests in this country. It's best to trust the local authorities and let them handle their procedures."

Reluctantly, Julian agreed to return to the interview room, leaving the precinct's bustling lobby behind. As they waited for more information about Camille's disappearance, his worry for her safety weighed heavily on him. The passage of time felt agonizing, especially as they navigated the unfamiliar terrain of the local law enforcement.

Sebastian, always the voice of reason, suggested a different approach. "Sir, perhaps there's something on the news?" he proposed.

Julian, desperate for any lead, nodded in agreement and retrieved his phone. His fingers danced across the touchscreen as he delved into the digital world, searching for clues or any piece of information that could shed light on Camille's whereabouts. Within moments, the screen displayed a breaking news report, its headline delivering a chilling revelation that sent shivers down Julian's spine: "Murder Shakes New York Apartment."

A video accompanied the article, displaying a chaotic scene outside an apartment building. Police cars and ambulances were stationed, their presence painting a grim tableau. The flashing lights and the urgency of the situation were unmistakable. As Julian and Sebastian watched, a growing sense of unease settled in their hearts.

Sebastian, always vigilant, overheard the unfolding discovery and couldn't help but add, "Isn't that Mr. Mitchell's apartment, Julian?"

Julian's face tightened as he confirmed Sebastian's observation with a grim nod. The video's focus zoomed in on a tragic tableau: paramedics solemnly wheeling out a body draped in a black body bag, carefully loading it into an awaiting ambulance. The image was jarring, a stark reminder of life's fragility.

A woman reporter, her voice trembling with the gravity of the situation, narrated the unfolding events. She spoke with the solemnity befitting such a tragedy, "Earlier this evening, police responded to a 911 distress call from a concerned neighbor who reported hearing a gunshot. When they arrived at the scene, they discovered a deceased individual inside one of the apartment units. At this time, details remain scant. We will continue to update our viewers as more information becomes available."

The revelation sent a wave of dread through Julian. The uncertainty surrounding the situation was unnerving, and a sinking feeling gripped his heart as he considered the implications of this chilling news. It was clear that something terrible had happened, and their world had been upended once again.

***

A few hours ago…

Camille's eyes fluttered open to a disorienting darkness. As her groggy senses gradually sharpened, panic surged through her. She attempted to move, but her body felt heavy, and she realized her hands were tightly bound to the arms of a chair. A cloth was wedged into her mouth, effectively gagging her and making it impossible to scream.

The room was devoid of light, leaving Camille in a state of near-blindness. Only the faintest sliver of light crept in from an unknown source, offering a mere glimmer of hope. It was hard to tell whether it was day or night.

Camille's heart raced, thudding like a bass drum in her chest. Every breath seemed laborious, and she strained to see any details in the room. The feeling of vulnerability was suffocating, intensified by the eerie silence that enveloped her.

She struggled against her restraints, her heart pounding loudly in her chest. With each frantic tug, the knots on her wrists seemed to tighten, the ropes cutting into her skin.

Desperation overtook her, and she started to squirm in the chair, attempting to free herself. The feeling of helplessness washed over her, and despite everything, she wondered who had orchestrated her capture and what sinister plans lay ahead.

Camille's mind raced as she fought against her bindings. In the oppressive darkness, the unknown threats that surrounded her became all too real, and she was left with a chilling realization — she was trapped and at the mercy of an unknown entity.

Her desperate efforts to free herself from the tightly bound chair continued as minutes passed like hours in the darkness. With each strained tug and twist, the knots on her wrists seemed to resist her every move, and a growing sense of frustration gnawed at her. But, surprisingly, she managed to remove the cloth from her mouth.

She coughed audibly and yelled, "Can anyone hear me? Please help me."

Her mind raced, determined to find a way out of this perilous situation, to uncover the identity of those who had orchestrated her abduction. The room remained shrouded in shadows, the silence broken only by her attempts to scream into the void, "Help! Can anyone hear me?"

Then, suddenly, the door creaked open, revealing a sliver of light that cast a silhouette across the room. Camille's heart skipped a beat as the silhouette of a man walked inside. His voice, filled with chilling confidence, echoed through the dimly lit space.

"Who the fuck are you?," she yelled, "Let me go, you asshole."

The man's voice remained eerily composed as he spoke, "I'm the one asking the questions here, Camille. You're not in any position to make demands. The game is just starting." He moved closer, casting a foreboding shadow that hung over her. "And I promise you, this will be a ride you won't forget."

Camille's eyes widened, a blend of fear and confusion clouding her thoughts. The man seemed to possess knowledge, something she hadn't fully grasped herself. She fought against her restraints, her gaze locked on the mysterious figure before her, her determination to escape and uncover the truth burning fiercely.

As the man stepped further into the light, Camille's eyes met his, and her heart sank. It was Lucas, but something had changed. His eyes held an unsettling, maniacal glint, a stark departure from the Lucas she had known. It was as though he had transformed into someone entirely different.

"Well...well...well... I've been searching all over for you, Eva," Lucas declared in an oddly high-pitched voice, sounding nothing like his usual self.

"Lucas," she began, her voice quivering as she confronted the person she once recognized. "This is not possible. I thought you were dead."

He chuckled as he retreated into the shadows, "Dead? Lucas is very much alive, you know."

"How?" she asked, her voice tinged with disbelief. "We received a call from the hospital."

"Oh, you got a call from the hospital," he taunted in a mocking, whiny tone. "And you believed I was dead? Well, sorry to disappoint you, but it was me who made that call."

"Lucas, please," she began hesitantly, her voice trembling as she confronted the person she thought she knew. "What's happened to you? This isn't you."

In response, Lucas – or whatever being now controlled him – fixed his gaze on her with a sinister grin. "Oh, but it is you, or should I say Eva?"

Camille's heart raced as recognition set in. She had hidden her true identity, but this version of Lucas, who now called himself Miles, had seen right through her facade.

Miles continued to circle the room, never once breaking his predatory focus on her. "You thought you could escape, that you could start a new life as Camille. But I found you. I always find you."

Eva's mind raced as she tried to comprehend the situation. Lucas had transformed into something entirely different, someone with a sinister and vengeful alter ego, Miles. She knew she had to proceed cautiously to survive and untangle the madness that surrounded them.

In the dimly lit room, Eva, now fully aware of the sinister transformation that had consumed Lucas, or Miles, locked eyes with the person who had once been her lover. Her heart pounded in her chest, and she understood the gravity of the situation.

"Why, Eva?" Miles hissed, his voice dripping with menace. "Why did you leave Lucas? What did you think would happen?"

Eva met his gaze, a mixture of fear and determination in her eyes. "I left because of you, Miles. Lucas, or whatever you've become, you turned into someone unrecognizable. A dangerous, unpredictable stranger. I had to protect myself."

The tension in the room thickened, and the weight of their shared history hung in the air. Miles's sinister transformation had set the stage for a chilling confrontation, and Eva knew that she needed to navigate this treacherous path with care and precision.

Miles paced restlessly, the room closing in on them with each step. "You thought you could just run away, assume a new identity as Camille, and I wouldn't track you down?"

Eva's voice quivered, but she held his gaze firmly. "I had no choice. I had to find a way to break free, to escape the darkness that consumed you."

The atmosphere in the room was thick with tension as they confronted each other, the weight of their shared truth hanging heavily in the air. The sinister alter ego of the man she had once loved had found her, and now, Eva's only hope was to navigate the treacherous waters of his mind to uncover the secrets that bound them in this twisted dance of fate.

Miles, standing right in front of her, fired another question, his voice laced with accusation. "So, why the hell did you lure Lucas to Paris?"

Eva's response was grim and to the point. "Because I'm in deep trouble."

Miles chuckled. "What a load of crap. You're nothing but trouble. Admit it—you missed Lucas, didn't you?"

Eva, trapped in this perilous confrontation with Miles, the dark and vengeful persona, knew that her survival hinged on resurrecting the man she once loved, Lucas. Her mind raced to find a way to rekindle the buried memories and forgotten moments that could bring back the person he used to be. The room seemed to close in further, their fates intertwined in a deadly dance, where the past and present collided in a high-stakes battle of wits and emotions.

Eva, her voice quivering but filled with determination, implored, "Miles, please, you have to remember." Her gaze locked onto his, searching for a flicker of recognition. "Think back to that night when we were stargazing at the planetarium. It was pure magic, a time when it was just Lucas and Eva, connected in such a beautiful way."

Miles struggled, his face contorted by the internal conflict of his two personas. The memories of that night at the planetarium hovered on the fringes of his consciousness, like a dream trying to break free.

Eva, desperation in her voice, continued, "And what about that little hidden bookstore we stumbled upon? You read me your favorite poem, pouring out your dreams and aspirations for the future."

Miles winced as those forgotten moments crept into his thoughts. The shadow of his alter ego began to waver, and the essence of Lucas emerged, if only for a fleeting moment.

In Miles's eyes, Eva detected a glimmer of recognition. "Lucas," she urged, "I know you're still in there. You have to fight against this chaos. Remember who you used to be."

Miles grappled with the two opposing forces raging within him, and the battle for control played out in the shifting expressions on his face. As the memories of their love and shared moments rekindled, the sinister facade of Miles started to crumble, revealing the Lucas Eva had desperately sought.

The room around them seemed to hold its breath, the very air heavy with the tension of this internal struggle. Eva clung to hope as she watched her plea start to break through the darkness, inch by inch.

Eva's heart ached with hope as she continued to speak, her voice acting as a lifeline thrown out to Lucas, who was deeply entrenched in the torment of his own mind. She was unwavering in her determination to reach the man she loved, no matter the cost.

Miles, still under the influence of his sinister alter ego, paced relentlessly, mirroring the chaos that raged within his mind. His movements were erratic, as if he were battling the voice of reason and sanity that Eva was striving to rekindle.

Eva's words seemed to agitate him further, and his actions grew more erratic, almost as if he had become unhinged. He snapped, his emotions spiraling into violence, and a chilling moment unfolded as he produced a gun, menacingly pointing it at Eva's face.

"Bitch! Shut the fuck up!" he snarled, his voice dripping with venom as he struggled to suppress the return of Lucas, the man he used to be. The room hung heavy with tension, teetering on the precipice of disaster, where one wrong move could tip the scales in a terrifying direction. Eva found herself trapped in a harrowing standoff, her life balancing on a knife's edge.

Eva, her voice a mix of sadness and sincerity, implored Miles to listen, to understand the reasons behind her choices, the love that had driven her actions, and the fear that had gripped her heart.

"Miles, I loved Lucas more than words can express," Eva began, her eyes locked onto his as she pleaded for comprehension. "But there were moments when he... when you hurt me. It wasn't you, Lucas. It was something else that took control, something I couldn't bear. I had to run to protect myself."

As she spoke, Eva's words carried the heavy burden of regret and unspoken pain. Memories of those difficult moments, when Lucas had become unrecognizable, washed over her, and she shared them with Miles, the embodiment of that darkness. The room, shrouded in tension and fear, bore witness to a desperate struggle for understanding and reconciliation.

Eva's voice trembled with emotion as she pleaded, "Miles, you have to find a way to tell Lucas that I'm so sorry. Leaving him was the hardest thing I've ever done, but I couldn't stay and watch him suffer. I had to protect myself, but I never stopped loving him."

In that charged moment, Eva wasn't just trying to convey her feelings to Lucas through Miles; she also yearned to bring some closure to her own painful past. She desperately sought forgiveness, hoping that a fragment of the man she had once adored still lingered within the tortured soul of Miles.

Miles, the dark presence that had consumed Lucas, blinked in disbelief. His grip on the gun loosened, and he gazed at Eva, someone he thought was forever lost.

"Eva? Is that you?" Lucas's voice quivered, torn between confusion and hope. Slowly, he lowered the gun, taking cautious yet eager steps towards her.

Eva, still wary but unable to conceal the tears welling up in her eyes, nodded. "Lucas, yes, it's me," she confirmed, her voice quivering with emotion.

As Lucas let the gun slip from his grasp, he rushed to her side, his trembling hands gently cupping her face. Eva initially flinched, the fear still clinging to her, but then allowed him to hold her. Their eyes met, and the intensity of the moment hung in the air.

"Oh, Eva, I've been searching for you," Lucas admitted, his voice a mix of relief and longing. "Where have you been all this time?"

Eva, her voice tender and reassuring, replied, "I've

been here all along, Lucas." Her words carried the weight of time lost and the hope of rekindled connection, as the two once-separated souls finally found each other again in the middle of their tangled past.

His expression softened as he gazed into her eyes. "I'm so happy you came back. I've been lost without you."

Eva couldn't help but feel moved by Lucas's raw vulnerability. She reached out, gently placing her hand on his arm, offering a comforting touch. "Lucas, it's okay. I'm here now. Just untie me, alright?" Her hope was that by helping him regain control and releasing her, they could begin the journey of mending the shattered fragments of their shared past.

Lucas carefully worked to untangle the ropes binding Eva to the chair, his fingers trembling with a mixture of concern and haste. As the last of the knots fell away, Eva quickly moved to free herself. Her heart raced with fear as she scrambled to her feet, just out of Lucas's reach.

Lucas, taken aback by her reaction, reached out a hand towards her. "Eva, what are you doing?"

Eva, her emotions in turmoil, managed to snatch the gun that had fallen to the floor during her hurried escape. Her hands trembled as she held the weapon, and with unsteady determination, she aimed it directly at Lucas.

Her voice quivered as she spoke, "I don't know you anymore, Lucas. I can't take any chances." The Eva he had loved and known had been tested and tormented, and she couldn't be certain if this was still the man she had once cared for.

Lucas, in a desperate plea, tapped his wristwatch and called out, "Millie? I could use some help here, please." His eyes darted toward the unseen presence he addressed, a perplexed expression on his face.

In the middle of the tension, the room bore witness to the clash of emotions and the tangled web of their complex history. Eva stood armed and wary, while Lucas, overwhelmed by a mixture of confusion and panic, reached out to the invisible entity that held the answers to their predicament.

Eva's eyes darted around the room, uncertainty in her gaze. "Who are you talking to?"

Lucas pointed to the Bluetooth device nestled in his ears. "Our AI assistant, Millie, remember? We created her together."

Eva's disbelief was evident as she shook her head, a touch of sadness in her voice. "Lucas, we never got to finish that project. Don't you remember?"

Lucas appeared shaken, confusion and uncertainty etching across his features. "What are you saying? I talk to Millie all the time. Look at the Bluetooth device." He reached up to take out the earpiece, but his fingers grasped empty air. His gaze darted around the room in bewilderment.

Eva's voice carried a hint of sorrow as she explained, "Lucas, you're not well. You're fucking insane. This is why I had to leave."

The room seemed to close in on Lucas as he grappled with the sudden change in Eva's demeanor. His world was already in turmoil, and the surreal weight of their twisted reality bore down on him, threatening to shatter his sanity. Hallucinations danced before his eyes, a chilling and eerie spectacle.

"No," he yelled, gripping his head with both hands. "This can't be real." His voice quivered with desperation as he struggled to hold onto his crumbling sense of reality.

In the middle of the chaos in his mind, Lucas heard a sinister whisper. It was Millie, his AI assistant, urging him to do the unthinkable. "You know what you have to do, Lucas. You have to kill Eva. It's the only way."

His grip on reality was slipping, and the sense of self was slipping away with it. It was no longer Lucas who gazed at Eva, but the sinister alter ego, Miles.

As he battled his inner demons, Eva tried to reason with him, her voice tinged with concern. "Lucas, please, you don't have to do this. We can find help. Just talk to me."

Lucas, or rather Miles, seemed beyond reason. His eyes reflected madness, and he grinned with that deranged, unsettling smile. He lunged towards her with menacing intent. Filled with dread and desperation, Eva closed her eyes, trembling as she pulled the trigger. Her heart weighed heavy with sorrow for the man Lucas once was.

The deafening gunshot reverberated through the room. As the echoes subsided, Eva opened her eyes to a chilling sight. Lucas lay on the floor, shock and agony etched onto his face, a bullet wound seeping blood from his chest. She approached him, her demeanor devoid of the love and concern that had once bound them. Standing over him, she watched as he struggled to draw breath.

With a cold, mocking tone, Eva said, "Oh, poor baby Lucas. In the end, you weren't too smart for me, were you?"

Lucas, or what was left of him, attempted to speak, but his words were choked by the blood that welled up in his throat. He gazed up at Eva, his life slipping away with every fading heartbeat. All he could do was listen as Eva, her voice taking on an eerie, childlike quality, whispered, "Night, night, Lukie."

With those haunting words, Eva became the last image etched into Lucas's fading consciousness as he slipped into the darkness. The room around them seemed to close in, shrouded in an eerie silence, as the darkness swallowed the chilling tableau.

CHAPTER 13: TRUTH OR DARE

At last, Julian ended up in a chilly, poorly lit interrogation room. It felt like he was stuck in a never-ending nightmare, and the weight of the whole situation pressed down on him, making it even harder to breathe. The room's walls were painted a dull, lifeless shade of gray, and the sole source of light came from a dim overhead bulb, casting eerie shadows on the walls. The worn-out table in front of him had seen better days, with countless scratches and stains marring its surface.

Julian shivered, not just from the room's temperature but from the growing anxiety gnawing at his stomach. He couldn't shake the feeling that he was in some kind of movie scene. The cold metal chair he sat on was far from comfortable, and it added to the unsettling ambiance.

Detective Anderson, a stern and straightforward officer at the New York Police Department, took a seat across from Julian. He could see the unease and fear in Julian's eyes. The detective didn't waste any time and delivered the shocking news about Lucas. Julian's voice quivered as he tried to make sense of it all, his disbelief evident. "Lucas? Are you sure it's Lucas? What happened?"

The detective's expression remained somber as he nodded. "I'm afraid it is, Mr. Laurent. We found Lucas dead in his apartment."

Julian's world seemed to spin. His mind raced, struggling to grasp the sudden loss of his friend. Questions flooded his thoughts, and he blurted out, "What about Camille? Did you find her? Is she safe?"

Detective Anderson's response was another jolt to Julian's already shaken world. "She's not Camille, Mr. Laurent. There never was a Camille. Her name is Eva Smith."

The revelation left Julian stunned, his mind grappling with the layers of deception and the mysteries that had enshrouded their lives.

Julian leaned forward, his eyes locked onto Detective Anderson, as he asked, "Tell me everything. I need to know the whole story."

He needed to understand more, to uncover the truth behind this bewildering turn of events. The dimly lit room felt like a confined space, suffocating with the weight of the unexpected truths that had come to light.

In the small interrogation room, Julian's mind raced as he grappled with the shocking revelation. He turned to Detective Anderson, his voice oozing disbelief, "So, you're saying Camille, I mean, Eva, has been right here with us all along?"

The detective's face remained stern as he reclined in his chair. "That's what it appears to be, Mr. Laurent. But can you enlighten me? How do you think it's possible?"

Julian let out a sardonic chuckle. "You really think I had something to do with this? That I played a part in whatever happened to Lucas?"

Detective Anderson leaned in, his gaze intense. "Well, you were there when Lucas got attacked, right?"

Julian hesitated, pondering the detective's question. Yes, he had been there, but he hadn't actually witnessed the stabbing itself. The whole night was becoming a foggy puzzle, and he was struggling to piece it all together.

"Fine," the detective pressed on, "consider this, Mr. Laurent." He set a laptop on the table and played a video clip. It was a security camera recording from the lobby of a building. The footage showed a disheveled Camille, or rather, Eva, exiting the building.

Julian's eyes widened as he watched the video. He could hardly believe what he was seeing. "When was this recorded?" he asked, his voice tinged with incredulity.

Detective Anderson closed the laptop with a grave expression. "Just a few minutes after Lucas Mitchell was declared dead."

The weight of what Julian had just witnessed sent a chill down his spine. The boundaries between truth and deceit had blurred to the point where he couldn't be sure whom to trust or what to believe anymore. The sterile room seemed to close in around them, the mystery deepening with each passing moment, and Julian felt a growing unease as he struggled to make sense of it all.

Julian's mind whirled, grappling with the detective's words. "So, how did Lucas end up in his apartment? I got a call from the hospital saying that Lucas was already dead," he questioned, his voice a blend of confusion and disbelief.

Detective Anderson leaned back in his chair, weariness in his eyes. "Well, Mr. Laurent, it's quite a bizarre situation. After his surgery, Lucas somehow left the hospital on his own. Hours later, he turned up dead in his apartment, the victim of a gunshot."

Julian audibly gasped. "He was shot?"

Detective Anderson's patience seemed to wear thin, his tone firm. "Yes, he was shot."

A knot of dread tightened in Julian's chest as he hesitated to voice the question he dreaded. "Was it Camille? Or maybe Eva?"

The detective sighed, his face reflecting the complexity of the case. "We're still piecing it all together, but for now, we have what we need from you. You're free to go. If we require more information, we'll be in touch."

Julian rose from his seat, a swirling mix of emotions in his mind. The events of the past few hours had unfolded into a tangle of mysteries and horrors, leaving him with more questions than answers. As he exited the interrogation room, an unsettling feeling clung to him, a sense that something far more complex and sinister lurked beneath the surface of this perplexing case.

In the dimly lit hallway, he glanced at his phone, contemplating who to call next. The weight of uncertainty and suspicion hung heavy in the air as he ventured back into the outside world, determined to unravel the mystery that had become his life.

***

Eva, known by one of her many aliases, had just pulled off a slick escape from the chaotic streets of

New York City. With the city's never-ending hustle and bustle as her backdrop, she moved like a true ninja, weaving through the urban labyrinth with grace, evading anyone who might have been tailing her.

As she made her way through the intricate subway system, her heart raced with a mix of excitement and fear. The clatter of the trains and the swarm of commuters provided her with the perfect cover, allowing her to seamlessly blend into the city's urban tapestry. Her steps were precise, each one meticulously calculated, and her eyes remained sharp, scanning her surroundings for any potential threats.

Despite the tension in the air, Eva couldn't help but flash a satisfied grin. She was thrilled by her flawless escape, amazed at how she had outsmarted anyone who might have been on her tail. She murmured to herself, "Eva, you've still got your touch."

The dimly lit subway tunnels stretched out in front of her, and without even thinking, she pondered her next move. A sense of intrigue sparkled in Eva's eyes; she had an unquenchable thirst for adventure, and this escape was merely the prologue. She wondered about the exciting escapades that lay on the horizon.

Continuing her journey through the complex

subway system, Eva's mind buzzed with curiosity. She couldn't resist asking herself, "What's the next big thing in store for me?" Her smile grew wider as she anticipated the multitude of possibilities that lay ahead.

Eva finally arrived at the airport, a place that represented her path to freedom. Stepping into the terminal, she was greeted by a whirlwind of activity. Travelers scurried about, and the continuous drone of overhead announcements filled the air. Eva did her best to maintain a low profile, concealing her identity under an elegant hat and oversized sunglasses, ensuring she blended seamlessly into the crowd.

Approaching the ticketing counter, a friendly agent welcomed her with a warm smile. "Welcome to the airport. How can I assist you today?"

Eva responded, her voice tinged with anticipation, "I need a ticket, a one-way ticket."

The ticketing agent studied her for a moment and then offered, "I have a business class ticket available for a flight to Cuba. Will that work for you?"

Eva's face lit up with a smile, her heart overflowing with happiness. "That's perfect," she said, relieved that her journey to freedom was about to kick off.

For as long as she could remember, she'd yearned

for this moment, the opportunity to break free from the relentless troubles that had dogged her life for years. Clutching her sleek business class ticket, she found herself swept up in a surge of excitement as she navigated the frenetic terminal.

The airport served as a mesmerizing crossroads for a diverse variety of humanity. Families shared teary-eyed goodbyes, adventurous backpackers eagerly set off on their journeys, and determined business folk dashed towards their gates with unwavering purpose. The rich aroma of freshly brewed coffee wafted through the air, accompanying the distant harmonious notes of a jazz band performing in a nearby café.

Eva's heart lightened considerably as she sailed through the security checkpoint without a hitch. Her years of practice had honed her self-control, and it was now paying dividends. She understood all too well that a single misstep could jeopardize her escape plan, so she remained vigilant.

Surrendering her passport to the immigration officer, she watched as he meticulously scrutinized it, his stern visage causing a flutter of anxiety. Mustering a casual smile, she braced herself.

"Where are you headed today?" the officer inquired, his tone dispassionate.

Eva's heart raced as she replied, "I'm off to visit some friends in Cuba."

The officer nodded, his gaze still fixed on her passport. "How long do you plan to stay there?"

Eva had prepared for this question. "Just a few weeks, perhaps a month. I've been missing them terribly."

At last, the officer tore his eyes away from the passport and met Eva's gaze. "Enjoy your trip, ma'am."

Eva expressed her gratitude and continued on her way, her guard remaining firmly in place until she had put considerable distance between herself and the checkpoint. Only then did she permit herself a relieved sigh, taking solace in the bustling ambience of the airport, which offered a veil of cover for her escape.

Eva strolled through the bustling airport terminal, taking in the vibrant array of shops and eateries that surrounded her. The duty-free store beckoned with its display of high-end perfumes, decadent chocolates, and luxurious goods, teasing her with the promise of a more opulent life. She couldn't resist the allure and paused at a nearby bookstore, her fingers grazing the titles of novels, each one sparking anticipation for the adventures and stories she'd soon embrace.

The evening sun bathed the terminal in a golden

hue, casting inviting rays that warmed her spirit. Eva's heart felt lighter than ever, embracing the freedom that lay ahead. Her thoughts drifted to an inevitable question: "What will my new life in Cuba hold? What exciting adventures await me?" Eva was en route to a brighter future, leaving behind the shadows of her past.

Eva eventually found a quiet nook near a massive window overlooking the bustling tarmac. She gazed out at the panorama, her mind racing with dreams of the new life awaiting her. The radiant sunlight poured in, casting a gentle, welcoming glow over the entire terminal. Passengers hurried by, their animated conversations blending with the soft hum of the airport's energy.

A cheerful couple seated nearby captured her attention. They engaged in an animated discussion about their upcoming vacation plans. Watching them, Eva felt a twinge of longing for the kind of freedom they seemed to be reveling in. Determined to ease her anxiety and make herself feel more at ease, she decided to strike up a conversation.

With a friendly smile, Eva turned to the couple and said, "I overheard your excitement about your trip—it sounds incredible! Where are you guys headed?"

The couple beamed, delighted to share their plans. "We're off to Hawaii! It's the vacation of our dreams," the woman replied.

Eva's eyes sparkled with genuine interest. "That's fantastic! I've always dreamt of visiting Hawaii. What's on your must-see list while you're there?"

As they chatted about Hawaii's breathtaking beaches, vibrant culture, and delectable cuisine, Eva felt a growing sense of connection with the couple. The worries that had plagued her began to dissolve into the background. The bustling airport provided a dynamic backdrop to her newfound friends, who graciously shared their enthusiasm and joy, making her feel more at home in that moment.

Eva's heart swelled with gratitude as she soaked in the ordinary moments, a brief respite in the middle of her tumultuous escape. The journey ahead was far from over, but these simple connections and the friendly banter she enjoyed were the little triumphs that fueled her determination.

She glanced at her watch, realizing that her boarding time was approaching. Eva weaved her way through the airport's hustle and bustle, her heart racing as she finally spotted her gate. Amid the bustling travelers, she felt a surge of anticipation as she stepped onto the aircraft. Her disguise remained intact, allowing her to blend seamlessly with the other passengers. The plane's engines roared to life, and with each passing second, Eva moved closer to her destination, leaving behind the city that had imprisoned her for too long.

In the exclusive comfort of the business class section, Eva savored the lavish treatment bestowed upon her by the attentive flight attendants. A warm, friendly smile graced her lips as one of them handed her a glistening flute of champagne, its bubbles frolicking in the crystal-clear glass. She took a sip, and the effervescent liquid tickled her taste buds, instantly brightening her mood.

With a contented sigh, she settled into her plush seat, enveloped by opulence. The cabin exuded a sophisticated ambiance, bathed in soft, inviting lighting that enhanced the feeling of relaxation. Leaning back, Eva allowed herself to drift into thought, her mind wandering aimlessly, unburdened by the worries that had plagued her in the city.

The aircraft's engines hummed, and with each passing mile, Eva moved further away from her past, her destination drawing nearer with every moment.

***

Eva had her trusty laptop right in front of her, and with a cheeky smile, she flipped the screen open. The soft glow it cast on her face gave her that cozy, late-night vibe. Like a whisper from fate, the thought surfaced in her mind—what lay ahead? The upcoming journey was on her mind, and it had her heart racing with anticipation.

Leaning back in her seat, Eva's gaze shifted towards the window of the airplane. The world outside was dark, punctuated only by a scattering of lights below, like stars on Earth. She couldn't resist striking up a conversation with the friendly flight attendant. Her charm just flowed naturally, as if she had a pocketful of charisma.

"So, how often do you get to hop around all these amazing places?" Eva was curious, and she couldn't hide it. The idea of globetrotting to different destinations seemed like a dream come true.

The flight attendant, equally interested in her passenger, responded with a warm smile. "Oh, quite often, ma'am. It's one of the perks of the job, seeing the world." She leaned in a bit, eager to share her own travel tales.

Eva's eyes sparkled with enthusiasm, and she gave an appreciative nod. "I can only imagine the incredible adventures you've had," she replied, hinting at her own intriguing life. Their conversation seamlessly blended with the soothing hum of the plane's engines and the calming ambiance of the cabin.

The flight attendant, while still keeping a watchful eye on her other duties, inquired, "Is this your first time in Cuba?"

Eva's face lit up, and she responded with a hint of excitement, thanks in part to the champagne she'd enjoyed. "Yes, it is! In fact, I was hoping you might have some great recommendations for me."

As the airplane soared through the night sky, Eva and the flight attendant chatted away, their voices dancing with the soft buzz of the cabin. The dimmed cabin lights created a cozy atmosphere, making it feel like a late-night chat with a friend. Eva had already enjoyed a glass or two of champagne, and it had put her in a cheerful, adventurous mood.

The flight attendant leaned in a bit closer, her eyes alight with the enthusiasm of sharing her travel insights. "Cuba is a fantastic place to explore. I'd recommend starting with Havana; it's like stepping back in time with its old-world charm and vibrant culture. The music, the architecture, and the people are incredible. And don't forget to try the Cuban food; the flavors are amazing."

Eva nodded eagerly, her curiosity piqued. "Sounds amazing! What else should I check out?"

With a warm smile, the flight attendant continued, "If you're a beach lover, Varadero is a must-visit. The beaches there are stunning, with clear blue waters and white sandy shores. It's perfect for some relaxation and water activities. And for history buffs, don't miss Trinidad; it's a UNESCO World Heritage site with beautifully preserved colonial architecture."

Eva listened attentively, mentally making a list of all the places she wanted to explore. "That all sounds incredible. I can't wait to dive into the Cuban culture."

The flight attendant was instantly charmed by Eva's enthusiasm. "You're in for a treat, ma'am. Cuba is a treasure trove of experiences. Just remember to embrace the laid-back island vibe, and you'll have a wonderful time."

As the flight attendant left, Eva shifted her focus back to her laptop. The plane's cabin was dimly lit, making it her makeshift work zone. Her fingers raced across the keyboard, a mischievous grin playing on her lips, hinting at the web of secrets and plots she kept close. The distant sound of clinking glasses and quiet conversations provided a background hum, like a world she'd momentarily escaped.

Eva's laptop sprang to life, revealing a chilling logo that sent shivers down her spine—a coiled serpent with gleaming scales, radiating an air of foreboding. She couldn't resist pausing for a moment to savor her achievements. Her journey had been a rollercoaster of dangerous twists and turns, a path lined with trickery, peril, and the pure thrill of outsmarting those who had underestimated her.

Her eyes remained locked on the sinister serpent symbol on the screen, satisfaction and curiosity mingling in her gaze. She reminisced about the hurdles she'd overcome, the bold risks she'd taken, and the allies she'd gathered along the way. With a quiet sense of pride, she pondered the winding road she'd traveled and the intriguing one yet to come.

Eva reclined in her seat, her heart pounding with excitement. The airplane's cabin had further dimmed its lights, casting a cozy glow on the rows of seats. The engines droned softly, creating a soothing background noise in the middle of her inner whirlwind.

Across from her, a fellow passenger was engrossed in a captivating novel, their eyes fixed on the pages, and another was sipping a glass of red wine, savoring each sip as they looked out of the window.

The scent of warm inflight meals wafted through the air, hinting at the culinary delights to come. It was like a snapshot of life at 30,000 feet, a reminder that the sky was filled with people embarking on their own unique journeys.

Lost in thought, Eva found her mind overflowing with ambitious ideas. She leaned back, gazing out of the window at the vast expanse of the night sky. With a confident smirk, she muttered to herself, "Seriously, could anyone doubt my ability to pull this off? My plan, it's practically a masterpiece, don't you think?" Her words were filled with a sense of triumph as she reveled in her own success, her voice brimming with satisfaction.

***

Eva was stuck in her airplane seat, feeling like time was crawling by. The plane's engines were making a constant, low noise in the background. She couldn't fall asleep, and as the hours passed, her impatience just kept growing. Eva glanced around the cabin, taking in the busy scene. People were chatting softly and their voices mixed with the continuous drone of the engines.

The passengers on the plane were all in their own little bubbles. Some were watching the latest movies on their personal screens, while others were deep into their books or working on their laptops. Eva sank even deeper into her comfortable seat, appreciating the soft velvety fabric under her fingers and the gentle vibrations running through the plane. It was a far cry from the tense and secretive world she had left behind.

The dim cabin lights created a cozy atmosphere, and the overhead compartments were filled with bags and suitcases. The whole place was a sea of people, each with their own stories and destinations. Eva's eyes wandered, observing the flight attendants gracefully moving through the aisles, offering snacks and drinks with warm smiles. The scent of reheated airplane food wafted through the air, a strange mix of pasta and coffee.

Outside the small window, the sky was painted in shades of dusk, with the sun setting in the distance. It cast a warm, orange glow on the wing, making it seem almost magical. Eva leaned her head against the window and gazed at the world below, a patchwork of fields, towns, and highways that looked like a miniature model. She was far from home now, on a journey to who knew where, but the adventure was just beginning.

Eva's mind wandered to the complex web of espionage and deception she had willingly plunged herself into. The shadowy figure on her digital display served as an ominous reminder of the treacherous path she had chosen. She was determined to navigate it with the utmost precision and caution.

As Eva reflected on her recent actions, she found herself in an emotional whirlwind, torn between disbelief and a strange sense of triumph. Her thoughts meandered to a specific memory from the past, a moment when Lucas had introduced her to his manager at the cybersecurity firm.

In that recollection, Lucas had exuded an air of professionalism, his voice steady as he introduced her. "Meet Camille," he had said, "an independent contractor I've brought in to assist us." The authority in his tone was undeniable as he added, "Grant her the access she needs, and together, we'll solve this."

Eva found herself pondering the ironic twist of fate that had led her to this moment. She had executed a masterful plan, secured the invaluable cybersecurity data while subtly orchestrated the stage for Lucas's eventual downfall. Her initial intent had never involved taking his life, but circumstances had relentlessly pushed her to a point where she felt she had little choice. She knew Lucas all too well, with his unyielding drive and unwavering determination. She understood that he would stop at nothing to unveil her secrets.

In the dimly lit airplane cabin, Eva reveled in the success of her sinister plan. A part of her relished her own cleverness as she posed questions to herself, her voice soft and filled with intrigue. "Did I actually pull this off? Fuck! I can't believe I managed to outsmart him," she mused, her mind racing with the satisfaction of her accomplishments.

As she sat there, the eerie glow from her laptop screen cast eerie shadows that danced around her, creating a surreal atmosphere. It was a constant reminder of the treacherous game she'd willingly dived into, a high-stakes affair that had far surpassed her initial expectations. The tension in the air was palpable as she contemplated her next move, fully aware of the steep price she'd paid for her triumph.

Eva's eyes darted around the cabin, taking in the subdued lighting and the hushed murmurs of her fellow passengers. Some were engrossed in their books or gadgets, oblivious to the drama unfolding just a few feet away. She adjusted her seat, her fingers tapping nervously on the armrest as she mentally reviewed her carefully constructed trap.

Outside the airplane window, a world bathed in the warm hues of a setting sun unfurled. The distant landscape, with its patchwork of fields and meandering rivers, seemed so far removed from the perilous game she was playing. It was a stark contrast to the cold, calculating world she'd come to inhabit.

The hum of the engines and the gentle rocking of the plane served as a backdrop to her thoughts. Her mind kept circling back to the people around her, strangers who knew nothing of the secrets and subterfuge that had led her to this moment. Each seat held its own story, its own silent narrative, and she found herself lost in the anonymity of the crowd.

Her heart raced as she replayed the intricate web of schemes she'd woven, trying to anticipate any unforeseen consequences. The danger of it all loomed over her, a constant companion on this turbulent journey. Eva knew that there was no turning back now, and she was determined to see her plan through to its chilling conclusion.

With a deep breath, she turned her attention back to her laptop screen, her fingers poised over the keyboard. The final act of her calculated move awaited, and she was ready to execute it with precision. In this confined space, where shadows danced and secrets lingered, Eva was the puppeteer of her own suspenseful narrative, ready to unveil the shocking climax of her dangerous game.

Eva's mind drifted back to that pivotal moment when she'd hatched and pulled off the bold hack into Lucas's ultra-secure systems. Crafting a message so tantalizing, it managed to lure even a cautious guy like Lucas. "The Obsidian Muse awaits your arrival," she'd written, her words acting like a digital siren in the vast sea of the internet.

The airplane's insides, bathed in a soothing, soft glow, stood in stark contrast to the calculated risks and intrigue that had defined Eva's journey thus far. Her fellow passengers remained blissfully unaware of the mysterious world she'd dived into, each absorbed in their own personal pursuits. The constant drone of the engines, coupled with the occasional rustling of in-flight magazines, formed an oddly tranquil backdrop to her covert mission.

As Eva peered out of the airplane window, her thoughts swirled like a hurricane inside her mind. The gentle, steady hum of the engines provided a comforting soundtrack to her deep contemplation. The past had a grip on her, dragging her thoughts back to the choices that had shaped this moment—choices tangled in a dangerous game and a painting called the Obsidian Muse.

Eva's mind wandered back to the day she had gotten her hands on that painting. It was like her ultimate guilty pleasure, a mesmerizing dark beauty she couldn't resist. She had discovered the tipsy artist in the charming, winding streets of Paris. He was an old fellow with hands that had seen a lifetime of toil and a voice that sounded like sandpaper on wood.

Against her better judgment, she allowed her curiosity to take over, her gaze sharp with intent as she engaged him in conversation. She acted like she was genuinely fascinated by his art. Their chat flowed smoothly, as if they were reciting lines from a well-practiced play. The old man began to share the tale behind the Obsidian Muse, a story of love lost and the depths of despair, making the painting even more enchanting.

Eva leaned in, her voice dripping with feigned curiosity, "So, tell me more about this Obsidian Muse. What inspired you to create it? Is there a deeper meaning behind those dark, captivating strokes?" Her questions seemed to bring a glint of joy to the old artist's eyes.

The scene around them was a snapshot of picturesque Parisian charm. Cobblestone streets wound their way through quaint buildings adorned with colorful shutters and flower-filled window boxes. The scent of freshly baked croissants lingered in the air, and the distant sound of an accordion playing a romantic melody filled the atmosphere.

Eva persisted with her inquiries, "And how did you come up with the name, Obsidian Muse? It's so mysterious and intriguing. Did you have a specific muse in mind when you painted it?" Her words hung in the air, as the old man's eyes danced with nostalgia.

He continued to share his secrets, recounting how each brushstroke had been a labor of love and melancholy. The story unfolded with every word he spoke, adding layers of history and sentiment to the captivating artwork. Eva was irresistibly drawn into the narrative, her curiosity deepening with each detail she uncovered. After some persuasive words and a modest sum of ten pounds, he had reluctantly handed over the captivating artwork, his eyes mirroring a hint of regret.

Eventually, Eva had led him to the river under the cover of night, their voices hushed, the only sounds the soft ripples of the water. She had put on an act, guiding him closer to the edge. And then, with a swift, calculated push, she had sent him tumbling into the dark river. His death was to appear as an unfortunate accident, and Eva had made sure of that. As she watched him disappear into the water, a cold sensation of remorse had washed over her, though it was quickly buried beneath her ruthless determination.

Eva couldn't help but revel in her own cunning, her voice filled with self-satisfaction. "Did you really think you could outsmart me, asshole?" She murmured to herself as she reminisced about the thrill of her accomplishment. Eva's mind was still buzzing with the thrill of her recent hacking victory. She was on a flight, lost in her thoughts, with the cabin dimly lit, creating an atmosphere of subdued secrecy. She leaned back into the plush leather seat, reminiscing about her triumph in the comfort of her high-tech haven in the sky. The private jet was a luxurious cocoon, a testament to her exquisite tastes, furnished with a collection of rare artifacts from her global travels.

Among her treasures, the Obsidian Muse held a special place. It hung on the wall, its dark and mysterious presence accentuated by the interplay of shadows, casting a mysterious spell across the cabin. Eva's fingertips grazed the edge of the painting, and a wicked grin crept across her lips as she admired the masterpiece that had served as both her weapon and her victory.

Eva reveled in the success of her intricate plan.

She had executed a brilliant act of subterfuge at the prestigious auction house, ensuring the painting's placement there. With the masterpiece strategically positioned, setting a trap for Lucas had become almost effortless. She had taken on the persona of Camille, a fictitious twin sister, and skillfully lured him in with a masterful illusion. The memory of her cunning artistry brought a sense of satisfaction as she gazed out of the plane's window, soaring above the world, a step closer to achieving her mysterious goals.

In the middle of the intricate dance of her sinister scheme, a complication had surfaced. Julian Laurent, an unexpected and persistent presence, had somehow entangled himself into the unfolding story. He'd proven to be a thorn in her side, but Eva had quickly recognized that he was also malleable, a pawn she could manipulate at will.

Eva's thoughts meandered through the delicate balance of deception and manipulation at the heart of her twisted game. Her success had been intoxicating, but the unforeseen emergence of Julian had added an intriguing layer of complexity to her grand design.

The surroundings exuded an air of opulence and mystique. The walls of the lavishly decorated room boasted priceless works of art, and the soft glow of antique lamps enveloped everything in a warm, alluring ambiance. Eva, ever the master puppeteer, sat regally in a plush chair, her fingers idly caressing a crystal glass. Her gaze was fixed on Julian Laurent as he boldly acquired her painting at the gala.

The auction room in Paris held its breath, and the silence was as thick as velvet, broken only by the faint rustle of fabric and the soft murmur of hushed conversations. As she watched Julian's every move, Eva's thoughts roamed, contemplating her next steps. She reveled in the intricacies of her malevolent design, savoring the thrill of the game she was playing, where every move, every decision, was a piece in her intricate chessboard of deception and manipulation.

Meeting Julian had thrown an unexpected curveball into Eva's carefully crafted plan. At first, she'd aimed to take Julian down, going as far as dispatching a group of bikers to get the job done. But fate had other ideas. Somehow, Julian had eluded the grasp of the hired assailants, slipping through their fingers like a wily fox.

Eva found herself reminiscing about that fateful encounter as it unfolded in her memory. Julian, the unexpected hero, had delivered a bone-crushing roundhouse kick that left the two menacing bikers crumpled on the floor, their aura of threat instantly deflated. Julian, standing tall, with his chest heaving from the exertion, had locked eyes with Camille.

As the dust settled, Julian couldn't resist a touch of playful banter, a mischievous smirk playing on his lips. "Did you ever doubt my heroic abilities, Camille?" he'd asked, his tone laced with a hint of flirtation. "You know, not everyone can swoop in like this."

Eva found herself wondering how that twist of fate had triggered a chain of events she never saw coming. Her flight was a stark contrast to the intensity of her memories. She was seated comfortably in the aircraft, surrounded by the soft hum of the engines and the muted chatter of fellow passengers. The view outside the window was serene, with fluffy clouds adorning the expansive blue sky.

In her unwavering pursuit of her goals, Eva had also dispatched a team of men to infiltrate Lucas's apartment. She had banked on the element of surprise to ensure a successful attack. To her chagrin, both Julian and his butler turned out to be formidable martial artists, putting up a fierce defense that thwarted her initial designs.

However, in the middle of the chaos and the tumultuous events of that fateful night, Eva found herself relishing a pivotal moment. In the middle of the struggle, her blade had unerringly found its mark, killing Lucas. It was a swift, covert action, a twist of fate that sent her carefully crafted plan spiraling in a new direction.

Eva questioned the unfolding of her strategy, her tone carrying a hint of satisfaction. "Who would have thought, huh? Lucas injured and my plan taking a different course? Things just got more interesting." Her voice resonated with a sense of triumph, her eyes gleaming with the success of her daring move.

The scene around her was one of chaos and uncertainty, with the shadows of the night deepening the sense of intrigue. Eva's calculated scheme had taken an unexpected turn, and the world seemed to shift in response, her victory pushing her ever closer to her ultimate goal.

Despite her initial attempt to eliminate Lucas, he had miraculously clung to life, surviving Eva's assassination plot. Her carefully crafted plan had unraveled right before her eyes. In response, Eva sought the services of a professional hitman to finish the job, taking advantage of Lucas's hospitalization.

Eva basked in the success of her cunning strategy, savoring her triumph over the unexpected failure. As she had engineered every step with meticulous precision, she had even gone so far as to pretend to be asleep when the hired assassin entered Lucas's hospital room.

But, to her astonishment, her well-thought-out scheme took an unforeseen twist when Lucas, driven by determination and survival instincts, sprang into action. In a bold move to thwart the assassin's mission, he created a commotion that alerted the hospital staff, shattering Eva's sinister plans.

The room in the hospital, once a sanctuary for Lucas, had become a battleground. Eva's momentary sense of victory had given way to frustration, as Lucas refused to be a mere pawn in her dangerous game. The sterile hospital environment became a symbol of her struggle, where Eva's intricate plot had been temporarily foiled, leaving her to regroup and adapt to the unexpected turn of events.

The news of Lucas's supposed death had swept over Eva like a tidal wave of relief. She believed, for a brief moment, that her troubles had finally come to an end. Little did she suspect that the whirlwind of chaos and intrigue was far from finished.

Eva reveled in the success of her cunning plan, watching it unfold like an intricate puzzle. As the news of Lucas's demise circulated, a sly grin danced on her lips, and her eyes glittered with satisfaction. "They'll never see it coming," she thought, as her mind swirled with the possibilities.

The message, "I know what you are," had initially sent chills down Eva's spine. When it first appeared on her screen, she had attributed it to one of her adversaries, an enemy from her shadowy past. But the unsettling truth was far more sinister. It was the malevolent alter ego of Lucas, the ominous Miles, who had masterminded her abduction.

Eva found herself wondering about the twisted games Miles had in mind. Her mind raced with questions, and she couldn't resist asking herself out loud, "What was his endgame? What did he want from me now?" Her voice quivered with uncertainty as she found herself, once again, ensnared in the clutches of this deranged personality she had barely escaped from five years ago.

In the middle of this new, unsettling reality, Eva had found herself teetering on the edge of danger, her past colliding with her present in a menacing dance. The room she was trapped in felt suffocating, its dimly lit corners concealing secrets that she was now forced to confront.

Yet, In the heart of this harrowing ordeal, Eva's brilliance and cunning proved to be her most valuable allies. She reveled in her ability to manipulate Miles, tapping into his unrelenting love for her. In the middle of the chaos and impending danger, she marveled at the fact that Lucas's affection for her remained unwavering, even in the face of dire circumstances. The intricate web of emotions and relationships that had woven her life together continued to unwind in ways she could have never foreseen.

Eva's mind buzzed with satisfaction as she wondered aloud, "Did it really work? Can I truly manipulate their emotions like a symphony, turning their feelings into my own instruments?" Her own voice, tinged with a hint of wonder, echoed in the room as she contemplated the complexities of her scheme.

Surrounded by the intense atmosphere of the unfolding drama, she saw her plan coming to fruition, a masterstroke of manipulation and intrigue. With each passing moment, she grew more and more confident in her calculated actions, which were set to alter the course of her entangled life forever.

Hidden behind her array of aliases and personas, Eva had expertly cloaked her true identity as the mysterious Shadow Serpent Syndicate. Within Lucas's advanced security systems, she reveled in the prowess that allowed her to infiltrate virtually any security system worldwide. Her digital wizardry made her a phantom in the world of ones and zeros, leaving no digital trail to trace her back to her real self.

The urge to voice her thoughts was undeniable, and so she did, victory lacing every word. "Did anyone see it coming, I wonder? They had no clue who I really was, did they?" Her words, spoken softly, were met with the silence of the digital world.

Eva had woven a super sneaky web of secrecy around everything she did, making it almost impossible for anyone to link her to the tricky crimes she pulled off. As far as everyone else was concerned, she was like a ghost, lurking in the shadows and hatching her wicked plans deep in her clever brain. No one had the full scoop on all the bad stuff she was up to, and that gave her the green light to keep on doing her shady business in the world of shadows. It was like a crazy digital maze, and Eva was the undisputed queen, her mysterious identity ruling the world of cybercrime.

Eva's mission was clear – to protect her secrets, her true identity, and to stay one step ahead of those who would dare to challenge her. She knew that in the vast expanse of cyberspace, her skills were her most potent weapons.

***

In the amazing city of Paris, Julian's return home was like a whole new chapter in his life. He used to be this cheerful and playful guy, but now he was different. He was feeling really sad, and it was pretty obvious to Sebastian. It's like a heavy cloud of sadness was hanging over Julian, and it didn't look like it was going away anytime soon. The change in Julian's mood and attitude was pretty clear to Sebastian, who had a keen eye for these things. It was like Julian was sinking into a deep, deep sadness, and Sebastian couldn't ignore it. The city itself was still as enchanting as ever, with its cobblestone streets and charming cafes, but Julian's transformation cast a shadow over their surroundings.

Julian had turned into a total loner. He'd lock himself in his room for days, hardly coming out. When he did, you could see he was living on junk food and alcohol. It was pretty shocking, and it worried everyone.

Sebastian, who was always loyal and cared about Julian, could see things were getting out of hand. He knew he had to step in before Julian got even worse. It was obvious that something heavy was weighing on Julian's mind, and someone had to be there to help him find his way out of it.

Picture Julian as this guy who used to hang out and be part of everything, but now he's like a hermit, just staying locked up in his room. And when he finally does show up, you can see he's eating nothing but junk food and drinking like there's no tomorrow. It's not good at all, and it's really starting to worry everyone.

Sebastian, he's like the kind of friend who sticks with you through thick and thin. He could see that Julian was in a really bad place, and he knew he had to step in. Julian was clearly carrying some heavy burden or sadness, and it was high time for someone to reach out and help him find his way back to the light.

In the middle of this emotional turmoil, Julian couldn't help but voice his inner turmoil with a series of poignant questions. "Why did she have to leave me, Sebastian? What did I do wrong? I thought we had something special. How do you move on from losing the love of your life?"

Sebastian, the ever-dutiful butler, offered a sympathetic nod while providing a tray of freshly baked croissants. "I'm sorry to see you in such a state,

Mr. Julian. But you know, sometimes life takes us on a wild ride, and we just have to hang on and enjoy the view."

Julian managed a half-smile, plucking a croissant from the tray. "You're right, Sebastian. Life's a carnival, and I seem to be on the dizzying teacup ride."

Sebastian chuckled warmly. "Ah, but the teacups can be quite exhilarating, can't they, sir? Now, shall I prepare some tea to accompany those pastries?"

Julian's heart felt a bit lighter as he munched on the croissant, savoring the comforting taste of butter and flakiness. "Tea sounds splendid, my good man. Let's put on the kettle and continue this thrilling circus act called life."

Julian's life had become a never-ending cycle of longing and pain. Each day felt like a repeat of the last as he lay on his bed, clutching his phone desperately and calling Camille's number over and over. But it was always the same result: the line was disconnected, a harsh reminder of her sudden disappearance.

He was determined to solve the mystery of where she had gone, no matter the cost. Julian spared no expense and enlisted the best cyber investigators in the business. These experts dived deep into the intricate world of digital technology, their dedication unyielding as they scoured for any hint of information that could lead them to Camille.

In his dimly lit room, Julian's phone's glow was the only source of light, casting eerie shadows on the walls. The air was heavy with tension, and the weight of uncertainty pressed down on him as he continued to make those frustrating phone calls.

Outside, the world carried on, unaware of Julian's relentless pursuit. Cars passed by, their headlights painting streaks of light across the window. The soft hum of the city's nightlife filled the room, serving as a stark contrast to the turmoil in Julian's heart.

His room, once a place of comfort, had transformed into a battleground of emotions. The soft, worn sheets on his bed now crumpled under his restless form, and the room was filled with the faint scent of his favorite cologne, a reminder of happier times with Camille.

Meanwhile, the cyber investigators tirelessly worked their magic, fingers dancing across keyboards, eyes fixed on multiple screens displaying lines of code and digital breadcrumbs. The atmosphere in their high-tech lair was intense, the hum of powerful computers and the soft clicks of keyboards providing a constant background rhythm.

Julian's determination was unwavering, and as he lay on his bed, he could almost feel the invisible threads of the digital world tightening, bringing him closer to the answers he so desperately sought.

His bedroom had become a dimly lit haven, with mysterious shadows playing on the walls. His laptop, a beacon of hope, sat atop his cluttered desk, casting an eerie glow. Torn between fear and urgency, his words tumbled out before he could stop them.

"What happened to Camille? Why has she gone completely off the grid?" His words hung in the air, as if he expected his room to reveal the answers.

As the days passed, the disconnection and silence were a constant torment, a harsh reminder of Camille's absence. In a race against time, cyber investigators tirelessly worked their magic. Their faces were bathed in the cool, blue glow of computer screens, their fingers danced across keyboards, following virtual breadcrumbs through the vast expanse of the internet.

Julian knew he was in it for the long haul. He couldn't just let go of the one glimmer of hope he had to find Camille. Determination was etched across his face as he watched the experts navigate the digital maze. In his heart, a silent prayer took shape, a hope that they would unearth the missing pieces of the puzzle, leading him back to the mysterious woman who had stolen his heart.

One of those relentless days when Julian had lost all track of time, Sebastian entered his room bearing a tray filled with breakfast. The morning sun gently filtered through the curtains, casting a warm, soft glow upon the room. Julian, lost in his ceaseless quest to reconnect with Camille, hadn't even noticed that morning had arrived. Sleep had become a distant memory, a state that seemed to elude him.

Sebastian, his face etched with concern, stood by Julian's side, attempting to coax his despondent employer out of bed. He softly prodded, "Mr. Laurent, it's time to get up. I've found something important."

Julian's response was laden with reluctance and sullenness. "I don't want to go anywhere, Sebastian."

However, the ever-resourceful butler had an enticing offer to present. He leaned in, his voice low and persuasive. "Julian, I've got a lead, something that could be a breakthrough in finding Camille. But I'll only share it if you agree to freshen up, get dressed, eat some breakfast, and come out with me."

Julian's annoyance was palpable. He let out a frustrated sigh, begrudgingly accepting the necessity of the situation. "Fine."

Julian slumped back into his pillows, his eyes blinking sleep away as he realized the importance of Sebastian's announcement. The room around him was a cozy mess, with scattered books, crumpled notes, and the faint scent of old coffee cups on the side table. The view from his window offered a glimpse of their sprawling garden, now bathed in the morning light, and the distant chirping of birds filled the air.

Sebastian smiled in satisfaction, relieved that Julian had agreed to the plan. He set the tray on a nearby table and, with a hint of mischief in his eyes, said, "Good choice, Mr. Laurent. Now, let's talk over breakfast, and I promise you, this lead might just bring Camille back sooner than you think."

Julian, now more intrigued than annoyed, sat up, rubbing his eyes. "You better not be playing with my emotions, Sebastian."

Sebastian found himself rushing to open the curtains and bring in more daylight. Soon Julian's room was bathed in the gentle morning light, where time seemed to stand still. The room exuded a sense of calm, in stark contrast to the turmoil that had consumed Julian's thoughts. With an air of reluctant determination, Julian was ready to take the first step towards the unknown lead that might bring him closer to Camille. It was a stark contrast to the darkness that had enveloped him for so long, and for the first time in a while, he felt a glimmer of hope that perhaps Camille wasn't so far away after all.

Sebastian lent a hand to Julian as he got ready for the day, making sure he looked presentable. Together, they headed for the door. Julian reluctantly agreed to munch on a croissant during the journey, a small concession given the circumstances. The contrast between the sleek waiting car and Julian's despondent mood was stark.

Julian hesitated for a moment before getting into the passenger seat. Sebastian, wearing a subtle smile, took the driver's seat, clearly in a good mood. Julian couldn't resist asking, "What's got you in such high spirits, Sebastian?"

As the car pulled away from the residence, Sebastian hummed a gentle tune, glancing over at Julian. He offered a cryptic response, "You'll find out soon enough, sir." The anticipation hung in the air, leaving Julian to ponder what awaited them on this mysterious journey. The car glided smoothly through the streets, and the world outside seemed to be holding its breath, just like Julian, as they ventured into the unknown.

As they left the house, Julian finally relaxed. The place had been feeling like a prison, so it was a relief to escape for a bit. He looked around at the passing streets, just to pass the time. But Sebastian, his loyal butler, had other plans. Instead of their usual route, they were heading straight for the gallery. Julian's curiosity got the best of him, and before he knew it, his eyebrow arched.

He turned to Sebastian and asked, "Why are we going to the gallery so early in the morning?"

Sebastian shot him a sly grin and said, "You'll see, sir." The car continued down the winding streets until it pulled up right in front of the gallery. Julian's interest grew even stronger. What in the world was waiting for him inside those walls? The gallery, bathed in the gentle morning light, held mysteries and surprises just waiting to be discovered.

Julian couldn't help himself and leaned in towards Sebastian, whispering, "What's the big secret, Seb? Is it a surprise art exhibition, or are we here to buy some fancy paintings?"

Sebastian chuckled, his eyes twinkling with mischief. "Oh, sir, you have quite the imagination. It's neither of those things, but you're in for a treat." Julian shrugged, deciding to trust Sebastian's sense of adventure. It was, after all, a welcome break from the usual routine.

Sebastian expertly maneuvered the car, bringing it to a stop right in front of the gallery's entrance. Everything was meticulously arranged, ready for Julian's grand entrance. As they both stepped out of the sleek vehicle, Julian immediately noticed that the gallery had been closed to the public. The private showing had piqued his curiosity, and he couldn't resist wondering what Sebastian had up his sleeve.

Returning to the gallery stirred a whirlwind of emotions within Julian. It was there that his fascination with that mysterious painting had first taken root, setting him on a path of both love and heartache. Julian had never anticipated finding himself entangled in such a situation, ensnared in a complex web of emotions, all because of a painting and the alluring woman it seemed to conceal. Was she Camille, Eva, or someone else entirely? Julian was adrift in a sea of uncertainty, and the weight of it all bore heavily on his heart.

Julian turned to Sebastian, his curiosity getting the better of him. "Sebastian, what's the plan here? This is quite the setup." His voice held a mix of anticipation and intrigue, eager to uncover the mysteries lying ahead.

Julian and Sebastian entered the gallery, and their footsteps echoed through the quiet space until they came to a halt in front of The Obsidian Muse. Julian's gaze lingered on the painting, and before he knew it, a sense of connection washed over him. The sight of the painting, shrouded in its ornate frame, sent a shiver down Julian's spine. Questions raced through his mind, and he voiced them with a hint of wonder, "Who is she, really? Is it possible she's been here all along, hidden in plain sight?" Julian was on the brink of discovering the truth, and the gallery's hushed ambiance only added to the mystique of the moment.

There was a strange feeling in the air as Julian entered the grand hall. The painting he had admired for so long seemed different, as if it had been altered in some way. Julian squinted at it, his brow furrowing, and he couldn't resist asking, "Sebastian, is it just me, or does the painting look different?"

Sebastian, the butler, wore a knowing smile and responded, "You've got a sharp eye, sir. Someone paid a visit late last night and decided to leave their mark, quite literally."

Julian's eyes widened in disbelief, and he inquired, "What in the world?"

Sebastian nodded, his expression serious. "Yes, sir. I thought it best that you see it first. There might be a hidden message or clue within these changes." The mystery deepened, and Julian found himself wondering who had altered the painting and what their intentions might be. The gallery, with its dimly lit elegance, became the center of an unexpected mystery, and Julian was determined to uncover the secrets hidden within the canvas.

Julian felt an irresistible pull toward the painting, like a moth to a flame. His curiosity burned with intensity. He couldn't resist moving closer, paying no mind to the rope barrier, until he was standing right in front of the enigmatic masterpiece known as "The Obsidian Muse." It was as if the canvas held a hidden secret, whispering to him in some silent language.

Amidst the swirls of altered brushstrokes, Julian's eyes locked onto a sequence of numbers and letters etched into the paint. They stood out starkly against the dark backdrop, an enigma that begged to be deciphered. He turned to Sebastian, his trusty butler, who was hovering nearby.

"Sebastian, do you see this?" Julian exclaimed, pointing to the mysterious markings.

Sebastian peered at the cryptic symbols, squinting

slightly. "Indeed, Mr. Laurent. It does appear to be a code of some sort. Quite peculiar."

Julian scratched his head, puzzled. "I wonder what it means. It's almost like a message hidden within the artwork. Should we try to figure it out?"

Sebastian raised an eyebrow, a twinkle of mischief in his eyes. "Well, Mr. Laurent, it could be a treasure map, or perhaps the secret to everlasting youth. Shall we embark on an adventure to decode this artistic riddle?"

Julian couldn't help but be drawn to the ornate frame of the painting, its intricate carvings telling a story of their own. He chuckled at Sebastian's playfulness. "I like the way you think, Sebastian, but let's not get ahead of ourselves."

The canvas had a rough and uneven texture, giving the artwork depth, and the colors were so vivid they practically leaped off the canvas. He was beyond excited and couldn't keep it to himself. "Sebastian, you genius bastard," he exclaimed, turning to his ever-faithful butler. "Get these numbers down, my man."

Sebastian quickly grabbed his notepad, jotting down the strange sequence of characters. As he finished, the thought surfaced in his mind, "Sir, this seems like some kind of location, doesn't it?" The puzzle pieces were falling into place, and the idea of a hidden destination piqued their curiosity.

Julian's heart raced as he stared at the altered artwork. This had to be a sign, a message he had to follow. He was sure of it. Sebastian had cracked the code in the graffiti clue, and as he shared the location, Julian's suspicions were confirmed.

"Sir, it's pointing to Havana," Sebastian revealed.

Julian's determination solidified, his gaze unwavering. "I knew it, that's where she's hiding."

A chuckle escaped Julian as the thought crossed his mind. "Sebastian, I never knew you had a talent for cracking codes. Maybe you missed your true calling as a secret agent."

Sebastian gave a sly smile. "Well, sir, one never knows when a butler might come in handy on a top-secret mission."

Julian laughed, feeling a surge of excitement. "Well, then, Sebastian, it looks like we're off to Havana."

Meanwhile, halfway around the world in sunny Cuba, the clandestine mastermind behind The Shadow Serpent Syndicate, lounged in a dimly lit lair. She was surrounded by an array of cutting-edge gadgets and computer screens, her eyes locked onto a live video feed from security cameras strategically positioned in the Laurent gallery. A sly smile curled on her lips as she fixated on the screens.

In the comfort of her plush ebony leather chair, Eva leaned back and scanned her high-tech domain. The room boasted sleek, black surfaces and walls adorned with numerous monitors, each offering a different view of the gallery. The atmosphere was thick with tension, the soft hum of electronic equipment creating an eerie yet exhilarating vibe.

Eva had meticulously tracked every move made by Julian and Sebastian through the gallery's CCTV cameras. She was confident that they were getting closer to her, and the elements of her grand scheme were falling into place like a meticulously crafted puzzle. She had invested countless hours in planning and orchestrating this intricate operation, and now, the pieces were aligning for a grand reveal.

Yet, beneath the layers of her criminal ambition, Eva's fixation ran deeper. Her eyes lingered on one particular figure, Julian. Her smile took on a more sinister edge as she watched him on the screen. Eva's obsession with him had just begun, and her motives remained a cryptic mystery, ready to be unraveled.

Before she knew it, the question surfaced in her

mind: "What is it about him that pulls me in? Is it love, or is there something deeper?" As the screens around her displayed the unfolding drama in the gallery, Eva's own personal agenda was slowly being entwined with the criminal plot she had so meticulously crafted.

*** THE END***

ABOUT THE AUTHOR

Kathy Winslower is a gifted storyteller with a passion for weaving tales of love, resilience, and triumph. With her captivating narratives and richly drawn characters, she takes readers on unforgettable journeys that explore the depths of human emotions and the power of love to transform lives.

Born with an insatiable curiosity and a love for words, Kathy began her writing journey at a young age, filling countless notebooks with her imaginative stories. As she grew older, her passion for storytelling only deepened, leading her to pursue a career as a novelist.

Drawing inspiration from her own experiences and the world around her, Kathy's writing is characterized by its heartfelt authenticity and emotional depth. She skillfully delves into the complexities of relationships, capturing the raw and tender moments that shape her characters' lives.

When she's not immersed in her writing, Kathy can be found exploring nature, seeking inspiration from the beauty of the world around her. She believes that every moment holds the potential for a story, and it is her mission to capture those moments and share them with her readers.

ABOUT THE AUTHOR

Kathy Winslower is a gifted storyteller with a passion for weaving tales of love, resilience, and triumph. With her captivating narratives and richly drawn characters, she takes readers on unforgettable journeys that explore the depths of human emotions and the power of love to transform lives.

Born with an insatiable curiosity and a love for words, Kathy began her writing journey at a young age, filling countless notebooks with her imaginative stories. As she grew older, her passion for storytelling only deepened, leading her to pursue a career as a novelist.

Drawing inspiration from her own experiences and the world around her, Kathy's writing is characterized by its heartfelt authenticity and emotional depth. She skillfully delves into the complexities of relationships, capturing the raw and tender moments that shape her characters' lives.

When she's not immersed in her writing, Kathy can be found exploring nature, seeking inspiration from the beauty of the world around her. She believes that every moment holds the potential for a story, and it is her mission to capture those moments and share them with her readers.

www.ingramcontent.com/pod-product-compliance
Lightning Source LLC
Chambersburg PA
CBHW061539190726
48289CB00004B/1101